SONG
OF THE
SIX REALMS

SONG
OF THE
SIX REALMS

JUDY I. LIN

FEIWEL AND FRIENDS
NEW YORK

A Feiwel and Friends Book
An imprint of Macmillan Publishing Group, LLC
120 Broadway, New York, NY 10271 • fiercereads.com

Our books may be purchased in bulk for promotional, educational, or business use. Please contact your local bookseller or the Macmillan Corporate and Premium Sales Department at (800) 221-7945 ext. 5442 or by email at MacmillanSpecialMarkets@macmillan.com.

Library of Congress Cataloging-in-Publication Data

Names: Lin, Judy I., author.
Title: Song of the six realms / Judy I. Lin.
Description: First edition. | New York : Feiwel & Friends, 2024. |
    Audience: Ages 13 and up. | Audience: Grades 10–12. | Summary:
    Seventeen-year-old musician Xue faces a lifetime of servitude until Duke Meng
    offers her freedom in exchange for serving as a musician in residence,
    but Xue soon discovers the Duke is a celestial ruler with ulterior motives
    and she must unlock her past to prevent an impending war in the Six Realms.
Identifiers: LCCN 2023035542 | ISBN 9781250871619 (hardcover)
Subjects: CYAC: Fantasy fiction. | Musicians—Fiction. | Indentured
    servants—Fiction. | Memory—Fiction. | LCGFT: Fantasy fiction. | Novels.
Classification: LCC PZ7.1.L554 So 2024 | DDC [Fic]—dc23
LC record available at https://lccn.loc.gov/2023035542

First edition, 2024
Book design by Maria W. Jenson
Feiwel and Friends logo designed by Filomena Tuosto
Printed in the United States of America

ISBN 978-1-250-87161-9
1   3   5   7   9   10   8   6   4   2

ISBN 978-1-250-35660-4 (Special edition)
1   3   5   7   9   10   8   6   4   2

For Lydia and Lyra,
the brightest stars in my sky

六界經
ON THE STRUCTURE AND ORDER OF THE SIX REALMS

The Three Heavenly Stars (of the Celestial and Spirit Realms)

太陽天君 The Sky Sovereign (The Sun), Ruler of the Celestial and Spirit Realms

玄女天后 Supported by the Sky Consort, Xuannu

靈光聖母 Guided by the wisdom of the Heavenly Mother of Numinous Radiance, retired to the Crystal Palace of Longevity

First Realm: 仙 The Celestial Realm

六正星 Ruled by *The Six Rising Stars* of the Celestial Court

太歲 Star of Protection: Trains the Celestial Army to protect and defend the Celestial Realm

天機 Star of Fortune: Maintains the Mortal Tapestry, ensuring threads of fate are aligned

天相 Star of Governance: Oversees the minor gods and the selection of tributes from the Spirit Realm

天府 Star of Ordinance: Carries out the decrees of the Sky Sovereign, ensuring the laws of the court are followed

天梁 Star of Pillars: Maintains the Spirit Tree, ensuring the roots are nourished

天同 Star of Balance: Maintains the borders between the realms

SECOND REALM: 精 THE SPIRIT REALM

Governed by the four major clans. Each clan has their own territories and areas of influence, as well as their own methods of governance. Most Celestials originate from the Spirit Realm.

花 *Flower Clan*

鳥 *Bird Clan*

樹 *Tree Clan*

水 *Water Clan*

THIRD REALM: 人 THE MORTAL REALM

A place of neutrality, Mortal lives are governed by the Celestials, and the afterlife is governed by the Demons in the Ghost Realm. Some Mortals may gain enough spiritual affinity to ascend to the Celestial Realm, usually by passing the Rite of Ascension.

玄炳皇 Currently ruled by the Emperor Xuanbin

THE TWIN DARK MOONS (OF THE DEMON AND THE GHOST REALMS)

太陰 The Moon Sovereign, Ruler of the Demon and the Ghost Realms

魔君 The Demon Lord, Second-in-Command to the Moon Sovereign

FOURTH REALM: 魔 THE DEMON REALM

六魔王 Ruled by the *Six Fallen Stars* of the Demon Court

貪狼 Prince of Wolves, once the *Star of Desire*

巨門 Prince of Suspicion, once the *Star of Movement*

七殺 Prince of Sevens, once the *Star of Solitude*

破軍 Prince of War, once the *Star of Destruction*

廉貞 Prince of Lies, once the *Star of Fear*

武曲 Prince of Snakes, once the *Star of Pride*

FIFTH REALM: 鬼 THE GHOST REALM

閻羅王 Overseen by *the Judge* of the Ghost Court

Where Mortal souls go after they die in the Mortal Realm. They pass through ten levels of judgment and punishments as deemed appropriate by the Judge before rebirth.

SIXTH REALM: 空 THE BARREN REALM

All that is known of this place is the *Four Planes of Emptiness*.

Those who are banished here never leave.

PRELUDE

ONCE THERE WAS A YOUNG SCHOLAR WHO WAS exiled from the imperial court after angering the emperor. He fled to the forest of Sanxia with only his beloved qín and the clothes on his back. He built a small hut out of bamboo and dug a garden for sustenance. Each night he practiced on his qín, for he could not bear to leave the music of his former life behind. He believed his only audience was the wild animals, but one day he glimpsed a woman through the trees. He picked up his qín and chased after her, but she was too quick and he fell, smashing his instrument on the rocks.

The next day he toiled in his garden under the hot sun and, exhausted, threw down his tools. There was no music to look forward to in the evening, and filled with bitter disappointment, he fell asleep under the tóng tree.

He dreamed of a beautiful woman playing the qín, singing in accompaniment with a lovely voice. He woke and saw a nightingale above him on the branches of the tree, but from its mouth came the sound that was like the plucking of the strings. He declared this a sign from the gods and used his ax to chop down the tree. From its trunk, he built two instruments. One he named after the sun, and the other, the moon.

The scholar returned to the capital and became a famous qín maker. His instruments were highly sought after, but he never parted with the originals he built from the tree in Sanxia. Even the emperor came to hear of him and asked him to bring the Sun and the Moon, so that he too could enjoy the pleasing music. But the scholar never arrived at the palace. He had disappeared, along with both of his qíns. Those lovely instruments were never heard from again.

There were rumors he may have been called to the Celestial Realm, reunited with the Nightingale Spirit who led him to the tree. Together, they played for the Celestial Court, and their music flowed through the palace. The Sky Sovereign, pleased with the music, made them both immortal, so they could delight the stars forever.

—"The Bird and the Scholar," common
folktale of the Kingdom of Qi

VERSE ONE

CHAPTER ONE

I WAS TWELVE YEARS OLD WHEN MY CONTRACT WAS purchased by the House of Flowing Water. Its complex was one of the grandest buildings I had ever seen, even among its competitors in Wudan's most popular entertainment district. The curved, black-tiled roofs were held up by red rafters, and lanterns hung from the corners of each tier, three floors in all. Its name was written in gold calligraphy on an ornately carved plaque that hung over the entrance.

We waited on the street along with others who sought admission, surrounded by their excited chatter. Guards stood watch in front of a barrier of golden rope, preventing anyone from swarming the doors too early. I had to crane my neck to look up the stretch of stairs leading to the main entrance. At the proper time, a bell rang somewhere above our heads, and the double doors were opened to reveal three elegantly dressed women.

They descended the stairs in a splendid procession, and even those who were passing by stopped to admire the marvelous sight. Their hair was artfully arranged upon their heads in sweeping waves, crowned with elaborate headdresses of gold and silver filigree. Jewels dangled from those waves, sparkling as they caught the light. Their robes cascaded down the steps behind them, glittering with embroidered fish. Every part of them was designed to draw the eye, to beckon one closer. What secrets might pass through those lips, curved alluringly in the corners?

"Who are they?" I whispered to Uncle, entranced.

"They are the adepts of the house," he told me, amused at my awe.

"Trained in conversation or music or dance. They are on their way to provide entertainment at a nobleman's residence or a lady's garden. One day, Xue'er, you'll become one of them." He smiled, eyes crinkling.

The guard lowered the barrier to let them pass, and they swept by us, leaving behind the slightest scent of floral perfume. I stared as the crowd parted for them. They were like the heavenly Celestials in Uncle's stories who sometimes graced the Mortals with their presence. It was hard to imagine that I, a quiet and awkward child, could ever belong in their midst.

THE OWNER OF the establishment, Madam Wu, was an imposing woman with sharp cheekbones and thin lips. At that time, her favored color was red. I would learn later she changed her surroundings to suit her whims and the fashions currently in favor, so she could always appear like a treasure contained within a jeweled box. To my young eyes, she seemed a phoenix, just landed upon the earth. She was dressed in scarlet, and upon her eyelids there was brushed pink powder in the shape of wings sweeping toward her brows. Her lips were colored a matching shade. But her touch was icy cold.

A thin stream of fear collected at the back of my neck as she lifted my chin with her fingers and turned my head one way and then the other. She opened my mouth and checked that I still had all my teeth. Uncle had told me she was the one I must please in order to gain admittance into the House. The rebellious, angry part of me wanted to jerk away. To behave in a manner that would cause offense so Uncle would be forced to send me back to our cottage on the outskirts of Wudan. The other part of me stayed still under her scrutiny, knowing that to behave in such a manner would be a poor way to repay how he had cared for me the past few years.

Her attention lingered on the scar upon my brow. Most people stared at it—some openly, others trying to avert their gaze, but their curiosity always drew them back. It cut from above my right brow, across the bridge of my nose, ending above my left eye. It used to look even uglier, the skin puckered and red, but had faded slightly in the past year. Still, a scar all the same, and one that could not be hidden by cleverly pinned hair pieces or adornments. It would be a blemish on my record in this place, where beauty was obviously held in the highest regard.

"There is potential for loveliness, without this." She traced the scar with her fingernail. "What happened?"

"Fell out of a tree," Uncle said gruffly. "Could have lost an eye, but she was lucky."

"Hmm." The mistress continued her consideration of me, unimpressed. "Can she read? Write?"

Uncle made a sound of offense. "She is my niece. Do you think I would neglect her education? Her calligraphy could use some work, but she has read and memorized the ten classics. She can recite three hundred poems from memory. You will not find her knowledge lacking."

"It takes considerable expense to train an entertainer," Madam Wu murmured, picking up a strand of my hair and examining it between her fingers. "Usually they come to me at five or six, when they are still malleable and not prone to bad habits. I can have my pick of the young scholars from the monastery or an eager apprentice of the Limen Theater. Why should I choose her?"

My face stung at her words, even though Uncle had warned me it

5

would be like this. A push and a pull, much like the rise and fall of a song. He assured me she would take everything under serious consideration, for she owed him a favor from many years ago. A play he had written for her had gained great repute, and she was even invited to the Eastern Palace to perform. It was with that success she was able to open her own house, growing it to the successful establishment it had become.

This is the way of the world, he had told me, before the carriage came and took us past the frozen lake and into the city proper. *What you offer and what someone is willing to give you. Know your worth.*

I stood there, trembling, as they joked back and forth, as she criticized every detail of my appearance and mannerisms. Uncle countered with a list of my supposed virtues, but still I was reminded of every one of my faults. If I was so worthy, then why wouldn't he take me with him while he was called away on his travels? If I had skills to offer, then why was I not suitable to be his companion? But I'd already made my protests, cried my tears, begged him to reconsider. There was no changing his mind. Not when it involved the capital, and the demands of a powerful emperor.

"You say she has an aptitude with the qín." Madam Wu clapped and a servant appeared almost immediately in the doorway. "Have her demonstrate."

A table was quickly brought out, the instrument placed upon it, and a stool positioned in front. I ran my hand over the qín and gently plucked the strings, getting accustomed to the feel. It was made of a golden-colored wood, speckled with brown whorls, strung with good-quality silk. Each qín was unique—playing a new one was like meeting a person for the first time. This one's sound was warmer in tone than my own instrument, but it was well cared for.

"You are her teacher?" Madam Wu poured a cup of tea for my uncle, placing it next to him as they settled upon chairs for the performance. Uncle betrayed nothing in his expression as he lifted the cup to drink, no hint of nervousness or doubt in my abilities.

"Me?" He laughed. "I do not hold my musical skills in such high esteem that I could hope to train someone worthy of your notice. Her skills have long surpassed my abilities. Her instructor for the past two years has been Kong Yang of the Shandong School."

Teacher Kong. My fingers twitched at the phantom pain that lashed across my knuckles, a reminder of the thin piece of bamboo he held at his back like a sword to use on his students. Arrogant, and fastidious in his devotion to technique, but the sounds that flowed from his hands . . .

"Kong Yang?" I heard the surprise in her voice. "If she is worthy to be his student, then why not become one of his disciples at the academy?"

"I believe she will receive a more well-rounded education at your house," Uncle stated, resorting to flattery. "I've no doubt once she comes of age, other offers will follow . . ."

She gave a harsh bark of laughter. "That may work on those who are dazzled by your many accolades, Tang Guanyue, but you and I know each other far too well for that."

"Of course." Uncle bowed his head. "There is a reason why not many of my associates are aware of her existence." Reaching into his robe, he pulled out the stone pendant that identified each of the citizens of the kingdom. One that stated our names, both family and given. My hands faltered and betrayed my nervousness, even as I continued the process of tuning the strings.

Madam Wu held it up to the light, examining the red mark struck across my family's name. I could see it even from across the room. A stain. Another blemish upon my record. One even more damning than a scar in a house of beautiful things.

"Her family?" she inquired.

"Her father was a minister who was loyal to Prince Yuan," Uncle said. "I once swore an oath before the Star of Balance that I was blessed to call him my brother, in this lifetime and the lifetimes to come."

"May he find peace in another life." She inclined her head, then sighed. "If—and this is only *if*—I were to admit her into my ranks, there is no guarantee she would ever be pardoned."

"You would be the one to give her the best chance at success." Uncle stood and bowed deeply. It hurt me to see him beg, for I knew his pride. The chance of me ever clearing my record was slim, but Uncle wished for me only the best opportunity. I was beginning to understand it now.

"I cannot make any promises." She stood and helped him up, alarmed at the display of reverence, gesturing for him to sit again. "That a rank such as the yuè-hù should exist in this enlightened time is a disgrace upon us all."

To hear it uttered felt like a slap to the face. A term that I'd heard followed with spitting on the street, a bitter reminder of what caused the execution of my father, mother, and brother. To have my family name stricken from the Book of Records.

"Guxue." She looked toward me then. "A fitting name for a poet's ward."

Solitary Snow.

It was indeed appropriate for someone who would never marry, never bear children, never have anything to my name. I would exist only to serve, to bear the punishment of the transgressions of my parents, unless the emperor or empress ever found me worthy of a pardon. I willed myself to remain still, even as tears threatened to overwhelm me. To wait, even as my hands shook in my lap.

Madam Wu considered me for a moment, then nodded. "For a student of Kong Yang, I will listen and see."

That was my cue. One chance to prove that I could be an asset to her establishment. I chose a song called "Morning Rain," which paid homage to the House of Flowing Water. The sound filled the small room, the notes quivering in the air like dew on a leaf. The song continued, imitating the sound of raindrops falling one by one, splattering on the stones below.

For all of Uncle's complaints about my calligraphy, my lack of finesse in pleasant conversation, my tendency to stumble when reciting poetry, I knew from the first moment I plucked the string of the qín that this was what I would master. This instrument of scholar-officials, the pinnacle of refinement, revered in stories as the one favored by even the Sky Sovereign himself. The qín was capable of elegance and meditation, or fury and dissent. Its seven strings could express so much in the grasp of a skilled musician.

The last notes trembled in the air before I dared to look over at my audience. Madam Wu had her eyes closed, like she was savoring the sound, a smile upon her lips. Uncle gave me a small nod, and I knew before Madam Wu said anything, she would take me into her house. I would join the ranks of the House of Flowing Water and leave my childhood behind.

CHAPTER TWO

UNCLE LEFT NOT LONG AFTER I GAINED ADMIT-
tance to the House, unable to delay a direct summons from the emperor
for too long. He promised before he left that he would visit when he
could. I managed to hold in my tears while we said our goodbyes and
only allowed them to flow when I could no longer see his carriage.

The House of Flowing Water was a city within a city, I learned. It
opened midday for a show that was accompanied by refreshments.
Soon after, the novices and servants would descend upon the hall,
scrubbing furiously to prepare for the evening performances. The
shows rotated by day of the week and were renewed each season, for
the mistress knew the audience was fickle and constantly clamored for
new delights.

The House employed a drum troupe, with dancers to accompany
their rhythms with cymbals or scarves. There were two groups that specialized in opera, as well as duos and trios who performed theatrical skits
wearing elaborate masks. Many of the performers could also sing and play
the pipa or the flute. In order to dazzle the eye with sets and costumes,
the House had an on-site group of seamstresses and artists responsible
for transforming the many spaces of the establishment to appear otherworldly. One day we could be in the dark and dreary realm of the ghosts,
the next in the fanciful realm of Celestials or the colorful Spirit World.

True to his word, Uncle came to visit me when he was able, when his
travels brought him back to Wudan. His visits broke up the monotony
of the days drifting into weeks, into months, and then years.

Uncle asked the same question, every visit, as he took me strolling through the market streets. He would look at me, and ask softly, "How are you faring in the House, Xue'er? Is the madam treating you well?"

I would respond the same way each time, even though it only contained a half truth: "Everything is fine, Uncle. They are very kind to me."

I could not say that the inhabitants of the House made me feel unwelcome—I was not shunned or made to feel lesser because of my status. Uncle had promised me that the House of Flowing Water would be a refuge, and it was. The term *yuè-hù* was banned within those four walls. I was regarded the same as any of the other novices, and told to call the mistress Auntie Wu, as she was referred to by all under her protection.

It wasn't that I was kept idle either. No, the days were busy and filled with lessons and tasks. My education on etiquette, history, and philosophy continued. I was instructed in the art of serving, and assisted in many of the other novice chores. However, I was not permitted to be in the kitchens, for my hands were deemed too precious to risk injury. As the years passed, I learned how to maneuver among the tables of the packed dining room, carrying large platters of food and drink. I learned how to pour tea and wine without spilling a drop. I could distinguish the roles and ranks of Wudan society, recognizing patrons from the details of their clothing and mannerisms. I knew how deeply to bow and how to cast my eyes down when speaking and being spoken to.

It wasn't that I was lonely either. I made acquaintance with an apprentice in the drum troupe who treated me almost like a little sister, and she would give me an extra bun with supper or sneak me an occasional sweet. There was another apprentice of opera who loved to listen to me practice, and would join her voice to my instrument in joyous accompaniment. But because of my personal history, hidden away from society in a cottage waiting for my father's transgressions to fade from the court's memory, I would often retreat into my books and music. An escape from the overwhelming noise and bustle of the House and the city. And it was because of those books and poems and stories that I felt a restlessness inside of me that grew with each year.

I wished to appear grown-up in Uncle's eyes, for him to know that I was furthering my education as he wanted. I hoped that one day he would see me as a worthy companion to take along on his travels. There were not many other opportunities afforded to those like me, and like many other children, to be refused something only made me desire it more desperately.

This year, though, marked my seventeenth year, and this summer's visit would be different from the ones that came before. For it was the year of my Jì Lǐ, the coming-of-age ceremony that all citizens of the kingdom underwent. In this house, it indicated our transition from novice to apprentice, from servant to performer, and Uncle had come to see it.

Auntie had given me a reprieve from my tasks for the little time he was in the city, and those days were among my most treasured memories. Eating red candied fruits on a stick that turned our tongues red. Burning our mouths on the soup that spilled out of the dumplings because of our impatience. A gift of a fan, upon which there were delicate plum blossoms, hand-painted, that I admired in the market.

"Let me tell you of the gossip from the capital," he said, laughing at my claps of delighted anticipation.

I never knew how much of his tales was embellishment or reality, but I clung to each word all the same. His stories of the princess and her assortment of exotic pets that roamed her private gardens, or the minister who commissioned a series of lewd stone sculptures that scandalized the court. His descriptions of them made me double over, chortling at the imagined sight.

Later, with our bellies full from the crispy duck and bitter greens of the kitchens, we played card games in his private suite at an inn down the road. Our reunions gave me a pleasant and familiar feeling, a reminder of my old life. That once I had a mother and a father and an elder brother, even if they were only vague smears of memory to me: a certain laugh, a strain of music, the scent of rain. Uncle was my connection to them.

Once our games were done, I knew that it was time for the request that came at the end of each of his visits. One that was just like his questions after my well-being. One that I both anticipated and dreaded.

"Show me what you have learned while I have been away," he instructed, wine in hand, expression serious.

I brought out my qín then, already prepared. I played through the repertoire that I had painstakingly practiced for the weeks leading up to this visit, each piece selected to demonstrate a new song or a particularly challenging technique. He listened intently, foot tapping along with the rhythm.

"Ah," he sighed afterward when the last strains of the melody were gone. "The qín is the instrument of your soul, of that I have no doubt."

His approval pleased me, for some part of me was still six years old and frightened at being away from home, and he was the one who made me feel safe.

"But the way you play . . ." He regarded me with all sincerity then. "It reminds me of 'The Ode to the Lost City.' The Poet Zhu's sadness upon realizing it was impossible to return to his homeland."

I had thought I was careful about how I portrayed myself, and yet I could not hide from him. My music betrayed my innermost thoughts.

"I only want you to be happy, Xue," he said softly. "If only—"

"I am," I interrupted him, wanting to be reassuring. Perhaps if I said it enough times, I would believe it myself.

"I have something to show you." Uncle stood. He lifted a large box onto the table and gestured for me to open it. "I encountered this during my travels, and thought you might like to see it."

With the size of the box, I had an idea of what it could contain, but my hand still trembled a little in anticipation. I slid off the lid to find the item wrapped in soft, blue silk. Slowly and reverently, I pulled off the cover to find a lacquered qín. One that gleamed a deep, rich red.

I lifted it out of the box and set it upon the table to examine each and every component. My fingers skimmed over the bridge shaped like a mountain, then to the other side, the dragon's gums. There were thirteen round pearl inlays, each shimmering with its own milky hue. Underneath, I checked the tuning pegs, as well as the pillar of earth and the pillar of heaven. Everything was as it should be. An instrument beautifully constructed at the hands of a master qín maker. Her artisan mark was etched upon the underside: Su Wei. A revered name in the musicians' circle. The beauty of it put my own practice qín to shame.

"'The Bird and the Scholar,'" I whispered, remembering the folktale that was one of Uncle's favorites.

"Su Wei was thought to be the scholar's apprentice," Uncle said with a knowing smile. "There are not many of these left in the world."

I plucked one of the strings, and the note quivered in the air.

A lump rose in my throat. I was afraid to speak. Afraid of what Uncle would say. I didn't know how I could bear it if this resplendent thing was only brought here for me to try and then be taken away. I could not believe that Uncle, even with his tendency to tease me, could break my heart in such a way.

I looked up at him, wordless, and he shook his head.

"Do not worry, Xue'er," he said gently, placing his hand on my arm. "It is yours."

CHAPTER THREE

THE NEXT DAY I WAS BATHED AND POWDERED, MY hair brushed with a hundred strokes and then oiled until it shone. With nimble fingers, Feiyun—my friend with a talent for the opera—pulled the dark strands into an elaborate knot piled high on top of my head, a hairstyle only befitting of a girl when she came of age. Then I was dressed in underclothes of midnight blue edged with gold, the colors in fashion that season. Gauzy fabric of a lighter shade, the pale blue of a cold winter sky, was draped around my shoulders and skirts, pinned into place until it felt as if I were surrounded by a cloud. My closest companions then each kissed me on the cheek, and sent me on my way with their blessings.

I joined the other two novices who were also coming-of-age, both boys, in the hall. Matron Dee, Auntie Wu's second-in-command, was the one to lead us up the stairs to the altar room, a sacred place usually forbidden to us. The room watched over the main hall like a star, windows open to look upon the space below. It existed as a reminder of the Celestials above, guiding us as we moved through the cycle of birth and rebirth.

We knelt before the altar, the three of us in a line. Above us hung the portrait of the Star of Fortune, the god who looked after our house. He held a book in one hand, a calligraphy brush in the other. His face was stern, for he was responsible for all of our fates—who we were destined to meet, influence, or marry. There were red strings draped over one of his arms, and to his left there was a laughing woman who held up the rest of the threads in her hands, surrounded by birds of all kinds holding the ends of the strings in their beaks. Some called her the Minor Star of Lovers, others, the Guardian of Dreams, for to love and to dream were the sustenance of Mortal existence. To his right was a man strumming a pipa with an expression of pleasant enjoyment. This was the Minor Star of Talent, worshipped by performers, who prayed his light shone upon them so they may gain recognition for their abilities.

This trio of Celestials were our spiritual guides, and so our offering table was well stocked. There were fresh-cut branches of wintersweet and sprigs of narcissus blooms. In the center of the table lay a plate of peaches, their ripe scent mingling with the incense, for these were the fruits most beloved by the gods. Beside them was a platter of pastries to sweeten their palates so that they may look upon us kindly. The third dish held an assortment of nuts so that they would enjoy each morsel, and never leave us and take away their blessings.

We waited in quiet reflection until the doors opened again, admitting Auntie Wu. To my surprise, Uncle was there beside her as well. He retreated to the side of the room to observe, and the ceremony began. For each of us, Auntie conducted the same steps of the ritual as we knelt. She sprinkled water in front of us, then burned a paper talisman of protection in a metal bowl. She walked around us so that the smoke encircled our bodies. Matron Dee recited the chants that heralded our coming-of-age.

For the two other novices, since they were boys becoming men, Auntie Wu draped black cloaks around their shoulders and placed black caps upon their heads. As she approached me, I looked down at her embroidered slippers, giving her the respect deserved of an elder.

Auntie spoke the words above my head: "At this time, presented before the gods, you are acknowledged." She slid the pin into my hair, where it snagged sharply. A pinch of pain, and then I was a woman. No longer a girl.

I thought the ceremony concluded, but she stepped aside, and a shadow passed over me.

"As your father acknowledged me as brother, so I acknowledge you in turn," Uncle's voice rumbled above me. I felt the envious gaze of the others, for they had no family to attend to them. There was a small spark of pride inside of me as I bowed my head before him.

"Thank you, Uncle," I whispered as he draped the cloak around my shoulders. I would no longer wear the short cape of children—instead I would have a full cloak that brushed against my legs as I rose to standing. Fur tickled the back of my neck. There was a weight to the cloak as I turned, the hem trailing along the floor. I would grow into it. My fingers touched the material. It was soft, smooth, luxurious. The embroidered design along the edge was of flowers, orchids done in silver thread.

We bowed to the gods first, then to the mistress of the house who had taken us in. We were now apprentices, capable of performing for our esteemed patrons if Auntie deemed us worthy. A servant placed a cup of wine into my hand, and the mood turned from serious to cheerful. The air filled with words of congratulations. The wine burned its way down my throat.

Uncle embraced me, his eyes shining with pride. In that moment, I felt blessed with his precious gifts. Seen, recognized, and loved.

I SAID GOODBYE to my uncle the next day, and he promised me he would return before the snow fell. I spent the next few months eagerly learning the nuances of my new qín, drawing out its unique sounds. I found myself wanting to prove that I was worthy of such a priceless instrument.

The next time Auntie called me to her study, it was at the beginning of autumn. I was certain it was finally my time to take on the apprentice role, for which I had grown impatient.

I entered the room after a quick tap of my knuckles upon the wooden door. Auntie sat at her desk, looking down at papers in her hand.

"Ah, Xue . . . ," she said, but it was more like a sigh. She lifted her hand and waved me closer.

I took a step forward, but she finally looked at me, and I saw her eyes were misty with tears. I had never before seen her lose her composure. It was the equivalent of a scream.

"A letter came from the capital, bearing sorrowful news," she said, voice quivering. "Your uncle's caravan was attacked by bandits on the way to Wudan. He died two weeks ago."

My knees almost gave way. If it weren't for the table beside me, I would have ended up on the floor.

"The House will take care of you, child. You'll still have a place here," Auntie said, in an attempt to be reassuring.

I must have said something to her afterward, or perhaps not. My memory of that afternoon was obscured whenever I attempted to look back, like the fog that would sweep over the lake unexpectedly when the winds shifted.

In a way, nothing had changed, and yet, everything had changed. I belonged fully to the House of Flowing Water now, bound in servitude until my death. It was time to set aside the foolish, secret dreams I had of traveling the world like my uncle and the wanderers in his stories.

I would respect his memory, and try to be happy.

THE ROUTINE OF the House saved me from disappearing into my sadness. New responsibilities awaited me as an apprentice. I was like a puppet being led along by the strings, performing the steps I knew so well with a hollow heart. For the afternoon banquet, I played behind a screen while the guests enjoyed a performance from our limber acrobats. In the evening, I was the music that trickled down from the rafters above, hidden from view, while patrons feasted.

The House of Flowing Water continued to entertain guests of high standing in society, and Auntie honed our reputations as a house capable of putting on grand shows just as well as intimate gatherings. She purchased the adjacent building, expanding the House into the inn business, with rooms made available for visitors who wanted to stay overnight.

The pain of losing my uncle became a quiet hurt, one that struck me unexpectedly whenever I read a passage that reminded me of his wit, or I thought I had caught his voice somewhere in the distance.

Though I'd been plagued by bad dreams ever since I was little, a new nightmare emerged: Me, searching for him in a crowd. Catching a glimpse of his face, and then losing him in the distance. Pushing past the sea of bodies that kept getting in my way, being swept back, again and again.

Xue! There's something I have to tell you! he would call to me. Then I would wake up, his voice still echoing inside of my ears and a brittle sense of loss inside my chest.

I devoted myself to the practice of the qín, spending most of my time in pursuit of the clarity of sound, the perfect technique and form. I cared for Uncle's gift until I knew it as well as my own body, its dips and crevices, the unique markings upon the wood.

I moved into the newly constructed women's quarters once they were completed, finally joining Feiyun and my older companions. The apprentices spoke of flirtations and secret notes and gifts from patrons.

Late night whispers when someone tiptoed in, a little tipsy from one of the many parties hosted by Wudan's literati. I watched as a few of them rose to the ranks of adept, butterflies among a field of flowers, gaining their share of devotees. Some of them fought one another in subtle jabs, sharp words or spilled paint, as strong personalities often clashed when they vied for the attention of a wealthy or esteemed guest. But most of them were never rude to me, even though they all knew my status as an Undesirable.

Perhaps it was out of pity. I knew that their chances to gain their freedom was a dream that hovered before them, a hopeful future soon within reach. If they earned enough to pay off their contract or caught the attention of either a devoted patron or an amorous suitor. Not like me, bound to the House until my death. Some of them distanced themselves from me, as if my social status was a condition that could be caught like a disease. Others tried to encourage me by using me as a willing canvas for their experiments with new shades of makeup, and they told me rumors of exiles who had found their way back into society and reclaimed their names.

They would often speak of Consort Yu, a favored concubine of the Xuanwu emperor with a notorious past. She was once a pipa musician whose yuè-hù status was struck from record when he became entranced with her beauty and brought her to the inner palace. The gossip raged through the kingdom when her past was discovered, and I found it laughable that they believed it could also one day be my fate. It would be just as likely for the Heavenly Mother of Radiance to bestow the title of Blessed upon me and lift me up among the stars to become one of the Dancing Maidens.

Some of them thought me shy, resigned to my fate, and therefore hesitant to participate in casual flirtations. But it wasn't that. I just never felt that tug they experienced when they found someone pleasing to the eyes. That fluttering in my belly eluded me, and never the sharp pull of the heartstrings that said the Minor Star of Lovers was attentive to my future. In this way, I drifted. Accepted, of sorts. Peered at the rest of the world from behind screens and doors. Watched as the guests laughed and feasted and enjoyed themselves. Waited nervously for the day when it would be my turn on the stage.

The restless feeling returned eventually. I should have been grateful, for the clothes on my back and the roof over my head, and yet I still felt that something was missing. It was not the warmth of a lover's touch or the call of freedom, just the knowledge that this was not where I was meant to be.

Even though I was surrounded by people, I could deeply relate to the words of one of my favorite poets, another concubine of a former emperor, trapped within the beautiful walls of the inner palace: *I am surrounded by many splendors, and yet I am alone.*

CHAPTER FOUR

IT WAS THE FIRST SNOWFALL OF THE YEAR. CRIES of delight filled the room as the windows were thrown open, letting the cold air in. A few of the apprentices yelped, but others laughed. Someone would, inevitably, make a joke about my name, as they did each year. We could look forward to the desserts made with warming ingredients, many hot cups of ginger tea, and red bean soup.

Serendipitously, the first snowfall coincided with the first day of the Little Snow on the solar calendar, which meant the House of Flowing Water was closed to guests for the afternoon. We spent the day preparing the house for the change in seasons: replaced the incense for a spicier fragrance that warmed the blood and invigorated the mind, pulled our winter clothes from our trunks, and aired out the heavier coverings that would keep us warm in the evening's chill.

We endeavored to keep our guests as comfortable as possible, and it took a considerable amount of fuel to keep such a large building heated. I swept the dried leaves from the garden paths, walking past the piles of chopped wood that were stacked against the side of the shed. The sun hung low in the sky and shone with weak, wavering light through the thin clouds. The air was still, expectant. As if all the birds and creatures knew the true beast of winter lurked around the corner, waiting to pounce.

That night was a significant evening for me, because Auntie Wu had finally selected me to perform in the main hall. Matron Dee had announced it at dinner the night before, and I was offered many congratulations by the other apprentices. The women's quarters were a flurry of activity when I returned to dress for the evening performance. There were fabrics, ties, and shoes strewn about everywhere. Open containers of cosmetics on dressing tables and hairpins that sparkled in the light. There was an atmosphere of merriment, interspersed with occasional bursts of laughter and giggles as jokes were made at one another's expense. We did not have to maintain our careful composure in here, for no one was watching to ensure we kept our decorum.

I slipped into a long, light green skirt with many folds. It was designed to drape gracefully over the stool that I would sit on. My jacket and sleeves were tight to the body, almost constricting, in order to not impede the playing of the qín. I looked enviously at the outfits of the dancers, with their shorter skirts and flowing sleeves.

The dance troupe was a colorful sight to behold. They each had a red blossom painted upon their foreheads, and their eyes were outlined in a dark, dramatic fashion. Their hair was pinned up in two loops, then bound with festive ribbons that trailed down the sides of their faces and brushed their shoulders. They wore red sashes wound around their chests that matched the embroidered edges of their skirts.

Auntie strode into the chamber, clapping her hands to capture our attention.

"We shall put on a good show tonight, my lovelies," she declared, for in speaking of things, she believed she would make them real. "Fortunes' blessings upon our house."

"Fortunes' blessings," all of us echoed in turn. The portrait of the Star of Fortune flashed in my mind. He was said to weave all of our Mortal fates upon the Tapestry of Destinies, and a part of me always found the thought uncomfortable. *Did our choices mean nothing when our fates were already knotted, predetermined before we even left our mothers' wombs?*

I took a deep breath and tried to brush away the thought. I could not let myself be distracted tonight.

The evening's festivities began, and the hall was filled to capacity. A typical sight upon the changeover of a season, as many were always eager to see the new performances, but it did nothing to ease my jagged nerves. I stood in the back, behind the carved wooden screens that blocked off a section of the hall and allowed performers to enter unobtrusively.

The first performance of the evening was an opera. A flute trilled in the background as two figures crossed the stage, footsteps light. I recognized Feiyun's voice immediately, even from behind her mask.

Our shoulders brush
A moment frozen in clarity
I recognize you
See myself in your gaze

Another woman's voice, low and husky, joined her in the duet as they both bowed to one another, then to the audience, who represented the gods they hoped would bless their union. They made quite a striking pair, dressed in wedding colors of red and gold. It was a love song, one called "Heaven and Earth," about a Fox Spirit who accidentally fell into the Mortal Realm—characterized by Feiyun's mask of white, red, and black—and the huntress who saved her from the fearful villagers. Even though their love was forbidden, they still married and performed the rites before heaven, committing themselves to each other. The Sky Consort herself took pity upon the lovers, and lifted them to the Celestial Realm, so they could be together for eternity.

Spirits were associated with nature, flighty and wild. Beings who absorbed enough of the cosmic energy to gain sentience, able to take on human appearance if they wished. I loved stories about them. Birds who became warriors. Fish that spoke in riddles. Stories that helped me traverse other realms. Focusing on the beauty of the words and the melody, I was able to breathe a little easier.

Then it was my turn to ascend the steps, my qín held against my heart. The room was filled with so many people, and yet all of their faces were a blur.

I sat on the stool and arranged my skirts around me, like the adepts had instructed. With my head down, I could pretend the screen was still there, separating me from the rest of the room. There was only the safety of the stage, and the performers I was to accompany. The two dancers glided forward and took their positions. One was dressed as a king of dynasties past, the other his devoted concubine.

"The Tragedy of Consort Xiang" was a sad story, as shown by the way the sound poured from the strings. No vocalist accompanied our performance, but it was the dramatic dancing of the figures on the stage that told the tale.

Swirling flowers, falling leaves, mark the days I've dreamed of my king but have not seen him

The pain inside like my organs severing, my tears leave ever-deepening scars . . .

I lost myself in the expression of the music, careful to ensure each note wept. My qín sang with an ache that manifested the concubine's longing. The king and his concubine danced around each other, always just out of reach, as the lament wove its way around them. The consort sank to her knees in despair as she realized the wind carried the king away from her. He was only a dream, a figment of her imagination.

When the last notes crept in, like the wind that swept through the bamboo grove where the concubine perished, I wondered what that all-consuming, gut-wrenching love would feel like. If there was such an emotion that would render me unable to live, I wasn't sure the gaining of it was worth the loss.

I joined the other performers to bow to the sound of enthusiastic applause. When I glanced up at the audience, some of them dabbed at their eyes or noses with their handkerchiefs, visibly emotional. I felt a little spark of hesitant pride in my chest. I had done my part through the power of the song. It was everything I thought it would be, what I had longed for: to be seen, to be acknowledged. Even though I was more familiar with poets of old than real people, even though I was not meant for love or a family of my own, I could pretend for a moment that I was one of them.

Once I was safely alone in the back hallway, I wept.

I knew my uncle would have wanted to be here. He would have sat in the best seat in the house.

I HID IN the shadow of the stairwell for a while longer, my face still hot from the excitement of my first mainstage performance. Closing my eyes, I took in the sounds of the house, like listening to an old friend. The clatter of the dishes being cleaned in the kitchens, the drums of the next performance shaking the floor beneath my feet.

Down the hall there was a thump, and then a soft cry. I wiped my eyes with my sleeve as I stood, setting my qín aside, and crept toward the source of the sound. It came from the hallway that led to the gardens, where the kitchen staff would bring out food for the outdoor banquets. I wondered if one of the servants had slipped and fallen, but to my shock I saw the back of a man in black robes. Not one of our staff, not with his top knot and the pendant he wore at his side. A patron, where he shouldn't be.

He shifted. A flash of red caught my eye, then a terrified, pale face turned in my direction. It was one of the dancers, her mouth covered by his hand. He struggled to keep her pinned against the wall. She saw me and then thrashed harder, cries muffled. He turned then and met my eyes. His lips pulled back in an imitation of a smile.

"I am the second son of Minister Jiang." He leered in my direction. "Scurry away, little one, and you'll find a fat purse sent to you tomorrow for your trouble."

I scowled. Some of these patrons sauntered in here as if they owned the establishment because they flung about a bit of coin. They believed our worth was measured by our price, and our only value was to do their bidding. All of us could tell stories about being pinched and grabbed by overeager guests. Those who ordered us about like servants of their own household. Gossip, too, was shared about other houses, owners who were less scrupulous with the rules, even though there were regulations and licenses that governed the entertainment and pleasure districts.

"Get away from her." I stepped forward. Out of everyone in the house, I had the least to lose from the confrontation of a minister's son. I was already an outcast from society, so what else could he possibly do to me?

He pulled the dancer to his side, twisting her arm behind her until she yelped in pain.

"Who are you?" he snarled. "How dare you speak to me in that manner!"

"I think you would do well to remember what sort of establishment this is," I said, trying to make myself appear as threatening as possible. "I saw Magistrate Qiu and Official Au in the audience tonight—if I scream and they come, I wonder whose innocence they will believe?"

"You . . . you wouldn't dare!" he sputtered.

I drew in a deep breath, but then a hand clamped down upon my wrist before I could scream. I looked up to see the impassive face of Matron Dee.

"Jiang Erlang," she said, stepping forward. "Please, let me pour you a head-cleansing tonic. I fear you've had a bit too much to drink."

"Old hag," he spat in her direction. "I am a customer. You exist to serve me, and I want this little morsel to myself. You want me to hire a private room? How much? I'll pay it!"

"We are not that sort of establishment!" Matron's voice was as sharp as a lash. Somehow she had procured a rod in her hand, and she advanced menacingly. "Go seek the pleasure houses."

Jiang Erlang's eyes darted to the weapon, then back up to the older woman's face to judge her seriousness. He cursed her ancestors under his breath and pushed the girl forward. She stumbled, falling to her knees, and he fled out the back door.

"H-he grabbed m-me." I finally recognized the girl as Anjing, one of the newer dancer-apprentices. Tears streaked her face. "I swear, Matron, I didn't—"

The rules of the House of Flowing Water were clear. There were legal distinctions between the types of houses and the kind of entertainment that could be provided within. To break those rules would subject the House to fines and the loss of its operating licenses, especially as many of its patrons were magistrates and officials. We received constant reminders to conduct ourselves accordingly.

"It's all right, Anjing," Matron said soothingly, bending down to help her.

I took that as my cue to leave, but then Matron Dee turned to me. "You're wanted by Madam in her office, Guxue. Immediately."

"Did . . . she say why?" I asked, more afraid of this sudden meeting than of that pathetic nobleman.

"You know she does not like to be kept waiting," Matron said, a note of warning in her voice.

Anjing mouthed *Thank you* behind her, and I gave her a quick nod before hurrying away.

CHAPTER FIVE

I RESCUED MY QÍN FROM WHERE I'D HIDDEN IT beside the stairwell and ascended, dread mounting with each step. I thought I had done well for my first performance, but there would only be one listener whose opinion mattered.

Madam Wu sipped tea at her desk, ledgers spread out before her. The beads of her abacus clicked rapidly under her fingers. While I stood there waiting, I distracted myself from my nervousness by admiring her treasures: embroidered wall scrolls depicting birds and flowers, a collection of small painted vases set in custom-built niches in the wall, a gilded bird cage in the corner where her parrot lived.

I fidgeted while she completed her calculations, reminded of how I had not even dared to lift my head when I first walked into this room. I recalled the intensity of her gaze, and I still withered under the same scrutiny when she finally acknowledged me.

I felt twelve years old again. Awkward and unsure.

Auntie stood, her appearance impeccable as always. She wore a green silk jacket with full sleeves and an undertunic of peach. Her skirt was of a paler green, a shade reminiscent of the highest quality of milk jade. But most splendid of all was the necklace she wore: a collar of thin gold filaments, upon which flowers with ruby petals and gold centers dangled. On another woman the necklace would have appeared gaudy, but it suited her.

"You've done well for yourself, Apprentice Xue," she said to me with a smile. It caused that tight knot inside of me to ease ever so slightly. A smile was a good sign, that it was possible she was pleased with me. She gestured then for me to sit down in one of the chairs under the painting of the Qinling Mountains.

I gingerly perched myself upon the chair as directed. She sat down opposite me, and immediately there was a servant behind us to pour tea into the already prepared cups between us.

"Your first public performance. No screen to hide behind any longer. How did it feel?" she asked. I felt as if I was being tested, and I did not like to be the sole recipient of her attention. It seemed to me like the threat of a very sharp knife.

I decided to be honest. "I was nervous, Auntie. But I believe I made only minimal mistakes." My palms began to sweat then, but I did not want to rest them on the finely carved arms of the chair. I furtively tried to wipe them on my skirts, then decided to sit on them instead, to resist the temptation to fidget further.

"Did you speak with anyone when you entered the hall, or when you were leaving it? Did you speak to anyone at all, anyone who is not currently under the employ of the House?" The questions came, one after the other, and the dread seeped back. How did she find out about what happened with the minister's son and Anjing so quickly? Perhaps the rumors really were true, that Auntie was actually a Tiger Spirit hiding out in the human world. It was why she appeared to never age, and why she could hear and sense the goings-on in any corner of her domain.

"Think," she urged.

"I . . . I spoke with Minister Jiang's son, briefly," I said. *Threatened him, more like.* But hopefully Matron Dee would explain it under a kinder light.

But Auntie waved her hand with a grimace. "Not him." Clearly she didn't have a high opinion of the minister's offspring either.

I thought back to after I left the women's quarters. There was nothing else that stood out. I'd kept to the back, like I'd always been told.

"There was no one else," I said.

"And does the name Meng Jinglang mean anything to you?"

I shook my head. A stranger's name.

"Funny," Auntie remarked. "He purchased your token tonight."

I stared at her, not understanding. Was this some sort of joke? A token permitted a patron to spend time conversing with an apprentice or an adept in private, but usually after they'd already met at an event where the entertainers were permitted to mingle with the guests. I'd always been behind the screen. Until tonight.

"You are not a girl known for . . . trysts," she said. "You've heard the cautionary tale of those who cast a net with their beauty? They thought they were pulling in fish, but dragged in an eel instead."

"Yes, Auntie," I said softly. I'd heard enough of that gossip as well in the women's quarters. Adepts who believed their lover was a wealthy merchant, but then discovered after it was too late that they had fallen in love with a fraud, a wastrel who had nothing to their name.

"He presented himself as a scholar, but with his bearing and the appearance of his companions, I believe he may be associated with the Meng family in the capital. A reputable family, generations serving the emperor in his army," she told me, tapping her finger on the table. "You must conduct yourself with the utmost care. Ensure that you do not give them reason to unfavorably compare our house to those of the capital, to find us lacking. Do you understand?"

"Yes," I whispered, still baffled.

"If he is indeed associated with the recently titled Marquis Meng, then there is great potential for us to make further connections with the family." She pondered aloud, already performing her calculations, and then noticed that I was still there, waiting for her dismissal. "He waits for you in the pavilion. I'll have the servants bring out an assortment of refreshments. Serve him well. Bring your qín, as he requested. One token, one stick of incense. If he asks for more, decline, say you are unavailable for the rest of the evening. Ask him to come speak to me again if he wishes to request another visit."

I tried to retain the instructions, inwardly already wondering how I would do this. If I was even capable of entertaining a patron. I thought I would have more time to observe how the adepts conducted themselves at parties or private events. Not thrown into my first meeting like this.

Auntie Wu waved me off. "Go."

I slowly lurched to my feet and offered a clumsy bow as I left the room, gathering my qín once again at the door. My heart beat so rapidly that I felt as if it would burst from my chest, as if I might expire and that would be the end of it. *Poor girl*, they would say about me in memoriam, *the stress of it was too much for her.*

I took a deep breath and tried to quell the panic that threatened to overwhelm me. What did the adepts say when the other apprentices would gather around them, asking questions when they returned from their visits? Some patrons wanted to impress, and would speak of their various exploits or show off their wealth in extravagant gifts. Others quoted poetry and spoke of love, demanded their devotion, and begged that their attention remained their own. What would he ask of me? I was then aware that I could appear disheveled, too sweaty from my earlier performance. What if I showed up and he turned away, repulsed by my appearance?

My feet took me too quickly to the back gate, then into the garden proper. I could not keep my mysterious patron waiting. The walled garden was small, but well maintained. The sound of trickling water flowed in the background, unseen, to soothe the mind as one strolled the garden paths. I spent many hours here, practicing for the flowers to hear, so that I did not disturb the others in the house. The moon hung overhead, a faded disk, almost hidden behind the clouds. The pavilion itself was lit by lanterns, so I could see the figure waiting for me there, his back to me.

From this distance, he did look like a scholar, as he claimed. His hair was pulled back in a topknot and secured with a jade pin, dark strands flowing down to his shoulders. The robe he wore was an uncommon shade of cerulean, edged with black and silver. His hands were clasped behind him as he looked up at the lanterns above.

Stones crunched under my slippered feet as I drew closer to the pavilion. He turned at the sound. My gaze swept over the dark brows, the high cheekbones, the serious set to his lips, before I sank into a deep bow. A greeting befitting the suspected son of a marquis. But I did not expect him to join me on the path, his hands to touch my elbows, to bring me up to standing. It was not how one behaved in Wudan's society. I drew in a sharp breath.

"There's no need for that," he said, but not in a tone of chastisement. He seemed almost . . . embarrassed.

I looked up, startled at the sound of his voice. Only my qín separated us like a shield, my fingers clutching it for comfort. Dark eyes looked down at me. He was younger than I expected, only a few years older than myself.

I knew there were eyes watching us from the main house, waiting to report back to Auntie. I was very much aware that I walked a fine line between impropriety and danger, and I could only rely on myself to navigate this unfamiliar path.

"I . . . I'm sorry . . . ," I choked out, and took a step backward. Until I was out of his reach.

He frowned. "My apologies. I am . . . unaware of how one should behave in such an establishment."

I stared at him, not knowing what to say. A military household, Auntie had speculated. It would make sense if he hadn't grown up within the confines of polite society. If only I could utter something clever in response, to lighten the mood, but my voice froze in my throat.

"Come join me," he said, after a long, drawn-out pause. He turned and went up the steps to the pavilion.

I had no choice but to follow.

CHAPTER SIX

THE SERVANTS HAD ALREADY PREPARED THE PAVIL-
ion prior to my arrival. Three sides were covered with heavy drapery so
we would be protected from the wind. A coal brazier burned in the corner, warming the space. There was a tray of sweets and wine on the stone
table, and beside it one stick of incense held in the beak of a carved bird.
But the scent of chénxiāng, meant to be soothing, was a clear reminder
of Auntie's instructions: one stick, no longer.

A stand for my qín was set up beside the stone table. I placed the
instrument into the wood frame, careful to secure it so that it wouldn't
be easily dislodged. When I turned back, my patron had already settled
on one of the stools. I hurriedly reached for the jar of wine. This, at least,
I was capable of.

Except he reached for the jar too, and our hands brushed against
each other. I snatched my arm back, and my sleeve almost spilled the
wine entirely. One cup fell across the tray with a clatter.

I winced. Again, another failure of my training. Matron Dee would
certainly have choice words to share about her disappointment.

"Apologies, my lord," I said hastily, gathering the cups. He opened
his mouth to speak, but I continued on. "Please, allow me to serve *you*."

He paused for a moment, then commented wryly, with a slight lift
in the corner of his mouth, "Twice I have blundered. I will learn to keep
my hands to myself."

It conjured up the memory of the drunk man fumbling at Anjing's skirts in the back hallway, and I hoped he would not see the resultant flush on my face. I kept my attention on pouring the wine.

Straighten your shoulders, tip the head, ensure your sleeves ripple downward. Envision yourself like a painting. Each curve of your wrist, lift of your arm, should feel like a dance . . .

Clearing my throat, I spoke again, offering the cup with a bow. "I hope the wine served at our humble establishment is to your liking."

He drained the whole cup in one gulp. I stared at him, not knowing what to make of this odd behavior. Perhaps all patrons had their . . . eccentricities.

"Admittedly, I would not know whether it is of the finest or the lowest quality," he said, setting it back down on its tray. "My tastes are not so refined." That slight curve at the corner of his mouth again. I could not tell if he was mocking me or himself.

"But I am not here for the wine." I waited for him to continue, to reveal the answer of why he had mysteriously requested my presence this evening. He smiled, leaning forward, elbows upon the table. "I was in attendance at your performance and I found myself entranced by your playing."

"That's very kind," I said, hoping to sound humble instead of simpering. I was not immune to praise. I wish I could pretend it was the artistic pursuit of musical perfection that motivated my playing, but a part of it was the selfish urge to be recognized for my talents. To have something that was solely mine.

"I have a deep appreciation for the music of the qín," he said, bowing his head. "You have made me an ardent fan of your musicianship. Permit me to introduce myself. My clan name is Meng, and the name my family bestowed upon me is Jinglang."

No title or rank, so I could not confirm for Auntie his relation to the household of the general.

"Lord Meng, I am honored to make your acquaintance." I poured another cup of wine, but it remained beside him. Untouched.

He picked up my token instead, on which was written the character of my name. "It was quite a challenge to convince your mistress to permit me to speak with you. You must be in demand."

I could not stop the laugh that burst out of me, unbidden, even as confusion fluttered across his brow as my hand flew to cover my mouth.

"You are not local to Wudan, and a new visitor to the House of Flowing Water." I spoke quickly, trying to recover. "I am but an apprentice. I merely accompany the performers. My role is to assist in elevating the story, playing but a small part."

"Ah, but it was not the dance that came first. The music was written prior," he reminded me, as someone who had a good grasp of court music and its history would know.

"The poem was first," I countered, then immediately regretted it. The adepts had cautioned the attentive apprentices against correcting a patron. One never knows when someone may take offense, especially for those not accustomed to being corrected.

But his expression was that of delight, not anger. "You're aware of the poem!"

"The House provides us a passable education," I informed him, not speaking the entire truth—as if Uncle would permit me to learn any song without understanding its origins and influences. It was a habit I'd continued with any new piece I added to my ever-growing repertoire.

"Of course," he said, nodding, as if confirming something for himself. "I don't know why I would have expected anything less."

Lord Meng plucked a date from the bowl before him and held it up to the light, reciting in a low voice:

Oh sweetness, preserved in fruit
How I wish to contain my love's attention
But only bitterness lingered
The impenetrable core
The inevitable goodbye

A poem that captured the feeling of barely contained longing, relegated to old textbooks after the emperors of the current dynasty placed value on restraint and propriety instead. Such passionate verses had been determined by the academics to no longer hold value. Even the commoner's version, the one performed tonight, lacked the beauty and agony of the original verses.

It was not a poem I would have expected to pass through the lips of a soldier's son. The way this young lord presented himself was a series of contradictions, each more confusing than the last. The words reverberated between us, creating an odd intimacy in the small space. The breeze caused the walls of the pavilion to ripple and shift, sending the shadows and light dancing all around us.

He spoke as if he understood the depth of that wanting, like he knew about the sadness of reaching for something impossible to obtain. But what could someone as privileged as him know what it was like to *want*?

"You'll find only sweet morsels here." I kept my voice light, wanting to shift the mood. "Our fruit is fresh."

That startled a laugh out of him, and I couldn't help but smile back. His amusement should be my only focus, the fulfillment of my role: to be good company.

"Would you play for me?" He waved his hand toward the stand.

"The lamentation?" I asked.

"Oh, gods, no!" He coughed. "Something more upbeat, something . . ." He gazed up at the sky, paused, then said, ". . . suitable for moon watching."

I looked up as well. The moon continued to be obscured by clouds. I was almost certain he was teasing me, but I couldn't be sure.

What, I thought, as I stood from my seat, *a strange man.*

I TOOK MY time checking and tuning the strings, while I searched within my repertoire to select a piece that would be able to hold his attention. A puzzle was what he offered me. A challenge, not unlike the ones Uncle had presented to me before, when he wanted reassurance that I was still receiving an education that met his standards.

This lord was a learned man, as apparent by his recitation of the poem and his knowledge of the origins of the concubine's song. The words were uttered with feeling, not a mere demonstration of rote memorization. Did he appreciate the loveliness of the words, or did he relate to the sentiment contained within? A great love, long lost?

The right piece came to me then.

I began, fingers gently caressing the strings, as soft as the snow that fell earlier in the day.

When the cicadas have quieted, the migrating geese begin their call
From my view upon the high tower, the land meets the sky upon the horizon
Both the Goddesses of the Frost and the Moon endure the chill
Hard to say who is the victor, the beauty of the moon or the frost?

The last note lingered like the frost in the air, a sign of winter's swift approach. From the top of my imagined tower, I slowly returned to my body as the music dissipated. Another poem that inspired a song, then a dance that was offered to the dowager empress as tribute.

"Your music transports the listener to another realm," Lord Meng said after a round of slow applause. "A transcendent interpretation of Poet Li's words."

I bowed my head, hiding a smile. I shouldn't be so drawn to his praise, and yet, it pleased me.

"When I was younger, I imagined the Celestials frolicking through the clouds," I said. *Snow trailing from the fingers of Lady Frost, illuminated by the Moon Goddess's mirror.*

"And now?" he asked.

"It reminds me another year has passed," I said. "While for the immortals it is a mere breath, a moment."

"Ah, but time passes for them all the same. I'd like to believe for humans the brevity of earthly existence creates greater appreciation for Mortal delights."

"If you are lucky enough to be born into such a household," I couldn't help but retort. Not all of us had the freedom of choice, to go where we wanted, to buy what we craved.

Lord Meng inclined his head and looked at me with amusement. "The lady offers a clever counterpoint. Your words draw blood."

The dramatic declaration made me chuckle. Was this what the adepts felt like when they entertained our guests? The playful word games and hidden flirtations?

"And yet, another reminder of time's swift passing." He gestured to the incense—another section turned gray and crumbled, fell to ash on the tray below. Only a few minutes remained.

For a moment, I wished the time within this pavilion could slow, be drawn out a little longer. I wanted to speak further of poetry and music with someone who understood.

"Your instrument . . ." He gestured at the qín on the stand. "The color of the wood is quite striking."

I ran my finger over the side, noting its familiar curve. The renowned qín makers specialized in particular types of wood grown in various regions. The hardness of the wood, the shape of the tree that it was harvested from, the time of year the tree was felled . . . all of it had an effect on the sound and quality of the instrument.

"Could you tell me, was it made by Su Wei?"

My stomach dropped at the familiar name. Uncle had warned me after he gave me such a precious gift. He said that people would come calling in search of these priceless creations. Some would offer me treasures in exchange, gold and jewelry and riches. Others would provide favors, promises of protection.

I asked him then why he wished to gift it to me, when it could fetch so much more on the market. Surely one of his friends in the academy would be worthy of such an instrument. He chortled then, and said to me with great seriousness, *I entrust this qín to you because you understand its worth. Someone very dear to me gave me this responsibility. To ensure that this qín is owned only by someone who would appreciate it.*

Some say Su Wei was the only artisan trained by the Nightingale herself, not the scholar in the story, that she had learned the way to infuse magic into the instruments she made. Others said that she had shaped instruments that would rival the beauty of the Sun qín and Moon qín. She lived many years ago, and her instruments had changed hands time and time again. Now there were very few of her creations left.

"You're a collector," I said. I could not hide the hurt in my voice. It felt almost like a betrayal, even though he owed me nothing, offered nothing but a purchase of my time and pretty words to entice me.

"I am looking for a particular instrument of hers," he said, expression changing to one of intent, revealing his true aim. "If you would only permit me to see—"

"You have wasted your funds and my time," I said, tight-lipped. I lifted the qín from its stand, held it close, protectively.

"Name your price," he said, voice taking on a desperate tone. "It is a matter of great importance. I must know if this is the one I am looking for."

"It. Is. Not. For. Sale," I said through gritted teeth.

The red dot at the bottom of the incense extinguished itself, sending a tendril of smoke into the air.

"I bid you good evening, my lord." With a swift bow, I was gone, and with great shame I felt tears prickle my eyes as I entered the safety of the building. At least they did not fall while I was still in his presence. I had held on to that shred of dignity.

It was the damned poetry that had made me feel as if I was speaking with a kindred spirit. But it was all a ruse, a pretense for the prize to be won. The adepts were right—every patron had a price, something they desperately sought from us. It was best for us to understand it.

I would not be so foolish again.

CHAPTER SEVEN

WHEN I ENTERED THE WOMEN'S QUARTERS, THE others immediately swarmed me, buzzing with excitement. At first, I thought they wanted to congratulate me about my first performance, but then the questions came swiftly.

"What was he like?"

"Was he handsome?"

"How did you know him?"

It was difficult to hide anything in the House. Everyone knew everyone else's business. I just never had anything of note to share.

"Our sweet Xue'er, finally growing up . . ." Feiyun placed her arm around my shoulders, and a flash of annoyance flared inside of my chest. I shook her arm off, but she just laughed while the others tittered at the face I made. Living together as long as we did, they were aware of my moods.

I could tell them it was not my presence the patron sought, but the ownership of my qín, except what would be the point? Most, if not all, of them would say I was foolish to turn down such an offer. To refuse all that money to keep a piece of wood . . . It would be unthinkable.

I splashed some cold water on my face to prepare for sleep, to cool down the embarrassment still burning my face. I should have been celebrating my successful performance, but instead I had to think of *him* and his outrageous request.

Some schools of music believed the qín had a soul, for it required the heart of the wood in its creation. The wood had memory, and it was the responsibility of the musician to honor the life that was taken in order for the qín to be made. When I was younger, I had been given the rare opportunity to observe part of the construction of a qín with a master qín maker. They were true artisans in the way they handled the wood. With reverence and respect.

While the rest of the house quieted down for the night, I spent time alone in the music room, cleaning the qín with a cloth. Wiping it until the surface shone so that I could rid myself of the ill feeling the evening's conversation had given me.

Not every artisan who was skilled at crafting the qín was capable of playing it, but legend said Su Wei was known to be a respectable musician. She was able to pair a player with the instrument most suitable for them, by listening to the style and expression of how they played. Her manuals on technique were still well circulated in schools.

Out of all the types of people whose lives revolved around the qín, from the most revered teacher to the common merchant who bought and sold them, there was no one more detested within the community than the collector. There were collectors who sought to round out their treasure vaults with one exquisite specimen crafted by each of the fifty qín makers who had obtained renown, their names revered by the three major music academies. Others searched for one or two master artisans and made a point of collecting all of their works that they were able to find.

Regardless of their goal, the results were the same: The qín were displayed as a demonstration of wealth and power, rarely handled. A waste of the harvested wood, the tree that had to die in order for the instrument to be made.

To a musician, this was sacrilege.

———

THE NEXT MORNING, Auntie sent me a summons to join her for the morning meal. My mood was sour, for I did not want to disappoint her. I did not want to know how the young lord had responded to my slight. He could have accused me of all sorts of things.

"Ah, there you are, Xue." Auntie gestured for me to sit down. We were in her receiving room. With her hair down over her shoulders, wearing only a casual morning dress, I could almost pretend she did not have that intimidating reputation. But I knew better than to let my guard down.

"Eat." She waved at the platters on the table with the book in her hand. I picked up a palm-size flatbread and munched on it quietly while Auntie frowned at the figures in the book, considering some calculation or another. I took a sip from the bowl of soy milk that was meant for dipping the flatbread in, and stirred some sugar in to make it more palatable.

When she was ready, Auntie picked up her own flatbread and turned her attention to me.

"Tell me everything," she said. "Leave out no detail."

So I did. I told her my recollection of the time in the pavilion, from the awkward beginning to the challenge offered, even the moments that made me cringe. Auntie listened carefully, only interjecting with a question or two. When I was done, I braced myself for her wrath. But instead she appeared thoughtful.

"A collector," she said, tapping a finger against her chin. "That aligns with my suspicions. Those who obtained noble ranks through military prowess often overcompensate in their attempt to ensure they fit in with the literati."

I remained quiet. The clashes between the factions within the court were often discussed and speculated upon by patrons who had political ties. Many influential people passed within these halls, and our mistress was a collector in her own way, of an eclectic assortment of people. She utilized them for her own purposes, which assisted her in gaining favors in the city and across the kingdom. But what did I care for these generals and scholars and their court games? The capital was as distant to me as the moon, as the Celestials and their crystal palaces.

"And it may surprise you that he was not dissuaded," she continued, barely containing her glee. "He requested your presence again tonight."

Ah, there it was. The reason why I was not punished for losing my composure and fleeing the pavilion, ending the evening on a bad note. The only thing that mattered was that our customers came back, again and again, to grace our halls and purchase our tokens and be entertained.

"I will not sell my qín to him or to anyone," I said to Auntie in a low voice. She'd never asked me to, but I dreaded that someday that request would come out of her mouth, and then I would be trapped.

She gave me a peculiar look. "I would not ask that of you," she said. "Your uncle . . ." A pained expression crossed her face, then smoothed away.

"Tonight you will perform for him again," she said, after clearing her throat. "A private concert in the garden. We will show him all that Wudan has to offer."

Another session in which I would have to dodge his advances, but do so in a way where he would not take offense.

There was no good reason for me to refuse, so I left the room alone with my swallowed protests, keeping my dark thoughts to myself. There were days when I was content in the role I played within the House, to stay behind the screen and provide pleasant accompaniment. Then there were days when I felt like I should step out into the garden and stand under the open sky and scream at all of the rules that governed my existence, like hands placed around my throat, slowly choking me.

I heard someone say my name, and I paused in the doorway to the women's quarters. They were talking about me inside.

"He's requested her again tonight."

"Cook complained that Auntie is expecting a banquet on such short notice."

"She surprised us all."

"I didn't know she was capable of it."

"It's always the quiet ones who surprise us."

"They have the most to prove."

Their comments flowed into one another, coming from familiar faces. The voices took on different tones, insinuations, and sneers. It had never been directed at me before, but it struck a tender part of me all the same. Especially as one of them was Feiyun, who I always thought was my friend. I realized it was all a falsehood, and I was surrounded by people who wore many masks. How they could offer pretty smiles and then wield words that dripped venom.

"Have you all said enough?" Someone grabbed my arm and pulled me out of the shadows. Anjing dragged me before them, even as I struggled to pull myself from her grasp. She scowled at all of them, teeth bared, incensed on my behalf. I should've been more upset that they believed I had so little to offer other than my body, but looking at their incredulous expressions, I just felt numb.

"We should be happy when each of us finds a possible future out of this house," Anjing declared, head high. "Do you imagine all of us will stay here forever?"

"Matron is here permanently," one of them said after a time. "I thought . . . I thought Xue's contract had a similar sort of agreement. They're the same type, after all."

"The same type?" Anjing's eyebrows shot upward. I tugged at her elbow, trying to get her to calm down. I did not like their attention. I did not like to be seen as competition. Some of them appeared contrite, while others folded their arms over their chests and said nothing at all, yet their expressions made their thoughts clear. But Feiyun was the one who I cared about the most, and she averted her eyes. I had stepped out of my place, disrupted the hierarchy of the House, and they despised me for it.

"Never mind," I said to her, repeating myself. "Never mind."

"You should care, Xue!" Anjing snapped at me. "You should believe that you are meant for more than this place. Take that opportunity if it's what you want, and get away from small-minded people like them." She turned and shot them a glare over her shoulder.

The cluster of people separated then, and I realized I was trembling a little.

"Don't let them get to you," she said. I knew that she was trying to be supportive, but I was too wound up in my misery to see it other than a different type of intrusion.

"You shouldn't have said anything." I brushed by her, reminded again of everything that bound me to this place. How I was like them and yet not like them. How I had thought I was finally advancing forward, that I would finally be an apprentice not only in name but in position, and yet the reality was I would never truly be free.

"This came for you earlier." It was Mili, one of the novices. She handed me a small bundle. The ties that secured the cloth were obviously loosened and then hastily retied again. "I couldn't stop the adepts from opening it. I'm sorry."

"Thanks," I mumbled, and turned away from her too.

I sat down on my bed and opened up the package. Inside were two books. I opened one and stretched it to its full length. It was bound in an alternating style so that it all unfolded in a long strip—a song manual. It contained instructions for how to perform the correct fingerings as well as an explanation of the associated poem or imagery—a way to learn a song without a teacher.

"Don't be too sad." Xidié, one of the older adepts, had come over, drawn by the earlier commotion. She did not participate in the speculation about how I may have gained the attention of my patron, but she must have overheard it in the tight quarters. More witnesses to my embarrassment.

"There will be others, in time," she added, placing a sympathetic hand upon my shoulder. "Nothing shows more sincerity than gold or jewels."

She had misread my shock for disappointment. I did not know how to explain that these manuals were priceless. To me, they were a precious gift, worth their weight in gold.

CHAPTER EIGHT

XIDIÉ WASTED NO TIME GATHERING A FEW OF THE others to her cause: defending me. Anjing became one of my most vocal supporters and shrugged off my thanks, reminding me I had helped her before.

They attended to me patiently, scrutinizing every detail with ten times the attention of Matron Dee. They argued over whether my coloring should be shifted to bold or subtle, if this or that color of fabric was flattering or washed out my complexion.

In the end they chose a pink outfit, a delicate shade that was like a blushing spring rose. I was loaned bits of jewelry: a bracelet of thin gold to be fastened high on my arm, a simple hairpin with a dangling pearl, and a fine jade comb affixed into my hair that was pulled into the shape of a flower. Each of them placed their mark on me until I sat before the mirror, wholly transformed.

My eyes, outlined with the technique they called phoenix wings, provided a subtle lift in the corners so that I appeared more alert. My scar lightened and blended with cosmetics so it was barely visible. The full curve of my lower lip was drawn into an enticing pout. I did not look like myself, and perhaps that would grant me the confidence to do what I needed to do tonight: stand my ground.

But in the quiet moment when I was left on my own to prepare for the evening, I could not resist opening the manual again. It was a most peculiar gift to give to an entertainer of a house, but a prized one to give to a disciple of qín music. My own notes on my repertoire were either collected on scraps of bamboo after my teacher's lessons or, the rare times I had access to a manual, copied by hand, and I was usually only given enough time to consult a section or two.

Wealthy scholars were able to pay people to transcribe the manuals completely and review them at their leisure. To have two of my own . . . something that I would have only been able to purchase if I'd made the right connections, and if I'd gained Auntie's permission to have funds to secure such a purchase. Years and years into the future. Did he know the value of what he gave so freely? Or was he so wealthy that this was an expense he could carelessly throw into the wind?

My finger trailed down the title of the song he had picked for me. The first, "Melody of the Water Immortals," the strings meant to be played like a waterfall. A song about loss, grief, and ghosts. The second, "A Song for Remembrance"—the story of a woman whose song remained, even though she had died years prior, crying out for vengeance. A furious piece, full of wild strumming and fervor.

It seemed like another puzzle for me to solve, the reason why he chose those two pieces in particular as gifts. Both songs originated as poems, reinterpretations of legends, then were accompanied with music. It showed he remembered the details of our conversation the previous night, and it made me feel slightly exposed. Like catching someone watching me from across a room.

A note fell out of the side of the manual. His writing was a confident scrawl.

I offer these with my most sincere apologies. I would be most grateful for your company this evening.

—Meng Jinglang

I knew I should grit my teeth and bear his presence tonight and never see him again, yet some part of my curiosity was piqued. At the song manuals. At the offered apology. What else would he ask of me?

I MADE MY way to the back garden in the early evening. The sun had fully set, and all the lights of Wudan were illuminated, glittering in the distance. I could see them from the second story as I descended the stairwell. The House was busy preparing for the evening's show, filled with lively sounds of chatter and movement, but when I shut the door behind me, the garden was quiet and dim, except for a row of lanterns lighting an enticing, winding path toward the back.

Last year, a chancellor visited with his wife from the capital. Auntie, knowing the wife's family was from the coast, brought in great tanks filled with various delights of the sea.

This year, for the New Year celebrations, carpenters were brought in to construct platforms in the courtyard, connecting them with rope. While the guests feasted, acrobats performed above their heads, and we were the talk of the town for weeks after.

I'd seen gatherings that were grand spectacles and gatherings that were small and intimate, like stepping into an ink painting. Tonight, the banquet was laid out in a hidden corner of the garden, where the hedges provided the most privacy. The background was a wall of climbing winter roses, white and delicate. There were sculptures carved from ice interspersed along the path. One, a dragon rolling toward the sky; the other, a phoenix diving down to earth.

Lord Meng waited for me at the table set up at the end of the path, the space lit up by the cheery fires that glowed within metal braziers. He stood as I approached, and bowed, the lights dancing across his face. I thought seeing him again would make me angry. Instead, I decided to hold on to the illusion, pretend we were meeting for the first time. He seemed eager to do the same.

As the evening progressed, my patron kept his word, and he was a pleasant and attentive companion. The awkwardness between us lingered for the first two courses, but then conversation flowed as steady as the dishes that came out of the kitchens.

The kitchens had prepared for us the famed Wudan banquet: eight cold dishes and sixteen hot dishes. Each of the courses was served on the finest blue porcelain, appearing as if they were carved from ice. Every course contained only one elegantly prepared bite: a crisp fried flower unfurled to hide the jeweled morsel of sweet taro within, a mushroom shaped like a hand, a meatball that melted on the tongue . . . Course after course, a sampling of the city's specialties.

While we ate, a musician had erected a set of cloud gongs a few paces down the path, the latest trend from the capital. He struck the ten bronze gongs of various sizes with small mallets, creating a cascading series of sounds that flowed around us like rain falling. It was an exquisite display, I admitted, even though I had already observed these events from the other side. To experience it for myself, all the tastes, sounds, scents, sights . . .

While we ate, I satisfied his curiosity about the running of a business such as the House of Flowing Water, about the ranks from novice to adept. I provided a comparison to the schooling of the scholar-officials in the academies, which he seemed to understand. He was also interested in the cooking skills exhibited in each dish of the Wudan banquet, and I tried to answer his questions to the best of my ability. But I noticed that he picked at his food and left most of his dishes unfinished, until I had to speak up. "Is the food not to your liking, my lord?" I asked, when another dish was yet again taken away half-eaten.

"No, no." Lord Meng shook his head. "I've been of poor health for some time."

He noted my look of alarm, and quickly added, "I'm well on the way to recovery, though some symptoms still remain. One of which is a weak stomach."

He refused my offer to have the kitchen send out lighter fare, and spoke of other things, obviously not wanting to discuss the topic further. Our conversation continued to flow smoothly after that, and we even engaged in a lively debate about which living poet was the most influential of the kingdom.

"I must thank you for the loan of the song manuals," I said to him after my belly was satiated.

"I hope my selection pleased you," he replied with a smile.

"They were lovely folktales," I said. "I was familiar with the story of the Water Immortals, but not the other. They will be excellent additions to my repertoire, for which I am most grateful."

He inclined his head. "I am glad to have had a small contribution to the addition of exquisite music in Wudan."

"I will copy them and return them to you in a timely manner," I said impulsively. The sips of wine that accompanied the meal were going to my head, casting everything in a golden glow. I decided that I could not assume it was a gift outright—originally I had believed what he had given me was also a copy, but upon closer examination I had seen additional annotations and fingerings. Notes made by the brush of a master.

The smile was replaced by a frown. "Was that what you've been told? My message must not have been clear. They were a gift. They are yours."

I did not know how to react to the sudden intensity of his gaze, and I did not want to know what the cost of accepting such a gift would be.

"It is . . . not something that is done here," I tried to explain to him. "I'm only an apprentice. I cannot afford the price of your favor."

"You believe I am bribing you!" He let out a harsh laugh and shook his head. "How low you must think of me, offering you nothing but insults again and again."

We'd been taught that inside these walls was a sanctuary from the dangers of the city, that we were here by the grace of our given talents, the blessings of the Star of Fortune. But sometimes the danger came inside, and I'd seen how easy it was to slip and offend, and be cast out of favor, disgraced.

"My lord, I am most appreciative of your gift," I said, attempting to pivot. "But—"

A scream pierced the serenity of the night, followed by the sound of something shattering upon the stones. We looked up to see one of our serving girls on the path, broken dishes at her feet. With horror, I recognized Mili. It must have been her turn to assist with the kitchens that night. Beside her was the player of the cloud gongs, holding up the small mallets in his hands as pitiful weapons.

Before them loomed a beast like nothing I had ever seen before. It looked like a giant cat, but I could see there was something . . . wrong with it, even from this distance. There were colorful protrusions that grew from its face like glass, gold, blue, and green. Its eyes were too large, the color a deep dark red, with a black orb in the center. Behind its body thrashed a long tail that ended with a tip of dangerous-looking spikes.

Such a creature existed only in books of legend, whispered over a campfire, passed down from our ancestors as warnings to their children. Not as a living, breathing specimen before me.

The beast threw its head back and gave a great roar that shook the trees. Mili cowered, backing up the path in our direction. The sound sent the musician running for the trees. The beast lunged, a blur, and batted at the man with its huge paws, sending him sprawling onto the path instead.

I shot to my feet, and beside me, Lord Meng was already standing. We were trapped. To our back there was the wall, before us the table. If the beast was to run up the path toward us, we would be torn to shreds. If we could scale the wall behind us in time—

The man tried to crawl toward the trees, but the beast flipped him onto his back. Then . . . all I could see was the movement of the beast's head as the man's arms and legs shuddered, then stilled.

Mili ran toward us, screaming, a high, tinny sound. She stumbled on the slippery rocks and fell, landing on her hands and knees. I cried out a warning as the beast lifted its head, attention drawn.

A growl reverberated in the air, low and sinister.

Then it lunged.

CHAPTER NINE

MILI LOOKED BACK OVER HER SHOULDER AND scrambled to her feet, terror contorting her features.

"Xue!" she cried out, tears streaming down her face. She reached out to me as she ran toward us, the beast rapidly closing the distance between them. "Help!"

I tried to throw myself forward, but hands grabbed me and pulled me back. The beast snapped at Mili, almost catching her arm, and she threw her body aside just in time. She steadied herself against the wall, and the beast growled in annoyance. It advanced upon her again, hackles raised.

Mili made a run for the house in another desperate attempt to escape, but the beast raised a great paw and batted her like a toy. She flew sideways, and her body struck the apparatus on which the ten cloud gongs were hung. The whole structure toppled. A sudden cacophony of sounds exploded as the gongs fell against the rocks, the frame, and one another. Some of the gongs broke off and rolled in every direction. The beast flinched, claws leaving deep grooves in the dirt, as it tried to put as much distance between it and the sound as possible. Which brought it farther down the path. Closer to—

"I'll distract it," Lord Meng said in my ear, in a cool, calm voice. "If you crawl under the shrubs and stay against the wall, it will be difficult for it to reach you through the branches."

I wanted desperately to see if Mili was still moving, if she had survived such a fall, but he held me back with one arm.

The beast gave a great huff and shook its head as the sounds faded. It raised its head again, sniffing the air, and then turned toward us. I looked around to see if there was anything within reach that could be used as a weapon. But there were only the flimsy plates, the ice sculptures, my qín on its stand . . .

"It will kill you," I gasped.

"It will try," he muttered, and then he strode forward to face the beast. Confident. Not as if he was walking toward his certain death by mauling.

I ran for the wall of the garden and the hedges like he told me to. Every instinct said I should run away as quickly as possible toward the house, but I couldn't help but look back. The beast gave another great, world-shaking roar, its attention diverted by the man who waved his arms above his head. Lord Meng would be devoured before I could even make it around the corner.

I had to *do* something. I could not leave him to die.

At my feet there was a glimmer of metal. I bent down and wrapped the string around my hand, lifting the gong off the ground. It had a good weight to it.

Lord Meng still had one arm up in the air. Was he so foolish he was going to try and fight the creature with his bare fists? My hand found a rock and I banged it against the metal as hard as I could. It made an ugly, jarring sound that rang in my left ear.

The beast flinched, then turned, eyeing me with hate. I struck the gong again and again, continuing to deafen myself in the process. I wished it all the pain and hurt, imagined the sound emanating from me in waves. Its paws scrambled upon the stones as it retreated backward, its lips pulled back from very sharp, bloody teeth with a snarl.

I forced it down the path, step by step, as it recoiled from the onslaught of sound.

"Keep going!" Lord Meng appeared beside me again. But this time, a strange light emanated from his hands. As he turned, the light changed, and he wielded a long, slender sword that shone in the darkness, soft and blue. I hadn't noticed that he was armed, but perhaps he had somehow hidden it within his robes.

I continued my determined banging of the gong, praying that it would give him even a slight chance against that ferocious beast. *Oh, Stars, hear my plea . . .*

He darted forward. The sword flashed, slashing across the beast's body. Lord Meng moved impossibly fast, dodging the attacks from those deadly claws that would have shredded him if they landed.

His sword struck true, time and time again, until the beast howled. It fell upon the stones before us and lay there panting, its blood running out from its sides as it drew its last breath. For a moment, I could have sworn that its blood looked silver.

Lord Meng stood over the body. His breathing was heavy from the exertion of the fight, his sword still pointed at the beast as if he feared it would rise again for one final attack, but his expression was regretful. He did not appear thrilled to still be alive, to have slain the beast and lived to tell the tale. His head was lowered, mouth moving as if he was praying. Why? It would have killed us both if he had not stopped it . . .

The gong fell down beside me as my hand let go, exhausted from the strain of holding it up. My ears still rang with that awful noise, and it made me dizzy and ill. The ground felt too soft under my feet.

Lord Meng was suddenly there above me, grasping my arms. His mouth moved, yet I couldn't hear him.

My head spun, and the world slipped away too.

———

I AWOKE STARING up at the ceiling of one of the house's private receiving rooms. Above my head was a carving of one of the Glorious Beauties of the palace, Consort Wen, who resided in the court of several emperors past. It was said the Minor Star of Music fell in love with her when he saw her portrait upon the Mortal Tapestry. He blessed her with the gift of song, and when she sang, flower petals fell from the sky like snow.

"Be still!" someone instructed me as I felt a pinch at my side. Needles were pulled away from acupuncture points on my face and my arms, and then Matron Dee was there, assisting me up. She gave me a cup of tea and bade me to drink with a stern look. I quickly took a sip, even though it burned my mouth.

My memory came back to me in bits and pieces. The night in the garden. The banquet with the gongs. The beast with strange protrusions from its body—

"My qín!" I cried out, spilling hot tea on my hand in the process. I noticed it lying against the wall, and sat back with a sigh. I set the cup on the table beside me, since I couldn't be trusted with it.

Matron gave me an odd look, then shook her head. She understood my peculiarities, having seen me grow up over the years. One of the apprentices had said she was like me, an Undesirable, and I wondered how she had received that punishment. She never spoke to me about it.

"And . . . Lord Meng?" My unlucky patron. Had he been hurt in the struggle?

"Madam is currently attending to the lord." There was a crease in the spot between her brows—something was on her mind.

He cut down that creature with a shining sword . . .

There came the sound of an argument outside the door, raised voices, then a moment later, Auntie and the lord in question came into the room.

"As you can see, she is fine." Auntie Wu swept her arm in my direction, and I detected a thread of impatience in her tone. Usually she was able to maintain her composure even with the most disagreeable of guests.

"My dear, your patron has been most insistent that he must lay eyes upon you to ensure you are alive," she said to me, her tone sweet, but I knew her temper was a quickly advancing storm. I knew she was analyzing the situation, attempting to see how she could prevent the news from spreading that someone had been attacked on the grounds.

Lord Meng came to kneel beside me, his expression earnest. "It would have devoured me if it wasn't for your quick thinking," he said. "I am in your debt."

"How lucky we were for your quickness with the sword!" Auntie exclaimed. "We were spared further loss of life. How unthinkable that mountain lions could be roaming the streets of Wudan. I should submit a complaint to the city guards that they've placed their citizens at such risk!"

I opened my mouth to tell her that it was no mountain lion, but a hand was placed upon my arm. I met Lord Meng's eyes, and he gave a small shake of his head. He did not want me to elaborate on what I saw.

He stood with a bow. "Madam Wu, I had requested a conversation with Apprentice Xue. If you will grant me the privacy of the room?"

"Of course." Auntie and Matron both bowed in turn, but I could tell by Auntie's downturned mouth that she was still not pleased. Before leaving the room, Matron met my eyes as well over the lord's shoulder.

Be careful, she mouthed.

No one had mentioned the death of the man in our gardens. I did not even know his name. Bile rose up in my throat, bitter and foul. I retched, covering my mouth with my hand so that it did not spill out.

"Easy, easy . . ." A steadying hand was placed upon my back, and a handkerchief appeared in front of me. I leaned forward and hung my head until the urge to vomit subsided. I swallowed and swallowed again.

"Not too fast," he cautioned as I struggled to sit up. He got me a fresh cup of tea, and it took me two tries before I could take it from him.

"You've had quite the scare," he said, sitting on the stool beside me, regarding me with concern.

I drank the tea so I didn't have to talk, let it wash away the taste in my mouth.

"What . . . what happened to Mili?" I asked finally, when I could speak again. "The . . . the girl who was with us."

"Ah." He nodded, and did not brush off my concern, for which I was grateful. "She was still breathing when I checked on her. They found her a physician."

"And . . . the player of the cloud gongs?" I asked, but already knew the answer. There was no possible way he could have survived. He shook his head.

"You didn't want me to tell them about the beast," I said to him, and it came out louder and more accusatory in the space than I expected. But I hardened my resolve, forced myself to look up at him, even if it might risk his offense.

"I—" he began, then closed his mouth. He seemed nervous somehow, less sure. He cleared his throat and tried again.

"I'm afraid I have not been entirely forthright with you," he said.

That much I could have deduced on my own, but I waited for him to continue. To admit to why he would go through all this effort to seek me out. My hand clutched at my wrinkled and dirty skirt, the lovely outfit that I had begun the evening in now bloodstained and ruined.

The illusion and grandeur of this house. His feigned interest in poetry and my music.

It was all a beautiful lie.

CHAPTER TEN

"I AM ACQUAINTED WITH YOUR UNCLE," LORD MENG said. "Our paths have crossed many times in the past few years." Seeing my shock, he continued. "He was close with my shīfù. I used to attend your uncle's poetry readings at the Fengshan Teahouse, when it used to be at the Yangzi River crossing."

To call another a shīfù, it meant they had completed the rites and sworn the oath that bound mentor to student. It meant that his mentor saw him as a successor to his knowledge, a worthy bearer of the teachings he was to bestow upon him. Almost as sacred as the bond between parent and child.

"What is his name?" I asked. I wondered if it would be familiar, for Uncle often told me tales of his travels. I never knew how much of it was embellishment, but I had clung to every word all the same. The many antics of the often controversial Third Princess. The minister who had peculiar . . . interests that would scandalize the court if they were ever uncovered. The gossip that would pass through the lips of the ministers and officials as they drank and feasted in the pleasure vessels that meandered down one of the kingdom's grand rivers.

"My shīfù is Gao Qiqi of the Shanyang Academy."

The man's name was not familiar, but the name of the school was. Uncle often referred to Shanyang wistfully, as a place where thoughtful musicians could gather to play and practice and learn from one another, but its doors had long been shuttered.

"He referred to your uncle as his zhīyīn, and due to my respect for him, I regard him as my teacher as well."

Zhīyīn, the form of highest respect that a musician can offer another. *The one for whom my soul resonates.* A bond of greater understanding. I'd only ever heard Uncle mention someone by that term once, but he never said their name. If Lord Meng was indeed speaking the truth, then why did he initially hide his association with my uncle?

"You play the qín then, if you attended sessions at Fengshan?" I asked. A twinge of jealousy flickered inside of me. The teahouse was a traveling one, its performers the most renowned across the kingdoms and its guests welcomed by invitation only. It quickly appeared one evening and then was gone the next.

"I am only a passable player of the qín," Lord Meng said, his expression sheepish. "Though I'm reluctant to admit that. My interest is in calligraphy and poetry."

None of it made sense. The scholars of the classics had their own schools and academies, their own preferred methods of instruction. Although those scholarly pursuits often crossed—for songs frequently referenced poems, and poems often referred to stories—I'd never heard of a qín master with a poet apprentice.

"Your qín is familiar to me," he continued. "It belonged to my shīfù. After his passing, I attempted to find it among his effects, and found that he had given it to your uncle. And so, I tracked it to you."

I felt a tightening at my throat, dread for what was coming. He would make his demands, he would provide some paper, some contract that proved my ownership of this qín was false. I would be forced to give it up. I would lose what was most precious to me.

"May I?" he asked, gesturing to the qín, *my* qín, leaning against the wall. I gave a small nod. He stood and retrieved it, set it across his lap. He handled it carefully, with a reverence that I appreciated. His attention traveled down the body of the qín, checking every detail. I fought to keep my hands still in my lap, even though every part of me wanted to snatch it out of his arms and run, not looking back.

"Along the side are cloud-streak markings," he said, without looking, fingers pointing at the ripples and smudges, formed during the crafting of the instrument. As unique an identifier as a birthmark.

"And underneath." He lifted it and stood the qín vertical, pointing at the underside where the wood curved. "Ice-split cracks."

Black marks trailed through the wood like blood vessels, as familiar to me as my own hand.

"Here, the mark of Su Wei." He tapped where her name was inscribed upon the back, then to the four words below. "And this . . . my shīfù's calligraphy. He carved it himself."

高山流水

I thought it was a reference to the pair of famous melodies: "Mountains High and Swift Streams." But now I understood it referenced the family name of the owner of the qín: Gao.

"I had thought to offer you a fair price for it," Lord Meng said, "but now I recognize there was a reason why it was given to you. He would have wanted it to be played as it was meant to be played—by a true master of the qín."

"I don't understand," I whispered. I could not bear to part with it, and yet I had to. I could not take what was intended for someone else. A qín passed from mentor to student—it had always been that way.

He stood up and, with both arms extended, offered the qín back to me with a solemn bow. "It is yours."

"Truly?" I could hardly form the word.

"There is no one it belongs to more," he said. His gaze was soft as he gently lowered it into my arms. A safe, familiar weight.

"Thank you," I whispered.

"When I first met you, I felt an affinity to your playing, and this feeling has only deepened with each meeting." He looked down at me, still speaking in that low voice. His arms were alongside mine, both of us holding the instrument between us. I felt the warmth of his body through the thin fabric of my sleeves.

"Your mentor . . . ," I said. "You mentioned he had passed as well?"

His arms dropped away from mine, leaving only cold behind. He turned away, until I could only see his profile.

"Did you not know?" His breath caught in his throat, ever so slightly, and I recognized it as someone who carried the same grief as I did. "He was with your uncle when they were cut down by bandits. They were traveling in the same caravan."

"I'm sorry." It was all I could offer. Those hollow words. What little comfort I could not give him. I hugged the qín closer to my heart.

The lord straightened then, adjusted his sleeves, and turned back to me. His eyes were still misty, and yet he set his shoulders with resolve. He addressed me directly then, looking at me as a peer would look upon another, instead of a patron owed his entertainment from a lowly apprentice. The corner of his lip curved up, the faintest hint of a smile.

"In memory of your uncle and my shīfù, I would like to extend to you an invitation, Lady Xue," he said, that earnestness returning to him again. The sincerity drew me in, even as I wanted to resist it. "Come join me as a guest at my family's manor. My father was also a connoisseur of the qín. I would love for its music to flow through the estate again, as it once had."

"I cannot," I told him, for my life was not my own. "I owe a debt."

"And I owe you my life as well," he said, more insistent now. The mist had cleared, and his eyes now sparkled. "Let me repay that in turn. Come play at my estate for a year, and I will pay out whatever you have left of your contract."

I stared at him, not knowing how to respond.

"I am an Undesirable," I said to him, when I finally found my words. "A yuè-hù. Your family's reputation would be harmed if you had someone like me in your employ."

"My family's manor is high up in the mountains." He responded quickly, no sign of retraction when he heard of the mark upon my name. "There we live a simple life, and care not for the past, current, or future intrigues of the court."

"My debt might be paid, but I would still have that mark on my standing, and have nothing to my name," I persisted. "If I remain in the city, I could build a following, a reputation, patrons who would be willing to see me perform."

A secluded, gilded life. A *safe* life.

"Is that what you want?" Lord Meng regarded me as if he could hear my thoughts, sense my hesitation. I had resigned myself to a life in the House of Flowing Water, had convinced myself this was the life I was meant to live; I had not dared to consider another route, a way out. "Then three years, if that's an agreeable term. You'll receive a good reference, and I will use my family's influence to find you a position in an academy. You will no longer be bound to any house. You will be free to choose your own patrons."

A promised freedom. What a prize to dangle before an apprentice.

I said the first thing that came to mind: "I do not believe you."

That startled a laugh out of him.

"No one would take a risk like this without there being more to gain," I continued. "There are many musicians at the academy and other houses. All of them could provide the entertainment or the . . . companionship that you seek."

I would not embarrass myself or the others of this house by entering an agreement that sounded too good to be true. One year or three. He should have picked a more lovely girl for that, someone more susceptible to his flattery.

"Gods, now I am certain you have spent time under his tutelage," he said, still chuckling. "The many hours we've spent debating over some minor point of philosophy—I can see his mannerisms in you."

My face warmed. Was he making fun of me again? Mocking how I'd lived, sheltered from the world?

"I do not mean it as an offense," he said, serious again. "Look, to prove my sincerity."

From his tunic he drew out a piece of paper, folded carefully, and presented it to me. I opened it and recognized my uncle's writing immediately.

Young Meng,

Since we last spoke there have been many things to share with you. With your shifù, we have traveled to the other side of the Yinyang Sea to consult the oracle there, following your father's path. It looks like your intuition was right. With his knowledge of the realm and the path he laid out, he was able to provide us with clues. However, the number of ravagers that were drawn to our presence has grown. It would seem our enemy has been alerted to our investigation. It is growing increasingly dangerous for us to be here.

I am concerned about Xue'er, on her own in Wudan. If anything happens to me, I leave her to your care. If you receive news of our deaths, you must continue to follow the trail and finish what your shifù and I could not.

> *Remember, the qín is the lock, but she is the key.*
> —*Tang Guanyue*

The letter did not lie—this young lord *had* befriended my uncle. I could almost hear his voice, speaking the words aloud, in a tone that he would reserve only for the closest of confidants. Someone he trusted.

I looked up at him, mouth agape.

"What sort of danger is he talking about? What was my uncle involved in?" All of these words, they made no sense.

"Come with me to my estate," Lord Meng said. "There, I promise you, I will explain everything."

Out of all of his promises, this was the one that weakened my resolve.

"Tomorrow," he insisted. "Tomorrow I will return with contract in hand and prove to you I am no liar."

CHAPTER ELEVEN

THE NEXT MORNING, LORD MENG MADE HIS OFFI-
cial offer to buy my contract from Auntie Wu. She sought me out later
that day to inform me of the news. I was practicing in my usual spot
along the side of the house, overlooking the garden. I found the music
room too small and too distracting—the practice room for the drum
troupe was nearby, and their sessions threw off my rhythm. Luckily for
me, the gardeners enjoyed my playing, and one of them had built me a
small lean-to to shield me from the elements.

"You made quite the impression on the young man," Auntie Wu
said as I quickly scrambled to my feet to greet her with a clumsy bow.
"Enough for him to offer a substantial sum to take you off my hands."

I'd never had the sharpness of Auntie's anger directed at me personally, and it made me flinch.

"It is an offer that I would be foolish to refuse," I said. Three years
of servitude in exchange for the possibility of a position in a govern-
ment academy, where a pardon could be eventually possible if I had the
backing of a court official. All in all, a good bargain she should appreciate. I had spent the previous evening restless in bed, mulling over the
lord's offer. Even as tempting as it was for him to buy out my contract, to
promise me the connection that his family would be able to offer, it was
the letter that swayed me. There was so little I knew of my uncle's life, so
many secrets that he kept to himself.

"I've seen many offers made by ardent young men in my time,"
she said, skepticism dripping from her voice. "They come courting,

bringing with them as many promises as flowers they could carry. Very few of these arrangements resulted in happiness for the man and the entertainer he whisked away."

"He did not ask me to marry him," I retorted, finding myself on the defensive. "I would not be so foolish to accept a marriage proposal."

"Then you are even more naive than I thought!" she snapped, her opinion of my impertinence clear. "A proposal, with a dowry and an agreement from your guardian, would require a contract drawn by the magistrate. You would be protected even if he were to change his mind. Your reputation would at least remain intact."

"Auntie, you and I are both aware beauty and charm are two virtues that cannot be attributed to me. My family name has already been stricken from the record. I have very little to lose when it comes to my reputation. Accepting Lord Meng's offer would mean that after those years, my life would be my own."

"And what then?!" She finally raised her voice. "After you've gained your freedom, how will you survive on your own? You will have no promised employment, no connections to a house, no position at a school."

This exasperation was unlike her, and an unwelcome thought wormed its way into my mind: Had she known that Uncle's life was in danger? Had she been aware of the threat that he faced?

"Did my uncle have enemies?" I asked her, and her face grew pale. She turned then to the garden, folding her arms over her chest, biting her lower lip. It was unsettling to see my mistress's usual calm be disturbed in such a manner.

Finally, she turned back to me, frowning, her words carefully chosen.

"Your uncle was a brilliant man," she said, voice low. "His skills with a brush, unparalleled. His wits, like a finely sharpened blade. He was able to ruin a man's reputation with merely a cleverly thought-out phrase. He'd made many enemies, but also assisted many in positions of power. A fragile balance that he always tried to carefully maintain, until . . ."

She turned her palms face up, mimicking something falling between her hands. Something shattering on the ground, irrevocably broken.

"I have upheld my end of the bargain," Auntie Wu said, clenching her jaw. "If you wish to go, I will not stop you. Whatever game your uncle wishes to involve you in even after his death, I wash my hands of it. Go and chase after his ghost." With a swish of her skirt, she left me there, unsettled by her words.

I only want you to be happy, Xue, Uncle's whispers haunted me.

I should have seen it, but I had been so caught up by the excitement surrounding his infrequent visits that I did not notice. When we ate in the market, when he purchased me small trinkets, when he listened to me play the qín. A worry slowly consumed him, one he was quick to brush away, to reassure me that everything was as it should be.

I should have seen it.

What else was left for me here, trapped as I was in this house, an Undesirable? If he wanted me to play splendid music until the end of my days, he should not have shown me a glimpse of a different life. He should have taken my hand and led me straight to the House of Flowing Water, left me in Auntie's care at the age of seven. He should not have kept me at his side for five years, told me about sleeping goddesses and otherworldly realms, taught me about poetry and calligraphy, given me all these fanciful tales and then bade me to stay still.

Whatever task he left unfinished, whatever burden he carried with him at the end of his life, I would help him complete it.

I owed him that, at least.

———

IT TOOK A few days to wrap up my affairs in Wudan. For the funds to be exchanged, for the contract to be inked and signed. Mili had experienced more of a mental shock than physical injury, and she woke from her daze two days later. She had no memory of the evening, of the attack, or much of what happened that day. I heard from the gossip shared among the others that Lord Meng's retinue had assisted with the "cleanup" in the gardens, and the reputation of the House remained intact. No further mention of the peculiarities of the beast, and I kept my speculation to myself of what I thought I had seen.

It seemed everyone believed my reason for leaving the House was for the comfort of a man. Even Xidié pulled me aside and cautioned me against relying too much on honeyed words, sharing what she had learned from the adepts who came before her. But my mind was set, no matter how some of them tried to convince me otherwise. Some of them just whispered about me, falling quiet when they saw me approach.

For some reason during those last few days, I thought of my family more often than usual. My spotty memory of them. How my father was constantly away, and how I would wait by the gate until he arrived, bearing gifts. Not so unlike how I waited for my uncle, years later. I recalled the sound of my mother singing as we gathered water from the lake. I would wake from my dreams, calling out for Mama, when that term had not passed through my lips for some time.

Then the carriage pulled up in front of the doors of the House of Flowing Water to take me away to the Meng Estate. Anjing squeezed me so tight I thought I would pop as she wished me well. A few of my fellow housemates leaned out from the second story balcony and waved colorful fabrics overhead to send me on my way. They whistled and laughed, creating quite the spectacle for passersby.

It was Matron who represented the House to see me off. Auntie had not spoken to me at all since our argument. She passed on a single message, that she had made inquiries in the capital. Marquis Meng had only daughters to his name, and who this man was, she could not confirm. She wished to protect me, even though I'd spurned her protection. I don't doubt she cared for me in her own way, more than I'm sure she was willing to admit. Even with that knowledge, I knew I still had to make my way to Meng Manor. To see what I could learn about my uncle and why he had entrusted this stranger to protect me. What task of such importance he had left unfinished.

Matron presented to me the contract that sealed my freedom, and then the pendant that identified me as a citizen of Qi, and permitted me to travel out of the city. She held my hands for a beat longer than appropriate, until I looked up at her, surprised.

"Be well, Guxue," she said. "Take care."

I understood then, and gave her a smile in return. As one who would recognize another, both of us bound by the same restrictions, and finding our own way out.

Then the carriage carried me away from my childhood and the city that I had known all my life.

The steady clomping of hooves accompanied the swaying of the small, cramped space. Beside me, my qín was wrapped and secured so as not to be jostled during the trip. I spent much time ensuring its security, as much effort as I spent awkwardly avoiding eye contact with my patron—and now holder of my contract.

But I needn't have worried. Lord Meng sat across from me, beads of sweat across his brow. He dabbed at his forehead with a handkerchief, his face pale. I finally had to inquire about his well-being, concerned that he would be sick over the two of us in the small space—which was not quite how I had envisioned this journey.

"Motion sickness," he told me. "I'm afraid I will not be the most engaging companion during our travels."

That was fine with me, for it gave me the quiet and space to reflect upon my decision. Every once in a while, I peered at the young man seated across from me. His eyes were closed, his head propped on one hand, lips pursed as if he was still in pain. The apprentices who had caught a glimpse of him had called him handsome—I supposed he was pleasing enough to the eye, if you liked the scholarly sort, with high cheekbones and an air of serious contemplation. I did not know what I liked and what I didn't like, only that there was more to him than how he presented himself, and the only thing I was certain of was that I did not trust him.

Who are you? I wondered as I watched him fall asleep, his face finally smoothing into peaceful rest.

The rocking of the carriage seemed especially soothing, and though I wanted to stay awake, to remain alert, I was having difficulty keeping my eyes open as well. A sweet scent drifted by in the air. A faint, floral perfume . . .

I decided to just close my eyes for a moment.

Only a moment.

INTERLUDE

BOYA WAS A MUSICIAN WHOSE SKILL AT PLAYING
the qín was renowned throughout the realm. He was in the service of
the emperor of Wei, whose headaches could only be soothed at the
sound of Boya's playing. But Boya tired of the life of splendor and finery,
for the emperor's mood shifted constantly.

One spring, the emperor's court traveled to Xingfu Forest, where
they hunted the elusive white deer. Boya withdrew from the camp in
search of solitude and ascended the stone steps toward the Yan River
lookout. There, inspired by the views, he began to play.

When he finished, he noticed he had an audience: a man dressed in
rough clothes, an ax by his side.

"I could hear the sound of the wind swiftly coursing past the stone
peaks," the man said in wonder, "and experienced the awe of those stone
giants watching over us."

Delighted, Boya launched into another song. When he was done,
the man spoke again. "I heard in your music the sound of the rushing
waters. The river thundering mightily through the gorge from the melt-
ing snow, barely contained."

The man introduced himself as Ziqi, a humble woodcutter from
Xingfu.

Every song that Boya played, Ziqi understood, almost as if he could
peer into his mind. From then on, every spring they would meet at the
lookout. Boya would play for his friend, who understood his music like

no other. It was only this yearly meeting that made his life at court bearable, and he longed for a simple life free of the emperor's service.

One spring, he ascended the steps eagerly, but Ziqi was nowhere to be found. When he inquired at the village, he was informed that his friend had died in an accident that winter. He cried bitterly and mourned for his zhīyīn, the only one for whom his music resonated throughout all the realms.

Boya dashed his qín on the stones and said he would play no longer, even upon punishment and threat of death from the emperor.

For what was the point of playing, if Ziqi was not there to listen?

VERSE TWO

CHAPTER TWELVE

WE TRAVELED THROUGHOUT THE DAY AND NIGHT, stopping only to stretch our legs and change horses. I attempted pleasant conversation with our carriage driver, but he responded in short, terse phrases, offering me even less information than my ill companion. The vague description he was able to provide me with was this: The manor was located north of Wudan, west of the Jili River, high up in the mountains. I realized my knowledge of the kingdom's geography was woefully inadequate—all of the history books were about wars that were fought over the fertile land in the river valley, and very little of my education involved the countryside and rural communities outside of the three largest cities.

It didn't take me long to discern that Lord Meng was genuinely affected by the swaying of the carriage, and it was not a polite lie to avoid speaking to me during our travels. No one was a great enough actor to fake the sheer relief on his face when we stopped to rest, and he was able to descend from the carriage with shaky legs.

On the third evening, we pulled up to the yard of an inn. Servants quickly came to assist us with the horses and carriage, and I had to react quickly to save my qín from their eager hands. Soon, our belongings were settled in our rooms, and a place set up for us in the dining hall.

A pot of tea was placed roughly on the table, some of its contents sloshing onto the surface. I stared at it for a moment, aware that I had become accustomed to the niceties of serving and presentation. The pot was lifted before my eyes, and tea poured into a pair of green glazed cups.

My mind snapped out of its stupor, and I tried to clumsily correct this improper reversal of roles. "Wait—"

He waved my hand away. "You'll learn on the estate we are much less formal than we must be to maintain appearances in society," he said, setting the pot down. "There's no need for that sort of distinction when I'm just as capable of pouring my own tea." He didn't seem to have taken offense.

Sufficiently chastised, I was glad for the interruption of small dishes being set upon our table by the server. I busied my hands with some watermelon seeds, the satisfaction of cracking them between my teeth and their salty flavor, discarding the shells. Soon, other dishes came as well: shredded bitter melon, a bubbling earthen pot of garlic black chicken, slices of pumpkin fried golden with salted egg yolk. I dug into the food eagerly.

I was already halfway through my bowl of rice when I stopped, noticing that Lord Meng had barely eaten.

"The food is not to your liking?" I asked.

"It's fine," he said, and picked up a few strands of bitter melon, placing them in his bowl. They looked sad and pale upon the mound of rice. "Travel is bad on my appetite, is all." I remembered he had mentioned his illness, and the effects on his body that remained.

I looked at the dishes he'd not touched and then at his bowl, then shook my head for not realizing. Calling for the server, I asked for vegetarian dishes to be brought out, stating that my lord had his dietary preferences and could not partake in any meat.

"My many apologies!" The innkeeper herself came to our table and bowed. "I was not aware that acolytes of the monastery were among us. I will have them prepared fresh and brought out."

Lord Meng did not correct the assumption that we were pilgrims, and soon there were more dishes that joined the others—braised mushrooms and tofu drizzled in flavored oil and blanched greens.

"You didn't have to do that," he said quietly. "I'm not that hungry."

"Well, you said that I didn't have to behave like your servant." I gave him a pointed look. "I don't like eating alone."

He considered this, and then chuckled. "I did say that, didn't I? Brought it upon myself." He reached over and picked up the serving spoon to scoop some mushrooms into his bowl.

"Yes, you did," I agreed, smiling back. I noted this small thing about my new patron, and puzzled over this while eating the rest of our meal. All of our interactions thus far were contrary to what my fellow apprentices and adepts had cautioned against. Where their patrons had expected deference or subservience, mine didn't seem to have the same expectation, and casting aside my training was proving to be . . . difficult.

"You look as if you are expecting the poor bird to come alive and fly out of the pot," he said, and I startled out of my thoughts, realizing that our table had fallen quiet for some time.

"I was just wondering why you are a vegetarian," I said, tossing forward the first question that came to my mind. It seemed a diet only for priests and paupers, and he was neither of those.

It was his turn to be taken aback, but then he provided an answer easily enough. "The soul moves through the cycle of death and rebirth. I do not consume the body of anything that contains the potential for spiritual ascendance."

"So that was also why you said a prayer after you killed that . . ." I paused, knowing that it was a lie, and yet not wanting to contradict him. "The mountain lion in the garden." I had wanted to ask about the events that transpired that night, but no suitable time had presented itself. Until now, I supposed.

"Ah." He leaned back. "You have questions."

"It was no mountain lion," I said, surprising even myself with my certainty. "There was something wrong with its eyes, and there were those strange growths." The almost human hatred contained within its gaze.

"You noticed," he murmured, like he was puzzled by this.

"I led a sheltered life, but not so sheltered that I would not know the sign of an animal who is . . . ill?" I told him, insistent on knowing more. "Is it a coincidence that it came to Wudan while you were there? Did it have something to do with my uncle?" I needed answers, the reason why I chose to uproot my life and follow him here, even if it resulted in the amusement disappearing from his expression.

"I made you a promise that I would tell you what I know, and I will honor that promise," he said, his gaze now shadowed. "Once we are at the manor, I can speak freely, but for now I ask for your patience."

He left the table soon after, and I cursed myself for being too eager. I endeavored from that point onward to be the most pleasant of traveling companions.

Just three years, I reminded myself. *Three years, and I will be free.*

TRUE TO HIS word, Lord Meng did not expect me to act like a servant. We ate each meal side by side. I learned we both liked a spoonful of sugar in our millet porridge in the mornings, and I took care to ensure each establishment knew of his preference for vegetarian dishes. He would order me a small dish of chili peanuts and roasted watermelon seeds when they were available, just because he knew I liked them.

Time stretched strangely on the road. It felt both too long and not long enough. I became accustomed to the quiet in the carriage, a different sort of existence compared to life in the House, where there was always noise and commotion and excitement.

When we rested, I would check my qín to make sure it was secure. Occasionally I would play, if it was deemed safe—guards followed us on horseback, for there were always dangers to traveling on roads that were lightly patrolled. They kept such a distance though, I would not have been able to recognize them. At times, Lord Meng would request a song or two. Our driver, gruff as he was, would pause in the care of the horses to listen to my music.

Many of those nights we spent beside the crackling fire, cups of warm tea in hand. Just the two of us.

"What is the estate like?" I asked him on one of those evenings under a canopy of stars, a little drowsy.

"It's high in the mountains and prone to fog," Lord Meng answered, dark eyes reflecting the flames as he extended his hands toward it for warmth. "It's . . . quiet. A place for peaceful contemplation."

"Sounds like the mountain monastery the emperor used to visit for his yearly pilgrimage," I said. A place to escape the summer heat and the bustle of the cities. I hoped he would mention something about the emperor, so I could deduce his connection to the court, but his responses were always elusive.

We spoke as well about poetry, about music, about the dialogue between verse and song, between melody and history. We talked about the library that his father built upon the estate, how he was a collector of music manuals. I learned he had a sister who had little appreciation for artistic endeavors, and a mother who focused more upon spiritual pursuits. He did not tell me if they still resided at the manor, and I had no idea what life would be like for me once we arrived there.

Would they accept me, an entertainer with nothing but a qín to my name? Or would they see me as an intruder, a disruption to their usual routines?

The closer we got to the manor, the more it seemed to weigh upon him. I could often see him frowning, chewing on the corner of his lip, as if there was a puzzle in his mind that he had to solve. He would often cast his gaze into the distance, fidgeting frequently, picking at his cuticles or a frayed thread on his tunic. But he never shared what plagued his thoughts, and the color never quite returned to his cheeks as the air grew thinner around us. When he did sleep, he was restless, twitching and mumbling.

Three weeks we spent traveling, stopping at inns when there were ones available, sleeping on the side of the road when there were not. Finally, we began our last ascent into the mountains. We were rocked and tossed about in that small space, my hands clutching the window frame so that I did not smack my head against the wood.

The road narrowed until it could only fit a single carriage. The trees pressed in against either side, thick and endless, towering over us. Fog swept in, obscuring everything around us, and cast everything in a gray, silvery light. It felt like we were floating amid the clouds.

Eventually our destination emerged from the mist. A gate of stone, and a name carved into one of the pillars.

夢幽府

The Manor of Tranquil Dreams.

A clever play on their family name, an echo of a dream.

We climbed out of the carriage a final time. Lord Meng stood for a moment between the gates, his eyes closed, and turned his face up toward the sky. As if gathering his inner strength for what awaited him.

The wind picked up, rustling the branches above our heads. It felt like ghostly fingers trailing through my hair. I was unsettled by the observation that came with the wind: The times he spoke about this place, he'd never once referred to it as home.

CHAPTER THIRTEEN

I FOLLOWED LORD MENG THROUGH THE GATE AND into a courtyard, walled on both sides by gray stone. Under our feet were white pavers that quieted our footsteps. There were white statues of various birds, carved in meticulous detail, interspersed in the space. There were peacocks, swans, owls, eagles, and sparrows, ranging in height from my hip to taller than my head, frozen in various positions—wings lifted and caught in flight, preening feathers or roosting upon a branch with eyes closed. It made an eerie effect, as if with one snap of the fingers, I would be surrounded with the flutter of wings and they would all ascend into the sky. I hurried my steps to leave this place, a sense of unease crawling down my back.

Through the next gate, the expanse of the estate appeared before me. There was a stream that snaked silver amid the grass, dipping down and curving around the hill. I saw pavilions in the distance, graceful rooftops and pillars that disappeared into the mist. Barely perceptible past them were the jagged shapes of mountains beyond. Everything was shrouded, muted in color. As if the fog leached it out, leaving only a pale imitation behind.

It was then that I realized what was causing my discomfort: There was no sound. No calls of birds or the drone of insects. It was a reminder we were far from the city.

If something happened to you, my mind whispered, *no one would ever know.*

Lord Meng was already halfway across the bridge that arched over the stream; I sped up again to be at his heels. The footpath snaked upward toward the entrance to the manor. White walls topped with black tiles separated the manor from the garden. Above the wall I could see the shape of the grand house beyond. As we drew closer, I saw upon the black double doors of the entrance gate were carved heads—stone lions with copper rings dangling from their fanged mouths. The doors opened when we walked up the gray stone steps. Two servants within bowed their heads and murmured greetings when we passed them.

I tried my very best not to gawk, though I couldn't help but look this way and that as we entered the interior courtyard. The manor was constructed in a traditional sìhéyuàn style, buildings surrounding a central courtyard. The wings were to our right and left, but the grand house stretched above us. There was a second story balcony, behind which was a line of long, skinny windows, covered with carved wooden shutters. The pillars, which held up the roofs of the covered pathways that ran along the side of the courtyard, were also carved in entwining shapes of sea serpents and dragons, birds and flowers.

It took me a moment to force myself to return my attention to the figures who waited to greet us in the courtyard. Three to the right, three to the left. Dressed in unobtrusive shades that ranged from pale blue to light gray—colors that Auntie would have criticized, as they washed out the warmth in anyone's complexion and left them appearing like wraiths. All of them bowed in sync.

"You may rise," Lord Meng said with a wave of his hand.

A man on the left took a step forward. He looked to be in his mid-thirties. There was something gentle in his features, in the graceful way in which he bowed first to his lord and then to me.

"Welcome home, my duke," he said.

Duke. The title struck me by surprise, and I could not stop the sharp hiss that left my lips. Only one of the servants glanced in my direction, a young woman, but she quickly looked back at the duke again when she met my eyes. He had not mentioned he was already the bearer of the noble title. I had thought, by the way he'd spoken of his father, that he was a lordling, still waiting for the title to pass to him. But he was truly the owner of this place and had kept it from me. For what purpose, I could not understand.

"Attendant Luo." The duke himself did not notice my shock. "I trust everything is in order?"

"Yes, everything is as it should be," Attendant Luo said. "Is there anything we can do for you or your . . . guest?"

The first impression matters. I heard Matron's cool voice, as she instructed us in our lessons on etiquette and manners. *Do not let them see you cower.*

I stood there and tried not to flinch as I felt all of their attention upon me. It was different when performing, when there was music separating me from everyone else.

"This is the Lady Guxue." The duke spoke to the staff with a voice that was used to being obeyed. I was not used to that tone of command. He had never spoken with me in that manner while we were on the road. "She will be my honored guest. I expect you to treat her accordingly, with respect and welcome."

They bowed in accordance. "Yes, sir."

"Danrou," he called out, and the woman who had looked at me earlier stepped forward. She appeared to be the youngest of the servants, not too far out of her adolescence. She was slightly shorter than me, with delicate features and watery eyes. "You will attend to the lady in the guest wing."

He then addressed me. "She has experience as a lady's maid, so you

92

will find her attentive to your needs. If you have any requests, you need only ask."

"I am happy to serve," Danrou said, and even her voice was sweet, matching her appearance.

"She will show you to your rooms. I hope you will join me for the evening meal." Without waiting to hear my response, he was already through the side doors, the other servants trailing behind him.

I was left alone with Danrou.

"This way, my lady." She gestured for me to pass through the opposite gate, taking me in a different direction altogether. "I will show you to the west wing."

"You can just call me Xue," I quickly corrected her. To be called a lady seemed like carrying a false title, for which there would always be consequences.

"I can only follow my duke's instructions," Danrou said, but then after a pause offered, "Lady Xue."

The covered pathway took us through another courtyard of carefully pruned trees. The lattice windows, cut every few steps into the wall, offered glimpses into the large garden that surrounded the manor house. In addition to the pavilions I saw, there were more bridges, stairs that ascended to platforms, pillars cutting into the sky, small groves of trees. All this space for just one household.

It was also difficult to know the size of the manor's interior, for the pathway led us past doors into other rooms, corridors, smaller courtyards. It seemed much larger inside than I initially thought. We passed no one on the way to the guest wing, and it seemed Duke Meng was not merely being humble when he spoke about his household being smaller than most. Perhaps it was difficult to keep staff in such a remote place.

Danrou pushed open yet another set of doors. Removing our shoes, we stepped onto the platform of a receiving room that felt as if it belonged to another manor. In comparison to the stark white walls, the walls of this space were lined with dark wood panels of an ornate pattern. Crisscrossing loops and curves that drew the eye, leading to the flower that was hidden in the center. Set into that pattern were small shelves on which pieces of art were displayed. In the center of the room, there was a low table, only high enough to reach the knee. Cushions for kneeling lay scattered around it. A bronze brazier hung from the ceiling, emitting a pleasant scent and warmth.

Even though someone had carefully paid attention to the pieces being displayed, I couldn't help but note that the large room felt strangely empty. It seemed not lived in, the furniture placed inside and askew as if as an afterthought.

I set my qín against the wall, and made a mental note that I would have to request a stand or some way of hanging it.

"Your bedchamber is through here." Danrou parted the bead curtain that separated the receiving room from the other rooms farther into the residence. "Could I draw a bath for you to wash off the dirt of travel?"

"Yes, that would be wonderful," I said, distracted by the appearance of the inner chamber. "Thank you," I added when I remembered, but she was already gone.

Most of the room was taken up by a large platform bed built entirely into the back wall. The wood was dark and red, polished to such a shine that I could almost see my reflection in it. I ran my finger over the blanket, marveled at the coolness of the silk that slipped over my fingertips. The bedcovering was dyed peach, embroidered in gold thread with floral blooms and green leaves. The canopy that was tied back from the posts was made of a sheer fabric, dyed a light green.

I sat down on the bench before the dressing table, admiring the craftsmanship. Vines were carved into the frame of the mirror, matching the edges of the table and the small drawers below. In my trunks there were a few pots of cosmetics, as well as hairpins and jewels that some of the adepts had gifted me prior to my departure. Remembering those women, I felt some sadness that I would miss out on the upcoming banquet for the Winter Solstice. I wouldn't be there to see Feiyun finally achieve the rank of adept, for it was whispered that she would be the next chosen to ascend. Maybe I was indeed a fool, like Auntie had believed, to cast aside that security and safety for the unknown. To cling to the memory of someone who I had thought a friend and who had obviously not felt the same.

I pulled open the drawers, absentmindedly considering how back at the House, three or four of us would have to share one table half this size. I heard the clink of something shift inside the lower drawer. Reaching in, my fingers touched something cold and thin.

It was a fine-toothed hair comb, gleaming in the light. The handle was a gold carving of a flower with a ruby set in the center. There was a good weight to it, showing it was made of metal of the highest quality, like something a true lady would own. She must have forgotten it in the back of the drawer when the rest of her belongings were taken away.

I wondered if the duke had received many guests like me previously. I wondered what she was like, this lady who'd stayed in these rooms before me. If she had walked through here like I did and marveled at the designs upon the walls. If she sat here upon this very seat and thought about her good fortune. But if she was happy here, then why did she leave? And where did she go?

"The bath is ready, Lady Xue!" Danrou called from the next room, disrupting my growing sense of unease.

It was not my place to wonder what had happened to those before me, if there had been one or if there had been twenty girls.

I dropped the comb into the drawer and quickly shut it.

CHAPTER FOURTEEN

I REMAINED IN THE BATH FAR LONGER THAN I should have, luxuriating after spending too long traveling with only cold water to clean myself with. When I stepped out, my fingers and toes were wrinkled, my limbs loose and languid, and I smelled sweetly of chrysanthemum. Danrou assisted me by covering me with a warm towel, which I hastily took away from her so that I could dry myself. She pursed her lips in disapproval when I told her I could don my own garments, but said nothing.

She had left an outfit though, hanging upon the dressing screen. One that was definitely not mine, as all of my clothing was crumpled at the bottom of my trunk. I lifted one sleeve, and noted how the fabric glided against my skin. Our House paid attention to fine tailoring, as the performances were known for the colorful variety of costumes that were created by the team of seamstresses under Auntie's employ. Matron had also instructed us on the quality of fabric, the detail of stitching, the fit of clothing that would tell us more about the background of the patron, subtle signs to indicate they were as they claimed.

Not my house any longer, I reminded myself as I pulled on the outfit and stood before the mirror. The style and cut appeared to be older, with flowing sleeves and a slimmer skirt—not a fashion typical in Wudan today.

My trunk was open in the corner, with all of my clothing taken out of it. My personal items remained within, separated into neat piles. I was accustomed to living with servants, but they were responsible for the care of the household: gardeners, cooks, housekeepers. None of them were lady's maids. I did not like the thought of a stranger touching my things.

I attempted to untangle my hair with my comb when Danrou appeared again, offering assistance.

"I'm not used to being attended by others," I told her. "I can manage myself, thank you." With the other women of the House, it was different. We helped one another, working toward the same goals. I did not like the way this made me feel. Helpless and out of sorts.

"On account of this being your first day at the manor, I will give you some time to become accustomed to our ways," she said stiffly. With a bow, she was gone before I could even apologize.

I'd made a bad impression. My new maid might be soft in appearance, but there was some spirit in her, which I liked. I hoped I could make it up to her.

BY THE TIME I made myself presentable, Danrou was there in the receiving room, waiting for me by the door. She gave me a look like how one might regard a snail in their path.

"The duke will be eating in the main hall this evening," she said. Even though she scowled at me, she was still pretty with her pale blue dress, a silver pin in her hair. I couldn't help but think she looked like she belonged to this manor more than I did.

I took my qín from its place against the wall, its familiar weight a comfort.

I followed Danrou through the series of pathways and hallways again until we returned to the central building, approaching it from the west. This must be the main residence, where the family received guests and resided.

We entered the hall, and my eyes were drawn upward again. The main section of the manor was a great room similar to the grand hall in the House of Flowing Water. The front wall of the first level was made of wooden screens that could be opened to the garden. The ceiling above had large beams, upon which lanterns were hung to illuminate the space. In the center of the room, a long scroll spanned two stories, hung from the ceiling: an ink painting of mountains and rivers. Other pieces of art were carefully positioned around the space—calligraphy plaques memorialized in gold, painted vases upon slender but no less beautifully carved stands, more statues of birds.

I thought I had understood opulence. But I could not have imagined this was how the Meng family lived, their obvious wealth dripping from every surface.

I was suddenly aware of how I must appear. The creases in my skirt. My plain jade hairpin and the rest of my hair flowing down my back. I should have accepted Danrou's offer to make me presentable. I wanted to turn back, to return to my room, but she was already up the stairs, waiting for me to follow.

I bit my lip as I ascended to the second story that overlooked the receiving room. There was a table set up there beside the railing. The duke was already seated, sipping from a cup. He gave me a nod of greeting, and gestured for me to take the seat in front of him.

"I invited you to dine with me," he said, noticing the qín. "As a guest. Not as a performer."

"Our bargain was that I was to be your musician, so I assumed . . ." I did not know then what to do. Danrou made the decision for me and eased the qín from my hands. She gave a demure smile, her demeanor distinctly different from how she behaved when we were alone.

I forced myself to move forward, one step at a time, until I found the stool on which I was supposed to sit. I wished I didn't feel so terribly out of place. The duke nodded in her direction, and with that silent command, Danrou was gone, and it was just the two of us left in this too-large and too-empty space.

"I hoped we would speak freely with each other like we did during our travels," he said, earnest again.

It was not what I expected. I thought our candidness while traveling was a temporary thing, an exception. I thought I would be tucked away into a room, brought out only when my particular skills were desired. When he noticed I did not pick up my chopsticks, he took the liberty of scooping what appeared to be a braised mushroom, carrot, and daikon dish into my bowl. Another gesture of intimacy that forced me to finally react instead of sitting there silent, stewing in my own thoughts. It was something that only my uncle had done for me before, and then came the flicker of a memory: his voice, coaxing me, *Try this, Xue'er, just a bite.* My uncle loved food and sharing new dishes with me.

I reached for some purple grain rice so that I did not have to look at him, worried that he would see for himself all of the emotions that bubbled forth unbidden. There was also steamed green bok choy, fried sweet potato, and some sort of orange blossom. All vegetarian, of course. I started eating so as not to appear like I was rejecting his hospitality, and realized that the dishes were quite good. Crisp where they needed to be, tender where they called for it, all well-seasoned.

"Is the food to your liking?" he asked. "I had Cook make a selection of her specialty dishes. If there are ones that you particularly enjoy, you can request that they be made again."

I nodded, mouth full of rice. No one had asked me that before. We ate what we were given. If this type of delicious food was what he was accustomed to, then no wonder he had no appetite on the road, when the offerings from the inns could at times be lacking.

"You don't have to be agreeable for my sake," he said to me, voice low. "If the food isn't to your liking, you can say so." He had misread, again, my quiet for discomfort.

I swallowed. His insistent manner made me anxious, and caused me to blurt out, "Why do you care?"

"Should I not?" He looked incredulous at the thought. "You are my guest."

"It makes me nervous," I said. "Not knowing." I felt like a string on the verge of snapping. Wary of saying something that would offend, and yet desperate to know the truth of why I was brought here.

"You want answers." Duke Meng poured himself more wine, then leaned over to pour for me, but saw I had not touched my cup. I needed to keep my mind clear, my focus on the purpose at hand.

"I don't know if you understand much of the entertainers' life," I said, wanting to see if he was truly sincere. "Madam Wu was not a harsh mistress. She was strict, true, but she protected us. She was fair. I ask that you offer me the same. You will see that I am willing to make myself useful, as long as you honor the terms of our agreement."

"Yes, we do have an understanding between us," he said stiffly. I could sense him withdrawing. It wasn't that I didn't appreciate the courtesy, but I would rather that the false niceties be discarded. Better that we establish this now before I grew too accustomed to his kindness.

"Come, walk with me," he requested.

We descended the staircase together, and instead of passing through the courtyard, he led me down a different hallway until we were in the main garden. I had expected the night to be cloudy, the garden to be dim, but the day's fog had cleared. The moon was full overhead, as bright and large as I'd ever seen it hanging over the horizon. The stars were scattered across the sky, an astonishing number of brilliant pinpricks across the swath of deep blue.

I had forgotten what the night looked like outside of the city.

I must have stopped unwittingly to gaze in amazement at the sight, for the duke also remained still next to me. The moonlight cast a silver hue over the bare branches of the trees, and the water of the stream shone with an ethereal glow. It looked like something out of a dream.

"I forgot how lovely the garden is during the full moon," he said.

"I feel as if I should have a brush in hand, like the poets of old," I said to him, still a little breathless. "To capture all of it this, preserve it in memory."

"*As a child I had no name for the moon, called it a plate of white jade. Suspected it may be a Celestial mirror, flying amidst the faraway clouds,*" he recited to the sky. A familiar poem, but the exact words of the stanzas that followed eluded me.

Uncle's voice came to me again, ringing as if he stood right beside me, as if I just needed to turn my head, and he would be there, encouraging. *Try to remember the next line. What is it? You know it. I'm certain you do!*

A lump rose in my throat. What was it about this place that kept conjuring up these memories that I'd kept suppressed for so long? Out of the city, away from the structure and busy routine of the house, my mind had space to wander, to roam too far into the past. Uncle's incessant questioning used to frustrate me as a child, but now I would give everything to hear him ask me once more.

Lord Meng was suddenly blocking the garden view, his expression one of alarm. "You're crying."

I wiped my eyes with my sleeve, not wanting to look at him. How ridiculous I must appear, crying at the sight of the moon.

"My uncle would have known the rest of the poem," I said, sounding wretched through my tears. Every time I tried to take a breath, I wheezed. "He died on the way to Wudan, on his way back to visit me."

I regretted the words as soon as I said them to the night. A secret source of my guilt and shame. Even though anyone would dismiss it outright, that little jagged edge still cut me every time I was reminded of it.

He touched my shoulder, offering a hesitant warmth, before pulling away.

"He would have liked to be remembered this way," he said.

I snorted. "Viewing the moon, and reciting poetry?" Even weeping, I could not help but offer a quip. A way to pretend that it did not matter so much to me, even though it was obvious it did.

Lord Meng only smiled. "That he passed on his love of poetry to you." He offered me a handkerchief, and I took it gratefully to dab at my eyes.

"Yes, I suppose that was very much like him. A font of obscure knowledge," I said dryly, and he chuckled, understanding what I meant about Uncle's tendency to lecture.

I squinted at the moon then, a nagging thought appearing in mind. "My last attempt at moon watching was with you, back in Wudan . . . but wasn't it a full moon then?"

"Was it? I do not recall."

I must have misread the calendar. Did a full month already pass?

"Lady Xue," he said, expression suddenly serious. "I regret . . ."

I looked up at him then, expecting him to tell me that he regretted bringing me here, regretted opening his estate to such a foolish girl, prone to tears.

"I regret offending you with the offer to purchase your qín, to not make your acquaintance first," he said, then gave me a tentative smile. "But I am glad you are here. It reminds me to look at things with new eyes, a different perspective. I am hopeful we can help each other."

"But I still don't understand," I murmured. "What does my qín have to do with anything?"

His expression darkened, like a storm cloud passing overhead. "For the past year, your uncle and my shīfù had been conducting an investigation of a . . . sensitive nature. I believe they found something on the way to Wudan, knowledge that was dangerous. Knowledge that got them killed."

CHAPTER FIFTEEN

I STARED AT HIM IN DISBELIEF.

"You're . . . you're speaking of murder?" I managed to choke out.

I had assumed the letter referred to a final request, one my uncle had entrusted to the duke to complete. Not mysteries left unresolved. This wasn't what I expected. I felt as if I was holding scraps of paper, snippets of a song, but unable to hear the full piece play out, understand its true meaning.

"I told you my shīfù was traveling with Elder Tang—your uncle—when they were accosted by bandits," Duke Meng said. "But the truth of it was that they were hunted. There was evidence that they were tracked through the forest by dogs. Nothing they had of value was taken. All of it was burned in their carriage, along with their bodies."

I covered my mouth, in shock at this terrible revelation. Hunted. Burned. Not a chance encounter, but something more treacherous.

"But who? Who would do this to them?" I asked.

"That is what I have been attempting to uncover for the past few months," he said, expression grave. "They had anticipated they were being followed. I was gathering help to find them when I received the news of their deaths."

His fist clenched at his side, and I could sense the undercurrent of emotion inside him, that he struggled to hold back even with the calm of his words.

"This was why you did not want to speak of it while we were traveling," I said. "You were worried that the danger may have followed you."

He nodded. "I made a promise to your uncle to keep you safe, and I intend to honor that promise. When we were attacked in the garden, I could not leave you there."

"I *knew* that wasn't a mountain lion!" I exclaimed.

"We call them ravagers," Duke Meng said with a grimace. "They're a species not . . . native to this area. They can be used as trackers, or worse, for those who have ill intent. They can be trained to experience bloodlust, with a taste for human flesh."

The explanation made sense, and yet, I was still unsure.

"I'm certain it is the ravagers that will give me the answers I am looking for," he said, words carrying a threat of vengeance. "Once I track down the hand that holds the leash, I will destroy it."

IN THE MORNING I woke to find someone had tucked a warming box at the foot of the bed, so my body was comfortable under the blankets. The dressing screen had been moved to this chamber, where another outfit was already hung. I frowned at them, not knowing how they could have prepared more clothes with my measurements so quickly. That was how the wealthy lived, I supposed, and I shouldn't be critical of the staff doing their jobs *too* well.

As I pulled on the shift and the tunic, I thought about Duke Meng's parting words last night. He would be gone from the estate for a little while, a few days, maybe more. He had asked for me to place my trust in him, that he was continuing the investigation. Although I asked what my uncle and his shīfù were looking for, he evaded my question.

Anything you need, he'd reminded me again, *ask Danrou to bring for you. She will assist you in navigating the manor.*

Maybe some would enjoy the experience of being waited upon, but it continued to make me feel uncomfortable. It meant someone was always watching me, moving around my rooms in the dark, rustling my blankets . . . I shuddered. I was used to being left alone, to come and go as I pleased, as long as I performed my duties and was present when and where I was expected.

Danrou brought me the morning meal on a tray: seaweed soup with tofu, roasted yellow yams, and three small buns with a black sesame filling. The porcelain bowl and plates were exquisite, formed in the shape of lotus leaves and glazed in green. She must have thought me ridiculous, lifting them up and marveling at the detail on the undersides of the dishes, but I didn't care.

When I returned to my room to find my slippers, the maid was there again, tying the curtain to the posts. I noticed she had also smoothed out my blankets, folded them a different way than I had already tidied them earlier. It irked me still, like an itch I couldn't quite reach.

"Give me a moment, my lady, and I will assist you with your hair," she said.

"That's quite all right," I said, attempting politeness again. "I would prefer to dress and bathe myself, and do my own hair."

Danrou pursed her lips again, a sign of her obvious displeasure.

"The duke has been called to attend some business," she said curtly. "I am to make you comfortable, ensure that you are ready for your . . . duties."

Perhaps I was overthinking it, but there was a way she said the word *duties* that made me believe she was insinuating other things. I was already used to how people viewed entertainers, and though the duke had promised that my status in his house was that of a guest, it was not a guarantee that those under his employ would view me in the same light.

"Well, since the duke is not here to ensure that I appear presentable,"

I retorted, "then we'll agree that for these few days while he is away, I can do those things on my own."

"As the lady wishes," she said, with a bow. "If you would like to leave the rooms, then please call for me and I will accompany you." Her tone made it sound like she would much rather do anything else.

"I . . ." I sighed, not wanting further confrontation, yet frustrated that we may have to do this daily song and dance. "I should be able to find my way around the estate without an escort."

She looked at me like I had grown two heads, and said slowly, as if speaking to a child, "The Meng Estate was built into the mountain-side and meant as a refuge from the weariness of the world. There are paths upon which the terrain could be treacherous, and recently there have been sightings of wild animals at the walls. Who knows what cave a beast could drag you into? Or what edge you could slip and fall off of?"

I didn't doubt she would love for one of those things to happen to me.

"I would be happy, then, for you to show me where I could and could not go, and I will endeavor to keep to those safe spaces," I said tightly.

"My lady." She dropped to her knees, startling me. "I have offended you somehow, and I apologize for it. Though you may be used to taking care of yourself, I am only doing my job. I would be chastised by Attendant Luo if I am found to be neglecting my duties. The blame would be upon me, even if you were the one who requested it."

Danrou sounded like she was on the verge of tears, and I quickly bent down to help her up, taken aback by this sudden outburst.

"I understand," I murmured then, giving up the fight. "We all have our roles to play. I am sure you are more than capable in your position. I will call when I am ready for you to show me the grounds."

With another bow, she was off, leaving me alone in the room. I sighed again, sitting down at the dressing table. It was then I realized that I had forgotten to ask her about the comb.

WHEN IT CAME time, I kept my word and requested that Danrou provide me with a tour of the residence. It was impossible to grow up in an entertainer's house and not have an appreciation for exquisite things. The House of Flowing Water carefully cultivated an image of elegance and beauty, all the elements balanced in perfect harmony: fire, air, earth, metal, water. From the incense flowing through the air, to the trickle of water in the indoor pond, the wood carvings of scenes such as *Nüwa Gifting the Breath of Life*. Whoever decorated the guest wing where I resided had an eye for such a balance, in the warmth of the wood and the softness of the fabrics, the nature motifs.

The rest of the Meng residence, however, was sparse in decoration—instead its elegance was in minimalism and contrast. Everything appeared to be like an ink painting, like the landscape scroll that adorned the receiving room of the main manor, shades of gray against white, outlined in black. Danrou took me then to walk along the south wing, where the kitchens were located and the servants resided. But in comparison to the kitchens of the House of Flowing Water, where the servants were constantly running in and out with supplies, ingredients, wood for the fire, the kitchens here were quiet.

In fact, we did not pass by many people while walking.

"Beyond the manor is the north wing," Danrou said, pointing down a hallway, past another small courtyard, and toward a set of great doors in the distance. "That is the private residence of the duke and his family, and is strictly forbidden to trespassers."

Such as myself; the warning in her tone was clear.

When we found ourselves back to the doors of my residence, I was eager to rid myself of my sour-faced guide.

"I will keep to the residence," I said to her. "You must have other tasks to attend to."

"Yes, lady," she said coolly. "I will take my leave, then."

I returned to the inner chamber with the restless feeling that I should be doing *something*. I picked out my belongings from the trunk and attempted to put them away.

I didn't like to look at the token with my name and the mark of the Undesirables, so I put it in a drawer. Next, my family pendant, a jade disc that was a reminder of the name that was lost to me. I held it in my hand until it warmed up with my body heat. If I closed my eyes, I could recall the feeling of sunlight that bathed my skin as I splashed in a puddle. The air smelled like fresh rain and dirt. The sound of my mother's voice calling for me. I held up a hand to block out the sun, but it was too bright. Her face was just a blur in the distance, and beside her, another figure. My father, perhaps? I tried to recall what they looked like, but their features eluded me. I dropped the pendant next to the token. Remembering hurt too much.

I had my selection of song manuals, scrolls, and books, which took up one shelf in the receiving room. My gifted cosmetics and jewelry went into the dressing table drawers. And that was it. All that I owned of any value in the world, except for the qín.

It still remained my ever, steadfast companion. From the shelf of music, I selected the book for "Melody of the Water Immortals." That gift which was too precious to me and scoffed at by the dancers. I turned to the first page and marveled yet again at the notations, recorded by a master.

I decided to treat this time as a gift. The time to learn a new piece, without the distractions of having other duties. Surrounded by music, the rest of the world fell away. I was no longer a girl orphaned, a woman lost. I was the song, spiraling upward. A water spirit, dancing in the light.

CHAPTER SIXTEEN

TWO DAYS I LASTED, PLAYING THE QÍN BY MYSELF, with only Danrou for company. Although she kept out of sight when I remained in the residence, when I approached the gate to the outside, she was there. I felt an ever-watchful presence, sensed her readiness to pounce upon me if I ever stepped out of turn. The windows of the residence only opened to other covered pathways. Even though they were lined with trees against the outer wall of the manor, I felt as if the walls were closing in.

I ate alone, morning, midday, and evening. I played the qín. I shifted my things from one shelf to the other. I flipped through the few books on the shelves. One, a collection of legends that seemed quite fanciful, stories of the Spirit clans and their various disputes. Another, a book of poetry from a poet whose name I did not recognize. But there were only so many books that I could read before I felt myself going cross-eyed, and so I stood and paced back and forth between the rooms until I could bear it no longer.

It was my contrary nature surfacing again. I practiced and untangled the difficult notes of music in solitude, for it bothered me for anyone else to hear me struggling over a new piece, and yet I craved the presence of others. I used to sit in my lean-to, watching the gardeners move about, trimming flowers and tidying the bushes, while I puzzled over a complex fingering silently upon the strings. There was nothing I liked more than to be unobtrusive, part of the bustle of the house and yet separate from it. There, but not there. Included, and yet apart.

In desperate need of a change of scenery, I carried my qín and the stand that I had requested and wandered into the hallway, in search of inspiration. The main gate out of the west wing was blocked to me, as my overzealous maid would definitely intrude upon my peace to ensure that I was not going where I was not permitted. It meant that I should explore deeper into the residence.

There was a hallway behind my inner chambers that led to a few storage rooms holding nothing of note. I found a smaller room that contained scrolls of calligraphy, but the dust upon them made me sneeze. It seemed like it had not been disturbed for a long time. Another covered pathway had a lattice window that peered into a small courtyard paved with stone, a large weeping willow in the center, and a bench underneath. Try as I might, though, I could not find the entrance to that courtyard—each of the hallways seemed to lead me away from it. All of them looked the same.

It was then that I realized I was lost.

I turned and walked down another pathway, expecting to find myself back in the main courtyard, perhaps. There was another set of doors through the inner wall, and I passed through them, certain this would be the way back. I went through the covered hall and emerged into a small garden. I gasped with delight at the unexpected discovery. This place had been neglected and grown wild. Matted greenery climbed the walls. Even this late into the season, I was surprised to see large and heavy blooms still hanging from some of the flower shrubs.

I found a space for my stand and the qín under the eaves, and stepped onto the pavers. It didn't look like it had been wholly neglected, for the path could still be seen, making its way through the garden. Some of the trees and the shrubs have been cut back and piled against the wall so that nature had not completely taken over this place. But I still noticed signs of disrepair. Crumbling pavers that had not been filled in. A hole in the wall that was hastily filled with large stones piled upon one another in a haphazard manner. The air smelled like dirt and decay and growth.

Trailing my fingers through the leaves, I thought I was lucky that the head gardener of the House of Flowing Water was never irritated by my presence. She was actually a lover of music, and said that the qín encouraged the plants to grow. I didn't know if that was true or not, but the house was frequently filled with the results of the garden's bounty. I often wished that I could assist them in pulling weeds and cutting branches and putting together the floral displays, but Gardener Guan scolded me from getting my hands dirty. She told me that I was to focus on keeping the flow of music, for happy hands resulted in happy blooms.

Here, this tiny garden filled with brambles, was a dream that I could finally pursue. I could learn for myself how to care for these plants. Armed with that resolve, I took another step forward, but my entire foot went into water.

Just my luck. I used my other foot to nudge some of the branches aside, and saw a pond back there. The ornamental edge around it had been broken through, and the water was dank and dark with algae. I wrung out my slipper and hobbled back down the path, where I found a bench covered with a layer of leaves. I brushed them aside with my sleeve and saw that the seat at least was dry. Putting my damp slipper back on, I went to retrieve my qín. At least I could make use of the afternoon and the warm weather to practice out in the open air.

"Melody of the Water Immortals" was a complex piece that pulled in figures of history, spinning a tale intermingling melody with poetry, one feeding into the other. The fingerings themselves were a headache to puzzle over, for I had only the descriptions in the text to guide me, and no teacher in front of me to demonstrate. A song in three parts, a phrase that repeated in one section was echoed in another, a melody that wound and unwound itself, offering a question that circled back.

Was it about a musician who, finding himself lacking in inspiration, traveled to the "edge of the world" to contemplate the waves, and then heard the waves sing back?

The song flowed forward and then pulled back, an unrelenting swell of sound that then fell back into something more tender. I closed my eyes to worry about the plucking of the gentle parts, played those phrases again and again, in order to coax more feeling out of them.

When I finally blinked my eyes open and looked up, I saw bright eyes staring back at me.

A girl was crouched in front of me. Part of her hair was pulled back high, the rest of it spilling over her shoulders—a hairstyle that was meant for young, unmarried women my age. She had smudges of dirt on her cheeks, stains on her knees and sleeves. Bits of leaves and flowers were tangled in her hair, like they grew there naturally. Woven bracelets made of grass encircled both wrists. She looked like she had just crawled out of the pond, feral. A ghost, perhaps, someone who had perished in this garden, looking now to speak to the living.

I screamed.

She screamed too, falling back, hands up in the air in defense. We stared at each other.

"Who are you?" I gasped, as I watched her fumble in the mud before standing up unsteadily. She tried to smooth down her skirts, but all it did was smear the mud further.

"I'm . . . Yingzi," she squeaked. "I was working in the garden when I . . ." She gave a small yawn. "When I fell asleep." She scratched her head.

I couldn't help but smile at her disheveled state. She looked much too real to be a ghost.

"You're one of the gardeners." I felt an odd sense of kinship with this girl, because she was hiding too, just like I was, from the rest of the house.

"Don't tell Datou." She made an X with her hands. "Please. She won't be happy I'm hiding out here again."

"Datou . . . your boss?"

"You could say that." Her eyes narrowed then as she regarded me. "Wait, then who are you?"

"I'm Xue." I gestured to the qín in front of me. "I'm a recent addition to the estate. I've been hired to play music for the duke."

Her mouth opened to an O of understanding as she nodded. "The duke does enjoy his music. Welcome."

I was eager to learn more. "Have there been other musicians then in this place, before me?"

"Only those who have been invited to play at the parties," she said, voice taking on a wistful tone. "There used to be parties here all the time, when the borders were open. The pupils of Elder Gao and acquaintances of the duke. They would play in the garden, with accompanying dancers."

The Elder Gao she referred to I suspected might be who Duke Meng called his shīfù.

"Used to be?" I questioned. If this was to be one of my duties, called to perform at these gatherings, I had to prepare myself for them. It was one thing to provide pleasant background music behind a screen, faceless, and another to be performing in front of scholars and nobles whose skills were likely to surpass my own. I found myself both dreading and looking forward to that challenge.

"You weren't informed before you were hired?" She stepped forward then, looking up the path to see if there was anyone coming, before dropping her voice conspiratorially. "There are no parties anymore. Not after the former duke was banished."

I shook my head, hoping that I did not seem too eager, too curious. In the House of Flowing Water, we were educated on history, but purposefully kept ignorant of what was happening in the current court. Auntie did not dare involve her entertainers in the schemes of politicians, lest she be accused of interference.

"He raised his appeal directly to the sovereign himself," Yingzi said, still keeping her voice low. "But it was taboo to continue the investigation into . . . you know . . . what happened with the Queen of Flowers."

None of these references made sense to me.

The girl's eyes widened. "You know nothing of this? It was a great scandal!"

I was about to ask her to explain, when I heard someone call my name.

"I must go!" Before I could say anything, the girl was gone, disappearing into the bushes. There must be a gate somewhere beyond the mess of greenery. I puzzled over her words. A scandal. The reason the duke took on the title even though he was so young.

Danrou made her way toward me, frowning.

"This is where you disappeared to?" she muttered. "It took me a while to find you. You shouldn't stray too far from your chambers."

"I'm still within the manor walls," I reminded her. "I appreciate the concern, but as you can see, I am well and whole and not ripped apart by wild animals yet."

She looked down her nose at my muddied garments. "Well, I am here to inform you that the kitchen has sent some refreshments for you. They're waiting for you in your rooms."

As Danrou turned to leave, she stepped into the same puddle that had dirtied my slippers earlier, and I swallowed a chortle in response. She picked up her foot and tried to shake it off, scowling. Served her right.

CHAPTER SEVENTEEN

THE TEA AND THE PASTRIES WERE A WELCOME DIS-
traction from the mysteries of the duke's past. My brief interaction with
Yingzi confirmed for me that the other staff of Meng Manor may not
be so opposed to my presence, that perhaps it was only my maidservant who found me particularly distasteful. Her demeanor remained icy,
even as she performed all of her duties without complaint.

It was when I saw her dusting the mirror that I was reminded of what I
had been meaning to ask her. To make conversation, to extend a friendly
gesture. It had only been a few days, and I had to try.

"I found this in the drawer," I said, reaching over and pulling it open.

Danrou turned away, annoyed at my disruption of her task. My fingers found the comb, at the very back, and pulled it out. I lifted it in front
of her face for her to see. She gave it a cursory, impatient glance, before
doing a double take. Her gaze sharpened, and then before I could react,
she snatched it out of my hand.

"You know who it belongs to?" I asked.

"Where did you get this?" she demanded, eyes wild. "Why do you
have it?"

I was taken aback by this burst of genuine emotion, and tried to reach
for the comb, to explain. She backed away, clutching it to her chest.

"This is not yours," she snarled at me.

"I just want to know who it belongs to," I said, startled by her animosity. "So that it can be returned to them."

Tears rushed into her eyes as she spat in my direction, "That would be impossible unless you know how to bring back the dead! My mistress is no longer with us, and now I have to serve the likes of *you*!"

Danrou rushed out the door, and left me staring after her.

A banished duke. A mysterious scandal. And now I realized I lived in the former residence of a woman who had died.

How much dark history did this place hold?

I DID NOT intend to upset my maidservant, and didn't dare leave the residence the rest of the day for fear of angering her again. A part of me felt sympathy for her. Her distaste of me made sense if she'd lost her original mistress to this place, and her resentment was understandable if she was unwillingly called to serve another.

I saw the things in the rooms under a new light. I imagined what the woman who once walked through these halls looked like. Graceful, confident, knowing her place in this world. It gave me a peculiar feeling, knowing that she may have chosen these items carefully, displayed them proudly. Or maybe she felt as empty as I felt, looking upon them. Someone passing through.

A wooden carving of a rose.

A plain-looking box, the lid opening to reveal an interior of glittering purple crystal.

A jade statue of a serene-looking woman dressed in flowing robes, a flute held to her lips.

She had slept in the bed I slept in. Ate at the table I ate at. Had she been a musician too? But Yingzi said that there was no one else hired previously. Duke Meng had called this the guest wing. I was too afraid to ask the one person who would probably know the answers, so I went to bed and had a night filled with restless dreams.

I saw a girl who emerged from the brambles, thorns protruding from her skin, vines spreading from her hair. Her eyes and mouth were dark, empty caverns, from which tendrils grew, and flowers burst forth in grotesque explosions of color.

Help, she begged, extending one arm to me, but I could not reach her before she collapsed to her knees. She had come from the earth and the earth took her back. I woke, gasping, calling out for Mili.

The sense of unease remained while I ate my cold breakfast that was already laid out on the table. Danrou was nowhere to be found. Just as well. I didn't want to wait for the manor to consume me too.

I tried the wild garden first, but there was no sign of Yingzi. I lifted my skirts and made my way carefully around the sunken pond, and found another path through the overgrown grove of trees behind. There was a smaller gate in the wall, and it was only secured by a flimsy latch. I opened it and stepped through, finding myself outside the manor walls.

I peered to one side, then to the other—I could not see anyone. This was my chance. I closed the gate behind me and hurried down the path, certain that I would soon be discovered.

But no one followed. My steps took me to another little bridge that curved pleasingly over the stream. Snow fell in large, lazy flakes, covering everything in a light dusting of white. Even with the snow, the sun still shone. Under my cloak, with my brisk pace, I soon grew warm. It was a picturesque scene, and I pretended for a moment I was in a painting, something named *Young Woman Admiring Winter Blossoms*, perhaps, before a shout disrupted my fantasy.

There were footsteps suddenly, appearing out of nowhere. A hand gripped my wrist with the strength of iron. I was spun around and looked up at a man who scowled at me with a ferocious expression.

"What are you doing here?" His other hand reached around and grabbed my shoulder, and with both arms he shook me hard. "You're not supposed to be here! Trespasser!"

"I don't know what you're talking about!" I managed to force out, terrified.

"Did someone bring you here to distract him from his focus? Did you think it would be so easy for him to fall for your lies?" His hands made their way to my throat then, and he squeezed. "Tell me! Who sent you?"

My only thought was survival. I tried to pry his fingers away from my throat, but he was too strong. I tried kicking at him, pulling his arms, but I was too weak. His face danced in front of my eyes as pinpricks of white began to cloud my vision. I would die there, in the garden I so wanted to see.

There were other voices shouting in the distance. "You're killing her!" I vaguely made out, before the pressure relented from my neck, and I could breathe again. My legs could not hold me up any longer, and I sank to my knees, taking in great gulps of air.

"She's *Mortal*," I thought I heard, but it must have been my panicked wheezing that jumbled up the words.

Someone touched my shoulder. I looked up and saw one of the most beautiful women I had ever seen, on one knee beside me. Her blue-black hair fell around her face in waves, and her brown eyes were narrowed in concern. With a start, I realized she was dressed in armor. Her chest plate was white and etched with silver, and upon her shoulders were curved pauldrons that were carved with designs like feathers; a silver cloak flowed behind her. She looked like she'd stepped down from the clouds, a warrior goddess come to save me.

In comparison, the man who tried to kill me stared down with anger that radiated from his body. It was then I noticed he wore armor as well, except his was gold, not white. Even if he still radiated rage, his appearance was striking, all harsh lines and angles. It hurt a bit to look at him. It was like looking into the sun.

"There's no reason for a Mortal to be lurking about the Meng Estate," he said coldly. "Who released you here?"

Mortal. There it was again. I hadn't heard wrong.

"Here, let me help you up." The woman in white assisted me. The bottom of my skirt was damp from where I fell, the snow having melted underneath me.

"Your name!" the man barked at me, his hand upon the hilt of his sword.

Maybe I'd somehow slipped upon the rocks and hit my head and hallucinated this entire scene. But I blinked, once, twice, and both of them remained, looking at me expectantly. Even my savior waited for an answer.

"I am Guxue," I said, trying my best to keep my voice steady. At least with Danrou, all she could threaten me with were her words. She had spoken of dangers outside of the walls of the manor, and I'd neglected to listen. But I didn't expect a threat to appear like this. Two shining beings who stood before me as if they stepped out of a painting.

"I was recently hired by Lord—I mean, Duke Meng. I'm here to play the qín for the estate."

"The qín!" The man scoffed, then pulled up my arm, wrenching it away from my body. His touch made me draw in a breath. His fingers were icy cold, as he examined my fingertips with his own, a feeling both intrusive and strangely intimate.

"Excuse me!" I managed to choke out indignantly as I yanked my hand from his grasp as hard as I could.

The woman raised an eyebrow. "Well?"

"She does have the calluses of a qín player," he admitted gruffly, but the gaze he cast upon me was still suspicious. "Why would Jinglang bring her *here*?"

"Let me apologize for this brute." The woman's face softened as she pushed him away. "My name is Lingwei. I am Jinglang's sister. This is . . . *Prince* Zhou Chenwen." There was a mocking emphasis on his title, though her expression was teasing, and the man rolled his eyes.

"I am nothing of the sort," he snapped.

Prince? I did not know the emperor had a son that was so close to me in age. This man that stood before me could not be any older than in his midtwenties. The last I remembered, the prince was a middle-aged man, with children of his own. This "prince" did not appear old enough to be anyone's father.

The duke's sister regarded me thoughtfully. "I'm more curious about how Jinglang managed to smuggle her in."

"This is all a pretense," the prince said, still huffing. "He wouldn't be so foolish as to bring a Mortal here at this time, not when so much is at stake."

"Tell me then, Guxue," the lady said, voice gentle and coaxing. "Where are you from? And who is the current emperor?"

I looked at her, incredulous, certain she must be teasing me as well. "I'm from the House of Flowing Water in Wudan, Lady Meng," I responded, careful with my words. "The Guanghu Emperor Xuanbin is nearing the thirtieth year of his rule."

The man let out a harsh laugh. "That is no lady, I assure you. And you, your master has trained you well in keeping up your lies. No matter. We'll see who is right when Jinglang returns."

"Call me Lingwei," the woman said, not so judgmental as the prince.

She grabbed ahold of my elbow then and gently steered me toward the manor.

I tried to protest, but she silenced me with a shake of her head.

"We will figure out what my dear brother truly wants with you," she said. "Then we'll see if we can figure out how to resolve this mess."

CHAPTER EIGHTEEN

THERE WERE SERVANTS THAT CAME IMMEDIATELY to greet Lingwei as she strolled through the main manor doors. Even though she refused the title of Lady Meng, she behaved as if she was the owner of the estate. With the brisk efficiency of someone who was used to dispatching servants, she sent them to bring tea and refreshments.

We sat once again on the second story of the manor house, where I ate with Duke Meng that first evening. This time the table was covered with an assortment of treats, displayed elegantly upon the black lacquered platters. There was a chewy rice cake rolled around a filling of pink gardenia jam, dried persimmon cakes sprinkled with sugar, and green bean pastries shaped like flowers that crumbled into sweetness when placed upon the tongue.

I popped another rice cake into my mouth while I listened to the two of them bicker. If I was soon to be sent to my death, then I might as well do it with a full stomach.

"The gall of Jinglang to bring her across the borders at this time," Prince Zhou said, spinning a dagger upon the table. He kept on glaring in my direction, as if he wanted me to be mindful that he could end me at any moment.

"He must have his reasons," Lingwei defended her brother all the same. She certainly didn't seem to take the prince seriously, so with her there, I was not as worried about his threatening demeanor.

"It's the flaw of anyone under the tutelage of the Star of Fortune," Prince Zhou said, his derision clear. "When your purpose is to look upon the threads of the Mortal Tapestry, it's too easy to be drawn into the entanglement of their short, momentary lives."

He speared one of the persimmon cakes with the point of his dagger and lifted it up. Sugar fell everywhere as he bit into it. He grinned at me while doing so, and I looked away. Childish behavior.

I didn't want to let his antics distract me from what I should be focused on. The terms they tossed about. Mortal. The Tapestry. Stars. I refused to believe that this wasn't some sort of great joke, that they wouldn't clap and chortle once they were finally able to convince me of this charade.

"Where did you meet my brother?" Lingwei asked.

"He watched one of my performances at the House of Flowing Water and requested a private audience," I said. "Afterward, he learned I was bound to the House by a contract. He felt for my plight and purchased it with the request that I return with him to the manor to play for him here."

That night when we spoke of his investigations into my uncle's mysterious death, he had asked for my discretion. He said that his staff were unaware of his comings and goings, and that he would appreciate if his connection with my uncle was kept quiet. I did not know if that extended to his family as well, so I wanted to be cautious.

"What did he tell you about himself?" she asked, the questions still coming in a steady stream.

"He said that although he was a poet, he had great respect for qín music, as passed down by his sh—his father," I said, correcting my slip.

"Well, there's a simple solution to this problem, isn't there?" Prince Zhou slammed a hand upon the table, making the dishes shake and me jump. He gestured in my direction with the dagger. "Have her prove it."

I glared back. His attitude was beginning to grate on me. "What would you have me prove?"

"Prove that you're a qín player of any worth." He shrugged. "Get your instrument and play for us, then we'll know whether you're a liar, or if you are truly as you say." He gave me a slow smile.

"That won't be a problem," I said stiffly. Had he asked me to do anything else, I might have protested, but I was confident in my ability to play my instrument. At least in comparison to any other apprentice musician of a renowned academy.

Lingwei was also in agreement to this demonstration of my skills, and was my escort back to my residence in the west wing. She stepped through the doors and regarded the room with a thoughtful gaze.

"It's been a while since I've come into this wing," she commented. "It's . . . emptier than I remember."

Perhaps I was wrong and Danrou had served her former mistress elsewhere. "Were these your rooms once?"

"No, not mine." She shook her head. "My rooms were in the north wing, with the family. These belonged to . . ." Her voice trailed off as she picked up the carving of the rose.

"A girl who should have never come here," she finished, voice hollow, lost to her memories.

Lingwei sighed then, and set the carving back upon its shelf. With a whisper, she uttered a name: "Ruilan."

"Who was she?" I asked. I couldn't help but be curious, even though the sadness was evident in the downward cast of her gaze, in the drooping of her shoulders.

"There were rumors she was a victim of the curse of the Meng family," she said, mouth twisted in a rueful smile. "The first of a long list of tragedies that have befallen us."

"Danrou said she died."

Lingwei's eyes narrowed. "Yes, that is what they believe. Ruined her good name, though she was innocent in all of this. But there's no reason for me to tell you any of this, is there? We'll return you home soon, and you'll forget all of this ever happened."

"You mean to send me home?" I winced at the high, pleading pitch of my voice. I should not beg, and yet I hated to think that this was all to be a fanciful dream. Everything would go back to the way it was, and my fellow apprentices would look upon me with pitying eyes. They would offer comforting words of sympathy but whisper about me behind my back. *She tried to leave but was sent back a failure.*

Lingwei met my eyes and said solemnly, without a hint of humor, "This is a dangerous place for someone like you."

Alarmed, I wanted to ask her what she could possibly mean by that, but she had already turned and walked out the door.

THE HAZE HAD cleared and the sky was blue when we returned to the garden again. Most of the snow had melted, leaving only dampness upon the stones to indicate that it had ever been there at all. The bridge we crossed was on the far side of the garden. The posts were carved cranes, the elegant curves of their necks holding up the banisters.

Prince Zhou was already in the pavilion, standing at the balustrade. I noticed the plaque at the entrance: *Wind-Swept Pavilion.* As we ascended the steps, I gasped when I finally saw the view beyond.

Gray cliffs reaching up toward the sky. Here and there, evergreens, their tops still shrouded in tendrils of mist. Part of the pavilion jutted out from the cliffside upon which it was built, and before us was a sharp drop into the gorge below. We were truly isolated out here, hanging upon the expanse between sky and breath. I took a step back, dizzy.

I set up my qín and my stand. Lingwei and Prince Zhou spoke in low voices while I focused on tuning my instrument. I had to give the right impression, ensure that I proved myself, that I was worthy of being here, worthy of being the duke's hired musician. Perhaps they thought I looked too young, that I could not be trusted with such a role. I set my shoulders then. I would prove them wrong.

I peeked at them once again. They made a stunning couple, standing side by side, white and gold. Looking beyond them, to the mountain view, and remembering the name of the pavilion, I decided that my piece would be "Riding the Wind." I called for their attention. After Lingwei settled upon the bench and Prince Zhou leaned against the post to listen, I began.

The melody was brisk. It danced through the air, like the flapping of the wings of the geese, making their journey through the mountains. Their orientation was always true, the longing for home contained in their chest. There was some lively strumming that showed off clever fingerings without appearing like I was too eager to please. But as I played, my thoughts meandered with the worry of being banished home.

Had I grown attached to this strange place? We should be deep in winter, this high in the mountains. I had thought underfoot there would be drifts of snow, but the air still held the sweet aroma of spring. Previously when I played in the gardens I was used to the buzzing of insects, the chirping of birds, accompanying my music. The household noises were lively too in the background—the sound of shoveling as the gardeners dug up tubers, the scurry of footsteps when the delivery boys ran up and down the path. But here, I had only the whistle of the wind sweeping between the cliffs. The music changed in my hands, became more frantic.

What happened to the girl who resided there and died? Why was there an unattended garden permitted to grow wild in the middle of the manor? What was the curse that had befallen the Meng family? And the question that kept surfacing, over and over again, as the sound grew louder from the qín: *What does he want from me?*

The trees trembled around us. The wind picked up, whipping my hair violently against my shoulders and my face. It was snowing again, chaotic swirls of white descending from the sky.

I should take shelter, but I couldn't seem to stop playing. The song kept pouring out from the qín, and there was power in it. It was wild . . . tumultuous . . . *free* . . .

A crash disrupted my concentration and my hands lost control. A string snapped and the music stilled, but my hands were clawed over the qín, the song still waiting for its ending. A restless feeling, like a moth trapped inside a jar, trying to make its way out. I looked up to see a large crack had developed on the stone table next to me—a rock had somehow landed upon it. Did it fall from somewhere?

Lingwei appeared perturbed, brows drawn together as she considered the crack upon the table. Prince Zhou's expression no longer had his typical resting smirk. He regarded me thoughtfully.

"How curious," he murmured. I did not like the way he looked at me.

"You've crossed paths with a Celestial before," Lingwei said. Her voice was once again steady, her expression calm, as if she'd found the answer she was looking for. "One that left a mark on you. It shows in your playing."

"Celestial? Those are just stories." It was my turn to scoff then. "I may come from a humble background, but we receive an education even in an entertainers' house."

Those were stories my uncle was fascinated with, stories he often told me even while I grew to an age where I no longer needed fanciful tales. So many of them now came to mind. The Heavenly Mother and her peach orchard. The Snake Spirit who was given the responsibility of the doorway between realms. The butcher who slayed four monsters that plagued the land and cleansed himself of the bloodshed he was responsible for. He was taken to the heavens when he was found worthy.

"A Mortal has not ascended for centuries," Prince Zhou continued to muse, as if talking to himself. "It would be very interesting to watch one pass the trials. It would be quite the spectacle."

"What are you two doing here?" a familiar voice called out from the garden. Duke Meng appeared then, an apparition that emerged from the mist. He had a look of irritation upon his face, and I was glad to see him. "Why are you bothering my guest?"

CHAPTER NINETEEN

PRINCE ZHOU WAS THE FIRST TO RECOVER, AND HE glanced over at me. "It seems we do owe you an apology after all."

"Yes, she is a lady welcomed to my estate, not here for your entertainment." Duke Meng frowned at them both, stepping under the roof of the pavilion. White flakes of snow dusted his hair.

"And you . . ." He turned to address Lingwei. "I didn't think you would indulge him in his antics."

"Antics?" Lingwei gave him a sideways look. "You convinced a Mortal to sign a contract, but you did not tell her who you are. You whisked her to this place, then left her alone under the open sky. You're lucky *she* didn't find her first."

I watched them as they threw barbed remarks at one another, voices slowly rising, tempers fraying.

"I don't need to justify to you or anyone else who I bring to my estate, what I do with my time, how I choose to occupy myself," Duke Meng said through gritted teeth.

Lingwei was unimpressed with her brother's temper. "You forget the decree from the consort. There is to be no travel between realms."

"I never forget who *you* work for," he snapped back. "I'm reminded of it every day. I'm not foolish enough to parade her around for the other denizens of the realm to gawk at. You saw her playing for yourself. She has the Spark."

"There are rules to this sort of thing, might I remind you." Prince

Zhou waded back into the fray. "And you know how much I detest the rules, but they're there for a reason, as you're well aware."

The way they spoke with one another revealed their history. They sounded like people who had grown up next to one another, squabbled and fought and laughed and hurt. A bond that could not be easily replicated or severed, as I'd seen for myself with those who had grown up in the House since they were children.

"We're here to let you know the tribunal has finally made a decision regarding our father," Lingwei said, voice strained. "He is to be executed after the rites of spring. Whatever you're working on to avenge him . . . it's a fool's errand, Jinglang."

Duke Meng's face still remained impassive at his sister's words. "She has nothing to do with our father. She will remain on my estate, and I will ensure she does not wander where she does not belong," the duke said with finality. "Do not forget, sister, that your welcome can be revoked. Especially if you choose to bring in *unwanted visitors*."

"I suppose that is a jab at me, then, brother?" The prince grinned, not at all perturbed by the harshness in the duke's voice, and just like that, the tension dissipated. The duke shook his head, and Lingwei rolled her eyes.

I watched all of this with growing frustration. They spoke about me and around me, yet they would not provide an explanation to their cryptic terms. I could not hold it in any longer.

"Will someone please tell me what you are talking about?!" I raised my voice, not caring who I was offending. "Who is the consort you're referring to? The empress? She has been dead for years! What sort of prince is he? He's not a prince of Qi, of that much I am certain."

The three of them turned to me, each eerily handsome in their own way. The way they moved, their way of dress, all of it pointed to a revelation I refused to acknowledge as real.

"Where am I?" I finally gasped, stepping back until I was against the balustrade. Until the cliffs were behind me, and there was nowhere to run. "Who are you?"

Lingwei turned to the duke, a veiled warning in her words. "You need to tell her."

A muscle in his forehead twitched as Duke Meng considered this. The prince nodded as well, stepping beside Lingwei, the two of them now in agreement. *Tell her, or we will.*

The duke ran his hand through his hair and sighed again. He walked toward me, even as I flinched and tried to move away from him, even though there was nowhere else to go.

"I had hoped to tell you in time, once you settled in." His tone was apologetic, his eyes sad. "This is my estate, and I do have a title—all of that is true. Except it is not in the Kingdom of Qi, nor any of the neighboring Mortal kingdoms. Those of us who inhabit this place are responsible for the fate of the living. In your world, you call this place the Celestial Realm."

I suddenly felt it difficult to breathe. I looked upon them, at their surreal beauty, and found myself laughing, on the verge of madness.

"Is this some sort of joke?" I examined their faces for a twitch, something to betray them and all of their lies. "This is a neighboring kingdom. Xia, perhaps, or even Tu, I could understand." I said it more to myself, to convince myself that this could be true. There were stories about women being abducted and sold across the border to become wives of mountain men. But did they live in grand estates such as these?

I had been warned about the wealthy and their eccentricities— perhaps this was another one of their tests, to frighten me, to ensure I would be loyal to them. I'd seen this play out before, when a new apprentice outshone the others, became favored before paying their dues. The pushing out was subtle, little jabs to remind them that they were different, that they couldn't quite fit in. Those tiny grievances would build up over time, until the newcomer eventually fled from the stress of it all. There were a few who would remain, stubbornly working at finding their place, and then over time, they would be accepted.

Sometimes it is smarter to yield, I remembered Matron's instructions. *Lest you find what remains of yourself being worn away.*

"I know I'm a sheltered musician from a small city," I said, dropping to my knees. "Have your laugh at me."

Except no one broke their seriousness. They still regarded me with concern, pity, apology. None of them stepped forward and admitted to the lie. I found anger rising up inside of me, hot embarrassment overriding my sensibilities. I should've stayed quiet and let the moment pass, let them have their fun, but I remembered Anjing's pale, terrified face. How disposable we were, at their expense. How we often had to be witnesses to their cruelties.

I shot to my feet then, a bit unsteady, advancing upon them.

"Prove it, then!" I jabbed my finger in the direction of Prince Zhou's face, already bordering on the hysterical. "Prove it, just like you wanted me to prove that I was capable of playing the qín. Show me that we are in the Celestial Realm."

I wanted to see that look of derision upon his face, to hear him scoff and tell me that there was no such place after all. That the Celestial Realm only existed in stories for children, in legends to keep them obedient and respectful of their elders. How pathetic I was to believe him, even for a moment, this little joke between friends. A harmless laugh to be had at the expense of a servant girl, whose fate was placed upon paper, contract signed and sealed.

But he gave me a nod and extended his hand toward me. For a

moment, I hesitated. Did he mean for me to take it? Then from his palm, there emerged a shoot. A tender green vine that emerged, winding itself around his arm. Buds popped from the branches, growing into leaves before me. From his palm, another tendril emerged; this time the bud formed into a drooping head, then the bloom unfurled before my eyes. A chrysanthemum, trembling upon the thin stalk. Yet even more terrifying than this sight of conjuring flowers from nothing were his eyes. His eyes flashed gold and there was nothing human about them, as sparks trailed through his hair.

Lingwei stepped forward then too, and she bowed her head, brought her hands up to her face . . . then she folded in upon herself. There was a brilliant flash that left dancing shadows across my vision, and in her place stood a swan. She extended her wings, and they were so wide they almost stretched from one side of the pavilion to the other. A gorgeous creature, with pure white feathers and black eyes that blinked at me with a soft intelligence. With a beat of those wings, the petals scattered from the hand of the prince, and as they fell to the earth, they disappeared into golden sparks.

I did not know what to say, could only gape.

Masters of illusion and spectacle had been given space to perform at the House for select shows. Those events dazzled, but observing from the balcony, one could see with perspective those were mere tricks. Sleight of hand, diversions of attention, shifts of perception. But this . . . what sort of marvel would this be called, if not pure magic?

Duke Meng approached me then, slowly. He took my hand, gentle, moving with careful intention, as if he was afraid I would flee.

I noticed then, with shock, the bright red smear of blood upon my palm. When the string snapped, it must have sliced my hand open, though I was numb to the pain. I tried to pull my hand out of his grasp so that I did not get blood on his tunic. But he put his other hand over mine, held me still, and I felt a subtle *push*. A sudden flare of warmth, enveloping our joined hands. He felt real, impossibly, unbearably real.

When I opened my hand again, the skin was smooth.

Healed.

CHAPTER TWENTY

I SWAYED ON MY FEET, AND THE DUKE CAUGHT MY arm, helped me to sit down on the bench. Another flash of light, and Lingwei was back to her human form. She seemed pleased that the truth was now revealed, but I was afraid of her too.

"You'll permit me some time alone to speak with the lady?" Duke Meng said to them. Lingwei nodded, while Prince Zhou gave me a little bow.

"I'll see you again," he said, flashing his white teeth.

"I'd rather not," I retorted back to that pretty face, which contained too much humor at my expense.

"Feisty, this one." He winked, undeterred, and Lingwei tugged at his arm. They left together, walking back toward the manor, the illusion again of a regular couple. *Mortal.*

I was left alone with the duke, who stood there wearing a guilty expression. The anger burned inside of me, almost choking me. His despicable lies. I hated it more than all of Prince Zhou's jokes; the duke had ample opportunity to tell me the truth of what I was walking into. Instead, he gave me a choice that wasn't really a choice. Another illusion.

"I want the truth," I said to him. "Tell me why I am really here."

He did not chastise me for being impolite, for daring to criticize him. Instead he just bowed his head.

"Everything I told you about your uncle and my shīfù was true. You saw it in the letter. He told me that you would be able help me, and he asked me to protect you. Bringing you here means I could do both," he said, appealing for me to understand. It incensed me further that he believed that he was justified in his decision to lie to me.

"You thought you could use me for your needs and then discard me," I spat. "You thought I was a poor Mortal girl, having to play for her keep, and you thought, how *delighted* would she be if I brought her to my Celestial manor. If I showed her my magic and my glorious world and made sure she would want for nothing. How grateful she would be, *should* be, how appreciative. She should be falling down at my feet in thanks!"

He stared at me, the shock plain on his face. It told me I had hit upon some aspect of the truth. I knew it from Prince Zhou's careless words, the way he spoke of *my kind*—short, insignificant Mortal lives. Not worthy of their consideration.

"That was not my intention," he protested, but I was not interested in his excuses. I saw each of his gestures, what I had misinterpreted as kindness, as manipulation. I should not have been lured by the story behind those sad eyes.

"I'm sure you have your reasons, whatever they may be," I choked out. "Perhaps they are even valid. But right now I do not want to hear it. Leave me to be angry. I deserve that, at least."

He closed his mouth. With whatever dignity I had remaining, I picked up my qín and my stand, and left him standing there in the pavilion by himself. Night was falling over the estate, and in the distance, I saw the rooms of the manor light up, one by one, as the servants passed through. It glowed like the moon.

I felt a sharp pang in my chest. This place was beautiful, but it was not the world I was meant for.

———

THAT NIGHT I could not sleep. It was another maid who brought my evening meal. When I asked her where Danrou was, she said that my maid was called away for another purpose. I picked at my food, having lost my appetite with all that had happened during the day. I tossed and turned in bed, but sleep would not come.

When sleep continued to elude me, I paced in my room. I don't know what I thought the Celestial Realm would look like. I had imagined a place of marble and gold, angles and lines, cold and austere. Not this elegant refinement, where the air lingered with the familiar scent of chénxiāng.

A desperate feeling struck me, the sense of the walls closing upon me once more. There was nowhere to go, nowhere to run. I found myself again with the only thing that comforted me. My qín in my arms, I shuffled my way down the long hallway, toward the small garden that was bathed in moonlight. I slipped through the hidden gate to the path beyond. This time, I turned the other way, down the path that meandered along the back wall of the manor to another pavilion at the foot of the mountain. I glanced up at the plaque.

待霜亭

The Pavilion of Expectant Frost.

There must have been a poet somewhere along the Meng family line to have named such a lonely corner of the estate.

I set up my qín on its stand. Back in the House of Flowing Water, whenever I grew restless, my garden lean-to was always my place of salvation. I liked to imagine the music drifting through the streets of Wudan, and hoped it would provide someone comfort. But here, who would even hear me, except the moon and the stars?

The moon was full again; the light reflected upon the water in the distance, and made it glimmer in the dark. How did time even work here?

Did this moon wax and wane like the one back home? Did the realms look upon the same moon, or was I under an entirely foreign sky?

My hands found the melody I sought. A slow, pensive plucking of strings. Each note lingered, like tears trembling upon eyelashes. I imagined the melody floating through the trees, calling for whoever was out there, willing to listen.

In the stillness of the night
Only the moon protests our leaving
I'm looking for you
Tell me you're coming . . .

The song told of two lovers who promised to meet each other beside the city walls. She sat in the boat, waiting for him to fulfill his promise, to take them away to a place where they could finally be together. The rise and fall of the boat was like the beat of her aching heart, uncertain if he would come, afraid he wasn't strong enough to leave.

I lowered my hands slowly, clinging to the solace the music provided, and then I heard it. A rustling. Behind me. Above me?

I stood up, trying to determine the direction the sound was coming from. Initially, I thought it was the sound of the wind, but it was too fast and too rhythmic, approaching swiftly from . . . the mountain.

Above me, the trees parted, and something shot through the canopy. A blur in the night. The shadows rippled, transformed . . . A dark, menacing shape loomed upon the wall. I shrank back, but it swooped down from the darkness, and it was upon me before I could even draw in a breath to scream.

You called me.

The voice was in my head, all around me. At first all I could see was the wide expanse of its mouth. It stretched too wide in a macabre grin,

142

a monstrosity beyond my comprehension. Too many rows of sharp, jagged teeth. Scattered around that wide mouth were a number of golden eyes, blinking at different intervals. Above that hideous visage were horns like a goat's, but its large head was attached to a body that was too small. A human-size body, with human hands that pinned my arms to the ground. I turned my head and felt something cold and sharp dig into my face.

The protrusions. Those strange growths of many colors that jutted out from its skin. Like the mountain lion that had attacked us in Wudan.

Hungry.

From that mouth came a long, long tongue that swept warmly across my cheek. Left a sticky residue. I shuddered.

I hope this one lasts a little longer than the one before it.

I gasped and remembered to fight. To kick at whatever I could reach.

You can hear me. Its smile grew wider, its many teeth clicking against one another. All of the pupils of the many eyes focused upon me. *I've climbed this mountain for days, came upon this place so full of sound and light.*

It placed one hand upon my chest and pressed down so that I felt as if my bones would crack open.

You are the shining thing in the garden. So ripe and filled with life. With the other hand it reached out and cupped my face, using a long nail that extended, claw-like, from its finger to stroke my hair. *You will satiate my hunger. At least . . . for a little while.*

I couldn't move, for fear it would crush me. I could only watch as it stretched its jaws wide above me, and I felt . . . a sharp tug, inside of my head. Not entirely painful. A slight ringing in my ear, the taste of blood in my mouth. My vision wavered, and I saw wispy strands of gray emerge from me and drift into its cavernous mouth.

The ringing in my ears grew louder and louder. The chill began in my fingers, crept up my arms, to my shoulders. My limbs grew heavy. Instinctually, I knew that soon I would turn into an emptied husk, a shell that was a physical body, with nothing left to inhabit it.

A blade emerged from its forehead, through one of its great eyes. From where it erupted, it leaked blood down its face. Silver, like it was weeping. It made a gurgling noise above me, thrashing in the air as it was lifted up, then thrown to the side.

The pressure eased from my chest, and those strands that left me rushed back in, sent me gasping as the sound returned to my ears and my vision suddenly sharpened. Returned again to a body that ached and was chilled and desperately needed breath. I gulped and gulped again, greedily, as if breathing for the first time. Like I had drowned and come back to life.

Hunger . . . My head was still filled with that dreadful longing. It was so terribly, terribly hungry. A dark void that could not be filled.

A warm hand touched my forehead, gently moved me so that my head was elevated, rested on something soft. It made it easier to breathe, so that the pain was not so overwhelming. The hand remained upon my forehead, emanating warmth. Until little by little, I felt myself again. I was once again Guxue, and not that creature filled with so much need.

"It's gone," the voice said above me, and I blinked away my tears to see two of him, then one, then two, and joined back together again. The duke. The liar. The savior. His hand cupped my cheek, and I was reminded of how that creature touched my face too. I flinched.

"Ruilan . . ." He called me by another name, and so much regret was contained in that simple utterance.

I realized then my head was cradled in his lap, and I struggled to sit up. He helped me into a half-reclining position, and I leaned upon one arm, too weak to stand, but not wanting to be sitting against him any farther.

"The feeling will pass," he said, stoic once again. He sat back. "Give it a moment."

I looked at him. He split into two again, then merged back into one.

"I think I may be sick," I warned him, before vomiting all over his shoes.

CHAPTER TWENTY-ONE

IN THE MORNING, DANROU RETURNED AS MY ATTEN-
tive maidservant. She waited on me, tight-lipped, offered no apology
and no explanation, yet I felt oddly glad to see her face. At least her
dislike of me was genuine, and that felt more sincere to me than anything else.

"The duke has requested you join him in his residence for the morning meal," she said, picking up the comb that was upon my dressing
table. Her eyes met mine in the mirror. *Do you want my help or not?* She
raised her brow, and I nodded, finally giving in. I sat there and submitted
myself to her administrations, partly because I was too tired to argue,
and partly because I understood she was right. She was doing her duty,
and I had to fulfill mine. Both of us answered to the same person.

"I am sorry," I said to her while she pinned up my hair, willing to offer
a truce. "I understand there will be time for us to adjust to each other,
and I would appreciate your assistance in learning how to best fit into
my role upon the estate, so that I may best serve the duke."

"Hmph." Danrou made a noise in her throat, but she didn't dismiss
the idea outright, so I would take that as a win.

"It's not my place to speak of these things," she said softly. "But if
you wished to give others the right impression, then the lady should be
mindful of her behavior."

"I would appreciate your advice, then, should you choose to give it,"
I told her, swallowing down my prickly defenses.

"The duke carried you back here last night." Her disapproval was clear, how it was *not done.* "I had warned you previously that there were dangerous places upon the estate, where someone of your . . . background should be wary of."

I understood then that Danrou was aware I was a Mortal, and that somehow, in this realm, Mortals were seen as lesser than. But last night's events proved that it was true. I was weak. No magical ability. No strength to face whatever lurked in those mountains.

Suddenly, that monstrous face filled my mind, and my stomach recoiled. The memory of the night crashed into me, until I leaned forward and pressed my hands upon the dressing table. Steadying myself as the nausea rolled over me, then receded.

"Should I tell him you are unwell?" Danrou inquired.

"No, no." I swallowed. "I'll be fine. Let's finish this."

"This does not change how I feel about you," she said matter-of-factly as she slid a pin into place and smoothed down a loose curl. "No matter what the duke's instructions are, we are ruled by the tenets of the Sky Sovereign and the Sky Consort. They have warned us about Mortal creatures like you."

"Understood." I was an interloper. Even though I wanted nothing more than to retreat to my bed and pull the covers over my head, I knew that the more ignorant I remained of what governed this different realm, the more danger I would be in. What would Auntie think of me if she ever were to find out the predicament I found myself in? I thought she would tell me she had warned me, but also tell me to survive. To thrive, to prove that she had once made the right decision to take me in.

We returned to the main courtyard, and I had expected we would pass through the main manor to the low buildings beyond, to the family wing. But instead, we went east, through a gate that had the carving of an undulating dragon upon it, surrounded by fish. Above the gate was another poetic name.

夢緣堂

The Residence of Fateful Dreams.

In this courtyard there was a path of crushed gray stones that led to the front steps. It curved around an enormous willow tree, slender new leaves just beginning to emerge from its gracefully drooping branches. The willow was one of the first signs of spring, and along the walls the bare shrubs were also starting to bud. In all appearance, this was a garden just coming to life after a long winter.

Only a few days on the Meng Estate, and I had passed through three seasons. Autumn falling into decay, the stillness of winter frost, and now the slow unfurling into spring. Somewhere there must be a garden that contained the vibrant blooming of summer. I should have seen this and recognized I was living in a place beyond time.

The receiving room was sparse and bare, white upon white. The doors and windows opened to let the slight breeze in. At the center was a bronze brazier, dominating the space with its size, and the slightly spicy, medicinal scent that emanated from the glow within. The only decorations were two matching scrolls of calligraphy, hung on either side of the wood lattice window that contained the design of the weeping willow, matching the tree in the courtyard.

It was a place devoid of personal touches. A place of austerity that bade you to lower your head and contemplate the questions of a Celestial nature: life and death, birth and rebirth. That matched the idea in my mind of how a Celestial should live, free from the distractions of worldly life.

The duke waited for me, sitting on a cushion beside a low black table decorated with gold scrollwork. A place setting in front of him, and another on the opposite side, just like how it was when we traveled.

"Please." He gestured for me to take my place. Danrou bowed and was dismissed.

I knelt upon the cushion, my head already a jumble of thoughts. There was so much I wanted to say, but when I met his eyes, his face wavered before me. The nausea returned stronger than before. A black wave descended across my vision, tilted the world so I no longer knew which way was up and which way was down. I tumbled then, through the darkness, with only the slithering ooze of that voice writhing around me.

I walked upon two feet once. Now my back arches, the barbs emerging from my changed flesh. Only the hunger propelled my search. I ran on four legs, claws digging into the earth. I might have had wings, long ago? What I used to be, I am no longer.

"Come back," a different voice parted the darkness. I saw his face again, and the darkness, still insistent, threatened to return me to that place.

"Guxue! You have to listen to me. Come back!"

It was his voice that pulled me back, calling me by name. Something familiar. I focused on his eyes, the small mole above his brow, the slight curl of hair at his ear. Those imperfections and differences that were unique to him, made him less like a feared Celestial, who held the fortunes of Mortals in his hand. More like the man who felt sick in a swaying carriage, arguing with me about poetry . . .

I let out a shuddering breath and the darkness receded. I leaned against his shoulder, too weak to care about the warning that Danrou gave me about propriety and behavior. Not when I knew how close I was to having my mind torn from me.

I felt the duke sigh, and then he brought a cup of tea to my mouth, poured a slight trickle in. I swallowed, my mind a little clearer. After he helped me with the first cup, I took the second cup he poured and sat up, and still, he remained beside me.

"Ravagers . . ." He began. It seemed that he was willing to give me an explanation then. A step forward. "They have a taste for the life force of all living things. It draws them down from the mountains. The wards around that part of the estate have been neglected for some time."

"A ravager," I croaked. "Like the beast that attacked us in Wudan."

He nodded. "I had forgotten you could see its form. A Mortal would only see the beast was larger and more ferocious than normal, nothing more. Yet you saw its true visage."

"Why?"

I pulled away so that I could look upon him, to see for myself whether he was speaking the truth. Or perhaps it was because being that close to him, it was difficult for me to keep my mind focused, yet I would never admit it.

"A Celestial's responsibility is to the Mortal Tapestry. Because of that influence, our very presence has the potential to reshape the fates of any Mortal that we encounter, however briefly," he explained. "You met a Celestial sometime in your past. It awoke something within you, the remnants of the magic that was passed on when the First Gods gave breath to humanity. We call this the Spark."

All of these terms made little sense to me, except that one thing I was certain of: I'd never met anyone who claimed to be a Celestial or had the potential to be.

"That's impossible." I shook my head. "I would have felt it somehow, right? That sort of encounter would have changed my life."

He shrugged. "It could have been as easy as bumping into them upon the street. It may have changed the path that your life had intended to follow, caused a deviation."

He must have noted the expression upon my face, one that resisted the thought of our lives being governed, predetermined by the Celestials, the thought that I had no choice in the matter but to be carried along.

"It's not necessarily good or bad," Duke Meng added gently. "Some would see it as a rare gift, a hidden potential." It was easy for him to say, for he stood on the outside of the pattern, looking in. He could see the true picture the strands formed, while I remained helpless, trapped.

"You should eat something." He picked up a bowl from the table and offered it to me.

I didn't see him gesture, but Attendant Luo was suddenly there, setting down a bubbling pot. The scent emanating from it made my mouth water. I took the spoon and picked up a bit of rice porridge. Better to be miserable with my stomach full than miserable and hungry.

I considered what he said while eating my fill of the thick porridge. It was salty and soothing, containing bits of purple yam and king oyster mushroom. It reminded me of what the House's cook would bring us when we were sick.

"You don't have to eat, do you?" I asked when I saw him stir his bowl of porridge, having also taken a serving for himself.

"No, I don't," he said. "But it's a pleasant enough experience. I appreciate the ritual and art of it."

I set my spoon down and sat up straight, regarding him with as much seriousness and sincerity as I could muster in my seventeen years of life. "I asked for your honesty, and I hoped you would be willing to provide it to me," I said. "Knowing what a ravager is does not help me understand why you brought me to this realm. What did my uncle's letter mean when he said I needed protection? The only time that I've encountered such a beast was when you appeared. It seemed likely that it was drawn to you, and if you left me there, I would still be safe."

He gave me a rueful smile and something pained flashed across his face. "Lost as they are to the infection that Turned them, some part of them must still retain the memory of their origins. Even though they would consume Mortal and Spirit life forces alike, it is the Celestial soul they crave the most. Because of your previous contact with the Celestials, it will hunger for your life force with equal fervor."

"What . . . *were* they?" I asked, afraid of the answer, even though I had suspected from my brief contact with them, the brush of my mind to theirs. The brief flash of sentient memory, before it was enveloped again by that ceaseless hunger.

"They were once like me," he said, voice low.

"*What I used to be, I am no longer,*" I whispered, remembering the words that echoed in the spinning dark.

"At first we had hoped once that the infection could be cured, that the ravagers could return to their Celestial form. But the Heavenly Mother has declared them incurable. They are to be eliminated immediately upon discovery, for their presence threatens the stability of the realms." He sighed. "Your uncle and my shīfù discovered more and more ravagers along the borders, making their way to the Mortal and the Spirit Realms. Someone is creating them, *causing* them to Turn."

Until they became those monsters that were amalgamations of different body parts, human and beast. They used to be ethereal and graceful, like Lingwei or the prince. I couldn't imagine how they could have morphed into their twisted forms.

"It's not so different from the Spark that resides within you, leftover from when the world was first shaped," Duke Meng explained. "This plague too was the remnant of the creation of the world. What we call the Corruption."

"But Celestials are powerful, immortal," I said. "They have the ability to shape and change the realms, to rule over and protect all living creatures."

"Ah." He shook his head. "That is where you are wrong, Lady Guxue. We have magic, true, yet we are not all-powerful."

From under the table he pulled out a book and handed it to me. The cover was plain, only the title upon it: *The Origin of the Six Realms.*

"This may help you in understanding how the realms are connected, how we are all reliant on one another. Whether Celestial, Mortal, or Demon."

"Thank you," I murmured. I supposed I shouldn't be surprised that with the existence of Celestials, there would also be the existence of Demons.

"No, thank *you* for speaking with me, even when informed that I brought you here under false pretenses," he said then, guilt all over his face. He leaned forward, sincere. "I have been to the Grand Library these past few days and consulted some old texts, to confirm what my shīfù had taught me, many years ago. I would be ever so grateful for your assistance in this matter. Please, join me at the Wind-Swept Pavilion this afternoon. Attendant Luo will come find you."

He took his hands in mine. I was suddenly taken aback again, by how easily he disarmed me, with his damned earnestness, with his devotion to his quest, with the warmth of his touch. My palm ached slightly from where he'd healed me.

"I said from the start. If I can help you, I will," I said slowly.

He grinned, and I found myself smiling back. Hoping I wouldn't regret whatever it was I agreed to.

INTERLUDE

On the Origin of the Mortal, Ghost, and Barren Realms

When the earth was formed, it was unstable, plagued with earthquakes and floods. Humans hid in caves and lived short lives of fear and woe. The first gods joined together and determined that a sacrifice must be made.

They drew lots, and it was the goddess Nüwa who was chosen. She went willingly, for she knew her sacrifice would ensure the stability of the earth. Her hair flowed into river streams, her bones formed the mountain ranges, and her tears filled the lakes. Her fingers held up the sky, and the earth was finally at peace.

The one who loved her, Fuxi, grieved for her, until it was revealed that the lots had been rigged. The Deceiver was discovered, and in a rage, Fuxi avenged Nüwa and cut off the Deceiver's head. The Deceiver cursed the humans as she died, for she knew the humans were Nüwa's precious legacy. This was known as the Corruption, for even in the brevity of human lives, they were cursed with famine and war and disease.

Fuxi then created the Realm of Ghosts, to purify and cleanse the souls of the suffering humans, so that they might live again in the cycle of rebirth.

As for the Deceiver, the Barren Realms were created to contain her. There is nothing there.

—From *The Origin of the Six Realms*

CHAPTER TWENTY-TWO

WHILE I WAITED FOR ATTENDANT LUO, I SPENT THE rest of the afternoon flipping through the text that the duke had given me. The stories were familiar and yet unfamiliar, especially the ones reminiscent of the tales told to me by my uncle. He made me remember them, had me repeat them back to him, again and again.

Did he know what fate awaited me, and was he trying to prepare me for the inevitable future? I thought he was just a lover of those old tales, but those memories had been cast in a new light. How much more about my uncle was I going to discover? And a hesitant whisper at the back of my mind: *Should I be afraid of what I will learn?*

When Attendant Luo came to fetch me, it was already late afternoon. The main garden was still shrouded in winter. Snow drifted around me, the trees now tinged in frost. I left a trail of footprints behind me, my breath fogging the air with each exhale. Yet, with just my cloak, I did not feel cold. It was as if I wandered through a mirage, the effect disorienting, and it made me quicken my steps as he led me to the Wind-Swept Pavilion.

This was where I'd learned of the existence of other realms. But instead of the view of the gorge and the mountains, there was nothing but swirling gray mist and fog. I could not see the manor in the distance, and the trees were only vague shapes somewhere beyond. After Attendant Luo left us, it felt like we were the only ones there, upon the edge of the world.

"I promised you an explanation," he said, more severe than I had ever seen him. "Will you entrust me with your qín?"

I set the qín upon the stand as he bade, wary of what he would do next. He sat down upon the bench, sweeping his cloak aside. He had tied his hair back, which sharpened his features, making him look younger.

"Your uncle's letter had spoken about the qín being a lock, and I had assumed it meant there was something contained within. Something hidden inside through magical means," he explained. "Yet when I held it, I did not feel that it had the potential to be a container. My next query was whether the qín itself would grant access to a place, if one played the right set of notes upon it."

"A doorway?"

"May I?" Duke Meng asked, gesturing at the strings. I acquiesced with a nod.

After a few moments to tune and familiarize himself with the feel of the instrument, he began to play. I recognized the melody after the first few notes. It was one of the most revered pieces of qín music, a classic most students should recognize. "Mountains High," the first of the pair of songs that were outlined in the Story of Boya and Ziqi.

The mountain's great peaks
Lofty heights and solitary cliffs
Reaching skyward

He played it competently, and he was, as he said, an adequate qín player. He was technically adept, but missing that emotional resonance that was required for greatness. That ability to reach into the heart of the audience, to soothe it or to pull it out.

As the last note faded, the duke frowned. "It is as I suspected. I feel . . .

nothing. If it truly had the potential to be a gate, the magic would have to be imbued into the strings, and I would be able to sense it."

He sighed then with obvious frustration. "It makes no sense! And yet, it does. The qín isn't the key, so it shouldn't open anything, but . . ." He rested his gaze upon me again. "Are you willing to play the song? To try?"

It seemed harmless enough. Even though I had no magic to call my own.

"I can, but . . ." In the distance, the mist seemed to move, to ripple and form different shapes. My ability to perform the song was not an issue—it was the fear that lurked at the edge of my mind. Worry that I would draw another one of those ravagers, that others would come—

"You do not have to be afraid of the ravagers," he said, assuring me. "The wards are repaired. I made certain of it myself. I will not fail you again."

I would have to trust that his words were true. He moved aside, and I took his place. I pulled the song from my memory. It began with low notes, a pensive reflection of how small and insignificant a person would feel at the foot of those great peaks. A reminder of Nüwa's sacrifice, where once she lay down and gave her body to reshape the earth. My fingers brushed against the strings, pulling out the sounds as wispy as the fog that swept down from the east.

"Look!"

Upon the edge of my qín, there were thirteen pearl inlays. Markings that helped with determining where to place the hands in order to play the correct notes. One began to rise from the wood, hovered in the air above, and emanated a soft glow. Duke Meng reached out to try to catch it, but it seemed to pass through his fingers. As the last notes of

"Mountains High" faded, the pearl lost some of its luster, and began to descend back into its hiding place.

But then I remembered the carving on the back of the qín. "Mountains High" and "Swift Streams." I quickly went into the next song before the pearl disappeared completely.

The silver stretches, a long ribbon unwinding
By the mountain stream, the qín plays, resounding

After the piece was done, the pearl was still there. Still real. I reached out and placed my hand underneath the jewel, where it fell into the crease of my palm. No bigger than my smallest fingernail.

Duke Meng met my eyes. Me with marvel, him with awe.

"It worked," he said, and it was his turn to be in disbelief. "Only when everything was in perfect alignment. The musician, the song, the realm. They hid it so well. There may be more, if we have the right songs to open them."

It did not surprise me, knowing my uncle's love of riddles, hidden in words and in song.

"What is it?" I asked.

"It's a memory jewel." He gently plucked it out of my hand and held it between his fingers. "Formed from the tears of a Celestial, usually associated with a state of heightened emotion. Sometimes they're kept so we can recall significant events in our long lives, but they've been banned for a while. It is against the tenets for us to dwell on these emotions. There's too much risk."

"Risk of what?"

"Of dwelling too long on earthly passions, distracting us from our role, resulting in a disturbance in the cosmic balance," he said, with great seriousness.

"Ah," I said. "Small, insignificant consequences." Then I realized I may have spoken out of turn, but he only smiled at me wryly.

"Shall we look and see what this contains?" he asked, and I saw hesitation flicker across his face, almost as if he was afraid of what could be in there.

"Show me," I said, sounding braver than I felt. But I needed to know what befell my uncle upon the road. "How do we look at what is hidden within?"

"You step into it," he said, as if it was simple, and held out his hand for me to take.

Sitting there in the pavilion, with him standing above me, I was struck with the feeling that *this* was the moment. This was my doorway to step through, the choice that would send me toward the answers I was looking for and entangle my life further with his. If all of my choices were woven into the Mortal Tapestry, was there ever another path of my life that would lead me anywhere but here?

I placed my hand in his.

THE WIND HOWLED as it rushed around us, sending my hair flying. The fog wiped out everything beyond the pavilion, taking even the garden away. The wind was so strong and sharp that I had to close my eyes, and when the noise died, I opened them to see we had been transported to another place entirely.

A bamboo forest surrounded us. The sun streamed through the leaves, scattering beams of golden light across the forest floor. Down from the steps of the pavilion, only a few paces away, was a hut. Before the hut was a small clearing with a table and chairs. Two figures sat there, beside a fire cheerfully burning in a pit, above which a pot hung.

One of the figures looked familiar, and then I realized with a gasp who he was. Dressed in black robes, the design of clouds upon the sleeves, his hair up in his typical topknot, happily regarding the table of food before him—

"Uncle!" I called out, already halfway across the pavilion in my eagerness to reach him. But I was pulled back, stopped by the duke, with a look of sympathy.

"He can't hear you," he said.

I turned to look back at my uncle. He looked so real, like I could run to him and embrace him once again. He would laugh and tell me how I'd grown yet again.

"But—" The image wavered then, like a stone dropped into a reflective pond.

"Be quiet!" the duke snapped, then softened his words when he saw my stricken expression. ". . . Or the memory will dissipate."

All I could do then was stand and watch. My uncle picked up his chopsticks and clicked them against the table, before leaning forward and picking up a piece of food. Beside him, another man played the qín, a delicate melody unwinding, accompanying their meal. This must be Elder Gao, the duke's shīfù, the one who loved my uncle and who my uncle loved in turn.

He was an older man, around fifty years of age. The gray hair around his temples gave him a distinguished air. He wore a black robe on which there was the pattern of geese flying.

"What is this?" Elder Gao said in a playful manner when he struck the last chord of the song with a flourish. "Do you recognize it?"

"Hmm." Uncle pondered this, thoughtful as he chewed. "I was too distracted by this delectable spread of food before us. Play it again?" He could not hide the slight smile that curled the corner of his lip. I saw it and knew that it was genuine, the way he cared for this man.

"I would have thought someone like you, a professed lover of music, would have recognized this straight away," Elder Gao shot back, a teasing lilt to his voice. "Even that apprentice of mine would know it, I bet."

Beside me, the duke shifted. I realized we had unwittingly drawn closer to each other, my hand still in his, leaning on him for support. Maybe I should've stepped aside, but the sight of my uncle talking and laughing before me was too much, and I was too weak to remain there without him pulling me back.

"You!" Uncle placed his finger against the mouth of the now smiling man, who could no longer hide his amusement. "Hush. Play it again!"

The two of them laughed as the notes of the song reverberated around them, and the sound began to fade. The mist crept in too, rising from the bamboo around them, sweeping in, until they were gone.

Too soon, we were back in the Meng Estate. The mist had cleared, and night was quickly falling. I wished the memory was just a moment longer so that I could see him happy and with someone he loved. Someone I'd never met, who I wished he had introduced me to. But I stood there, holding the hands of a stranger, my desperate wish unanswered.

I looked over at the duke, not knowing where to begin, but then I noticed the paleness of his face, the blue-purple tinge of his lips. He opened his mouth, but no sound came out, and his eyes rolled to the back of his head.

He fell, taking me with him, and I could not bear his weight. All I could do was guide him to the ground, against the table, so that he did not hit his head.

"Help!" I cried out. "Someone! Help us!"

CHAPTER TWENTY-THREE

IT WAS A GUARD WHO FOUND US, HAVING HEARD MY cries. She fetched Attendant Luo, who directed more guards and servants to assist in carrying the duke to his residence. I followed behind, not knowing what to do. If I should stay and wait for him to wake, or if I should go.

"You should return to your residence, Lady Guxue," Attendant Luo said, hands upon the doors, blocking my entry. I was not welcome in there.

"Will you let me know when he wakes up?" I asked. "Please."

He looked at me for a moment, considering me, before nodding. "I'll send word with Danrou when the duke is awake."

I turned to leave, descending the few steps into the courtyard.

"Wait!" he called out. Then, dropping his voice, he said, "You don't have to worry. The duke gets these . . . spells sometimes. He will recover with a night's rest. I will pass on your concern—it will comfort him to know that you asked after his well-being."

I bowed, and returned to my own residence like I was instructed. I gripped the memory jewel in my hand still; I had picked it up from the floor of the pavilion. I was afraid to lose it, knowing how precious it was. I placed it carefully in a wooden box, and slid it into the very back of the drawer.

I lay in the dark for a while, remembering how my uncle looked, spending time with the man he loved. There was a tightness in my chest.

How wonderful it must be, to have someone who loved you and who you loved in return.

THE NEXT MORNING there was no word from Attendant Luo. Danrou only gave me a baleful look when I inquired about the duke, as if she blamed me for her master being in this state. Which, I supposed, was true.

I tried flipping through the book on Celestial history again, but found some of the sections quite dry. I didn't want to sit there and be still, not when I recalled that the duke mentioned there may be other jewels hidden within the qín. I looked upon my instrument again, and noted something that I had not seen before: There were two other inlays in the qín that seemed to be of a different color from the rest. I thought it was just because of the variations in the type of pearl that was used, but something about those two caught the light in a different way. I was almost certain that those two must be the remaining memory jewels, and I was eager to find out if I could unlock the other songs that would open them too.

I held the qín close as I hurried to the secret garden in my residence, hopeful that I would encounter Yingzi as well, so that I would have company. When I entered the garden, I called out her name, but no one answered. There was only the slight rustle of the wind through the dried leaves. I worried for a moment about playing here alone, the duke no longer here with me. He had said the wards would hold, but . . . no, I had to go on, even through my fears.

I tried the easiest solution first. Playing "Mountains High," followed by "Swift Streams." Even as I plucked the strings, I knew that nothing was happening. No shivering feeling, no jewel rising from the wood. It was only a lovely pair of songs for an autumn morning.

I thought back to the memory that we'd witnessed, and it came to me. The melody that Elder Gao played—a puzzle within a puzzle. One step leading to another. That melody had to be the key for the next jewel. The duke had said, *Everything needed to be in alignment—the song, the player, the realm.*

I tried to recall the strains of it, attempting to stumble through each note, but my recollection was imperfect. I had only heard a snippet, and I had to play both songs in order for the qín to release the jewel. So that must be what I should find next, the book that contained this mystery piece. But how was I supposed to find a book I didn't even know the name of? I chewed on my lip, my predicament heavy upon me.

"Hello!" A cheerful greeting came from the trees as Yingzi emerged from the grove. She walked so quietly, I had not heard the gate opening. "May I join you?"

"Of course," I said. "But you may have to provide me a song to play, to distract me from my worries."

"Taking requests?" She clapped, delighted. "Yes! I . . . Ah . . . Oh! Do you know 'Sunny Spring'?"

She closed her eyes and made an attempt at humming the melody. I hid a laugh at her sincerity as she meandered and then stopped, making a face.

"I'm not good at music at all," she grumbled. "But you know what I'm talking about, right?"

I was charmed by this girl. She still had bits of leaf stuck in her hair, no doubt from her tendency to hide in the bushes from her supervisors.

"Yes, I know it!" I assured her. I was surprised that she knew of this piece, when she said she wasn't a musician herself—it had originated as a folk song in a small kingdom that was long conquered.

I played the lighthearted tune, utilizing most of the higher notes of the qín. My fingers danced over the strings, conjured up the feeling of lying in the sunshine in the garden. The plucks upon the strings indicated the birds that jumped and swooped from the trees or circled lazily overhead. It was such a happy song, full of light. When I first entered the House of Flowing Water, I recalled the dancers had prepared a performance for it for the Spring Festival. How they laughed and spun, flowers streaming from their hair. Like goddesses, celebrating the return of the long days of sun.

I missed those women of the House. I missed the other music students. I wondered if they missed me too, if my leaving was felt by any of them. The thought made me sad, and the notes trickled down quietly to a stop.

Yingzi sat up with a frown. "What happened?"

"I'm sorry, I got distracted," I told her. "I was thinking of . . ." *Home*, I wanted to say, but the word didn't seem right.

"When I first came here, I was lonely too," she said.

"You're not here with your family?" I asked. She seemed so young, like me, but here, it was hard to tell how old anyone truly was, being Celestials.

"Those of us from my clan who are picked for the Celestial Path are chosen very young. We spend most of our childhood in training, then we're sent here, so that it's easier for us to adjust," she explained. "Easier for us to learn the routines of the new realm and the estate."

She was like me after all. Having to move and settle in to a new place.

"You're from the Spirit Realm," I said, trying to understand.

She nodded. "It's the highest honor to be chosen." She waved her hands. "My family will be provided for, and it makes me happy, knowing that they are taken care of, like they take care of me here."

"I see," I said. I couldn't pretend that I agreed with their beliefs, since I knew so little about them.

"Is it not the same in the Mortal Realm?" she asked. "Do your clans not have to pay tribute to those in charge?"

I thought about the emperor's many palaces. The Blue Palace of the capital, the Winter Manor in the south, the garden resort on the island in the Summer Sea. The servants that followed his family here and there, that took up every moment of their lives. All of the retinue of the royal family, and all of the nobility who traveled with them as well. Those servants too must have obligations to their families, money to be sent back home, people they wanted to protect.

"You're right," I told her. "We call them by different names, but the process is the same."

"I chose to come here," she told me, her eyes bright. "So that my sisters do not have to. It's not so bad here, really, living on the Meng Estate. The duke—" She stopped herself with a shake of her head. "The former duke was always kind to us."

"What happened to the former duke? Why was he banished?"

"There was . . . a dreadful thing that happened," Yingzi said, clearly uncomfortable. "When it did, it sent reverberations throughout the realms. But the former duke did not agree with the Sky Sovereign's judgment, and he pleaded with him to continue the investigation. But when the sovereign refused, the duke continued the investigation in secret. When that was discovered, he was stripped of his title, and then imprisoned in the High Tower."

"What dreadful thing happened in the court?" I asked, knowing that it must have been terrible to bring down the wrath of the sovereign.

Yingzi opened her mouth to speak, but voices came from the corridor.

She looked skittish and leaned in, dropping her voice to a whisper, "We're not supposed to speak of it any longer. It's been banned, but there should be a copy of it in the library. Ask Zhuxi for *Twilight's Begonia*. Remember, only Zhuxi, no one else, and tell no one that you met with him." There was an urgency to her tone, a warning. "They don't like it when we disturb them at work in the library."

"Wait, how do I get to the library?" I asked. With Danrou still lurking, watchful of my every move, she'd probably hinder rather than help me.

"Take this corridor past the Hall of Heartfelt Dreams, and then you'll be in the north wing," she explained quickly as the voices grew louder. "Avoid the door with the bird on it, turn left instead and down the side corridor with the white lanterns. Find the bamboo door."

She jumped back, raising a finger to her lips. "Don't tell anyone I was here." With a wink, she was gone.

I had a feeling I'd made a friend. Someone who didn't quite belong. Someone like me.

BY THE TIME the gardeners discovered me in the garden, I tried to look as innocent as possible, tuning my qín. They pushed a wheelbarrow full of tools between them, and greeted me with bows.

"Lady Guxue," the older woman among them said. "Were you here with someone else?"

"You can call me Xue," I said, repeating myself endlessly despite knowing that my request would be politely ignored. "I was just practicing. Talking to myself."

"I am head gardener Tong," she said.

I wondered if this was the one who Yingzi had nicknamed Datou, "the boss." I couldn't help but chuckle, then tried to hide it with a cough.

Gardener Tong politely ignored my awkward coughing as she frowned at my surroundings. "Danrou has sent us here to clean up the garden. Looks to be in worse condition than when I saw it last."

"I won't be a disruption to your work, then," I said, standing and picking up my qín. As I walked past them, I asked, out of curiosity, "What happened to the wall? It must have been quite an explosion to leave a hole of that size."

"A tragedy," one of her underlings spoke up, while the other person spoke at the same time, voice shrill, "Someone Turned ravager here."

Gardener Tong gave them a sharp look. "We don't speak of that anymore!" Then, turning to me, with a milder tone, she said, "Apologies for my staff. They should not be spreading rumors."

I returned to my residence, puzzling over this. There were many things in this manor that the staff did not speak of, their fear evident in their whispered tones and sideways glances. A vast estate, magnificent at first glance, but the more time I spent here, the more I noticed wild gardens, emptied rooms, and dusty corridors. A crumbling sort of opulence.

What else would I uncover, hidden within these walls?

INTERLUDE

On the Origin of the Spirit Realm and the Founding of the Celestial Court

Over time the earth became populated with humans, spreading into various areas upon the land. The children of the gods became restless, and were split into two factions. Some desired a life free from human influence, for they tired of watching over mortals' well-being. Others believed humanity was the essence that held the earth together.

Those who desired freedom created a realm of their own governance, from the four founding clans: under the sea, rooted in the earth, high in the air, and hidden in the hills. So they became the Water, Tree, Bird, and Flower Clans. But over time, they found that their magic grew weaker, for they could not live in isolation. Consulting their father, Fuxi, who still ruled over the Ghost Realm, they learned Nüwa had known that the gods had a tendency to be selfish, and tied their life force to the survival of humanity.

The clans came together and found a solution. From each of their families, they would select tributes, and from those, the ones with the greatest propensity for magic. These children of the children of gods would be given the mantle of caring for humans, ensuring the survival of the clans. They were given the name Celestials and strengthened with the pooled magic of the clans.

They would become bearers of the sacred duty of protecting the realms.

—From *The Origin of the Six Realms*

VERSE THREE

CHAPTER TWENTY-FOUR

I REMAINED IN MY ROOM, READING, UNTIL DANROU left to take laundry to the south wing, then hurried down the northern corridor—the way that Yingzi had pointed out to me. Before I turned each corner, I would furtively stand and listen for footsteps or voices. Luck was on my side this time. The corridors were empty.

The north wing, I noted, was definitely grander than the other wings, meant for the family of the lord of the manor. The inner courtyard was larger than others, a place of gray stone and carefully manicured trees. But there was a stillness to it, an emptiness, like no one had resided there for a time. I walked past the door with the carving of a heron on it that Yingzi had mentioned, another equally poetic plaque beside it: *The Residence of Hopeful Dreaming*.

I found the side hallway with the lanterns and felt a bit like an intruder, tiptoeing through. My shadow was long and dark against the row of bamboo on the other side of the balustrade. Every rustle caused my heart to beat faster, afraid of being discovered. I was almost running when I reached the end.

The door had a carving of bamboo on it, just like Yingzi said. I slowly pushed the door open, unsure of what I would discover on the other side. When I stepped in, my eyes widened as I took in the room before me.

It was like walking into another world. Large lanterns hung from the rafters, illuminating the space. The room was narrow and long, larger than it appeared from the outside. Along the wall were shelves filled with books and scrolls. In the middle of the room, there were wooden stands upon which treasures were displayed. I approached one to admire the forest scene of small foxes and wolves cast in bronze, amid a grove of crystal trees atop which tiny jade birds perched.

I was so entranced that I did not hear the approach of slippered feet until someone spoke right beside me. "May I assist you?"

I jumped and then was immediately afraid I would knock something fragile off a shelf, and overcorrected myself with a swing of my arm. I fell instead against the bookshelf, slid ungracefully halfway, and sent a few books and scrolls tumbling to the ground in the process.

"I'm so sorry!" I dropped to my hands and knees to pick up the books, my face hot with embarrassment.

"Steady now . . ." The man helped me up and took the books from me to return them to their proper places on the shelves. He was in his late thirties, if I was to guess, with a round face and a serene expression, and he appeared to be unbothered by a stranger blundering into this sanctuary. I dusted off my sleeves and straightened my skirt, but I still felt like a mess next to him.

If I were to envision what a Celestial would look like, it would be like him. Not a strand of hair out of place, parted and tied neatly atop his head with a green ribbon. His robes were a light shade of green. He looked like someone who had never experienced the absurdities of life, someone who drank clouds and walked upon the moon.

"Are you Zhuxi?" I asked.

"At your service." He gave a small bow and looked at me curiously. "The lady knows my name."

"I was told you would be able to help me find what I am looking for," I told him. "You are the librarian?"

"You could call me that," he said with a smile. "I assist in the maintenance and cataloging of this place, but I also curate and preserve."

"Is it a museum, then?" I said.

"A little bit of both, a little bit of both." He nodded. "This place is called the Archive of Dreams."

"Dreams? Whose dreams?"

His smile widened. "That's the important question, isn't it? Everyone dreams, across all six realms. From the Heavenly Mother to a wandering ghost."

I thought the name of the manor was a play on the duke's title, but it seemed it was more than merely clever wordplay after all.

"The duke is . . . responsible for these dreams, then?"

"Yes, he manages the Dreaming, where dreamers go when they are sleeping. He ensures no one is trapped in the tangles of a dream or enthralled by a particular memory from which they do not want to wake."

"The Dreaming is an actual place a soul can travel to?" I asked, not understanding. I shivered at the thought of being trapped in a dream, unable to return to my body, lying there in the real world.

"It's more of a . . . path, you might say," Zhuxi murmured, brow furrowed as he considered my question. "A path that connects all six realms. But it's easy to get lost, if you don't know your way."

"How strange," I said, then quickly corrected myself. "I mean, it's . . . difficult to comprehend, with my limited understanding."

"Dreams are just another type of thread that holds up the Mortal Tapestry," he said, not unkindly. "The duke assists the Stars with ensuring that Mortal fortunes are aligned."

So we were influenced by our dreams to follow our destinies, whatever path Fortune had decided we should walk.

I must have made a face, because Zhuxi chuckled. "You're wondering if the entire course of your life has been mapped out. If there is even such a thing as free will."

I bristled at his nonchalance. "It's easy for you to say! You're a Celestial, able to influence and see the course of dreams. You can decide what our fates look like. You have all the control."

"Oh, that's where you're wrong." He tsked, amused at my outburst. "I was once a Mortal, like you."

I gasped at this revelation. "You're from the Mortal Realm?"

"A long, long time ago," he said. "The former duke found me caught in the Dreaming when I was young. He freed me from my nightmare. I woke up remembering who he was, and what he said to me. I made it my life's work to pursue all the texts that referred to the Lord of Dreams, and my stubbornness caught the eye of the Star of Fortune. I had strayed from my intended path, and so the Celestials found me and gave me a choice: attempt the Trial of Ascension, or cross the Bridge of Souls."

"Become a Celestial or die." I scoffed. "That's not much of a choice."

I tucked away that bit of knowledge, the realization the Bridge of Souls was an actual place. The stories referred to it as the path that the recently deceased used to enter the afterlife. I'd even heard of the Trial of Ascension. This must be the "trial" Prince Zhou mentioned before. A Mortal could attempt to endure challenges set before them by the gods, to prove they were worthy of becoming a Celestial, to live a life immortal, free from earthly worries. Except it seemed to me that in the Celestial Realm, there were ranks, roles, responsibilities. It did not seem a life of carefree pleasures, of philosophical contemplation, like the sages spoke of.

"It is a curious existence, isn't it?" Zhuxi said. "But I wanted to see where this choice would take me, so here I am. I'd like to know how your thread has strayed as well, and what your choice would be, when it comes time to make it."

"I wasn't given a choice—" I said too quickly, before I realized that this could be seen as a complaint, and that it could get back to the duke. "Never mind. I didn't mean it."

"We will always choose, one way or another." He regarded me, more serious now. "The choice will come to you."

"What about Ruilan?" I asked him. Something terrible happened to her, and I was too afraid to find out what it was.

"Ruilan . . ." He blinked, then shook his head, the corners of his lips dragging into a frown. "She was a sweet girl. Meant as the duke's future bride when she came of age. The duke, his sister, and Ruilan . . . they used to be inseparable. What happened to her was tragic."

If they grew up together, she must have lived here for a long while. I'd heard of such a practice for the daughters of nobility in Qi, for a girl to be raised in the household of her intended—her life no longer her own.

"What happened to her?" I asked, interest overriding caution. I wanted to know the fate that had befallen the girl who lived in my residence before me, for part of me feared that was what awaited me also. If the duke ever grew tired of me, if I failed him . . .

"She Turned," he said gravely. "She became a ravager."

I could not help the sharp intake of breath, the shock that ran through me. A transformation from girl to beast, to that monster without conscious thought, driven by the urge to consume. No wonder they did not want to talk about her, and why the duke seemed so stricken when we discussed the ravagers.

"The tragedy was not that she Turned, even though that was awful in itself," Zhuxi said after a pause. "The tragedy was that she willingly chose it."

"To become one of those monsters?" I shook my head. "No, I can't imagine anyone choosing that for themselves."

"Her maidservant, her closest confidant, was the one who reported it. She found her mistress weeping, overtaken by emotion. Heard her state that she would rather Turn than go willingly to her doom. She witnessed the change and called for the guards to contain her before she attacked. They cornered Ruilan in the garden, but she jumped off the Platform of Forgetting before anyone could stop her." He shuddered.

"Where did she go?" Celestials couldn't die . . . right? Even though her escape was via a platform with that ominous name.

"No one has seen her since. The platform was once a portal between realms, but those routes have been closed off for a while. Anyone who recklessly enters now . . . who knows where they might end up? It's possible she survived, but the poison eventually eats away at the Celestial form and then the inner core of magic."

"But why?" My voice grew higher. "Why did she do it?" My heart ached for that girl. There must have been a reason to choose such an unspeakable fate. *She was the one who Turned in the wild garden,* I realized. She was the one the gardeners spoke of. Would Danrou have been her maidservant? That must be why she reacted in such a way when I found one of her mistress's things.

"I don't know." Zhuxi sighed. "An investigation was done. The case closed. There was speculation, of course, of interference. Some said it was an attack from the Demon Realm, but there were no signs of Demon activity on the grounds.

"But we shouldn't speak of such unpleasant events," he said, with a shrug. "Tell me, what are you looking for?"

It reminded me that I should be focused on my purpose for being here, rather than distracting myself with stories of those long lost. "I am looking for some songbooks—the duke had mentioned his father was a collector of music," I said, as casually as possible, wondering if he would indeed listen to my request as Yingzi said. "The songbooks for *Mountains High* and *Swift Streams*, as well as *Twilight's Begonia*."

"The latter may prove a bit challenging to find," he said with a nod. "Anything else?"

"I'd like to learn more about the Celestial Realm in particular, if there are any books you would recommend for one wanting to obtain a basic knowledge of this place. My education has been . . . lacking in the area." I had the time, after all. Might as well use it for something practical.

"That, I can definitely obtain for you." Zhuxi said, confident. "I just need a few moments."

"Thank you," I told him. I'd been stumbling around in the dark. I felt as if I had gained some precious ground, someone who might be able to illuminate my way and provide some guidance toward the answers that I sought.

I retreated out of the way and hovered by the shelves. I wondered what a catalog of dreams would even look like. What would be contained within? But the books that I glanced at appeared not to be related to dreams at all. *On the Lineage of the Water Clan of the Trueform Sea. Folk Songs of the Sparrows. Memories of the Windy Palace.*

A book fell from the shelves. It must have been knocked askew when I bumped into the shelf. I bent over to pick it up.

A Tangle of Dreaming.

I put it back where I thought it fell from.

Zhuzi returned after what felt like ages, depositing scrolls and books into my waiting arms.

"What should I call you, my lady?" he asked. "I do not know your name."

"I'm Xue," I told him, already expecting he would tack on the false title that the duke had given me.

"Ah, Xue. I'm pleased to meet you," he said with a smile and a small bow. "I hope you will return again soon. I don't get much company here."

I grinned back. "I'm sure I will."

Leaving the library, I felt more hopeful than I had in days.

With my head down and arms full, I was not as careful this time navigating through the manor's winding halls. I was halfway across the courtyard when I heard the thump of boots, and before I could react, I was surrounded by soldiers.

"Stop!" one of them shouted. Two of them pointed the sharp tips of their spears in my direction, barring my way through. These soldiers were dressed in silver, helmets obscuring half of their faces. They approached me menacingly, tightening their circle, until I was closed in.

There was nowhere else to go.

CHAPTER TWENTY-FIVE

I ONLY HAD MY SCROLLS AND BOOKS IN HAND. Nothing to defend myself with. All I could do was stand there and cower, wait to see what they wanted from me. I supposed I could have protested my innocence, told them that I was here upon invitation from the duke. But I was caught in the throes of a memory long forgotten, of soldiers marching through a wooden gate. The sound of my mother, screaming, as they dragged my father out of the house and locked him in chains.

"Kneel," the one who seemed to be in command ordered me. With rough hands suddenly upon my shoulders, pushing me down, I had no choice but to fall to my knees.

The ring of soldiers parted, admitting a woman into the circle. She loomed above me, expression haughty. She wore a pale blue dress that glittered when she moved, and behind her trailed a cloak of soft gray feathers. Sweeping out from behind her ears, feathers adorned her hair as well, accompanied by sprigs of branches that resembled bones. Silver earrings like teardrops dangled beside her face. She looked as if tendrils of frost should follow her footsteps and ice crystals should bloom on everything she touched.

"Let me look at you." Her voice was as cold as the harshest winter. With two fingers, she pinched my chin and tilted my head back. She examined me, turning my face from side to side. Judging by her smirk, she found me lacking in some way.

"So . . . you're the Mortal who my son smuggled into the realm. The one who made him overexert himself. Bring her to the receiving hall. I'll figure out what to do with her there." With that, she turned and strolled out of the courtyard, her retinue of guards leaving with her.

The two guards who remained hauled me through the corridors, until we arrived at the Hall of Heartfelt Dreams. All of the doors and windows had been thrown open, the late afternoon sun streaming through. There was a chair moved to the center of the room, upon which the woman had settled. She watched as the guards ripped the books from my arms and dropped me to the floor unceremoniously before her.

"Even with the Meng family being brought so low by recent events, I did not think there would be others who would take advantage of my son's vulnerability." She looked at me as one would regard a smudge of dirt that had marred her bejeweled slippers. "It is a clever scheme though, to send a Mortal. Knowing that, as the one who handles their dreams and their innermost desires, he would be sympathetic to their cause. I suspect you concocted some sort of pathetic story, a tale of woe that appealed to his kindness, so that he would bring you to the estate."

"I've done nothing of the sort," I muttered, unable to stay silent, even though I knew it was smarter for me to stay quiet.

"You will speak only when spoken to, Mortal!" The butt of a spear struck my back, and I fell forward onto my hands and knees. "You will give Lady Hè the respect she is accorded."

"No, let her defend herself." The lady waved a hand in the air and smirked. "I'd like to hear her stories. She seems like she would tell a good one." The guard bowed and backed away.

I slowly straightened again, smoothing down my skirt in an attempt to recover my dignity. My hands trembled only a little.

"Your son was the one who brought me to the estate," I said. "When he wakes, you will be able to ask him."

"He will tell me what he believes when the time comes," she said. "With his softness, he will make excuses for your presence. I will do what needs to be done. He'll thank me later."

I'd met people like Lady Hè before. Noblewomen who swept into the House of Flowing Water, tempests of noise and fervor, demanding that everyone pay attention to their suffering from some perceived slight. Their wastrel sons spent all of the household funds on wine and song and amusement, but they would never be at fault. No, it was the temptresses, the ones who dragged these sons in, corrupted their gentle spirits and forced them to spend the money on the various delights of the entertainment district.

When I looked upon her face, all I could see was ugliness. It disappointed me a little, to see the same sorts of characters in the Celestial Realm, that this place was not above the petty feuds of us Mortal beings.

"Now, tell me," she commanded, voice dripping with disdain. "What sort of story did you use to convince him to bring you here? That you needed protection? That the world was unfair and cruel to you?"

With each word she uttered, each insinuation, my disgust grew. These people were supposed to be what we aspired to? The ones who had transcended beyond the immaterial, the ones who were pure of heart, worthy of immortality? What a joke.

My derision must have shown on my face, because she rose from her chair, furious. It always made arrogant people angry when they could not provoke the reaction they wanted. She wished for me to grovel, to beg for her forgiveness. Well, I would not give her the satisfaction of seeing my fear.

She scowled. "You dare *laugh*?" She raised her hand as if she was going to strike me.

"Everything my lady said is true," I admitted quickly. The hand lowered, but I wasn't done yet. "My contract belonged to the House of Flowing Water in Wudan, and your son purchased it. He now owns my contract. I am his, so in a sense, we are family." With my hands folded, I touched my forehead to the backs of my palms, and bowed at her feet, the greeting to an honored elder. A grandparent. "It seems, Lady Hè, that I should be referring to you as Aunt instead?"

There was a muffled gasp from one of the guards, a murmuring that rippled through them. With my head still lowered, I knew that I had struck a nerve. The victory was short lived, because her nails dug into my shoulders and she yanked me to standing. She leaned her face close to mine, so that I could see the fury in her dark eyes, her composure lost.

"How dare you insult me?!" she screamed. "I am a High Priestess of the Ordinance!"

She struck me across the mouth, hard enough that my head snapped to the side, blood blooming on my tongue. "I could have you whipped for your insolence!"

"Mother!" A high voice called out behind me. "What are you doing?"

I turned to see Lingwei. Instead of armor today, she was dressed in red robes, her hair tied back with a red ribbon.

Lady Hè's shoulders still shook with anger. "I'm disciplining the servants. I should have stepped in when your father was taken away and come back to clean up this place before your brother further destroys the reputation of this family."

"Jinglang has his own reasons for bringing her here," Lingwei said, even though barely a few days ago she herself had questioned his reasons. But with the way she pulled me away from her mother, the divide within this family was clear.

"He acted recklessly, foolishly," Lady Hè spat. "He already defied the tenets by traversing the borders between realms, in direct violation of the orders from the Sky Consort herself. As the acolyte of the Star of Balance, *you* should be the one reprimanding him!"

"Don't tell me how to do my job." Lingwei's lips tightened into a thin line. "You have your duties, and I have mine. I know very well where my loyalty lies."

"Daughter . . ." Lady Hè's tone softened then, as she stepped forward. "I know you are angry with me, but I had to report it. He had lost all sense, and I did it to protect your brother. To protect *you*."

"Let me clean up this mess before anyone discovers it," she continued briskly, her attention upon me again. She narrowed her eyes as she pointed her finger at me, and I knew she would love nothing more than to strike me again. "I'll send this one for a month's penance in the Caves. That should be enough to show the sovereign and the consort our contriteness for letting this intruder slip into our midst without the proper clearance. If we are lucky, the Meng Family will not receive another mark to our standing."

"You renounced this family, remember?" a cool voice said from the doorway.

All heads turned to see the duke. He stood on his own two feet, Attendant Luo beside him. But with the slow way he walked toward us, it was clear that each step pained him.

"This is not your temple, and we are not your followers," he said. "You have no say in what goes on in these walls. Not anymore."

"Jinglang, you're still ill." Lady Hè was gentle, the perfect illusion of a caring mother. "Let us speak of this when you are of clearer mind."

"My mind has never been clearer," the duke said, his contempt evident. "When you reported Father and sent the Ziwei Guard after him, when you damned him to the tower, that was enough. Go back to your temple. We have no need of you."

Two spots of red appeared on her cheeks, her mask quickly slipping as her voice rose again. "I am still your mother! I am the one who birthed and raised you. I will not be spoken to in this manner!"

"Then I'm afraid I will continue to be a disappointment," he said softly. "Guards, please escort my mother and her unwelcome companions out."

"I'm not done!" Lady Hè's tone sharpened. "You will listen to me, Jinglang. Your harboring of a Mortal girl has already been reported to the consort. In two weeks' time, we will celebrate the Spring Festival at her palace. She has summoned all of you there—including the girl."

With a flick of her wrist, a scroll appeared in her hand. She extended her arm, offering it to the duke, who refused it. Lingwei took it instead.

"I hope whatever . . . talent she possesses, that it was worth it to bring her here," she said with a sneer. "Or else she will be thrown from the Cliffs of Sundering. There will not be much of your pet to save after that."

"Get. Out," the duke said through gritted teeth.

With a swish of her cloak, Lady Hè was off, her silver guards flanking her. Attendant Luo retreated as well with the duke's personal guards, until it was only the three of us left in the hall.

Lingwei frowned, placing a hand on her brother's arm. "She will punish you for that."

He sighed, shoulders drooping. "I know." Then he turned to me. "I'm sorry you had to witness that . . . unpleasantness."

"Family can be complicated," I replied quietly. After a pause, I asked, because I had to know, "What are the Cliffs of Sundering?"

Duke Meng and Lingwei wore mirrored expressions of distaste. "It used to be a route to travel between realms. With the restrictions at the borders, it has been sealed," Lingwei explained. "It's now a method of punishment. It strips the essence of a Celestial away, until they are returned to what they used to be." Was this similar to the Platform of Forgetting that Zhuxi had mentioned earlier? But I didn't dare to mention it, remembering Yingzi's warning that I should keep any visits to the library to myself.

I asked the question I never thought to ask before: "And if a Mortal were to pass through it?"

After a pause, the duke answered. "It would tear you apart until nothing is left. You would cease to exist."

So that was what their mother wished upon me. A horrible, torturous death.

"Understood," I murmured.

CHAPTER TWENTY-SIX

THE THREAT WEIGHED UPON ME. WHAT REMAINED of my bravery drained out, leaving me feeling small and chilled. I rubbed my arms, shivering. Reminding myself that I was still made of flesh and bone and blood.

"We'll make sure it doesn't happen to you," Lingwei said, noticing my discomfort. "We have two weeks to prepare. We'll do all we can to help you."

Then she turned on the duke, chastising him. "Do you understand now that you need our help? Chenwen and I are willing to assist you in whatever foolish endeavor you are pursuing, brother. Don't shut us out. Not when someone's life is at stake, and we have a chance to save her this time!"

Emotions flitted across his face. Anger or irritation, I could not tell.

"You're right, admittedly," he finally said, resigned. "I cannot do this alone."

"I will return tomorrow." Lingwei reached out and grasped my hand, gripping it tight. I could see some of the duke in her features. "We will keep you safe, Xue. I promise you that."

I managed to squeak out a thanks as she let go. When she walked past her brother, she thumped him in the back. "Tell her what she is up against. Tell her *everything*." With a burst of light, she was gone. I caught a flash of white wings in the distance. The duke stared at the empty doorway for a moment longer, pensive.

"Let me walk you back to your residence," he said, turning back to me. Then, hesitantly, he added, "If you are not still angry with me?"

I didn't know why he would care about my feelings. I'd spent much of my life being shuffled from one place to another, living at the whims of others. My feelings had never been taken into consideration.

I turned to pick up my books from the table where one of the guards had placed them, giving me a moment to consider what I was going to say.

I decided to tell him the truth.

"No, I'm not angry any longer. It's taken some time to . . . adjust to my new reality. I know so little, and there is much more to learn."

We walked down the corridor, the walls of the manor looming above us. The stars winked overhead, distant and cold. The snow fell again around us, soft and silent. It reminded me that I was very far away from everything familiar to me.

I felt like I was locked in a labyrinth from which there was no escape. I would be trapped here forever in these winding halls.

"I thought I was keeping you safe," he said. "Now I realize that was the wrong assumption."

"Well, I would also like to live a little longer, if that's possible," I joked half-heartedly. He rewarded me with a small smile in return.

A brisk wind swept down the corridor, blowing my hair into my eyes. I shivered, teeth chattering slightly, and clutched the books tighter to my body, as if the thin volumes could protect me from the chill. I wished I had my cloak—I had not expected to still be outside after dark.

"Here." He stopped in the shadow of an evergreen, and placed his own cloak around my shoulders. It settled around me, still warm from the heat of his body. It provided a small bit of comfort, for the moment.

"Thank you," I mumbled, touched by the gesture. He was still watching me, eyes glimmering in the dark, like there was something else on his mind, but then he turned and we resumed the walk to my residence. The snow continued, heavier now, blowing directly in our direction, and it made my hair damp, my face wet as if soaked in tears.

We stopped below the awning of my residence's gate, momentarily sheltered from the snow. The lantern hung high above us, encircling us in a small pool of light. I pulled off the cloak, ready to return it to him, but he cleared his throat before speaking.

"You told me you believe I purchased your contract to save you from your circumstances, but I wanted to tell you that wasn't the case." His words caught in his throat, as if it pained him to speak. "It's not you who needs me, Lady Guxue. *I'm* the one who is in desperate need of *your* help.

"I believe if I am able to figure out the culprit behind my shīfù's death, then I will be able to find the evidence needed to exonerate my father as well," he continued, his expression anguished. "He will be executed soon if I fail to find the answer."

I would have given anything to be able to prevent my parents' execution, but I had been too young and too helpless. "If only I am able to do more," I whispered.

His gaze slid down to my cheek then, and guilt flared in his eyes. Guilt, regret . . . a history still unknown to me. "She hit you."

I was suddenly very much aware we were standing on these small steps, altogether too close. I should step away; I should slip through the gate and leave him there, and yet . . .

He reached out and his fingertips touched my skin. Slowly, ever so gently, as if he was handling a precious thing, he cupped my face in his hand.

I froze under his touch, that too-intimate sensation. He closed his eyes, and warmth spread across my face. His magic seeped into me, a feeling I recognized, as it took away the pain. I was glad then he could not see my expression.

For a moment, I'd thought he was going to kiss me.

And for a moment, I'd wanted him to.

When he opened his eyes again, he swayed a little on his feet.

"My lord?" I caught his arm, alarmed. Worried he was going to fall again, like when we were in the pavilion.

"No, no, I'm fine." He reached out and caught himself on the wall. "I'm just weak. Weak and useless."

"It seems to me you are caught in difficult circumstances," I said, not wanting to offer judgment, when he seemed so eager to provide it for himself.

"I . . ." He turned back to me, and we were suddenly too close again. I was near enough to see his lashes skimming his cheeks, and I knew that he was aware as well, his words swallowed before he spoke. He fumbled for his cloak, and I gave it to him. He stepped back, leaving the appropriate distance between us.

"There is only one more thing I wanted to say," Duke Meng said, after regaining his composure. "I will make you a promise. If you help me with removing the memory jewels from the qín, then I will release you from your contract. Regardless of whether we solve the mystery or not. You can return to the Mortal Realm and the life you were intended to live. My shīfù's name still has some influence in the Kingdom of Qi—I will ensure our bargain is kept."

It was, once again, not what I expected. The freedom that I desperately wanted was within reach. If I proved myself in the academy, then I could finally remove that red mark upon my name. I could once again be a commoner, a traveling musician, free to go where I wanted, free to keep the money that I made, free to love and choose who I wanted to marry. I would finally be able to live my life, like my uncle had wanted me to. It seemed the best way to honor his memory.

But to merely accept his offer did not seem like it was enough. I only had the sincerity of my words, the commitment to my oath.

"I, Guxue, once a member of the House of Flowing Water, swear upon the memory of my ancestors that I will assist you in completing this task," I told him. "If you will keep your promise in turn."

There was a prickling upon my arms, a different sort of sensation than his magic, the feeling that someone was watching. Someone greater than us both, paying attention to this moment in time.

"And I, Meng Jinglang, the Keeper of the Dreaming, make this vow to you." The duke's voice deepened as he touched his hand to his heart, sealing the bond between us. "You will safely return home once the last jewel is extracted. This is my promise."

DANROU AND I still existed at an impasse. She treated me coolly but politely, and I no longer protested what she perceived as her required duties. She must have seen me return to the residence with the duke, but she did not share her criticisms this time.

Pulling out my hairpins, she ran the comb through my hair, easing the tension in my scalp.

"Could you tell me why the duke is ill?" I had secured an understanding with the duke. Now if I could get to know my patron better, maybe I could help him in other ways. I didn't like to owe a debt, even if it was only one that I imagined.

"A Mortal would not understand," Danrou said dismissively, but when I pressed further, she told me, "Celestial powers are tied to their inner core. This is developed through the practice and cultivation of magic. One of the punishments to the Meng family was the stripping away of that power. The sovereign only allowed the duke to keep enough of his essence to fulfill his duties as the Keeper of the Dreaming, and no more. Any additional use of magic would come at a cost. It would cause him pain, or, if he exerted himself too much, harm his very being."

I nodded, appreciative that she told me even this.

She sniffed. "He should rest and not waste his energy on a Mortal girl. *That* is my opinion."

So much for our truce, but at least she'd given me an answer.

The following morning, Lingwei appeared at my residence while I was still eating. She brought an entourage with her, their cheerful chatter filling my residence. My chambers suddenly became a lively place. Someone carried over a full-length mirror and I was made to stand before it with my arms outstretched, while measurements were taken of my proportions.

During all of this, Lingwei sprawled out on a reclining bench, eating sliced pears with her fingers. She looked the very picture of indulgence in her cream-white robe, embroidered at the edge with small gold leaves. She wore a matching sash across her chest, and gauzy fabric draped over the wide skirt, which was a lovely shade of pink.

"Is all of this truly necessary?" I asked when my arms grew tired of being held up, and my body continued to be poked and prodded.

The head seamstress at my former House—a woman in her thirties who we called Fourth Aunt—was able to squint at us with one eye and a length of string. She kept all the measurements in her head, without writing anything down. It seemed like even in the Celestial Realm, they required ten people to do the job of one—they buzzed around me like a hive of bees.

"I don't know." Lingwei shrugged. "This is Chenwen's doing. He said that if we were going to enter the consort's palace, we needed to do it in style."

"Chen—I mean, Prince Zhou. He's coming too?" My face twitched as I tried to refrain from frowning. Our first impressions of each other was quite poor, and I did not think he would be interested in helping me. Unless coerced to do so by Lingwei.

She giggled at my expression, not offended. "He's sharp-tongued, but he has a tender heart. He's very invested in your upcoming *debut*."

Finally, the seamstresses completed their task. They bowed to Lingwei and exited the room.

"I'm sure he will enjoy the spectacle of my body being thrown off the cliffs," I muttered to myself, pulling my sleeves back.

"The practice is barbaric." Lingwei grimaced. "It's one thing to undo the making of a Celestial. It's another to render a living thing soulless."

Danrou appeared in my chamber, placing a letter upon my dressing table. I saw my name written upon the folded paper with a confident hand. "Beg pardon, my lady. A letter came for you, and a stack of books that I have left on the shelf in the receiving room."

Lingwei leaned forward, obviously curious, then sat back, interest lost when she recognized the writing. "It's just from my brother. He must have overexerted himself again. He's fond of writing messages even when the physician tells him to rest. He's always thinking too much." Her attention returned to the platter of fruit.

I sat down on a stool, unfolded the paper, and began to read.

Lady Guxue,
I hope you will not take offense, but I noticed the books that you were carrying yesterday when my mother so rudely accosted you. If you are interested in Celestial history, I have included some volumes from my

personal library, should you be so inclined to read them. I've selected scholars whose writings are matter-of-fact, but known for their concise summaries.

I extend my apologies for not being able to assist with the preparations for your introduction to the court, as I have been told I must remain in my residence for the next few days or suffer further injury. I assure you my sister and Chenwen have a keen understanding of the workings of the realm and you are in excellent hands.

As to our agreement, I believe another song will provide the answer that we seek. The challenge will be to determine which song is the appropriate selection. As your musical repertoire is far greater than mine, I await your suggestion as to what we should attempt next. But once again, I will ask for your discernment and discretion in that matter and that you do not speak of it to anyone, even to Lingwei or Chenwen.

If you have any other requests, you only need to pass a message through Attendant Luo, and I will endeavor to be of assistance.

Respectfully Yours,
Jinglang

CHAPTER TWENTY-SEVEN

WHEN I FINISHED READING, THE PAPER FOLDED upon itself into the shape of a boat, then disappeared. Winked out of existence by magic, leaving only a few sparkles upon my lap. It seemed the duke was not opposed to me borrowing books from Zhuxi's library then, so I took it as permission that I could return to the Archive of Dreams again.

While Lingwei was there, I decided I should consult her on the matter of this upcoming visit to the consort's palace. I didn't even know how to begin, to behave as expected. This morning I had attempted to read one of the books that Zhuxi had provided me, a slim volume that I thought I could quickly flip through, titled *Handbook of the Celestial Realm*. The chapter titles though, I found, were quite the mouthful. They included gems like *The Treaty of the Clans: On the Selection of Tributes from the Spirit Realm* and *The Mortal Potential and the Trial of Ascension*. The titles, ranks, and roles were already confusing enough.

I turned back to Lingwei. "Tell me . . . who must I impress to escape being unmade? Is it the consort who would decide whether someone could remain in the realm?"

I picked up half of a liánwù with my fingers and took a bite of the crisp, bell-shaped fruit, waiting for her answer. It filled my mouth with sweetness. Out of all of the food available at the manor, it was the fruit that was particularly delicious. All of it perfectly ripe, juicy or crunchy or soft, whatever it needed to be. That was one thing I would miss when I eventually returned to the Mortal Realm.

"The entirety of the Six Realms is overseen by the Sky Sovereign and the Sky Consort," Lingwei explained between bites of more fruit. "Most of the minor gods maintain the realms, performing their usual duties. Then there is the Celestial Court, which oversees the fortunes of Mortals and Spirits. Judgments are determined by tribunal, a smaller representation of three of the stars, but the sovereign and the consort may weigh in on the decision."

"I've been deemed a trespasser," I said flatly. "And for this, I will be punished." Even if I was deceived. It did not seem like it mattered.

"Our best chance is to present you as a Mortal Tribute," Lingwei said with a thoughtful look, chewing on a strand of her hair. "Every so often, a Mortal is deemed worthy of presentation to the court for an evaluation of their talents. A temporary residency may be granted."

"And that's different from a Spirit Tribute?" I asked, having seen the same term in the book, but not understanding exactly what it meant.

She nodded. "Very good! Every year, the Spirit Realm sends ten tributes with potential to the Celestial Realm. They care for the estates, and those who wish to remain will become apprentices under a star. If they demonstrate enough potential, they will ascend through the ranks."

"You were once a Spirit, but now you are a Celestial?" I said, trying to understand.

"Jinglang and I . . . we're a little different," Lingwei said. "Some of us were born in the Celestial Realm to Celestial parents. But there are not many Celestial children now. This is why we require the tributes from the Spirit Realm."

"Why?"

The question seemed to make her uncomfortable. "There's been a lot of speculation as to why. Some believe it's because of the Corruption; others believe it is Demon influence. There are also those who believe it's because the Sky Sovereign's power is waning, and it is time for a new age."

Demon. I wondered, did the existence of Celestials necessitate the existence of Demons? Like the philosophers said, there was always light and dark, good and evil, life and death.

"It's why those of us who are of a marriageable age are expected to wed. It's why Chenwen is my betrothed." The way she said it was like pointing out that the sky was blue. As if it was a matter of course to be told who you should marry, who you should commit yourself to and have children with. It was confusing to me, for even in an entertainers' house, we spoke of love. We witnessed genuine connections between patrons and adepts, guests and apprentices. We'd seen many true-love matches that received Auntie's blessing. In the Kingdom of Qi, other than the royals and nobles of high rank, marriage was possible between anyone who was of age and willing to enter into such a partnership. It signified the joining of two together, the formation of a new household. Children was one of the happy possibilities, but not the goal. The only barrier to such a union for the commoners was a societal rank, like mine. The security and protections of marriage are inaccessible to the Undesirables.

"You . . . love him, then?" I inquired, even though it was a personal sort of question. Somehow I did not think Lingwei would mind.

"Do I love Chenwen?" She seemed puzzled by the question. "It does not matter whether I love Chenwen or not. It is a betrothal that was predetermined by the Star of Ordinance to be a good match."

But . . . You have to share a household, raise children together," I said. "Does it not matter whether you enjoy each other's company? That you use your own judgment to determine if it will be an amicable match?"

Lingwei laughed, but it was a bitter sound. "Look at my mother and father! Their union resulted in two Celestial children, so they have done their duty. Now Mother returns to her temple, where she can continue to be fawned over as High Priestess, and Father, well . . . he found fulfillment in maintaining the Dreaming, the role he was given."

But was he happy? Content? Maybe I was the foolish one, to believe in love and happiness. When I left safety and security behind to chase my freedom.

"We cannot hope to educate her on all the intricacies of the Celestial Realm in an hour." Prince Zhou walked through the doorway with his usual loose stride. "We would bore her to death." He still spoke in that infuriating, mocking manner.

"Chenwen!" Lingwei turned to greet him with a smile. "I was just telling her of our betrothal. I don't think she approves."

"Oh?" He raised an eyebrow. "Does she not believe we are a suitable match?"

"Marrying for duty and children are for those of noble lineage," I said, and I couldn't help but be a little snide. "Not for us lowly Mortals. We dare to aspire to love matches. A companion to make the rest of our short, dreary lives more bearable."

"Love!" He scoffed. "You are correct. Love is something only afforded those with brief life spans. We care for millions of Mortal lives and their resultant fortunes. We cannot be influenced by such base emotions. The entirety of the realms would collapse."

"Some would say love is a strength," I replied, not willing to yield.

"Then you haven't read this yet." He tossed a songbook upon the table, one that he must have seen on the shelf in the receiving room where I had placed it last night. *Twilight's Begonia*. The songbook Yingzi recommended I try to find, some part of Celestial history that she thought I should know.

"You should play it, and then you will understand how Celestials cannot afford this type of weakness." He smirked. "Lingwei, come help me select the fabric for this Mortal girl's outfit, so we can at least give her somewhat of a fighting chance."

ANNOYED, I TOOK the songbook and my qín out to the wild garden again, though it did not appear quite as wild as before. I was beginning to see this place as *my* garden, even if that may not have been the most prudent, considering that I knew eventually, I must leave it.

Time passed so strangely there. How it seemed to be going by so quickly, and yet every day was the same. I felt I should delight that I had fine clothes to wear, delicious food to eat, a lovely residence in which I could rest my head, and yet I was still discontented. Because I knew how easily it could all be taken away, to have everything and everyone you know be gone entirely. I was still too young and unsettled.

To chase those thoughts away, I read through *Twilight's Begonia*. Tentatively, I followed the instructions, line by line, slowly plucking out the melody, then its counterpoint. It was a slow, haunting song, with moments of quiet contemplation, but also discordant sounds full of heartbreak and devastation. It was beautiful, tortured, and challenging to learn. I knew I needed to spend quite a lot of time on it before I could play it as it should be played, and I savored the challenge.

This time, I sensed her before I saw her, noticing movement through the shrubbery. Yingzi gave me a tentative smile as she approached.

"You found the song," she said, pleased.

"It's as brilliant as you said! I appreciate you recommending it." Then I noted her usual ragged appearance, with her rolled-up sleeves and muddied hems. "Working again today? Can you take a break and talk with me for a little bit?"

She gave a happy nod. "Of course!"

I stood up and stretched, rolling out my shoulders and the tightness in my neck from sitting hunched for too long.

"Will you show me what you're working on?" I asked. "Are you still working in this garden, or did your boss send you elsewhere?"

"I go where I'm needed," Yingzi said, gesturing for me to follow. The path was tidier now, weeds pulled and the overgrown grass cut back. "I spend time here because it's quiet."

The earth was disturbed here and there, holes dug waiting for more plants to fill them in. Many of the hedges had been trimmed back, the garden slowly regaining its former glory.

"I was away for some time," she said softly, surveying her surroundings. "It's sad to see that it wasn't maintained while I was gone, but I'm happy they're fixing it again."

Maybe she had been ill. That could explain why she always seemed so pale and skittish.

She looked at me shyly. "Because of *you*."

"I wouldn't say that," I quickly corrected her, shaking my head. "But since they're seeing it being used again, it reminded them that this place shouldn't be neglected any longer. It must have been quite the sight to behold before."

"Oh yes!" she exclaimed, throwing her arms wide. "In this corner, the ground slopes downward, so because of the better drainage, I was able to plant these yangmei trees. And over here, these climbing vines love the heat of the rocks. They have really gorgeous orange flowers, except for the year we had snails—"

I was happy to listen to her chatter about the plants she loved. It gave me a brief reprieve from the upcoming event, from my worries about my presentation, how I should behave before the others of the Celestial

Court. I still needed to figure out how to unlock the next memory jewel in the meanwhile. Duke Meng seemed so confident that the answer to exonerate his father was contained in these jewels.

There was so much to learn and so much to do in so little time.

I feared we may be running out of it.

INTERLUDE

暮色, 海棠香 (*Twilight's Begonia*)

Shunying, the Flower Queen, beloved to all under her care

Sweet-scented begonias crowned her hair, white lilies bloomed wherever she stepped

At twilight she tended to the most fragile of those among her clan

He appeared then, in the moonlit grove. Promises exchanged, words of love spoken

Until the daylight's cruel reveal: He wore the Crescent Mark upon his brow

His dominion over the Demons and ghosts ensured their love impossible

For long ago, the Jade Sovereign's harsh decree, the split authority of the realms ensured

Demons and Celestials were never to join, for a Great Calamity would result thereafter

Believing love should triumph over all, the Flower Queen petitioned the Sky Sovereign

She would relinquish the throne, and join the Court of Demons

But the Sky Sovereign feared the promised Calamity, and imprisoned her in the tower high

The Moon Sovereign raged and waged war against the heavens, to rescue his beloved

The world ripped asunder; Celestials, Spirits, and Demons slain

A thunderous wailing filled the realms

Blood ran down the steps of the Sovereign's golden palace

Mortals and ghosts wandered lost, with no one to shepherd them

The Flower Queen looked down upon the devastation and despaired

She declared the price of love too great, and flung herself over the tower's edge

The Moon Sovereign could not bear the loss

Grief overcame him and he Turned

Horns erupted from his head and back, upon his face grew ten pairs of all-seeing eyes

Six clawed hands and three pairs of silver wings, a monstrous abomination

He devoured ten thousand and ten thousand more

Until all joined to rein in the ravager beast, and cast him to the Barren Realm

Listen! His howls can be heard over the mountains, and his many children haunt the realms

Remember! Bloodred begonia blooms at twilight

The remnants of a love, a warning

Seven emotions corrupting forces forbidden to those who aspire to ascension

Duke Meng,

I appreciate the addition of the volumes from your personal library. While I know the selections were chosen for their brevity, I found most of them to be a bit dry. Your notations were amusing, however, and spared me the time spent on understanding the history of

the war between the Fox Family and Tree Clan. I also did not grasp why the Water Clan seemed keen to fight with everyone, but we have similar conflicts between kingdoms in the Mortal Realm as well. It seems many of our stories of the flighty and good-natured Spirits were wrong. I wish I could someday look upon the Spirit Tree. How fascinating it would be to catch a glimpse of all those fortunes!

Upon the prince's recommendation, I have begun to learn how to play "Twilight's Begonia," which was quite the tragic story. It made reference to several events that I do not understand and I hope you could provide some illumination:

Who is the Jade Sovereign, and what caused the split between the Celestials and the Demons?

Was the Moon Sovereign the original ravager? Does this mean that Demons can Turn as well?

Which seven emotions are the texts referring to? And why were they forbidden?

Finally, I have attempted to work on our shared puzzle, but have experienced no success so far. I had hoped the joining of "Mountains High" and "Swift Streams" would provide us another pleasant result, but it seems we will have to try other tunes.

I have another thought to share with you, but I am unsure if it is safe for me to share it here. Please advise.

With respect,
Xue

Lady Xue,

Those are excellent questions that have been the subject of debate by scholars across all of the realms without resolution. In brief:

Although Celestials live a long life, their powers eventually fade. Even the sovereign is not immune from this. The Jade Sovereign was our ruler prior to the assignment of the Sky Sovereign, and he was the one who oversaw the split of the Demon Realm from the Celestial Realm. The reasons for which will be outlined in the volume of the Histories of the Celestial Court *that I have provided.*

Demons and Celestials have the same origins, so they are susceptible to the same poisons. Although I have not seen a Demon ravager, I believe that they must be able to Turn as well. After the Moon Sovereign became a ravager, sightings of them increased a hundredfold across all the realms. His death caused a rift, from which we are still seeing devastating effects.

Since you mentioned you have read The Origin of the Six Realms, *you will understand the beginnings of this history. The treatise that I've included will explain how this resulted in the laws of the present time, but the seven emotions are:* **Joy, Anger, Sadness, Fear, Love, Hate, Desire.** *Currently, the Faction of Tranquility are in power in the court, and they believe in shedding the influence of emotion, for it is the root of Corruption. The Faction of Transcendence believes in the good in Mortal existence, and that the fullness of those experiences is what brings fulfillment to all living forms, especially for those who care for the fortunes of Mortals.*

For discreet communications, let me think on this. I will find a way to ensure we can speak in confidence while I remain in seclusion.

Respectfully yours,

Jinglang

INTERLUDE

ON THE FORMATION OF THE
DEMON REALM

At the height of the Jade Sovereign's rule, an opposition was formed from a section of the Celestial Court. They opposed the many restrictions imposed by the court on Celestial behavior. They presented a list of demands to have freedoms similar to the Mortals they cared for: the ability to travel between realms freely, to marry and have children with whom they chose, and to be able to remove the mantle of Celestial responsibility when they grew weary of the role.

Previous attempts at change in the court were swiftly eliminated, but this time the rebellion was helmed by the Star of Protection, the Jade Sovereign's second-in-command, whose frustration at the restrictions could not be overcome. With the support of half of the Celestial Court, their petition could no longer be ignored.

But the Jade Sovereign refused to change, fearing this was a sign of the Great Calamity. The gods too were split, unable to care for the realms as they should. The conflict resulted in one hundred days of lightning and thunder, under which the Mortal Realm trembled, fearing the end of days was upon them. The civil war was only stopped when the Heavenly Mother came out of seclusion from her Palace of Longevity and brokered an agreement. This was known as the Divide.

A mirror realm was created to oversee the Realm of Ghosts, and the Star of Protection assumed the title of Moon Sovereign, taking six stars of the court with him to the newly formed realm.

In the Celestial Court, they were acknowledged as the Fallen.

The Moon Sovereign embraced instead the name Mortals gave to the darkness and the unknowable, the ones who watched over them in the deepest part of the night:

Demon-born.

—From *Histories of the Celestial Court*

CHAPTER TWENTY-EIGHT

I SPENT MOST OF MY MORNINGS WITH LINGWEI, while she taught me the intricacies of behavior within the Celestial Court. How to walk, how to bow, how high my arms should be when speaking to those of different ranks, the appropriate terms of address. It was very similar to the etiquette lessons I'd had to undergo at the House of Flowing Water, and I learned them quickly.

Afternoons were spent practicing the qín, which most of the time I did in the wild garden. Sometimes Yingzi would be there, other times it was just me. The gardeners always left me alone if they found me there, and even if I tried to speak with them, they only gave one- or two-word answers before leaving. Lingwei had tasked me with choosing the songs for my performance at the Spring Festival, stating she knew nothing of music. The duke also had no suggestions of his own, and said that he would leave it for me to select pieces I would be most comfortable with. I had narrowed my selection down to a handful, but had yet to make my final decision even as the date approached.

In the evenings I read the volumes that I obtained from Zhuxi and Duke Meng. It was here I fully appreciated Uncle's careful education. He'd taught me how to read quickly and how to retain and recall the information rapidly. I asked Danrou for ink, brush, and paper on which I could take notes, and she provided them for me in my receiving room. I had begun to fill the room with items of my own, including a space on the wall for my qín, and had requested that the incense in the braziers be replaced with something less sweet.

While my days were busy, I was often unsettled at night. As I lay in bed, the worries surfaced, and I found it difficult to sleep. Sometimes, I would hear the sound of a xiao in the distance. Another lone musician, seeking comfort in the middle of the night. The sad, soulful melodies of that bamboo flute would often coax me to sleep.

But sleep too brought another sort of burden. I continued to be haunted by strange dreams. Most of the time I wandered through the corridors of the manor, chased by a thick mist from which ghostly hands emerged that tugged on my hair and pulled at my clothes. Sometimes my uncle appeared, reaching out for my help, but the earth cracked between our feet and he fell into the rift. I would wake choking on tears, pale light of the morning peeked through the shutters.

One of those nights, I fell asleep exhausted, and found myself in the sculpture garden. I walked between the bird statues, admiring and yet repulsed by their almost lifelike poses. I kept catching movement out of the corner of my eye, and yet when I spun around, the garden remained still.

Before me there was a statue of a swan. It reminded me of Lingwei when she . . . transformed, and I was suddenly consumed by a need to touch the stone. To ensure that it was truly cold and lifeless under my fingers, or to see if it was made of something else entirely.

My fingers touched something warm and feathered. With a gasp I stared into dark eyes, blinking and alert. Its wings unfolded from its body and covered the entirety of the sky. I found I could not move, could not open my mouth to call for help even as I screamed inwardly. I stood there, as it raised its head over mine and threatened to peck out my eyes.

"Be careful!" Someone pulled me away from that menacing form, and I fell against them. The shadow of the swan swept overhead.

I looked up to see . . . the duke. Dressed in a plain black robe, hair in a simple topknot. Looking like he once did while we were on the road. It brought on a sudden feeling of familiarity. He had saved me yet again, in the waking world and in my dreams.

"Are you real?" I wondered aloud, realizing I had missed speaking to him these past few days. I had missed the sound of his voice. I straightened and pulled away from him at this embarrassing realization.

"Sort of," he said, amused. With a wave of his hand, we were no longer in the sculpture garden. We were in a small courtyard. Between us, a stone table and stools appeared. "I didn't expect to find you here."

"What do you mean?" I asked, confused. "You appeared in *my* dream."

"I'm the Duke of Dreams." He poured me a cup of tea and nudged it in my direction with a finger. "Sometimes a dream is so strong, it pulls me in."

"I did not mean to!" I protested, mortified that he might believe I conjured him so desperately.

He frowned, considering this in his usual serious manner. "It may be due to our close proximity that your dream was particularly strong. But you helped us solve a problem: You requested a way through which we could communicate, and no one can overhear us in the Dreaming."

"Does this mean . . ." My face warmed at the mention of our *close proximity*. "Do you peer into everyone's dreams?" I frantically thought back to the previous dreams I'd had since entering the manor, if there were any improper thoughts or desires that were revealed through those dreams.

Now it was his turn to appear mortified. "I only intrude when someone is lost in the Dreaming or when the dream may tangle a section of the Mortal Tapestry."

"It feels so *real*." I did not want to dwell for too long on the thought of him traipsing through my dreams, and lifted up the teacup instead, marveling at the weight of it.

"Lingwei and Chenwen demonstrated their own Celestial affinities, and, well . . . this is mine," he said. In the blink of an eye, the table was sudden laden with all of my favorite dishes. Sweet potato covered in sticky strands of honey, crispy lotus root chips with green onions, and of course a dish of watermelon seeds ready for cracking. I couldn't help but smile at this shared memory.

We spoke then of my questions. I endeavored to understand Celestial history and behavior. I felt as if I had traveled to a foreign land in a way, and remembered what my uncle had always told me of his encounters with envoys from differing nations.

Here, in that strange space of the Dreaming, where it could look like anything he imagined it to be, it was as if we had returned to the peculiar intimacy that we shared around the campfire.

DURING THE DAY, we still communicated with letters that were often accompanied by books and scrolls, delivered by the ever-patient Attendant Luo. I flipped through his recommended "livelier reportings" on the history of the Celestial Realm in the time of the Jade Sovereign, by a Spirit scribe whose commentary was often delightfully sharp. There was an official document cautioning Celestials not to fall under the "Mortal affliction" of the seven emotions, as well as a wall scroll that had a painting of the Garden of the Spirit Tree, because I had expressed curiosity about that place.

Through my reading and our late-night conversations, I grew to understand Prince Zhou's perspective and Danrou's remarks. To them, to become a Celestial was to aspire to transcend the corrupting forces of the seven emotions. Through the devotion to their duties, the cultivation of their life force, immortality was to be their reward. It seemed a terrible way to live a life eternal, even as they called it a "worthy sacrifice." But with the reverence with which Yingzi spoke of the tribute process, it was clearly the highest honor to their clans, and something beyond my comprehension.

I was also curious to learn more about Elder Gao, the man who was beloved by my uncle, even though we never had a chance to meet. He did not have the same aversion of Mortals as the rest of them, but what brought them together? I clung on to Duke Meng's stories of the time he spent listening to them when they performed and debated in the teahouses. Those memories, though, brought about a shared sadness that neither of us were ready to face. Not while his father was still in danger.

It was in the Dreaming that my impression of the duke slowly changed. He was no longer the holder of my contract, the one who held my fate in his hands. He somehow became Jinglang, clever and insightful, still with that self-deprecating humor that I had grown to appreciate. Even though I would never dare call him by his name.

It was a secret I carefully carried inside of my heart. Only for me.

THREE DAYS PRIOR to the Spring Festival, my mornings were returned to me, for Lingwei was satisfied after a series of quizzes and demonstrations that I would be presentable enough. When I was in my receiving room gathering my songbooks, I saw Danrou in the courtyard, speaking to Prince Zhou beside the gate. His guards were also present, leaning against the wall. Her eyes, though, were entirely for him. She laughed at something he said, and even from this distance, I could tell there was a lightness to her expression that I had never seen before. A smile that she had never offered to me; she was usually so careful and guarded.

Danrou must have felt my eyes upon her. She gave a quick bow to the prince, who also noticed me as she hurried down the path toward my residence. He threw a salute in my direction, and I resisted the urge to roll my eyes. I managed a half-hearted wave instead, and he grinned at me, unperturbed by my rudeness.

"Lady Xue!" my maidservant said when she reached me, her voice high. There was pink in her cheeks, and her hair was slightly wind-blown. With the way she carried herself, she always seemed older than I was, but right now, she appeared like just a girl. "Was there something you needed from me?"

"No, I was just about to practice," I said. "What did the prince want?"

"We were making delivery arrangements for your festival outfit," Danrou said. Then, perhaps in an attempt at kindness, she added, "It's a splendid creation. You have no need to worry."

The thought of the celebration turned my stomach. "That's not what I'm worried about," I muttered. I already knew my appearance did not matter. I could walk in wearing an ensemble to rival the consort herself, but if my music failed me . . . well, it was off the cliffs I would fly.

"My lady has been practicing for days," Danrou said. "If I may offer my humble opinion?"

I regarded her warily. Her dislike of me was so obvious—why would she suddenly be so eager to help me?

Danrou cast her gaze down, suddenly shy. "I only ask for a favor in return."

That made more sense. A trade. "What do you want me to do?" I asked.

"I'm aware the prince already has his intended . . . but I have become a great admirer of him these past weeks," she said breathlessly. "If there is an opportunity for me to speak to him privately in your residence, I would ever be so grateful."

"Like you said, he already has his intended," I said flatly. The woman who I had begun to regard as my friend.

"I'm already aware of my lowly status in the realm," Danrou whispered. "I just want to give him a memento."

"I cannot force him to speak with you," I said, still guarded.

"You don't have to." Her face lit up, since I did not refuse. "You can ask him if he is willing to speak with me. That's all I wish. A chance."

If the prince was an honorable man, he would refuse this, but it offered an opportunity to satisfy my curiosity. Was he truly honor bound, committed to his Celestial duty? And besides, if he did turn out to be a scoundrel, I could always let Lingwei know. She would make the decision, ultimately.

"Fine," I agreed. "I will ask him, and if he is willing, then I will step aside for you to have your moment. *Only* if he is willing."

"Oh, thank you!" She gripped my arm in a rare show of genuine emotion. But only a beat later, she realized who she was speaking with and snatched her hand back. I watched, amused, as she bowed, in an attempt to regain her composure.

"I know my lady has been struggling with which piece to select for your performance. I am familiar with all of the songs that have previously passed through these halls, and a popular one was 'The Night-Blooming Flowers.'"

"I'll consider it," I said, then as to not be rude, I thanked her.

"Tomorrow the prince will return, and I'll ask you to honor your promise," Danrou said, and left quickly, as if afraid I would change my mind.

I decided then it was time to pay a visit to Zhuxi, who had been sup-plying me with songbooks. But I had promised Yingzi I would play a few songs for her. When I peered into the wild garden, she wasn't there, even after I called her name. I encountered one servant on my way back, who was busy sweeping the corridor.

"The girl who is usually in that garden—" I pointed at the open gate. The servant girl looked up at me with wide eyes, appearing almost frightened that I was speaking to her. "The one called Yingzi? If you see her, could you pass on the message that I will not be there today?"

She bobbed her head and said in a squeak, "My lady, I don't know anyone named Yingzi."

I frowned. "She's responsible for odd jobs around the garden, wher-ever she's sent."

"Apologies, my lady. It may be because I'm new at this post." She trembled a little, afraid of my reprimand.

"It's fine." I went on my way, not wanting to cause trouble for her. They all seemed afraid of the head gardener, who did appear stern from my brief encounters with her. I hid a smile, thinking about how Yingzi always jokingly referred to her as Big Head.

Whenever I passed over the threshold of the north wing, I quick-ened my steps, afraid Lady Hè would appear again, and that this time Lingwei would not arrive in time to save me. But I made it to the bam-boo door unscathed, and called out a greeting. Zhuxi was tidying the shelves in the back, and came out to listen to my request.

"A lovely choice, my lady," he said. "Let me go find it for you."

I added another two manuals to his list before he went on his way through the stacks. Like my previous visit, I couldn't help but look upon the shelves, to see if there were any books or scrolls that caught my interest. The song library within the estate was quite extensive—not surprising considering what Jinglang had said about his father's appreciation for the qín.

Again that memory contained in the jewel surfaced. The reason why I kept on playing and then discarding this list of songs. I still had not found the song that I was looking for. The more I remembered of the memory, though, the more it wore away at me. Their obvious affection for each other. How they must have known each other for a long time, and yet Uncle never introduced us, never trusted me with that piece of his heart. That hurt me more than I wanted to admit.

The melody sang in my mind, that song Elder Gao wanted my uncle to guess. Only a few notes, rising and then dipping downward. He wanted to tell me something with this memory, but what?

"You're humming 'Geese Flying Southerly,'" Zhuxi said behind me, books in hand. "A piece from the Kingdom of Wan."

I stared at him. That title. A classic. One I'd never played myself. That was why I did not recognize it, but I must have heard someone else play it long ago.

"Please." I grabbed his sleeve, not caring that I was being rude, and he was startled by my sudden eagerness. "Tell me you have the scroll."

"Yes, I believe I do."

The details slipped together in my mind. The geese embroidered on Elder Gao's robes. The memory's association, a tender moment. I finally recalled when I'd last heard it. When Uncle brought me to Wudan, to listen to my first performance at the academy, Teacher Kong had played it onstage. I'd admired the range of notes that could fly from such a small instrument.

You will be up there someday, Uncle had promised me. *Playing on a stage, for all to hear.*

My uncle was speaking to me through these memories, telling me to look closer, to pay attention. I did not doubt it now—he believed I would have the answers for these riddles.

When Zhuxi returned, I gave him a quick embrace, unable to contain my excitement, almost snatching the book from his hands. I ran all the way back to my residence, not caring if anyone noticed.

There was only one person I wanted to talk to.

CHAPTER TWENTY-NINE

I MUST HAVE BEEN SUCH A PECULIAR SIGHT, WALK-ing with the book in hand, pacing my room, mumbling to myself. I read through it once, then again, playing in the air as if I balanced an invisible qín on my lap. The notes rang through my head clearly, exactly as they appeared in the memory.

I grabbed my qín from its place on the wall and hurried through the corridors as if a ravager was biting on my heels. I did not want to play the song without him.

No one stopped me as I stepped through the gate of the Residence of Fateful Dreams and banged on the door with the great tree carved on it.

Attendant Luo opened it almost immediately, surprised to see me. "Lady Guxue!"

"I must speak to the duke!" I demanded.

"I was just about to come find you," he said with a bow. "My lord is no longer in isolation. He told me to invite you to dinner."

"Well, let her in!" I heard a voice call from inside the residence.

With another bow, Attendant Luo pulled the door open and let me through.

Jinglang was in his study, and as I entered, he placed his brush back down upon its stand.

"Is something the matter?" he asked, seeing my expression.

It was different seeing him in person, even though I'd had his voice in my mind for so long through his letters and in my dreams, but I did not let the sudden nervousness overwhelm me. Instead, I said quickly, "I found the song. I figured it out!"

"You did!" The excitement flashed across his face like lightning, matching my own thrill at the discovery. He closed the distance between us. "Are you able to play it?"

"I just need a moment to review the annotations again, if you are willing to flip the pages for me," I told him, my heart beating fast. This had to be it. I'd tried many songs, so many frustrated hours spent learning, reviewing, discarding. I thought I would break, if this was another disappointment.

"Come to the pavilion," the duke said.

I followed him through his study and the door beyond, into a personal courtyard that was simply a small stone pavilion within a grove of trees. I recognized it immediately as the courtyard we spent most of our time in while in the Dreaming. A familiar place, though I had never physically set foot here before. I set up my qín while Jinglang procured a table for the book. He sat beside me upon his own stool, then flipped to the first page and held it open.

I took a deep breath, and began.

"Geese Flying Southerly" was a slow tune about the passing of the seasons, about how the geese continued to fly home each year. But this time, their home was lost to them forever. The qín called out forlornly, like the calling of the geese to one another. Love and longing, the deep sensation that something was missing. That home was no longer a place they could return to. Only the memory of what it felt like remained. The mournful sound of the wind accompanied their restless flight, their internal compass no longer orienting true. They would be wanderers forever.

The marking began to glow, and the jewel rose from the surface as the rest of the song played out. The last notes of the qín faded, and Jinglang reached out to take the jewel.

"Well played," he said softly. "Are you ready to see the next memory hidden within?"

I was about to nod, but Attendant Luo stepped in. I had not noticed he was even there, so intent was I on the duke. "Wait, my lord, you must conserve your strength," he cautioned. "The Spring Festival approaches. Are you sure you want to risk another exertion of magic so soon?"

Jinglang considered this for a moment, but then set his jaw, determined. "We will do this now. There is no time to waste." He extended his hand toward me, a question in his gaze.

If he was willing to risk everything, even his own celestial being, then how could I not?

I stepped forward and placed my hand in his.

The memory unfurled around us, this time like a spread of ink across a white canvas. The room fell away, taking Attendant Luo with it. The only thing that remained was the duke, standing beside me, my hand holding his.

We stood in a forest of pine, sunlight streaming down around us through breaks in the treetops. The air smelled like fresh rain and earth. The serene vision was disrupted by shouts in the distance. Two figures raced through the trees, their footsteps urgently pounding the dirt path. One of them dropped to the ground, panting. The other spun around, facing their attackers.

"Stay back!" He extended a sword in hand, shining like a beacon before him—Celestial magic. The other figure was crouched, his back against a tree. His breathing was heavy, like he could go on no longer.

Slowly, the duke shifted us so that we faced the clearing and could see the full scene. I recognized then the man against the tree: My uncle.

A small figure also stood beside him, someone who he shielded with his arm. A child, slight of form, clinging to his side.

A girl with braids, crying.

That girl was me.

With a start, I looked closer at the details of this forest, at the man who stood protectively before them. Elder Gao. But I had no memory of this forest, no memory of being chased. I could not remember ever meeting *him*.

A low growl reverberated in the air, and then through the trees, a shadow crept closer and closer, until its true form emerged into the clearing. Another ravager. It had a boar's head, with an elongated snout, and the curved tusks from its mouth were the length of my arm. But its body was lithely muscled, with the characteristic orange and black stripes of a tiger. Its front legs had cloven hooves, yet its back legs ended in giant paws. A barbed tail lashed violently behind it. A senseless mishmash of various animals, some recognizable, and others unknown to me.

It stalked toward the three figures, its sheer size making them appear so small. It did not seem to care about the weapon pointed at its face, not when one of its teeth could rival it in size. I wanted to shout, scream, as if it could prevent that beast from attacking them, and I had to bite my lip hard to keep still.

I knew I lived through this. I stood there now, revisiting this memory of the past, but I did not want to witness whatever terrible thing that was about to happen. Jinglang gripped my hand tight, bringing me back. I looked at him and he gave me a nod, reminding me of our purpose.

We were here to remember.

Pay attention, I told myself. *There is something significant in this moment.*

The tiger-boar stamped its right hoof in the dirt. Once, twice, powerful enough that the ground trembled. It lowered its head and growled, then charged, scattering clumps of earth behind it. With a yell, Elder Gao raised his weapon to the sky, then brought it down upon the tiger-boar's head. The ravager veered at the last moment, the blade caught in the curve of one of its deadly tusks, and sent it spinning into the air. It struck the man with the side of its head, and his body flew through the trees. He hit one with a thud, then landed on the ground and was still.

I was the one who squeezed Jinglang's hand then, to prevent him from rushing forward.

The ravager threw its head back and let out a bellow before turning again, this time pointing its tusks at the other man and the girl. My uncle pushed her behind the tree, trying to protect her the best he could, while he stood up on shaky legs. He leaned heavily toward one side. His left leg was bloodstained, barely able to hold his weight, and yet he protected her. Protected *me*.

The ravager swept him aside easily. The girl rushed forward with a scream, trying to help him, and the tiger-boar turned its head. She was caught upon the deadly tip of its tusk, and was flung into the air. Her body arced, and the beast opened its terrible mouth, ready to tear her apart.

There was a yell as Elder Gao returned to the fight. A branch flew, striking the beast in the back of the head. The ravager turned and roared, preparing to charge again, but the blade came down in the spot between its eyes. There was only smooth skin there, no spiny bristles, and the sword sank into the ravager's face. It thrashed, but the man pushed his entire body weight into the thrust. The life slowly faded from the beast's eyes as it knelt, then collapsed onto its side.

Behind the body of the ravager, my uncle was on his knees. He held my broken body in his arms. My head lolled to the side, revealing bloody scratches all along my face, and a particularly deep gash on my forehead. Uncle wept, rocking me back and forth, and then I saw a thick branch that had pierced my side when I'd landed. A dark red stain spread from that point, a fatal wound. I was dying, my lifeblood dripping to the forest floor.

Elder Gao knelt beside us, expression grave.

"You can heal her . . . please," Uncle begged, sobbing.

"Her fortune splits at this point," Elder Gao said. "It is up to you to make the choice. If she lives, her life will be full of trials and tribulations. That is the price of someone who is Celestial-touched. If you let her go, she can drink the cup of forgetting, cross the Bridge, and start anew in a different life."

Uncle looked down at me and brushed my matted hair away from my cheek. "Will she one day know peace?" he asked.

"The road will be hard, but there will be an end," was the answer.

"I'm not ready yet to let you go . . . ," Uncle whispered. "Forgive me, Xue'er." He looked up and nodded, tears still in his eyes. "I want her to live."

"And so it shall be."

Elder Gao laid his hands upon my chest, and a rush of magic poured from him into me. Gold sparks streamed in a torrent from his hands. An echoing ache resounded in my chest, some part of me that still remembered that moment, the sensation of healing. The wound at my side knitted closed, the blood disappearing back inside of me. He raised his hands and held them over my head, where the sparks continued. The scratches on my face sealed and smoothed. The gash above my brow thinned. What looked like a star flared upon my forehead, then disappeared into the scar that still remained. I looked peaceful, sleeping there.

"The ravager attacks are worsening, Guanyue," Elder Gao said. "This area is no longer safe. We will have to find another sanctuary. Especially for her, now that there is a part of Celestial magic inside of her."

"The best place for her would be in Wudan, I know." Uncle sighed. "Surrounded by Mortals. They would not be able to follow her scent there as easily. This day was coming, but I did not want to accept it." He placed his hand upon my head, his heartache obvious.

"If you wish to join her in the city . . . ," Elder Gao said slowly, even though his reluctance was apparent.

Uncle shook his head. "They will try to hurt you through me. It would put her in danger as well." He struggled to stand with me in his arms.

"I'm sorry, my love," Elder Gao whispered. "I wish it were different."

Uncle looked up at him with so much love in his eyes, and recited: *"There is much to ponder with this brief existence, difficult to find those who can comprehend such thoughts, but in writing these words . . . they echo in the mountains to you."*

"Boya broke his strings and refused to play again," his love spoke back with the utmost tenderness, "for there was no one else who could understand him in all the world."

They disappeared then, back into the mist, until I too returned to my body. I'd heard for myself the pain in Uncle's voice, could almost feel how torn he was to send me away to the city. I thought he'd left me behind for his adventures, but now I understood he did it to keep me safe.

I folded upon myself—it hurt, knowing that what I had believed to be true all this time was not. That he did care, that he had wanted to keep me for as long as he could, and he risked his life for me. Even though it put his life and the life of his beloved at risk, he still came, year after year, to make sure I was safe.

"Lady Xue . . ." The duke spoke beside me, concerned.

"He didn't leave me," I blubbered, knowing that I was not making much sense. "He didn't leave me at the House because he didn't want me."

Jinglang was suddenly there, his face before mine, staring intently into my eyes. He was so close, I saw myself reflected in them. "He frequently spoke of you," he said, breath stirring my hair. "I knew he regretted leaving you behind. He spoke many times about how, when all of this was over, he would bring you to their house. You would be a family again."

His words made me sob even harder, and I felt myself being pulled to him. With my face pressed against his chest, I heard the steady beating of his heart. Even though it was improper, even though this was something that I shouldn't accept, I still leaned into that warmth.

The reminder that for this moment, I was not alone.

CHAPTER THIRTY

AFTER I COMPOSED MYSELF, JINGLANG CALLED FOR Attendant Luo to bring me a basin of water and a cloth to wash up with. I was sure my eyes were swollen from crying and my appearance a mess, but inside me there was a stillness I had never felt before. It was as if I had been wrung out and emptied. Cleansed.

When I returned to the receiving room, there was a table laden with many dishes. At the sight of the food, I was suddenly ravenous. I ate fried dumplings with a chewy outer shell, the interior a taro root filling, salty and sweet. I drank hot-and-sour soup filled with lily flowers, black mushrooms, and bamboo shoots. I crunched on pickled chili cabbage and daikon, all accompanied by warm, fluffy rice.

I ate for the soothing comfort, for something to distract myself from feeling too much. Too intently. The duke didn't say anything during this time, only provided his quiet company.

I was thankful for this slight reprieve. That he was giving me space to remember, to grieve.

When the fruit was brought out, I was ready to speak of what we had learned. I nibbled on a piece of watermelon, recalling with amusement how at the House we were taught to eat delicately, so that our makeup and outfits would remain pristine. Watermelon was a poor selection, the way it dribbled and got on everything. But the duke had already seen me sick, sobbing, angry. Whatever good impression he had of me would have been tarnished long ago.

He finally spoke, his gaze cast downward, not meeting my eyes.

"I know you've thought me less than forthright with you since our first meeting," he said, words awkwardly strained and formal. "But I wanted to offer an explanation."

"Go on," I said after a pause, once I realized he was waiting for my permission to continue.

"From my earliest memories, Celestials have been taught our responsibility as stewards, to care for the Mortal and Spirit Realms at a distance," he said. "That there were limitations to the capability of Mortal understanding due to the brevity of their life spans. We were told the seven forbidden emotions were sowed in the Mortal Realm, where the Corruption has fully taken root."

It was written in all of their texts, their handbooks, the distinction of what made someone Celestial. In their choice of words, *ascendance, elevation, purification*. We knew this even as Mortal children, in our stories about the Celestials and their sacred duty. They were often portrayed as sage and wise, having risen above humanity's burdens.

"I've since learned it is not true!" He leaned forward then, eyes flashing, with a fervor that startled me. "Ever since I began to learn from my shīfù, it was different from what I expected. Different from the books and scrolls. I thought I was able to discard my prejudices, yet I still failed."

I noticed how tightly his hand clutched his cup, how he uttered those words as if he was holding back a great wave of feeling that would soon break.

"I thought by telling you only part of what I knew, I was protecting you from the realities of the Celestial Realm," he continued. "Instead, I was following in the footsteps of my shīfù and your uncle. I was doing to you exactly what they did to both of us. Because of their attempt to keep us safe, we are now ill-prepared for what is coming."

"What exactly were Elder Gao's responsibilities?" I asked, having a sense of it, but not understanding it fully.

He looked surprised. "Did you not know? He is the Star of Fortune, responsible for the Mortal Tapestry. He came to power in a time when those of the Celestial Court used to have to pass the Rite of Tribulation, to fully experience the burdens of the Mortal life before they could become a true Celestial. He's taken on many forms: an almost-king who wanted for nothing, a fisherman who was at the mercy of the sea, a gravedigger who was reliant on the strength of his body to feed himself. He's lived it all, knowing of joy and hurt, loss and desire. He taught me there is nothing more precious than a Mortal soul."

My mind conjured up that stern face, the portrait hanging above the altar in the House of Flowing Water. The red threads that dangled from his fingers, to bring together or to sever. It was not how I imagined he would be, not in alignment with the one who laughed and joked with my uncle. Somewhere during his travels in the Mortal Realm, they met and fell in love. A Celestial and a Mortal man. The rules broken. A love forbidden.

"But . . . you're the Duke of Dreams," I said, not comprehending. "How can you be the apprentice to the Star of Fortune?"

"My father was meant to be the duke for many years longer," he replied. "When he was banished, his role could not be left abandoned, but his apprentice was also caught by the intrigue and punished. I was the one who was found to have the greatest affinity for the Dreaming, having grown up on this estate. The threads of the Mortal Tapestry and the roads of the Dreaming . . . they're not so different after all." He gave a rueful smile.

"Did you want to?" I asked. He was handed a responsibility different from what he had expected from his life. Did he resent it, see it as a burden?

"We learn early on that it's not about what we want or do not want," he said. "But I accepted it all the same. It was another way to look upon the pattern of the tapestry that emerges, another way to watch over those souls as they live and move on, as their Mortal cycle maintains the energy that holds the realms together. It was why, knowing what I know of my shīfù, I could not comprehend why he gave up that responsibility."

"He gave up the role of the Star of Fortune?" I had initially thought he was banished, just like the former duke.

"Yes, for Elder Tang," Jinglang said, his expression unreadable. "He gave up his Celestial core and shed his magic, so that he could live in the Mortal Realm."

"Do you . . . hate him for it?" I asked softly. If he thought his shīfù gave up everything to be with my uncle, that he gave up everything in pursuit of love, against all of their tenets, he must have believed his shīfù had lost all sense.

"I did, once," the duke murmured. "But I no longer believe things were as simple as that. Here, come with me."

He stood, and I followed him. Attendant Luo had somehow obtained my cloak. He handed it to me and I shrugged it on. Once we walked out of the residence, I understood why he had fetched it.

The main garden had changed again. Frost hung in the air, wrapped around the branches. Crystal shards that glittered when we breathed, white mist from our exhalations. The sun was a weak, pale orb in the muted sky. We walked over one of the curved bridges and took the path that led away from the Wind-Swept Pavilion. There was a series of steps that we ascended to a platform that overlooked the gorge. Except the gorge was once again shrouded in swirling mist, so we could only see vague tree-like shapes in the distance. In the middle of the platform was a stone pillar, upon which were markings that I could not read.

"I brought you here to my estate because I once thought that if you were under my protection, I could shield you from what is coming." He looked down at me, serious. "But instead, all I've done is put you in danger. You've met my mother . . . She is currently the leader of the Faction of Tranquility, and I've made you her target. You know what she thinks a Mortal's life is worth."

Reaching down, he took my hand and enveloped it in both of his. "I've had a lot of time to think about it while I was in seclusion. To consider what we discussed previously. I rescind my previous promise, Lady Xue, and now offer you this: If you want to be rid of the Celestial Realm and all of its intrigues, if you want to return to Wudan—free of all of this, your memory emptied, a new student of the academy—then tell me. I will take you back this very moment, no matter the cost. Just tell me."

I looked into his dark eyes, earnest and pleading. I knew he meant every word. He was giving me a way out. He would risk the wrath of the Sky Consort, the punishments his mother swore she would bring down upon my head. He would bear it all to return me to the Mortal Realm, if I only said the word.

I placed my left hand upon his, turned my right so that I was now holding his hands in my own. He gazed at me, wordless, waiting for my response. I felt something quiver inside of me, like a string gently plucked, waiting for another note to be played, for the melody to be concluded.

"I know what it is like to be kept in the dark. It's a terrible feeling of helplessness. They wanted to protect us, and yet they could not protect themselves in the end. Now we have to continue as they asked. Work together, and not make the same mistakes they did," I told him. "I'm only a musician. The intrigue of any court is beyond me, and yet somehow my thread of fate pulled me here. I believe this is where I'm meant to be, and I'll help you see it through."

His smile crept in, like sun peeking through the clouds, and I wished I could see this more often. The humor that was present in his letters more accurately matched the person standing before me now.

"Now, what is it that has caused the unrest in the Celestial Court?" I asked. "And what does it have to do with the memory jewels?"

Jinglang dropped his hands and stepped back, and gestured for me to do the same. He lifted his palms to the pillar, and I saw the sparks of his magic. The pillar rose slowly, breaking away from the platform, until a circle was left below it. A portal of some sort. I peered down, and I could see the swirling mist below.

The image cleared. "The Kingdom of Qi!" I gasped, recognizing it from the maps that I'd studied during my lessons.

"You've read *Twilight's Begonia*?" he asked.

I nodded. I'd studied it carefully, considered it as a potential piece to unlock another jewel, but it had not revealed anything. It was a sad tale, one of warning and woe.

"The death of the Flower Queen caused even deeper divide between the realms," he explained. "There were those who believed that Demons were the source of the Corruption, that they could no longer be trusted with the Realm of Ghosts—if the Moon Sovereign was able to become a ravager, then we were all at risk. The reports from our spies in the Demon Realm have all observed chaos as their princes devour one another in an attempt to seize power."

The histories I studied demonstrated that everyone, from Celestials to Demons, were all vulnerable to the same struggles that represented weakness in the Mortal Realm. They all fought for territory, for power, for resources. The old poems outlined a truth no one wanted to acknowledge: We were all Nüwa's children, for good or for ill.

"Here is the route my Father took through the Kingdom of Qi." With another gesture, the portal showed a red path through the kingdom. It began in the capital, then south, toward the Summer Sea. It curved then along the river through the Silver Mountain Canyon, and farther north to Wudan. "Through the Dreaming, he discovered there have been increasing reports of ravager sightings in the Mortal Realm, causing unrest. Tracking where they had originated, he found something troubling. The barrier that protected the rest of the realms from the Barren Realm had been breached, just large enough for something—or some*one*—to pass through."

"The Barren Realm . . . the sixth and final realm," I said, trying to recall specifics.

"It is there that dwell the monsters, the ageless, the deathless, the ones impossible to kill. Sent there to roam the four jagged planes for eternity. A ravager is a mere reflection of them, a fraction of the size and strength of the original Beasts of Corruption that threatened to tear the sky from the earth."

I couldn't imagine that there could be monsters even more grotesque and terrifying than the ones we'd already met, or that there were immortal versions of them, impossible to kill. I felt queasy, recalling the sensation of my life force being drawn out of my body unwillingly, my mind being separated from my body.

"My father believed someone killed the Flower Queen and set the unrest in the Demon Realm in motion. The Moon Sovereign was one of the most powerful beings across all of the realms. It would have taken a lot of power for him to lose control."

"Someone from the Barren Realms?" I asked softly.

The duke nodded. "The oracle who lives beyond the Yinyang Sea confirmed it. The Deceiver has returned. Maybe only a remnant of her, a shadow of her power. Small enough to squeeze through that crack in the barrier, but she's here for her revenge."

The Deceiver. The Origin of Corruption. The one who almost destroyed the world. Feared even by the gods and back to finish what she started.

CHAPTER THIRTY-ONE

THE KINGDOM OF QI RIPPLED IN THE PORTAL, EMA-
nating a soft glow. The mountains and rivers of my realm, the cities and
towns that contained so many Mortal lives.

"It cost my father his freedom when he went to the Mortal Realm
to search for evidence that the Deceiver has returned," Jinglang said,
voice tinged with sadness. "He petitioned the sovereign for an audience,
begged him to raise the alarm that the Deceiver had escaped. He was
warned that to continue down that path would be foolish."

With another wave of his hand, the Kingdom of Qi was gone,
replaced by an image of what appeared to be a white tower, but when
I peered closer, I saw that it was a pagoda. Seven stacks of seven-sided
rooms, from the largest at the base to the smallest at the peak.

"He would not stop his appeal to others of the court, and soon
after . . . Ruilan Turned, and he was certain that meant he was getting
closer to uncovering the truth. He was preparing to submit an appeal to
reopen the investigation into the Flower Queen's death when my mother
accused him of causing unrest, and he was sent to their temple. Or more
specifically, into this tower." The duke's mouth twisted. "The Tower of
Suffering."

"That's an . . . ominous name," I said, already dreading to hear what
was contained within.

"Celestials are sent there as a reminder of what would happen if
the Corruption spread across the realms. Throughout each level, they
would experience each of the forbidden emotions."

I could not understand why their punishment would be to endure the emotions that were innately woven into our brief Mortal existences. Why they feared it so.

"Most don't make it out." He waved a hand again and the tower disappeared. "They're consumed by whatever lives in the tower. Its past inhabitants, the strange forces that power it . . ."

"Your father survived."

"He was deemed too dangerous to remain in the Celestial Realm, on the brink of Turning. So they kept him locked in the tower until they could determine his fate, and if he were to Turn, well . . ." He shrugged. "There's no one there he could harm, right?" His eyes glittered as he stared down at the portal as it faded back to mist.

I placed a hand upon his arm, reminding him he was not alone.

"This is where she jumped," he said, voice hoarse. "She didn't deserve what happened to her. She did it because she didn't want to harm anyone else."

Ruilan. Her memory, her presence, haunted these halls. I couldn't help the twinge of envy to hear her remembered with such affection, even though she was gone.

"You think she was forced to Turn?" I asked, wishing I could take on some of his obvious pain, help him find a resolution.

"I don't know . . . but I know she wouldn't have done it herself." He gritted his teeth. "It could have been anyone. A servant. A visitor from the court. A friend. I've walked that day a thousand times in my mind, trying to recall if there was anything out of the ordinary. And I'm certain the same person or persons is involved in my shīfù's murder, because he was also getting dangerously closer to the truth."

Bit by bit, piece by piece, I was putting together the bigger picture. It made sense why he was so paranoid, hesitant to involve even his own

sister in his investigation. The way he became more and more with-
drawn the closer we got to the estate, because it was a reminder of all
that he had lost.

Someone killed his betrothed, framed his father, and murdered his
shīfù.

Someone who may still be here now.

EVEN THOUGH I wanted nothing more than to spend the next few
days poring over scrolls and books to find the song that would unlock the
final jewel, I still had to prepare for and survive the Spring Festival. To
make my presentation before the Sky Consort, and see if I was worthy to
remain in this realm. As I practiced, I tried not to think about the Cliffs of
Sundering, to imagine what it would feel like to disappear.

Lingwei came to me in the morning, dressed in her full outfit of
white armor, holding a spear.

"Sadly, I will not be able to accompany you to the palace like I had
originally planned," she said apologetically. "I was called to assist with
the palace guard, for there have been more sightings of pesky ravagers
again."

I dreaded the thought of the evening without Lingwei's company. I'd
hoped she could be there for me to rely on, to warn me if I was behaving
in some offensive manner.

She laughed when she saw the expression on my face. "Oh, don't
pout! Jinglang will ensure you get there safely. He will be the most steady
and *serious* companion. And I'll make sure Chenwen says a good word
or two on your behalf. The consort dotes on him. He's her favorite of the
princelings. Can you imagine? Him as the next sovereign?" She let out
another hearty laugh. I forced my mouth into an imitation of a grin yet
could not find humor in it.

I was still glum after she left, and used the time to run through my repertoire once again, letting the music soothe my unsettled mind. I'd selected choices in the standard progression as taught by my teacher at the music academy. Three pieces: first, *the call*; second, *the question*; and the finale, *the answer*. I'd been taught the pieces should follow a coherent theme, should evoke different moods, and yet not be so contrasting as to spoil the effect.

After making my deal with Danrou, I was surprised to find that my relationship with my maidservant had taken a turn for the better. She was somewhat pleasant to me, her frosty demeanor slightly melted. If she was truly willing to be my ally, then I could meet her halfway by learning the song she gave me.

True to his word, Prince Zhou personally delivered the outfit I was to wear for the evening, and brought his personal staff to prepare me. Though my worry still lingered, I knew this was the most suitable time for me to fulfill my promise to Danrou.

I spoke with him about it before he left to leave me to the administrations of his people.

"She wants to talk to me?" He raised a brow. "Whatever for?" He seemed surprised, which improved my impression of him slightly.

"She said she was grateful for your previous assistance on a personal matter," I told him, using the words she wanted me to say. "And wished to extend her thanks with a gift."

"I understand." Then with a smirk, he added, "It looks like I will have to break the heart of another admirer, as I am ever so devoted to my dear Lingwei."

I rolled my eyes then, any goodwill toward him dissipated just as easily.

"I'm sure your ego will remain as bloated as ever," I said. I could acknowledge he was pleasant to look at, but our personalities clashed too much for me to want to spend more time with him than necessary.

His grin stretched even wider. "One cannot help the beautiful face they were born with."

I glared at him. "Don't . . . don't give her too much hope," I couldn't help but add, even though I knew that my words were meaningless to him. Even though I had not known Danrou for very long, I saw her hopeful expression. She may appear guarded, but I suspected when someone got past her walls, she would be devoted.

"Off I go, then." He clapped his hands, and then my preparations began.

I was bathed, scrubbed, perfumed. Hair trimmed, plucked, brushed. Face massaged, powdered, painted. I was wrapped in various lengths of fabric—an undercloth of bright yellow, then each additional layer lighter in material and lighter in color, until I was surrounded in the wispiest cloud of white. I felt as if I was walking through sunbeams. Around my shoulders was draped a shawl that shifted from red to purple, trailing down my back like streaks of color in a sunset sky. On my feet I wore red slippers embroidered with silver thread. Around my neck they fastened drops of sparkling white and red jewels. They attempted to place rings upon my hands, but that I stood firm against, for I did not want the weight of them to affect my playing.

Prince Zhou was waiting for me in my courtyard when it was all done and, seeing me, declared me presentable. Danrou stood behind him with a secretive smile. Whatever conversation she had with him, it seemed to have gone well. I could only hope I made the right decision, and I didn't affect his relationship with Lingwei.

"I wish you good luck, Lady Xue," Danrou said softly, giving me a bow. She would travel with some of the other Meng family servants to bring gifts to honor the consort. I was still hopeful that we would learn to get along with each other in time, even though we would never be friends and confidants.

The prince walked with me to the main gate to meet Jinglang. We passed through the sculpture garden, which I had not entered since the first day I arrived and visited only that one time briefly in my dreams. As dusk took the light of the sun away, leaving the garden in twilight, I glanced back at the manor. It loomed in the mist, and the windows were lit up one by one, as if the house was bidding me farewell. I shivered, hoping that wouldn't be true. I wanted to return here again, unscathed and whole. Or did I want to go back to Wudan? My memory of my past life seemed hazy now, like the fog had seeped into my mind as well.

"Does she not look radiant, brother?" Prince Zhou announced when we approached the duke, waiting beside the carriage. As if I was some prize to be on display.

"She looks . . ." The duke inclined his head and seemed to consider this flippant question seriously. "She looks nice." He met my eyes and then looked away. Inside, a part of me warmed at the flicker of appreciation in his gaze.

"Just the words a woman would want to hear," the prince commented dryly. "Mortal or not." He turned to me and offered his arm. "Are you certain you want this wooden block to be your escort? I promise I would be a considerably more lively companion."

"I would rather not be in attendance at all, considering my life is at stake," I retorted. "But if I must, I would certainly not want to spend the evening with *you*. Didn't you say you have other ladies to fawn over you while Lingwei is otherwise occupied?"

"Her words cut me like a dagger!" Prince Zhou clutched his chest dramatically. "I am wounded, Jinglang! Save me!"

If there was one positive thing I could say about the prince, it was that for all of his antics, he remained unperturbed by whatever I had to say to him, however offensive I might be. He seemed to delight in receiving insults and jabs at his expense.

"Shall we?" I stepped closer to Jinglang, and he gave me a tentative smile. He helped me up the steps of the carriage, my hands full with the qín, and left the prince to his histrionics.

CHAPTER THIRTY-TWO

I HADN'T CONSIDERED HOW WE WOULD ARRIVE AT the palace of the consort. The carriage itself was relatively normal, made of a wood so dark it was almost black. It had a red roof and a carving of a dragon that arched above the door.

But it was the creatures I glimpsed out of the window that made me gasp.

To call them horses would be like calling a lion a housecat. They were great golden steeds, with the thick, muscular body and black hooves of a horse, but they had the head of a dragon, with long white antlers and shiny black eyes the size of a fist. Although they appeared rather docile as the driver hitched them to the carriage, one of them tossed its head and gave a powerful snort. They seemed like they could break free easily.

Seeing my discomfort, Jinglang reassured me these were docile Celestial animals.

"These are the qílín," he said. "Horses cannot travel the great distance required to reach the consort's estate."

With a turn of his hand, a ball of flame appeared in his palm. He blew at it, and it ascended above us like a star, settling into the lantern that hung from the roof, illuminating the small space.

Sometimes life in the manor was full of mundane events and chores, to the point where I could almost pretend it was a regular Mortal household. Then things like this happened, reminding me again of where I was, and that here, magic played a part in every aspect of life.

He leaned over and closed the shutters, explaining with seriousness,

"It will be easier if you do not see how quickly the qílín are able to travel."

The carriage rumbled, and then the sensation of being thrust into the air made my stomach drop. I was thankful then that the duke had the foresight to close the shutters—if I saw the trees and stars hurtling past me, I might have been sick. My hand clutched the side of the wall, grasping for something to hang on to.

I glanced at the duke, who sat there, serene. He didn't seem as ill as I remembered when we first traveled together.

"Were you truly motion sick before?" I asked, a little queasy.

The duke quirked a corner of his lips, amused at the memory. "I had to ensure we were hidden from the All-Seeing Eye that guarded the borders of the Celestial Realm. It expended my magic quite considerably."

"You risked so much to get me here," I said, aware of how little I'd known back then. *Was it worth it?* I could not bring myself to voice the question. "If I survive tonight, I will ensure that it is returned to you in kind. I will find the song to unlock the next jewel." I wanted him to know I had not forgotten what was required of me. Auntie's lessons came to mind again. To prove my worth after this hurdle, and then the next.

Instead of the approval I expected, he looked worried. "Is there something not to your liking in your residence? The food? If there is something that is missing, then you just have to ask."

"No!" I exclaimed. "It is wonderful, truly. I want for nothing. I only want to make sure I am not a burden—"

He cut me off before I could continue my thought. "You are not a *burden*." A pained expression crossed his face as he leaned forward. "I would never want to give you that impression."

I was taken aback by the intensity of his reaction. "I . . . I assure you, I know my place."

"Who is saying that to you?" he asked, his voice rising. "Is it Danrou? Gods, I should have known. I could replace her with another if you would like—"

"It's not her." I could admit that she had at times made me feel lesser than, unwelcome, but what would that achieve? "Danrou is pleasant enough. We get along. I'm only speaking of the reality of things."

What I was and what I was not.

"What reality?"

"You are a Celestial. You will live a far longer life than I could ever imagine. I'm only a brief moment in your existence."

I saw then the brevity of my life compared to his. A bee buzzing by in the garden, busily working on building its hive without knowing who was coming to harvest the honey that I so carefully made. I was the strike of the match, a flame that burned bright and then was quickly extinguished, until all that remained of me was smoke.

"I see." He leaned back in his seat. "You believe us to be heartless, emptied of feeling. Maybe even incapable of it."

"Those are your tenets, are they not? Outlined in the treatise you sent me," I told him. "If I knew I had eternity before me, I would certainly live my life differently."

I had angered him, I was sure of it. But for what reason other than bringing the truth to the forefront, I could not tell.

"What would you do, then, if you could go anywhere, do anything that you want to do?" he asked, a strange light in his eyes.

"I . . ." I did not understand the question. He was in a peculiar mood tonight, but if he wanted to know, then I should address his question with solemn consideration. "I want to be a traveling musician, just like my uncle was a traveling poet. To learn how to write my own music, maybe even make an attempt at my own poetry. To decide where I want to go and what I want to do. To . . . to know my life is my own."

"That sounds like a life worth aspiring to," he said, and he did not seem so angry anymore.

"Maybe it will all remain a dream if I do not survive this night." I shrugged. "But that is what I want."

"You *will* succeed," he told me softly. "Of that I have no doubt."

THE REST OF our journey ended all too soon, and the carriage slowed to a stop. There was a rap on the door, and it opened to reveal a servant dressed in festive red, who greeted us with a deep bow. He assisted me in descending the steps, balancing my qín in hand.

There was almost too much for my eyes to take in—the palace was the grandest structure I had ever seen. It appeared to have ten stories, each floor ablaze with light from what appeared to be hundreds of red and gold lanterns. Banners trailed down from the eaves, riotous with color. Music floated toward us upon the air, an ensemble of pipes that played a merry tune.

I swayed upon my feet, my heart beating too fast within my chest. There were so many people talking, laughing. Others walked past us, strangers with striking appearances, dressed in resplendent hues. They moved as if they floated, graceful in stride.

How could I ever aspire to impress this glittering, gleaming throng? How could I even *dare*?

"Steady . . ." Two hands clasped my arms, and Jinglang stepped between me and that whirling, too-brilliant crowd, acting as a shield. "I'd forgotten how the palace could appear to someone not used to its appearance. Breathe."

I could not. My breath was shallow, my face hot. I was at risk of float-ing away.

"Look at me." The duke touched his forehead to mine, until I was forced to look into his eyes. "As a child I had no name for the moon, called it a plate of white jade . . ."

He recited the poem that he had once mentioned, back when I did not yet know who he was. I forced myself to listen to the steady rhythm of the words, the images conjured—of toads that took a bite out of the moon, of the archer who shot down the nine sunbirds—and slowly, I was brought back down to earth.

"I can't do this," I whispered. My feet still felt rooted to the ground, and I was sure if I took a step they would buckle. I had played for so long behind screens, for my music to drift out as pleasant accompaniment. Even during the dance, I was to the side of the stage, while all of the eyes, all of the attention, were on the two figures dancing. I told Lingwei I did not doubt my ability to play the qín, but here, I was certain I would prove myself a liar.

Jinglang turned his head so that his lips were beside my ear, so I could feel the warmth of his breath. "Look at them. They believe them-selves to be better, but they couldn't be more wrong. Their eternity is spent trying to obtain and hold on to more power, more prestige. Trying to impress one another, trying to outwit one another. You wield true power, Lady Xue, for Mortals are capable of feeling what they could never even imagine. They rely upon Mortal art, Mortal music, to comprehend only a fraction of what it is like to truly live. They are afraid that there is something missing inside of them. Sometimes . . . I am too."

It could be that he said those pretty words to convince me to go on, to avoid execution, but I felt that he spoke from his heart. I sensed his words were true. I had to persevere, I had to continue, to prove that I deserved to remain here, to fulfill my promise to my uncle. To *live*.

I took a shaky breath and pulled back. Took a better grip of my qín, so it did not slip through my sweaty palms. "I'm ready."

"I'll be there in the crowd, listening. You won't be alone." He gestured toward the steps, bowing slightly. Letting me take the lead.

Together, we walked toward the entrance.

CHAPTER THIRTY-THREE

WITH EACH STEP WE TOOK, I FELT THEIR EYES UPON us. My brief moment of insecurity had drawn their attention; they stared, turned, and whispered to one another as we passed them. I stood straighter, tried to hold my head up high.

The hall that awaited us at the top of the steps was a splendid sight. A tree grew in the center, gleaming gold. Its long branches were covered with white and pink flowers, each with red and yellow centers. On its lower branches were green leaves and large orange apricots, the biggest I'd ever seen. The ceiling was covered in greenery, draping from the rafters, all at various peaks of flowering. Purples and pinks and blues and yellows dazzled my eyes. The air was heady with the scent of blooming flowers and ripening fruit.

"What do we do now?" I whispered.

"Soon we will be called to greet the consort and present our gifts," he whispered back, and nodded toward the stage at the back of the room, past the great tree. Another set of stairs rose to the platform above, and there was a large throne there, currently waiting for whoever was coming to claim it.

Tables were set up on either side of the room, with cushions to kneel on behind them. A few of the Celestials had already taken their places, drinking wine and speaking to one another. Behind them, their servants or bodyguards stood, watchful and waiting.

I saw Lady Hè enter with her soldiers. She was dressed in a gray sheath, which showcased her tall and slender form. A long silver robe composed of many layers trailed behind her, catching the light. Feathers were braided into her hair, which she had left long, falling in waves almost down to her waist.

A servant approached the duke and said, "Please, Duke Meng, right this way," and led him to one of the tables at the side of the room.

"I'll require another cushion," Jinglang requested.

The servant's eyes widened as he glanced at me. "This . . . this is not done, my lord."

"This is what I require," he said, voice ringing with the sound of command.

"Yes, my lord." The servant ducked his head and scurried away. I stood there, awkward and painfully aware of my lowly status.

"You didn't have to do that," I muttered. "I would have been fine with standing behind you."

"If we are to ensure the consort sees you as a valuable addition to the realm," he explained quietly, so that no one else could overhear, "the first impression you make cannot be as my servant."

That made sense, and I was sufficiently chastened. I was glad then that Lingwei wasn't there to watch me fumble yet again. She would have been embarrassed at the waste of all of those hours she had spent attempting to educate me on court decorum.

When the servant came back with the cushion, I knelt beside Jinglang with my qín, head lowered, trying not to stand out.

It felt like time dragged on forever as we waited for the hall to fill. I half listened to the conversations around me, people greeting one another, inquiring about this or that. It was all dreadfully dull, polite talk. Until finally, a woman appeared at the top of the stairwell and clapped her hands twice, and the hall quieted.

"Xuannu, the Transcendent, the Consort of the Sky Sovereign, the

Last Star of the Dawn. She brings the light that illuminates the morning. All hail."

"A hundred thousand years to the Sky Consort!" everyone in the hall declared, a resounding chorus.

And then the consort herself descended from the sky. Behind her trailed plumes of many colors, orange and red and pink and purple, like the sunrise she was responsible for bringing forth each day. Upon her head she wore a high golden headdress, sparkling with gems of many colors. As she settled upon the throne, the carving over her shoulder came to life. The phoenix unfurled from the stone, became a living creature. It preened itself with its beak as it shed its gray appearance and became as colorful as the consort, its long tail trailing down to the ground.

"Peace be with you," she declared. "I am grateful for your attendance at my celebration. As we delight in the welcoming of a new year."

The herald stepped forward again, announcing the next arrival: "The Sky Sovereign Chidi, the Glorious Sun which shines upon the realms, the Heavenly Ruler. All hail."

"A hundred thousand more to the glorious Sovereign!" the hall thundered.

There was a flash of light, so bright I had to cover my eyes, and when I looked back, he was already seated there beside the consort upon the massive throne. Upon his head he wore a guan, from which dangled twenty-four tassels of jade, symbolizing the solar terms that governed the year, from Spring's Arrival to the Frozen Earth. He wore a suit of red armor, and from his shoulders streamed a robe of umber on which gold dragons were embroidered. The dragons shifted and moved, and I blinked, certain I was seeing things. But no, a second look confirmed for me it was real—those dragons did ripple and move upon the fabric.

I could not find the words sufficient to capture the dazzling splendor of the sovereign and consort of the Celestial Realm.

"Another year at last," the Sovereign proclaimed, his deep, resonant voice booming above the heads of the crowd. "A cause to celebrate. Join us to welcome the morning, the dawning of a new year, for the sun will always rise upon the Six Realms. I so will it."

"It has been spoken," everyone said in a chorus.

The procession of gifts began immediately. The herald called out a name, and that person rose from their seat. They ascended the stairwell and knelt before the great throne, spoke words of good fortune. Their attendants came up behind them and brought forth their treasures. Black winged steeds captured from the northern mountains, presented by the Bird Clan, whose envoys all wielded feathered fans of an assortment of colors. The Tree Clan envoys wore mossy green cloaks that trailed behind them like spiderwebs, and presented a rare gem unearthed from their mines, said to glow red near sources of Corruption. The Water Clan was an intimidating procession of soldiers, their blue armor glassy and translucent, reminding me of sculptures carved from ice. They brought a bone flute imbued with a ghostly soul that only played haunting tunes by the light of the moon, said to be able to ward off those bearing ill intent to the player.

Treasure after dazzling treasure was brought up and then taken away. Then the herald called for the Duke of Dreams.

I rose with him, felt the intensity of all of those eyes like pinpricks. I chose to keep my eyes forward, to keep my steps steady. I ignored the whispers that flowed through the hall as we approached the throne, repeating Lingwei's careful instructions in my head.

I managed to ascend the steps without slipping, even though I was sure I was on the verge of collapse. At the top of the platform, the duke bowed, and I sank to my knees. I pressed my hands to my forehead, arms raised high, then I bent and forward and brought my head toward the earth. Bowing to the heavens with reverence.

"What is it you brought today, Jinglang?" The voice of the consort sounded like wind chimes, light and tinkling.

"May your rule be long, Consort," he spoke above me. I did not dare to lift my head and remained there, prostrate. "During my last excursion to the Mortal Realm, I encountered a musician who had a talent for the qín. When I heard her play, I was certain she was Celestial touched. As I knew you had an appreciation for the qín, I thought you might enjoy her playing."

"But there was no record of the admission of a Mortal girl into our realm," the consort said, tone slightly sharper. "You are aware of the rules, are you not?"

"I had thought to keep her hidden to surprise you, Your Highness," he said, and he dropped to one knee beside me. "I know now that this was foolish. I will accept any punishment that you deem appropriate for this transgression."

The sovereign laughed. "Now, now, Jinglang! There's no need for this seriousness, not when we are in the midst of a celebration."

"Rise, Mortal one, and let me look at you," the consort's voice rang above my head.

I slowly got to my feet, but kept my gaze lowered upon the red tail feathers of the phoenix that brushed the ground before me. I could feel the creature regarding me with its uncanny stare.

There was a rustle of her skirts as she stood over me. With one finger, she tipped my head back, and I looked up into her eyes. I saw the blue of a clear sky, the movement of clouds, the sunlight streaming through them. It was dazzling and terrifying, all that was contained within. As if her eyes could illuminate everything that I hid deep within and expose it for everyone to see. Every dark and terrible thought, every betrayal and secret kept.

"Bring her instrument. We'll see if she is as you say." Her finger dropped from my face, and I could breathe again. I gave a sloppy bow and turned away, my face burning. Out of all of the Celestials I'd met, she was the most formidable, the one I could truly call a god.

When I returned to retrieve my qín, Danrou was there to assist me. She gave no indication that she noticed how I shook slightly as she helped me set up the stand and brought a bench for me to sit on. After she was done, she bowed and retreated to stand behind the duke, who was given a seat beside the throne platform.

I was in the very center of the room. I felt the presence of the tree rising behind me, its branches reaching above my head. My insides felt like water as I went through the motions of tuning. As if I were somewhere else, out of my body, watching myself prepare to play.

Until I could not avoid it any longer. I lifted my hands, and strummed the first note.

CHAPTER THIRTY-FOUR

THE FIRST SONG I CHOSE PAID TRIBUTE TO THE
Celestial Realm and also to the duke, who brought me here. I hoped he
would recognize the melody, a reminder of the first gift he ever gave
me—the first song manual I ever owned.

"Melody of the Water Immortals" was a piece composed of three
parts, all inspired by the story about a man who stood at the edge of
the world and begged the sea for a song that would win the heart of the
woman he loved. The sea heard his story and gave him the melody to
accompany the poem "Reflections Upon Water and Sky" by the Poet
Wen.

The song was as gentle as the words themselves, a reflective melody
of notes that repeated in a cycle, like the waves of the sea.

A late-night guest approaches on the water, riding a red carp

*A mythical bird and twin cranes announce his arrival from a
faraway land*

The air stills, the freshness of the rain clears the sky

The solitary radiance of the moonlight can be seen over a great distance

Fog skims over the mountain tops like strands of fine hair

From the cold strings of the qín, the sound of a fragrant spring emerges

Darkness of the evening obscures the beauty of the mountains

Moonlight fills the boat like scattered pieces of jade

As the poem went on, after years of being with her, the man realized why she was initially reluctant to be with him—she was a Water
Immortal, destined to live forever, while he had a fading, Mortal life,

until all that remained was his song and a memory for her to grieve. At the end of the poem, she traveled to the edge of the world, to return his song to the sea.

While the last notes trembled in the air, and I returned to myself, I looked up and met the eyes of the duke. He gave me a small nod, a smile that indicated he remembered the reason why I chose this piece. Something tender ached in my heart. I cared so much what he thought. Perhaps too much.

"Well done!" I tore my gaze away from him to regard the consort applauding from her throne. "You exhibited restraint during the sections of their mutual longing. I am surprised to see someone as young as you demonstrate the ability to control the rise and fall of the song so well. Do you have another piece prepared?"

"Yes, Your Highness." I bowed my head. "I have two more pieces to complete my performance, if it so pleases you."

"Continue." She gestured, settling back down upon her seat. The phoenix was now on her lap, and she petted the length of it. Each time she stroked its back, sparks danced from her fingertips.

Before the next song, I pulled my sleeves back and ensured they were fastened appropriately. This was a song that required powerful movements, and I had to be prepared to strike the strings precisely, or else the sound would be lacking. Even though the qín was not a loud instrument—not as capable of commanding a hall as its cousin the zhēng—it was still able to conjure images of thunderous storms and roaring rivers.

My world shrank down to only the seven strings and my ten fingers, to the entirety of my soul laid bare for the listener to hear. The second song I chose was "A Dream of Butterflies." The opening was delicate, a light plucking of the strings. The sound then built upon itself, until it evoked the fluttering of a thousand wings flying over the heads of the audience.

The song told the story of a poet who had a dream he was no longer a man, but instead flew through the forest as a butterfly. He wove in and out of the flowers, and marveled at the sight of the other butterflies. When he woke, he pondered: Was he a man who dreamed of becoming a butterfly, or a butterfly who dreamed of becoming a man?

It was one of my favorite pieces to play, for it was vibrant and joyful. I envisioned ribbons of colors spilling forth from the qín, as vivid as the many banners that hung in the palace.

When the final note faded and I dared to look at the crowd again, it was still Jinglang's face I sought first. He was smiling fully now, clapping along with the rest of the guests. A sign I was still performing well, and it pleased me to see it.

"Wonderful!" The consort's delight was evident, and I was relieved that another song had received her approval.

For the last song, I hesitated. I could play "Plum Blossoms Three," three variations on the sweet-natured beauty of the plum blossom. Or I could play the song that Danrou recommended, the one that had once entertained the Celestial Court. I decided to heed her advice. If I was to remain at the manor, at least then she would recognize I had taken her suggestion into account.

I took a deep breath and stilled my mind as the hall faded away from my notice. The sound that came from the qín was the feel of the evening breeze, the sway of the flowers below the deep indigo sky as they reached up toward the moonlight. "The Night-Blooming Flowers." A Flower Spirit danced, accompanied by the song of the nightingale. She only sang for the one she had grown to love, the one ever so present in her heart. All of the other flowers had fallen asleep, but sleep eluded her.

> *The fragrance drifting upon the night*
> *I sing to the night blooms*
> *Only they know my dreams . . .*
> *How I love the vast stillness of the evening*
> *And the singing of the nightingale . . .*
> *I embrace the one that I dream of*
> *Kissing the flowers as if I am kissing her*

I poured myself into the song, imagining myself as the Spirit spinning, fingers held up to the moon. The music wrapped its strands around me, the melody a caress. It sang of love at a distance, of soft and tender wanting.

Applause filled the hall even before I lifted my hands off the strings. I had poured my all into this performance, everything that I had. My head buzzed with the dizzying feeling of accomplishment, the overwhelming rush of relief that it was over. But when I looked at Jinglang, he wore a stricken expression I had never seen before, and he did not meet my eyes. He pushed away from the table, and it gave a loud screech as it scraped against the floor. He staggered to his feet, a shattered man, barely holding himself together. The applause slowed to nothing as members of the audience stared.

"My . . . my apologies, Your Highnesses, for having to take l-leave during your celebration. I f-fear I am feeling . . . unwell." He stumbled over his words, like he was about to be violently ill.

"Of course, Jinglang!" The consort looked down at him, alarmed. "Shall I send for the physician?"

"No, please, don't let me disrupt the festivities," he said quickly, and he turned and strode toward the exit, as if he couldn't bear to be there a moment longer. He brushed by Danrou. Everyone watched him leave, but she alone kept her eyes on me.

She grinned then, slowly. A smile that stretched from ear to ear, unable to contain her triumph.

I knew perfectly well then what had happened.

I had been betrayed.

All the warmth and good feeling that had bloomed in the wake of my performance drained out of me, leaving only a sense of dread. I had done something wrong, but I did not know what. Only that I now stood alone to face the judgment of the consort, when the duke had told me he would stay.

"Now rise, Mortal," the consort commanded.

I forced myself to move, even as my mind remained in chaos. I stood in front of my qín, hands clasped before me, awaiting her decision. Would I live another day, or had I doomed myself to death by the Cliffs of Sundering?

"Your name?" she asked.

"I am called Guxue," I responded, casting my gaze downward, like I was instructed by Lingwei.

"You may look upon me when I am addressing you," the consort said, and I lifted my gaze to meet hers. I watched as she descended the steps slowly, shining with a soft glow. Her sleeves trailed behind her, the color of pale dawn light, awakening the world from its slumber. *Celestials are splendid in appearance*, I reminded myself, *but they are also fickle and cruel*. We were pets to them, like how Mortals in turn would regard dogs. We may please them, but it was a fondness rather than respect.

"I am pleased with the way you performed. Jinglang was right in what he saw. There is a Spark in you. A connection between the playing in your audience that felt like a communion of souls." She smiled at me, gorgeous and terrible, and I trembled before her. The phoenix swept down from the throne like a living flame, and landed upon her shoulder.

I performed the half bow of acknowledgment. "Thank you, Highness."

"I will bestow upon you the name of Jiaoliao, Winter's Wren, a song-bird that sings the most pleasing tune. To honor the lineage of Lady Hè, who brought you to my attention," the consort proclaimed. "Because you have pleased me, I will grant you an invitation to the palace when you are ready to perform again. A set of your choosing."

I sank to my knees and performed the bow of deep respect, touching my forehead again to my clasped hands on the floor. I should be happy at this, thrilled that my music had so moved her, that I had survived to this point. Yet all I could think of was Jinglang's expression as he fled the hall. The hurt and the devastation I saw there.

"We are grateful for your blessings and this highest honor." There was a brush of feathers against my arm, and Lady Hè's silver robe glittered in the light as she settled into a bow beside me. Her hand clamped down on my wrist as she pulled me to stand. She kept that careful pressure upon me, just on the cusp of pain, to remind me who was in control.

We were dismissed, and Lady Hè led me to her table. I was forced to kneel upon a cushion beside her, and given a plate of my own. The gift-giving ceremony continued. The courses had moved to desserts. Roasted chestnuts sweetened with syrup. Hot red bean soup warmed with ginger and other spices that tingled my nose. Various types of dried fruit dusted with sugar.

"You'll accept the hospitality of the consort if you know what's good for you," Lady Hè murmured next to me. She maintained a pleasant expression on her face, but her tone was cold and forceful. "Eat."

A command, not a suggestion, so I ate. I placed a piece of fruit upon my tongue and let the sugar dissolve, but all I tasted was sourness. The ache of being left behind, to be subject to the attention of the woman who had only ill will toward me.

"You did better than I thought you would," she said, still speaking through that placid smile. "I had hoped to witness your demise, but you held your tongue and did not pierce my pretty lie. I can acknowledge you're made of stronger stuff than I originally anticipated."

"I'm sorry to disappoint," I said, knowing it was petulant, and yet I did not care.

She let out a bark of laughter. "Yes, initially I thought you would be like that Ruilan. A delicate flower, so easily crushed by the weight of the world."

My heart twisted again, remembering how the duke had called out her name when he held me after the ravager attack. Ruilan, the memory of whom seeped into the very walls of my rooms.

"You know of her, right? Jinglang's betrothed." Her voice was sneering. "A tribute from the Flower Clan. Why Jinglang's father wanted our lineage to comingle with that tainted family, I will never know. If he had listened to me, then things would have been very different." Instead of disappointed, she sounded oddly triumphant, like she was pleased things had turned out this way. Her husband banished, her intended daughter-in-law dead.

I stirred the bowl of red bean soup with my spoon, watched the pieces bob up and down as she continued to talk. Her insistence that it was just a matter of time before the sovereign would see her loyalty, and her clan would be returned to their former glory.

"Join me and redeem yourself," she offered. "We always welcome those who are willing to devote themselves to the cause of the Faction of Tranquility. If you are willing to rise above the lowly status of your birth and discard the burden of the Mortal Affliction, then someday you may be selected for ascendancy. You'll find yourself pure, renewed.

"What do you say, Guxue?" Lady Hè grinned, showing two rows of perfect, white teeth. Her eyes shone with the devotion of a zealot. "Are you willing to take a step toward transformation?"

CHAPTER THIRTY-FIVE

I STRUGGLED TO MAINTAIN CONTROL OF MYSELF. My face, my body, my words. I wanted to scream at her, to ask her if she actually believed in all of her self-righteous lies. But most of all, I wanted to hit her. I wanted to return that slap she gave me upon our first meeting, to have her feel that pain blossom on her face, and let her know what I thought of her "offer."

Instead, I ducked my head and remained demure, forced myself to speak quietly. "I will have to respectfully decline. I would not want to lower the standards of your illustrious ranks by joining them."

"I'll have someone break all of your fingers," she said coolly, without missing a beat. "We'll see how well you'll be able to impress anyone then."

That was the true face behind Celestials' polite smiles and exquisite outfits. It was the baring of teeth, the brandishing of a dagger. Any of them would be willing to slash my throat and stand over my bloody body, grinning all the while.

"High Priestess!" an overly enthusiastic voice sounded behind us. I'd never been happier to see Prince Zhou.

"I don't believe this is your seat, Your Grace," Lady Hè said with narrowed eyes.

Goose bumps appeared on my arms, sensing the animosity rise between them. I knew somehow that her hatred of the prince was even deeper than the one she harbored for me, and my curiosity was piqued even in this dangerous spot I found myself.

"The duke has need of her, therefore I must deprive you of her pleas- ant company," he said, maintaining a cheerful demeanor, and gave a mocking bow.

"I'm not done—" Lady Hè hissed, but I needed no other encourage- ment. I was already halfway to my feet, rescuing my qín in the process.

"I must insist," Prince Zhou said forcefully, and placed his hand upon my arm. "The duke is waiting."

Lady Hè's face turned faintly pink at this obvious slight, but I did not see her response as we were already walking down the length of the hall, then through the double doors. I welcomed the cool night air and stopped at the railing, trying to take gulping breaths as my legs quivered with fear. He pressed his hand against my back, and though I wanted to tell him to keep his hand to himself, I saw how serious he appeared. Like I'd never seen him before.

"Walk," he said, voice low and urgent, even as he gave a pleasant smile and nodded at a passing couple who glanced at us with interest. We moved again, quickly, down the steps. "Walk as if your very life depends on it."

WE STOOD UPON the platform where the carriage had left us earlier. The moon was a crescent above us, partially obscured by misty clouds. The palace was still as magnificent as ever, but now that I had escaped it, it would forever loom ominous in my memories. As the place where I was brought forward and judged.

I waited for the appearance of those great golden steeds, but instead the prince brought his fingers to his lips and whistled. For a moment, there was nothing, and then a giant bird swooped down from the sky. It was the size of a carriage, about the height of two people.

I stumbled back and screamed, remembering the ravager that almost drank my life force dry, but Prince Zhou's hand covered my mouth, obscuring the sound.

The bird folded its wings against its body and stood there, looking down at us with too-intelligent eyes. It was impossibly large. I did not like the sharpness of its brilliant yellow beak, as if it could take off my head in one bite. It preened at its dark brown plumage, speckled with gold. Upon the feathers of its chest was the shape of a white star.

When Prince Zhou was certain I would not scream, his hand dropped from my face.

"What . . . what is it?" I asked.

"*She* is our transport back to the Meng Estate," Prince Zhou said.

"What do you mean?" I regarded the bird, still preening its wing. "Where's the duke?"

"I have no idea. I only said that to get you away from *her*," the prince told me, amused by my discomfort.

He returned quickly to his usual flippant self, behaving as if nothing and no one could bother him. "I flew here on a conjured sword. This is Lingwei's trusted mount, Bailu, whom she has graciously loaned us for the evening."

The bird, having heard her name, looked up and regarded the prince with a chirp.

"Unless you want to fly with me on the sword." He lifted his brow suggestively. "I will have to hold on to you tightly, for fear you may lose your balance."

"Why must you be like this all the time!" I snapped, finally at my limit. Between his lewd insinuations and Lady Hè's threats and the duke's disappearance, I felt as if I was on the verge of collapse.

"Bailu it is, then!" he said cheerfully, and whistled again.

Bailu bent her head forward. Prince Zhou snapped his fingers and my qín floated above me, before settling upon my back. It was secured to me with strands of conjured rope before I could mutter more protests. I was helped onto Bailu's back with a push from the prince. Her back was broad, and shifted under my feet from side to side as she tossed her head. The prince vaulted up and stood beside me.

Prince Zhou gestured, and a golden collar settled around Bailu's neck and golden reins appeared in his hands.

"You'll want to hang on to me," he said, glancing over his shoulder at me, but without the smirk now. He tugged on the reins and we rose into the air with two flaps of those great wings. I tried to keep my balance, standing on top of the bird's back, and placed one hand upon the prince's shoulder to steady myself. It was disorienting as we flew over the treetops. I tried to look back at the palace, but as we moved swiftly away from it, the feeling made me so ill I had to use my other hand to grab his arm so that I did not topple over.

"It takes some getting used to," he said, a little sympathy in his gaze.

I forced myself to look up as the trees flew past us, and we broke through the clouds. I gasped at the view before us. We hovered in the air under the dome of the night sky. The stars were brilliant, countless, dazzling my vision. We moved forward now, and the clouds beneath us clustered together in a stream, like a road pointing the way, and at last the dizziness subsided.

"It's breathtaking," I mumbled, reluctant to admit it.

"To a Mortal, I suppose, this would be impressive," Prince Zhou said.

"Even you cannot spoil this for me," I told him. I craned my neck as far back as possible to follow the stream of stars that arched overhead, like a bridge across the sky.

He chuckled and then glanced at me again. "I did not mean for it to be rude. I travel this way when I desire solitude. It's a familiar sight for me."

I wanted to say something sharp again, because he always enjoyed goading me into reacting. But instead I sighed. I should make peace with him. For he was the one who saved me tonight, even though he could have left me at the party to continue to be tormented by Lady Hè.

"Thank you for rescuing me, Prince Zhou," I finally told him, even as it grated me to say it.

"You can call me Chenwen." He said with great mirth. "I like to be called by name when a pretty lady insults me."

I scowled at him. I doubt he would ever stop being so . . . infuriating. Then, before I could respond, he added, "I thought you were handling yourself just fine. The entire hall could tell that Her Eminence was on the verge of strangling you, and the consort would have been most displeased if you were to die during her celebration."

"You're not an admirer of the High Priestess, then?" I said. Interesting.

He shrugged. "Who knows what sort of person could be swayed by that viper's lies."

"I thought you would be, considering the two of you appeared to follow the same tenets," I commented.

"And what tenets would those be?" he asked, head pivoting in my direction, suddenly curious.

"Believers in the 'Mortal Affliction.'" I could not even utter those two words without disgust rolling off my tongue.

"Ah." He snorted. "It may surprise you to know I have very little in common with Lady Hè. She tried to drown me when I was young."

"But you're a Celestial," I said, not understanding. He should have been welcomed into those illustrious ranks.

"I was abandoned as a baby. Appeared one day floating in the reflecting pool of a palace garden. The consort was the one who found me. She took pity on my pathetic appearance and took me in as her ward. When I was still a helpless child, the Ordinance soldiers seized me, and Lady Hè pushed me into the River of Cleansing that ran through the temple gardens. She thought I was Demon-born, a spy sent to destroy them."

"Did they ever find your parents?" I asked, horrified that they had tried to do that to one of their own, and a child, no less.

"I was the result of a forbidden tryst between a minor star who worked in the Grand Library and a visiting Flower Spirit who had a broken betrothal." He tried to keep his voice light, but I stood close enough to see the twitch of his jaw that made it obvious he cared. "They were both executed for breaking the tenets."

"I'm sorry."

"They broke the rules, knowing the cost if anyone ever found out. I was the consequence."

"If your parents were murdered because of these tenets, how could you follow them? How could you be their enforcer?" I blurted.

"I do what needs to be done," he said grimly. "To protect those I care for."

"And who do you care for?" With the way he presented himself, it seemed like he cared for nothing and no one. But I was beginning to suspect it was all a ruse—that he cared in a way that necessitated hiding his true intentions, for the sake of survival.

He smirked then, the stars reflected in his eyes, and said, ever so softly, "Jinglang. Lingwei. Ruilan. The three of them, I would die for." He made it sound like a joke, a trivial thing, but I knew he meant it with the entirety of his being. "I owe them a debt. I caused the divide in the Meng family. The former duke saved me, and spoke for me against his wife."

Except Ruilan was gone now. He could not protect her. Something else shone in his eyes—a glimmer of sadness.

"I was wary of you because I thought you were like the type of Mortals that usually made their way into the Celestial Realm. They want nothing more than to shed their Mortal shell. They always believe they are able to endure anything to remove themselves of the taint of human emotion," he said. "But not many of them can withstand the Trial of Ascension. When faced with the weight of all they despise, they cannot bear the burden of it."

In the texts I'd read, the Trial of Ascension was vaguely referred to, but there was no description of the process of it. Only that it was one of the most painful tests to be experienced, and that very few ever survived it.

"But they would become Celestial, would they not? If that is their goal, what is wrong with that ambition? Is it so different from the Spirit Tributes?"

"You've been studying." He nodded, acknowledging my efforts. "Spirit Tributes are selected young, tested for their Celestial potential. They're trained for the role, prepared, and their cultivation begins when they are sent to the Celestial Realm. Naturally, those with greater affinity for the role will advance through their training. It takes decades, if not centuries, of cultivation. It's the brevity of Mortal life that puts you at a disadvantage."

"You could fail then, after centuries of cultivation," I said. "You could fail to become a Celestial."

"Yes, I suppose you could."

With a cry, Bailu began her descent, and we passed through the clouds. Beneath us a river snaked through a vast gorge, and then I noticed the estate in the distance. I was almost relieved to see it.

"It does not seem fair," I said quietly.

He did not ask what I was referring to. Whether it was the short life of Mortals, or how centuries of study and training could not guarantee that a Spirit could become a Celestial. Or that a baby could be abandoned at birth, even though a Celestial baby sounded like a rare and precious life. All of it seemed unfair.

Chenwen jumped off Bailu's back, and extended his hand up toward me to help me off the bird.

"Be careful, Xue," he said, addressing me for the first time by name. "The thread of your fate brought you here. To this estate, to Jinglang's side. I do not know why. I am only certain of this: Someone on the Meng Estate caused Ruilan to Turn. If you are involved in some ploy to harm him, then there is nothing that will save you from my wrath."

"I was brought here to help him, not harm him."

"Then we will get along, you and I," the prince said with a wry smile.

He was still holding my hand, a moment longer than necessary, searching my face as if looking for an answer there.

"Jinglang has been lost for a long time," he finally said. "He needs to find his way. If you are truly here, as you say, to help him, then help him."

"How?"

"That I cannot tell you, only that I would owe you a debt too if you can resolve whatever burden he has forced himself to carry."

With a bow, he returned to stand upon Bailu, the golden reins once again in his hands, and then they were gone.

INTERLUDE

ON THE SUBJECT OF MORTAL ASCENSION

It is well known that the Mortal Realm is where the remainder of the Corruption lingers. It cycles through the Mortal kingdoms, causing war and strife. With the brevity of their existence, they suffer through all of the forbidden emotions, and it is through this suffering that they enter the cycle to be cleansed and begin anew. It is the Mortal essence, the cycle of birth and rebirth, that powers the realms. We should all be aware of this. Though Mortals' lives are brief, some may still shine with brilliant possibility.

In the wisdom of the Heavenly Mother, she extended the grace of the Trial of Ascension as her final blessing. For Mortals who devote their lives to the pursuit of transcendence, who are willing to discard the trappings of Mortal existence, they will be offered the Trial.

They will undergo great pain, the highest peaks of suffering, endure physical, mental, and spiritual agonies, and emerge anew.

Inside every living soul there exists a Spark.

A Celestial potential.

—From *Handbook of the Celestial Realm*

CHAPTER THIRTY-SIX

I MADE MY WAY BACK TO MY RESIDENCE, FEELING A weariness in my soul that I had not felt before. I wondered, briefly, where the duke was, though I suspected he may not want to see me now. Though we unlocked two of the three memory jewels, we had made no progress in resolving the mystery of what was contained within them. I'd survived the performance, and yet offended the duke. I did not know how he would treat me when he saw me next, if he believed that I chose that song on purpose to spite him.

In my receiving room, I untied the knots that allowed me to carry the qín upon my back, set it carefully in its place on the wall. Returning to my inner chamber, I sat at the dressing table and pulled the pins out of my hair, letting it fall in waves around my shoulders. I brushed my hair to ease the tightness on my scalp and tried to let the repetitive motion soothe my messy thoughts.

I heard the sound of the xiao again, low and melodic. This time, it was close. Almost like it came from just over the wall. I stood, drawn to that irresistible melody. Was it magic? I didn't know, only that it beckoned me to heed its call.

My feet followed the sound down the corridor and into the wild garden. Although it was no longer wild.

I shouldn't have been surprised when I saw Jinglang standing there. He was the one who played the flute, who was capable of drawing out such sadness. Grief and remembrance. I could almost taste the salt of tears whenever I heard it, lulling me to sleep.

He must have loved her deeply, to be able to play like this, I realized.

The song ended, and he turned to see me there. He looked as if he wanted to say something, but the words were caught in his throat. I knew the weight of that loss, the weight of that grief, and I could not bring myself to ask him why he left. He just looked like he needed me, so I walked to him in the moonlight, closing the distance between us.

I put my arms around him and said nothing at all.

Around us, the snow began to fall, silently and steadily. The tree branches glimmered once again with frost. Everything was quiet and still except for the rise and fall of our breathing. It was as if there was only the two of us in all the world.

With the span of several breaths, I felt his arms go around me, hesitant, returning my embrace. There was the warmth of his breath upon my hair as he rested his cheek against the top of my head.

"This was where she Turned," he said, after what felt like a long time.

"Ruilan?" I asked. Her name like a stone cast in a still pond, sending out ripples in its wake.

"The garden was where she was happiest," he said. "Most Flower Spirits have an affinity for plants, but she truly had a gift for growing things. If I wanted to find her, I knew she would be here. Hands in the dirt, never caring how she appeared."

I could almost see it, the way this garden would have bloomed if there was someone carefully tending to it. A Spirit who spoke to those flowers like her own children. Riotous blooms that spilled over the walls, that strained for the sun, overtook the trellises. Even in its neglected state, its former glory was still obvious.

"I ordered this place to be closed in, because I could not bear to see it, knowing she was no longer here," he said, still speaking into my hair.

Perhaps I should not be here, holding on to a man whose heart did not belong to me, but I also could not bring myself to pull away.

"You cared for her very much," I said, even as it hurt to say it.

He pulled away then, as if reminded of the distance that should be between us. Jealousy rose up inside of me, that ugly feeling. They all said Ruilan was a gentle, lovely girl, that she was too soft for the world and the world was too cruel to her. That the Meng family owed her a debt that could never be repaid. I braced myself for the inevitability of what was to come. To be told I was someone who dared to want something that was impossibly out of reach, someone who could never be mine.

"Lingwei told me earlier today I was being foolish," he said. "I did not understand what she meant then. But I knew it when I heard you play her song, and that's why I left."

"What do you mean?" I whispered, wanting it to make sense. Wanting him to do it quickly and sever whatever it was that I felt growing between us.

"She always sang that song to herself when she worked in the garden. "The Night-Blooming Flowers." When you played it, all of those memories came back. I couldn't protect her." His shoulders drooped then. "Did you hear the rumor? They all say she made the choice to Turn, because I was the one who was about to break our betrothal, and doing so, I broke her heart."

"Was it true?" I asked. I couldn't see him discarding his duty and his responsibilities. He was the one who took on the role of the Duke of Dreams, even though he had been apprenticed to become something else. Even though he never mentioned the loss, I knew that he was committed to his shīfù's teachings, that he wanted to assist in the making of the Mortal Tapestry.

"Celestial marriages are not for love, but for children. We all

273

understood that, but she told me she could never be that person for me. She had no desire to bear children. She did not want to be with any man, and so she asked me to let her go. I had known it for a long time that she cared for me the same way I cared for her," he said slowly, insistently, as if he was desperate for me to finally understand. "Do you know now what I mean? I care for her like I care for Lingwei, like a brother's love for a sister."

"Oh." That was all I could say.

He turned back to me then, and I should say something, yet I had no words. My mind still wondered what he meant by telling me all of this, and I was still in disbelief his love for Ruilan was a very different type of love than I had thought it to be. He took a step closer and carefully placed his hands upon my shoulders, held me so delicately, like he thought I would break free and run.

My heart beat a little quicker at his touch.

"This is where you would ask me, if it was something you wanted to know . . ." He hesitated, then with that slight quirk to the corner of his lip, went on. "You could ask me, 'And how is that different from the way you care for me, Jinglang?' and I would have an answer for you."

I sensed his nervousness then, this fragile feeling blooming between us, and I hesitantly returned the smile. "And how is that different from the way you care for me?"

"Jinglang," he prompted, and it was I who tried to pull away, because he asked for too much, because he teased me like this, when I'd never felt this way before for anyone.

Gently he pulled me back, shoulders shaking now with mirth. "You would ask everyone on the estate to call you by name, but you would not address me by mine."

All I could think of was Danrou's reprimands. The way she continually reminded me of my status, of all that was *proper*. Then I thought about how she looked after I played the song, when she had asked me to trust her, then stabbed me in the back. I thought about the judgment of all of those Celestials, and anger flared inside of me. What was the point of propriety when they already believed that I was less than, that I was impure? I had behaved carefully in such a way all of my life, followed every rule of survival, and it wasn't enough. It would never be enough.

He noticed my change of mood then, and his expression shifted from teasing to serious. "If you don't feel the same—"

I reached up and pulled him toward me. Damning us both to this feeling. When our lips touched, it was hesitant at first, unfamiliar. Then it quickly grew to something deeper, the yearning having finally found a release, like a plant reaching for the sun. His hands tangled in my hair, pulling me closer as well, returning my urgency.

We broke the kiss a few moments later, and he had that small smile on his face. One of secret knowing. Still with that smile upon his lips, he cupped my face with one hand and brushed my cheek tenderly with his thumb. I knew he was reminded of the last time he touched me like this, after Lady Hè struck me.

"Xue'er . . . ," he said softly. "I care for you in a way where I look forward to your letters, found myself pacing my room if one arrived late. I care for you in a way that I find it impossible to pay attention to anything else when you are in the room. I care for you in a way that I fear what the court and what my mother might do if it were ever discovered. I care for you, and I am afraid."

He closed his eyes and drew me closer, so that I settled against him, my head on his shoulder.

"I am afraid they will do to you what they did to Ruilan. When she was brought to the Meng Estate, my father placed her hand in mine and told me it was my job to care for her now. I don't know why she took to me then, but she followed me everywhere. To the point where those who knew us called her Yingzi, my little shadow, and I promised I would keep her safe—"

"Wait," I interrupted him. I pulled away and looked at him warily, half convinced I had misheard. "What did you say she was called?"

He looked down at me, puzzled. "Yingzi."

My throat was suddenly dry. "You said she spent most of her days in the garden, planting things in the dirt?"

He nodded.

"And . . . did she have a mole, right here?" I pointed at a spot upon my cheek, just below my right eye.

"Yes . . ." He pointed at the same spot on his own face.

"That's impossible," I whispered. "I met her here. In this garden. She called herself Yingzi. She said she took care of this garden, in particular."

He looked stricken then. "You met her? How?"

I quickly explained to him what I remembered of her, in as much detail as I was able to recall. Her flightiness, her eagerness to hide from others.

"My father spoke of this before," he said, rubbing his temple, thoughtful. "Similar to the magic of the making of memory jewels. Dreams . . . they're not so different from memories, after all."

He began to pace then before me, muttering to himself. "He said sometimes a violent event, one that evoked great emotion, could create a split in the soul. A shadow memory. This garden was where Danrou said she witnessed Ruilan Turning after she found out I was rescinding our betrothal. It made no sense for her to Turn, because it was what she begged me for, what we agreed on, and yet . . ."

He stopped and asked, "Do you know how to play the xiao?"

I nodded. Even though it was nowhere near my ability with the qín, I still retained some of that skill.

"Can you play 'The Night-Blooming Flowers'?" His words took on a slight edge of desperation. "I'll try to use it to find what remains of her."

I nodded again. He conjured the xiao into his hand and handed it to me. I brought it to my lips. Blew one practice note, winced, and then tried again, until I found the opening of the song.

How I love the vast stillness of the evening
And the singing of the nightingale . . .

CHAPTER THIRTY-SEVEN

THE TREES BEGAN TO SWAY IN THE SMALL GARDEN, then tremble. Leaves tumbled and swirled, skittering across our feet. Above our heads, the sun rose and set and the moon rose and set. I could feel that shift of magic, pulsating through the notes of the song.

I closed my eyes and recalled my memory of Yingzi. How she showed me her beloved flowers. How she pruned their stems carefully, plucked out any of the wilted heads, cleaned them by hand. How she called them all by name.

I embrace the one that I dream of . . .

I opened my eyes again as the song drew to an end. Jinglang stood there with both of his hands turned up to the sky, light and shadow dancing across his face. Stars shifted in his eyes, and he appeared like a god, like something wild and mesmerizing.

Somewhere through the trees, a voice sang thinly, echoing back: *"Kissing the flowers as if I am kissing her . . ."*

Yingzi—*Ruilan*—the girl I met in the garden. She stepped into the clearing, beneath the sky that was now a brilliant canopy of stars. She nodded at me in greeting, then turned to Jinglang with a smile.

"Took you long enough! I knew you would find me."

He stood there, rooted in place, staring at her in disbelief.

There was a peculiar quality to her appearance. The starlight seemed to catch in her hair, making her glow. She appeared almost translucent, not like she had appeared before in the garden. She had always been a little sleepy, slightly distracted. It made sense then, why the servant girl didn't know her when I asked after her, why she always hid when the others were around.

"You jumped off the Platform of Forgetting," he choked out.

"Did I?" Yingzi lowered her head sadly. "I'm the memory of her before that. I remember being worried for you, those days. After you found out about your father's punishment. After they sent him to the tower and threatened him with your safety. The chain the sovereign made you wear when he made you swear your allegiance . . . I was scared for you then."

"But what happened to you?" He stepped forward. "Why did you Turn? Tell me what happened!"

"She brought me news that you were about to break off our engagement," she said. "I was happy, but she did not like to see me happy. She said her mistress would not be pleased. I did not care. I had finally achieved my cultivation and formed my own inner core. She could not control me any longer."

"Who?" Jinglang's hand clenched into a fist. "I'll kill her."

"Danrou," I whispered, the name already formed on my tongue. What I'd thought was grief lashing out was actually guilt.

"Yes, my friend." Ruilan turned to me. "She pushed me down. She said all of their hard work would be for nothing, and that it was my responsibility to marry the duke. But then it did not matter, for I would be punished." Her hand went to her throat, as if it pained her to remember.

"Danrou's hands changed into claws, even though she was only a sparrow. It was like nothing I had ever seen before. I realized then she had already been changed into a Celestial. She was stronger than I expected. She forced me to eat it, forced it down my throat, and I changed . . ."

"What?" Jinglang asked. "What did she make you eat?"

"*Bloodred begonia blooms at twilight,*" she quoted. "That is the Celestial poison. Why it was banned. Why they don't want you to remember . . ." She began to fade, even as Jinglang reached for her, trying to keep her there. Her hands passed through his, and she shook her head sadly.

Until she was only a pale specter, disappearing into the night.

Jinglang fell to his knees and wept.

Petals rained from the sky, as if the manor cried along with its duke. I placed my arms around him, giving him whatever comfort I could offer. As his tears soaked into my shoulder, I stroked his hair, reminded of the time he had once done the same for me.

SOMETIME AFTER, JINGLANG brushed the leaves from his knees and stood again. I rose with him. He seemed troubled as he took the xiao from me and vanished it back to whatever place it was summoned from.

"She would not have wanted to hurt anyone," he said. "She always told me if she Turned into a ravager, she wanted me to stop her."

"It seems like she took it upon herself to ensure it," I said. When cornered, the ravager Ruilan transformed into jumped off the Platform of Forgetting, that's what they all said. "She mentioned that Danrou forced her to Turn, but there was a mistress involved. Someone who gave her direction."

"I had suspected her involvement for some time, but she's been cunning," he said, eyes flashing. "There have been no signs she has completed her cultivation. She has not yet requested to begin the process of her transformation, where she will be presented as a Celestial before the court. As to the identity of her mistress . . ."

He shook his head, then continued. "She has always been a great admirer of my mother, being that they both were born of the Bird Clan. But what did my mother have to gain from Ruilan's Turning . . . ? She'd already won. She proved her loyalty to the Court of Stars by bringing my father to judgment. It makes little sense. Ruilan's Turning only caused further unrest, and suspicions that Demon spies walked among us."

"Danrou believes she has driven a wedge between us with Ruilan's song," I told him. "If we let her continue to believe it, then maybe she will lead us to the person with whom her loyalties lie."

Jinglang pondered this. "I'm not a strategist. Lingwei has always been the more cunning one in our family. But it is worth a try."

I remembered what Chenwen said when he flew with me back to the estate, when he warned me what he would do if I were ever to betray Jinglang. Even though Jinglang's relationship with Lingwei appeared to be tenuous at times, it was obvious they still cared for each other.

"If you are looking for evidence to exonerate your father, then it sounds like you have to go against the court, maybe even the sovereign himself," I said. "It would be prudent to involve those you can trust. You cannot do it alone."

"I've been a fool to believe I could save my father on my own." He sighed. "Now I'm afraid that it will soon be too late."

"As long as he still lives, there will be time," I told him. "You will find something—even if it only delays his execution, it will at least give you more time."

He pulled me close. "I'm grateful for the threads of fate that brought us together," he said to me. "It feels easier now, not having to face it all alone." He kissed me again, and this time it was sweet and lingering.

But all the kisses in the world could not change what we both recognized.

We were running out of time.

JINGLANG ASSURED ME that he would handle Danrou, and when I woke up, there was another maid who attended to me. We agreed that the best course of action would be to swiftly solve the riddle of the third memory jewel. I'd learned so far that I was Celestial-touched and that my thread of fate had deviated. I could not eat, for I felt the heavy sense of unease, the feeling that something terrible was about to happen, but I could not stop it. All I could do was wait for Jinglang to come back to me again, because he said he would do as I suggested and seek out his allies.

I forced myself to put brush to paper again, to note all of the things that I remembered from the second memory. I felt the quote Elder Gao recited to my uncle had to be the solution to finding the next song. *They echo in the mountains to you* . . . The two scenes had involved their love for each other, one of deep understanding, just like the connection between Boya and Ziqi in the stories. They were said to be friends, lovers, and oftentimes both.

I had to go find Zhuxi again. He had assisted me in figuring out the previous song, and with his access to the vast collection of music, he would likely know what I was searching for.

I took the back way again from this wing to the north, mindful still that I was accessing a place that was forbidden to me. I thought it best to keep this knowledge to myself, so that it could not be taken away.

I knocked upon the door, urgently, and he opened it after a time. He greeted me with surprise, and I realized that this, to him, might appear inappropriate.

"I could come back later," I offered, suddenly wondering if I was disrupting his daily routine. But like usual, he welcomed me into the library graciously.

I inquired about any songs that referred to Boya and Ziqi, whether in the music or the accompanying texts. He considered this with his brow furrowed.

"I could think of hundreds of songs, perhaps thousands of texts, that reference their legend, directly or indirectly," he said wryly. "Is the lady looking for something more specific?"

How could I explain the puzzle I was trying to solve without letting him know the purpose? But I decided it was better to be direct than to waste what little time we had.

"The poem I'm looking for ends with, '*but in writing these words / they echo in the mountains to you*,'" I said. "Have you heard of it?"

Zhuxi considered this for a moment before holding up a finger. He turned and walked down the stacks. I assumed that he somehow was able to recall where the reference was in this meticulously organized space. I already knew his mind was as vast as a library in itself.

He reemerged with two scrolls in hand. "I believe one of these might be what you're looking for," he said. "They contain the reference to that snippet of poetry you mentioned."

I gave a deep bow of respect, to the point where he gestured for me to stand, embarrassed.

"Please, do not. I am happy I can be of service," he said.

"You have helped me more than you can ever know," I insisted. If I had to wander these stacks, searching through the shelves, I would be there years later, not any closer to what I was looking for.

He inclined his head in acknowledgment.

"How long have you served the Duke of Dreams?" I asked, suddenly mindful that I did not know very much about him. I'd always rushed in here, demanded things of him, then rushed out again.

He considered this for a pause before responding. "A few hundred years," he said. "I was born in the Kingdom of Zhu."

"The lost kingdom," I said, remembering it from the history books. The kingdom had ended tragically, with a violent coup and the slaughter of thousands.

"Yes," he said, wistful. "The tragic Mortal propensity for violence."

"Are you . . . happy here?" I asked tentatively.

He glanced at me, surprised, and then gave a slow, understanding grin. "I struggled with that very question for the first few years. What did I give up when I decided to face the Trial of Ascension? But now it's been too many years. That life belonged to someone else, long ago. I am here, protecting the Mortal Realm in my own way. By assisting in the cataloging of its art, by ensuring the dreams of Mortals are cared for."

I felt a pang inside of my chest at the thought. He may be able to describe it flippantly, as a life lived long ago, but my brief existence in the Mortal Realm was still clear in my memory. It could be extinguished easily. To these Celestials, I was a breath, a moment. Soon in the Mortal Realm, there may be no one left to remember me either.

"What happens to Demon dreams?" I asked him, another question to satisfy my curiosity.

"Long ago, there was no such thing as the Demon Realm or the Celestial Realm," he replied. "Everyone's dreams were cared for by the duke. That is still the case, but the dreams of Demons are buried deep in the vault below our feet." He tapped his foot against the wooden floor.

"The duke's role in maintaining the realms is essential," Zhuxi continued. "Without the Keeper of the Dreaming, the realms would collapse into one another. Ghosts would haunt the Spirit Realm, and Mortals would be devoured by the monsters from the Barrens."

Disturbed by the thought of that imagined catastrophe, I bowed and took my leave, the two scrolls in hand. On my way out, the title of a book glimmered in the light from the lantern, catching my eye. The one that fell at my feet the first time I visited the archives. *A Tangle of Dreaming*.

Zhuxi's comments had made me curious about the duke and his abilities. I took the book with me to read. Another way I hoped to understand him.

INTERLUDE

A History of the Dreaming

It is known that the weaving of the Mortal Tapestry has grown increasingly challenging the past few centuries as the population of the Mortal Realm has grown. The role of the Duke of Dreams has been ever so challenging to fulfill. The Dreaming is intimately bound to the maintenance of the Mortal Tapestry, threads woven in opposition by the Star of Fortune.

But the responsibilities of the role are significant, and finding those who possess the ability to control the Dreaming without being lost in it has been difficult. To avoid the entanglement in Mortal dreams without experiencing their influence requires a strong will and a deep inner well of magic, for here Corruption has a powerful hold. It feasts on the fears and anxieties of Mortals and spills over into the waking world if there is no one to keep it in check.

As a particularly somber example, when Jinxin, the Third Duke of Dreams, was consumed by the Dreaming, it was said that her loss caused the fall of the Kingdom of Zhu, thirty years before its intended demise. The unraveled threads took centuries to repair.

It is important now to test all Celestial-born, or those with potential for ascension, and mark those with an affinity for walking in the Dreaming, to ensure there is always an heir to this role, in case the current duke is lost.

—From *Handbook of the Celestial Realm*

VERSE FOUR

CHAPTER THIRTY-EIGHT

WITH MY MANUALS IN HAND, I HURRIED TO MY RES-
idence to retrieve my qín. While I was in my chambers, I thought of
Danrou. About the secret she hid from everyone. She had snatched that
comb out of my hand, on the verge of tears as she spoke of Ruilan. Did
she regret what she had done to her mistress, the one she had taken
care of every day, watched over every waking moment?

I pondered this even as I set up my instrument in the garden. Ruilan's
garden. What did Jinglang tell me? Only in the throes of the greatest
despair, a rush of strong emotion, will the soul split into two. One part
of her remaining here, waiting for someone to listen to her story, for the
truth of what happened to her to be discovered.

On a whim, I played "The Song of Remembrance." This was the
other piece that Jinglang had gifted me, the second day when I turned
down his offer to purchase my qín. It seemed apt for this place, a story
about a woman and the remnants of her song that lingered even after she
was gone.

Here I am but you are no longer . . .

When I opened my eyes I saw him there, lips curved again in that
secret, knowing smile.

"I thought I would find you here," he said.

I stood slowly, gripped by a strange fear that he would see things
clearer after a night's rest, realize that what had happened in the dark
was only a moment of weakness. See me for what I truly was in the cold
morning—a Mortal girl, with her short, firefly life.

But he closed the distance between us and greeted me with a gentle brush of his lips against mine, his eyes soft with warmth.

"So I did not dream it," Jinglang murmured. My hand found his, glad that I wasn't the only one who'd worried it was all imagined.

"You've arrived just in time," I told him. "I am about to see if one of these songs will be able to release the last memory jewel. You'll turn the pages for me again?"

He nodded, bringing over the small table and stool that I had requested be set up under the eaves.

"I had Attendant Luo bring in Danrou to assist him with a project at my residence," he said to me as I skimmed through the manual. "He will ensure she is watched, and anything she does out of the ordinary will be reported back to me."

"I'm worried about what she is capable of," I whispered. She had hidden it so well, all this time. Still served, continued her duties, as if nothing had happened. As if she did not hide the darkness inside of her.

"Tonight, I have invited Lingwei and Chenwen to the estate," he told me. "You had suggested I should seek help. Will you join us? We will drink in memory of shīfù, and I will tell them all we have found."

"Of course," I said, pleased he had taken my suggestion into account.

The next song I played was "On Listening to the Qín," a classic tribute to the legend. A reflection for the player of the qín, similar to the poet dreaming of becoming a butterfly. My progress was slow, the notes halted and unsure upon this first practice. I committed myself to playing each note, relying on the feeling inside. There was no echoing response, no insistent tug like I had felt previously when the magic contained in the qín answered. What remained was only disappointment.

"Well?" Jinglang regarded me, and I could sense his eagerness.

"Not this one, but . . . maybe the next will give us what we are looking for."

The second song was "White Moon, River Overlook." Framed around a classic poem, four traditional characters in each line, nine lines in total. A musician takes a qín on a boat and plays an ode to the moon. It is there he meets the woodcutter, listening from the shore, drawn by the longing in the notes. A wistful search for someone who could understand him. From the first notes, there was familiarity to it, like I'd heard this song before, somewhere, long ago.

I thought of those I'd played for. My uncle, who listened with careful attention. Ruilan, who danced as if the music found new meaning through the expression of her movements. Lingwei, who had no interest in music, but patiently sat through my practice sessions. Chenwen, who admitted to grudging appreciation for my playing. And sitting before me, Jinglang, who looked upon me with wonder. I played for them all, the people I cared for, the ones who listened and gave me what every musician craved—an understanding, a resonance, as if for a brief moment, we shared the same dream.

A bell rings from the temple, through the mist
Flying geese and tracks scattered in the snow

The jewel floated above the qín, emanating the same soft glow. Slowly, it drifted downward and settled into my palm.

I worried what this memory would reveal. For a moment, I considered taking this jewel and running, throwing it into the gorge. Despite what Jinglang would think, if he would hate me for not following through, if I would doom myself to never having my freedom. But I was certain that what was hidden in this jewel was nothing good.

"If you were not the Duke of Dreams, who would you want to be?" I asked, suddenly desperate to know. "If you were not responsible for the Dreaming, where would you go?"

I half expected him to laugh, to give a flippant answer, but he replied without hesitation: "I would listen to you play the qín while drifting down the Huali River. I would eat watermelon seeds with you in one of Wudan's finest teahouses, try that spicy noodle dish that you mentioned occasionally craving . . . Before, I couldn't understand why shīfù would be willing to leave the Celestial Realm for the brevity of a Mortal life. But I understand him now."

My heart ached still, remembering what Elder Gao had given up. A life immortal, his Celestial purpose, for my uncle's love, only to be murdered. A lump grew in my throat.

"Soon this will all be over," Jinglang said, placing his hand on mine. "Once we get to the root of the treachery, I'll protect you from whatever may come."

I managed to force a smile, even though I was struck with sadness. "Open it," I said.

"Together." The jewel suddenly became hot, pressed between us, and we were thrust into the memory.

There was no slightly shifting mist this time. We fell into the midst of battle. There were shouts, the sound of weapons striking one another. There was the scent of blood in the air, and on the ground before us there were the bodies of horses. They looked like they had been gored by wild beasts, their sides a bloody ruin.

Jinglang's grasp tightened on mine, and I turned to see my uncle and Elder Gao, leaning against the back of the carriage. They each held swords in their hands, my uncle hesitantly, Jinglang's shīfù with the practiced air of experience. Except his sword no longer had that glow I saw in the previous memory. He had no magic at all. His hair and beard had changed from black to pure white. He looked aged. Mortal.

This must have been after he accepted his punishment, stripped of his title and retired with my uncle. Only to be attacked in the forest. This had to be the final moment of their lives.

A growl rumbled beside us. Another ravager, advancing upon them. And then another guttural moan, approaching from the left. They were surrounded by creatures that defied Mortal comprehension. A deer with antlers that reached toward the sky, but it only had one eye in the center of its long face. The other was a horse with stripes like a tiger, but short, curved horns that protruded from the side of its head like a mountain goat. The deer opened its mouth and let out an inhuman scream.

The sound of music came drifting through the trees, at odds with the violent scene before us. A figure walked through the bamboo forest, dressed in flowing green robes, as if he sprouted from the forest itself. Upon his lips was a slender flute, and he played a slow, mournful melody.

The ravagers snorted and turned their heads, listening to that otherworldly song. There was magic in the sound of the flute—it called to them. It calmed their minds, made them lower their heads obediently. Like trained animals, obeying their master.

The man's face came clear as he stepped closer. I recognized him with a gasp.

Chenwen.

Prince Zhou.

"Why?" Elder Gao cried. "Why must it be you?"

Chenwen strode forward, his face stern. The ravagers flanked him, monstrous creatures waiting for his signal.

"Because you lied," he said simply.

"We did it to protect you!" Elder Gao insisted.

"Don't." Chenwen's face was stony, his voice cold. "I don't want to hear your excuses."

The memory narrowed then. We spun toward the corner of Elder Gao's eye, collected into a single tear, witnessed the formation of the jewel firsthand. We lifted into the sky and flew through the clouds until we came upon the rooftops of the city I knew so well. Wudan. There, we fell, flew past many lit windows with people talking, dancing, singing, until we hovered above a garden.

Below us, we saw a figure—me, practicing, chewing on the corner of my lip as I played the qín. Then we shrank into a small jewel and landed upon the qín's marking. So that was how the final memory jewel had come to be.

We returned to our bodies with a gasp.

Jinglang looked stricken, shadows under his eyes. "It couldn't be him," he whispered. He reached out and steadied himself on my shoulder, like the revelation was too heavy for him to bear. "It couldn't be Chenwen."

"I don't understand," was all I said, all I was able to say. How could the final memory jewel reveal this?

A sudden wind picked up in the garden. The leaves rustled, the branches swayed back and forth. The manuals were blown off the table and struck the ground one by one. Jinglang bent down and picked one up. I gathered the other two, dusted off the dirt the best I could.

Beside me, Jinglang remained silent, and stared down at the book in his hand intently. As if he expected it to suddenly speak to him.

"What's wrong?" I asked, disturbed by the look on his face. I almost said, *You look like you've seen a ghost.* But in the Celestial Realm, there were no such thing as ghosts . . .

"Where did you get this book?" he whispered. I recognized the cover then: *A Tangle of Dreaming*.

"I got it from Zhuxi," I said. "At the Archive of Dreams."

"That's impossible!" he snapped, his sudden anger lashing out at me like a whip.

"I—" I faltered. Danrou had said the north wing was banned to visitors; was he upset that I had trespassed in an area of the estate that was not permitted to me? "It was Ruilan who sent me there. She told me to go and find him, to ask for *Twilight's Begonia*. He's been helping me find the songbooks."

The anger shifted to confusion, then to pain. "You couldn't have spoken to Zhuxi. He was my father's apprentice. They threw him off the Cliffs of Sundering, called him my father's collaborator in creating unrest in the realms."

"I spoke to him earlier this morning," I said in disbelief. "He handed me those manuals."

"When the tribunal investigated my father, they tore through the residence for evidence of collaboration or communication with the Demon Realm," he continued. "They said they found it here. A portal to the Demon Realm."

Even though nothing that happened in the Meng Estate should surprise me anymore, I found myself not knowing whether to laugh or to weep.

"Walk with me." I grabbed his hand. "Let's see for ourselves."

Jinglang let me lead him down the corridor, and with each step, my heart grew heavier. These Celestials and their lives immortal, their long memories. I'd only caught a glimpse of their existence, and it already seemed unbearable. All their pent-up longings, their unfulfilled desires, their hidden heartbreaks.

What were their memories, if not ghosts of a different form?

CHAPTER THIRTY-NINE

THE COURTYARD OF THE RESIDENCE OF HOPEFUL
Dreaming was still half in shadow, even though it was supposed to be midday. Most of the time I hurried through this place, fearful of being discovered, but now, paying attention to my surroundings, I could see the remnants of the raid that Jinglang had mentioned. Statues toppled, trees cut down, debris piled in the corners . . . How had I not noticed this?

But when we entered the bamboo hallway, I already knew that the archive was gone. Before, the path was cleanly swept and tidy, the bamboo green and healthy against the wall. Now part of the railing that protected the bamboo was broken, fallen against the wall. The tiles were cracked underfoot, uneven.

"The condition of this place . . ." Jinglang pulled away from me and reached out to touch the scorch marks upon the wall. "The estate is tied to the magic of its owner, and with my abilities restricted, I repaired what I could and had to let the rest fall to ruin." It was obvious he blamed himself, saw all of this as a clear sign of his failure.

"Once you find the evidence to exonerate your family," I told him, "then you can work on restoring what you are able."

He had no reply. I turned my attention to the door instead. It hung sideways, almost split in half, the intricate carving upon it ruined. I was the one who reached out and pushed it aside, wary of what I would discover within.

The room was a ruin. Shelves were toppled over, collapsed on themselves. The once lovely, delicate treasures were on the floor, smashed and destroyed. The scrolls of calligraphy and landscapes that hung on the wall had been torn down and were covered with dirty footprints. There was no scent of incense, no trickle of soothing water, no slight tinkling of wind chimes. I ventured forward, down the full length of the room. It was once filled with books, scrolls stacked upon one another, following some unknown method of cataloguing that only Zhuxi understood.

"They burned it all," Jinglang said behind me, his voice slightly raspy with emotion. "They tossed all the scrolls of dreaming into the vault, and burned the rest. The entirety of his collection, his catalogs of music and poetry and history, destroyed as evidence of Corruption."

"I saw what it looked like whole. So many stories and poems and songs contained within this room . . ."

I despaired at its loss. At how much a labor of love this undertaking had to be, even for a Celestial with magic in his grasp. It made me angry. They saw all of these books as worthless, easily discarded, yet they were incapable of creating their own.

"But the books he gave me were *real*." I turned to him, insistent. "You turned the pages for me yourself. *Twilight's Begonia, White Moon, River Overlook*. They were real!" I'd held them in my hands. Touched them. Read from their pages. Were they just a dream as well?

"The books!" His eyes lit up as he pulled *A Tangle of Dreaming* once again from his sleeve. "This was my father's. It contained all of his notes on navigating the Dreaming. Some part of his magic or Zhuxi's magic must still remain here. I thought it was lost forever when they tore through these archives."

He opened the book and the pages began to turn of their own accord, faster and faster, gaining speed, until it was a blur. Then, as soon as it happened, it stopped, remaining open on a single page. We both leaned forward.

"'On the formation of memory jewels,'" he read aloud.

A memory jewel is formed from the experience of powerful Celestial emotion. That memory is expelled in the form of a tear and contains a shard of the Celestial's soul. There are many purposes for the capturing of these memories, such as passing knowledge from parent to child or teacher to student. A jewel may lie dormant and is only accessible to its owner or its intended recipient, carried away or protected as a treasure. Other times, the memory becomes tied to a particular place, made unwillingly, sometimes unknowingly, by the Celestial it originated from. I call these portals "slivers."

These moments are controlled by an alternate self, usually created by great loss and suffering—perhaps as a way for the Celestial to endure that traumatic event. It is unpredictable who the memory will accept into that other place, though as a Keeper of the Dreaming, I've encountered them many times in my wanderings. Perhaps they sense who I am and they believe I will listen to their stories. For memories often influence dreams, and dreams sometimes are not so different from memories.

But whether it is a jewel or sliver, its magic is ultimately tied to the Celestial it originated from. If that Celestial fades, the jewel and the sliver will also be no more.

Our eyes met above the book.

"This means . . . ," he said, breathless, almost as if he was afraid to utter it. "This means they might still be alive."

"If your shīfù still lives, perhaps my uncle does as well," I gasped.

"When they told me his carriage was burned, his body was unrecognizable. They identified him only because of his belongings. His books."

Jinglang's face lit up with the possibility.

"And Ruilan . . . ," he said. "Ruilan may still live. The Flower Clan petitioned for one of their own to investigate, claiming mistreatment, and the Acolytes of Protection and Balance searched the realms upon direction from the sovereign. They never found her body . . . nor Zhuxi's. The cliffs may have removed his Celestial form, but he may be somewhere out there, perhaps Mortal once more, having forgotten who he used to be!"

We laughed then, held one another, filled with hope that this might be true. But our delight did not last long.

"Someone took the time to burn the bodies in the carriage so that it appeared as if shīfù and Elder Tang were dead," Jinglang said, solemn once again. "It could be Chenwen, but what he hopes to gain from this ruse, I do not know."

"And we also have yet to find out who Danrou is loyal to," I added, then I remembered. "Danrou once asked me for a private audience with the prince. This was right before the party. Do you think it could be related?"

"Tonight I was going to place my trust in Chenwen." He frowned. "But I think it is time that we figure out where his loyalties lie, once and for all."

I RETURNED TO my residence and sent away my maid, requesting some time alone. Chenwen's face kept coming up in my mind. Resolute, cold. Different from his usual careless persona. It was all a ruse, to hide his true intentions. Jinglang seemed shaken by what was revealed in the memory jewel, and he had known the man all of his life.

Yet, nothing seemed to align quite right, like a shoe that chafed, slightly too tight. It wore at me the whole time I spent preparing for the evening, because I also remembered the way Chenwen looked at me after we rode Bailu back to the Meng Estate. *The three of them, I would die for.*

I braided my hair and coiled it atop my head, securing it with a pin— one of my own, gifted to me at the House. Tonight, it felt like I would need all the lessons of my life. The stories Uncle taught me. The ways to hear what remained unsaid from Auntie. And my music. The discipline it took to sit there, day after day, night after night, line after line, until the right notes rang true and my body could instinctually recall the movement of a particular piece. I needed to apply the same discipline now, play that memory in my mind, again and again, until I could find the answer.

There was a reason why Elder Gao sent that jewel to me, why they hid them inside *my* qín, why my uncle mailed the letter to Jinglang to start him on the journey to retrace their steps. To find that the Deceiver was free from the Barren Realm.

Was Chenwen under the influence of the Deceiver? Perhaps this was their way of warning us that he was not to be trusted.

I dressed in an outfit of light purple that reminded me of dusk, the color of the horizon right when night was beginning to fall and the stars just appeared in the sky. A color evocative of dreams.

From my dresser drawer I pulled out the three memory jewels. I slipped them into a pouch, and hid it within my sash. It made me feel safer, as if some part of my uncle was accompanying me to face whatever was going to happen tonight.

My maid bowed at the door. "It's time, my lady."

With a hesitant glance at my qín, I left my chambers. Without it I felt naked, defenseless. The dread seeped into me as the night quickly settled around the estate. The lanterns had already been lit, illuminating my way, and yet I still rubbed my hands together, folded my arms across my chest in an effort to keep warm.

I thought the maid would lead me to the hall, but instead, we walked to the north. The gate to the Residence of Hopeful Dreaming was open, and the courtyard had been completely changed from earlier in the day. The leaves were swept, the broken branches removed, the statues cleared. Three figures stood before the doors of the receiving room, talking to one another.

Chenwen. Lingwei. Jinglang.

They turned to look at me as I walked toward them. Lingwei, wearing a smile of welcome. Chenwen, his usual smirk. Jinglang, solemn, and yet a hint of warmth in those dark eyes, something reserved just for me. They appeared like three shining stars, impossibly beautiful. So much so that my Mortal heart ached.

Why? I wanted to shout at Chenwen. *Just when I saw you as an ally, and perhaps even a friend?* My face ached from holding my own smile, my pretense that nothing was wrong, that everything was as it should be. That this was just a gathering between good friends.

Lingwei stepped forward and embraced me, like she hadn't seen me in months, instead of only one evening. *Was it just one night ago I played before the consort?* The palace felt like ages ago.

"I had no doubt that you would make it through," she said. She turned to the prince beside her. "Right, Chenwen? We had no doubt."

"She did well." Chenwen nodded, but of course couldn't resist adding: "I doubted. But only a little."

"Even though I faltered, she did not." Jinglang stepped forward then, and inclined his head toward the prince. "And I must thank you for bringing her back safely."

"You insult me!" Chenwen patted his shoulder with a laugh. "Why such stiff politeness between old friends?"

"That is why I brought us all here, friends old and new, to celebrate tonight," Jinglang said softly. "Once, we had the tradition of sharing a drink to welcome the arrival of another spring. I hope to resume that tradition with you now. Shall we?"

He offered a hand to me, and that slow, irresistible smile.

Lingwei looked at me with delight.

Chenwen arched a brow. "New friends indeed, brother!"

I took Jinglang's hand and stepped closer to him. To be acknowledged, to not be hidden away as a secret. Even though we never spoke of what this new, fragile feeling was growing between us. Never gave a name to it.

Let me remember this moment.

One sweet, precious moment.

Before it all fell to dust.

CHAPTER FORTY

WE STEPPED OVER THE THRESHOLD AND INTO THE receiving room. These rooms were always dark, the doors shuttered whenever I hurried past. What did Ruilan call it? The door with the carving of the bird. The long-legged heron, with its graceful neck, standing in the rushes. After we entered, the doors shut behind us, and we were given our privacy.

Built into the far wall was an ascending series of platforms starting from waist height. On these platforms there were statues of various sizes, interspersed with candles. As the candles flickered, the faces of the statues came into light and then dimmed again. It gave an eerie effect, like the statues were blinking, opening and closing their mouths, caught between light and shadow.

My eyes were drawn to them. Human forms and animal forms, all sorts of shapes. A dragon. A fish. A snake. A turtle. A monkey. Representations of various beings throughout the realms. But their features appeared smeared and incomplete, half-formed, like someone had shaped them from clay and then forgotten to finish them. Like they were made by a child's hand.

"The Wall of Dreamers," Jinglang murmured beside me. "This, at least, the Ziwei Guard spared."

I felt Lingwei come up beside me, Chenwen at her side.

"The three of us were Celestial-born," Lingwei explained to me. "We knew nothing about the bond of family, only that we would grow up on this estate until we cultivated enough magic to become an acolyte or an apprentice. Ruilan, though . . . she remembered what it was like to grow up with a family, and she tried to make us into one."

"This was where she made us take an oath, that we would protect one another," Jinglang said.

"Remember how she trotted behind you, Jinglang?" Chenwen said, chuckling. "She barely reached your shoulder then."

"And when you tried to shoot those thorn arrows at her, she turned them into flowers." Lingwei giggled. "She was so happy. She started calling you Elder Brother, because you also wielded flower magic."

Those who were Spirit-born usually retained their Spirit abilities even after they ascended to their Celestial form, I remembered from the texts. The Celestial-born could specialize, but their affinities were heavily influenced by the parents who birthed them. It made sense then that a child of Lady Hè, like Lingwei, would retain the ability to shapeshift into a swan.

"We'll remember her now," Jinglang said to the wall. "And all we have lost." He let go of my hand and reached for the sticks of incense that were stuck into the brazier set in the center of the wall. An altar. In his hand, a flame flickered, and passed onto the sticks of incense, until their tips glowed red.

The mood grew solemn as we each accepted a few sticks of incense. We turned to face the wall. This, I knew the ritual of—it was similar to how we prayed to the gods in the Mortal Realm. How we prepared our offerings, and let the smoke take our messages up to the Celestial Realm. How funny it was to me now to discover Celestials did the same. Not so different above as it was below, after all.

"All of us dream, whether Spirit-formed or Mortal-born," Jinglang said. "This is the other side of the tapestry, the river that feeds the roots of the great tree, the alternate path that holds all six realms together."

There was a peculiar echo to his voice, a magic that made it seem like all of the eyes of the statues, their unfinished faces, turned toward us, even though they did not move. The flickering flames stilled when he spoke, pointed upward, as if listening to his speech. As if they were all listening.

It felt like something ancient. Something that existed before Mortals built walls to huddle behind. Something that called to the inner well inside of us. That primordial magic that gave us breath and life.

"First we breathed, then we dreamed," Jinglang murmured, then bowed his head, raising the incense up to the sky. We echoed his words in turn, mirroring his actions. Then Lingwei guided me back, away from the altar. Jinglang was the first to go up and place his incense back into the bowl. The smoke drifted upward, further blurring the faces of the statues.

How strange, I thought. *These candles have no smoke.*

Jinglang stepped aside, and it was Lingwei who went up next. She bowed reverently toward the altar.

"Father, I hope you can hear us," she said to the statues. "Lost as you are, forgive your daughter for being too weak to save you."

I glanced at Jinglang, but his gaze was downcast, his attention drawn inward. Contemplating something.

Lingwei moved to stand beside her brother, and then it was my turn. I gazed up at the rows upon rows of statues, representing all the dreamers. I raised my hands up and then bowed, hoping to appear half as graceful as Lingwei when she offered her prayers.

"For your protection while we sleep," I murmured, "I thank you."

I slid the incense into the waiting bowl, and then stepped aside. Finally, Chenwen strode forward. He looked up at the wall, face impassive and unreadable. As serious as he'd ever appeared before. He bowed his head, saying nothing, keeping his prayers to himself. Then he reached up and placed the incense into the bowl.

The candle flames suddenly flared brightly, and then swiveled to the right. Jinglang's shoulders tensed, and I sensed the change in the air. Shadowy hands shot up from the ground to grasp Chenwen's wrists, and hands reached from the statues, growing longer and longer, pressed down on his shoulders. Hands pushed and hands pulled, until he was forced to kneel.

Lingwei gasped and tried to move forward, but Jinglang raised one arm to stop her. From his hand extended a long sword, just like the one he used to cut down the ravager back in Wudan.

"What are you doing?" There was no accusation in her voice, only confusion.

I tugged on Lingwei's arm and shook my head. "Wait," I said. "He's going to talk to him. You'll see."

"Talk to him? It's a strange way of talking," Lingwei mumbled, but stayed back, a hand in her sleeve. I was certain she would pull out a weapon if anything went amiss.

Chenwen turned to look at Jinglang, but instead of the anger I expected, he was smiling. He didn't struggle in the grasp of those shadowy hands. He only gazed calmly up at the man he called his brother, waiting for his next move.

"Even though Shīfù already gave up everything for a life of quiet obscurity, you still had to chase him down. You refused to give him and his beloved peace. Why?" Jinglang spoke in a steady manner. I admired his ability to keep his emotions in check. Anger burned in my chest. If there was not the hope that my uncle was still alive, I would have put my hands around his neck and tried to force it out of him myself.

"You found out?" Chenwen said, and he looked . . . relieved? Then his expression changed to one of shrewd consideration. "But because my head is not severed from my body, then you know that they still live."

"You wish to bargain for their lives?" Jinglang said, disgusted.

A lock of hair fell across the face of the kneeling prince as he pulled and tested those shadow bonds, but they tightened around his wrist and his arms, held him fast. He still retained every bit of his dignity though, as he straightened up once again.

"Chenwen . . . what did you do?" Lingwei asked, fear creeping into her voice.

"He somehow learned how to harness dark magic," Jinglang spat. "He's gained the ability to control the ravagers and bend them to his will. He tracked down my shīfù and Xue's uncle in the Mortal Realm, faked their deaths, and took them somewhere. To what end, I do not know." His eyes narrowed and he said through gritted teeth, "But I will find out. Who do you work for?"

Jinglang raised his sword so its point was under Chenwen's neck.

Chenwen's eyes shone as bright as the glowing blade. "I swear allegiance to no faction. I don't care about who takes control of the court or the maintenance of the tattered Mortal Tapestry. All I care for is justice."

"Justice!" Jinglang scoffed.

Lingwei trembled beside me, face still in disbelief. "You . . . you have evidence of this?"

"I worked with Jinglang on retrieving the memory jewels hidden in my qín," I told her gently. "I saw the memories too."

"Did you have a hand in Turning Ruilan?" Jinglang leaned forward and pressed the cold blade against the prince's throat. "Did you?"

Chenwen said nothing, but he began to hum a tune. One that I recognized, for I learned it not that long ago.

Listen! His howls can be heard over the mountains, and his many children haunt the realms

Remember! Bloodred begonia blooms at twilight . . .

"Now is not the time for your jokes, Zhou Chenwen!" I raised my voice, desperate for him to listen to reason. "You profess you are willing to die for the people you love, so why? Why do this?"

Chenwen regarded me steadily and said, "I was a baby that was found in the reflecting pool of the palace. The son born of a forbidden union. But they lied to all of you. The Sky Sovereign. The Consort. My mother was the Flower Queen and my father the Moon Sovereign."

A chill seeped into his gaze, and the corner of his lip pulled upward. A feral imitation of his usual mocking grin.

"That is what your father uncovered, in his desperate search for the truth." He twisted his neck in an unnatural manner to look at Jinglang, to witness for himself the horror that spread over the face of his dearest friend. "I am the Great Calamity. Soon to bring destruction upon all the realms."

The words rang in the air, heavy with a terrible truth. The dire prophecy. In his eyes, I could see the tendrils of a blue flame.

"Demon fire?" Jinglang whispered. For a moment, the sword shook, and I wondered if he was going to do as he threatened. Put an end to it all.

Beside me, Lingwei tensed, like a cat waiting to pounce.

Then the sword dropped to Jinglang's side.

"If you are the Great Calamity, then I am the Deceiver Reborn," Jinglang snarled.

Chenwen was shocked into speechlessness, regarding him as if he had sprouted two heads.

"I thought initially that you killed them. You killed the elders for discovering your secret, who your parents truly were. But that didn't make sense, especially now that I know my shīfù may still be alive. Why did you not come to me?" Jinglang began to pace around the room. "We could have discussed it. Found you a way out of the Celestial Realm, somehow hidden your trail. There are many corners in the Six Realms in which a Celestial could hide!"

Lingwei folded her arms across her chest and scowled at her betrothed. "You," she said, with as much venom as I'd ever heard in her voice. "You *fool*. We call the illustrious High Priestess *Mother*. Do you think we care about lineages and bloodlines?" Her anger shifted to sadness with that final question, and she appeared like she was on the verge of tears.

The prince looked upon the two of them with wonderment, the blue having faded from his eyes. He seemed like he still had not regained his ability to speak, which might have been the greatest wonder of all.

With a loud crack, the door suddenly flew open and slammed into the wall. A cold wind swept around us and blew into the room, making all of the candles flicker and sending the shadows dancing across the ceiling.

Attendant Luo strode in, guards spilling into the room around him. He dragged Danrou behind him and thrust her before us, her hair askew around her shoulders, her clothing in disarray.

"This one was found putting something into the wine," Attendant Luo reported, voice impassive. "The first sign that she was behaving out of the ordinary."

Jinglang watched the maid's face, as if searching for a particular reaction. Danrou fell to her hands and knees. "Please, my lord," she begged. "I can explain."

He appeared like a judge, similar to the portrait that I once saw of the Star of Fortune. Stern and untouchable, unaffected by emotion.

"Tell me, then," he said, and only the slight clench of his jaw betrayed what he was trying to hold back. I could only imagine all the questions he wanted to ask, to rip an answer out of her. "What do you have to say for yourself?"

CHAPTER FORTY-ONE

DANROU RAISED HER HEAD, HER GAZE DARTING TO each of us in turn. First to Lingwei, then to me, finally to Chenwen, who still knelt upon the ground, trapped by his strange bindings.

"Prince Zhou?" she gasped.

"Don't look at him," Jinglang commanded. "Answer me."

"I . . . I only wanted to add some s-sweetness to the wine." She stumbled over her words, lower lip quivering. She appeared pathetic, not understanding why she was experiencing such rough treatment.

"Show me," Jinglang asked Attendant Luo, who strode forward, a pouch in his hands.

Danrou crawled toward me, eyes shining with unshed tears. She reached out with one hand. "Please . . . Lady Xue. I know I was unkind to you, but please, have mercy . . ."

"*Mercy?*" His voice was like thunder, and the manor around us trembled, sensing the fury of its lord. "When Ruilan was afraid, did you show her mercy?" He ripped the pouch open and red petals scattered from his hands to the ground, like drops of blood. The candle flames flared behind him, leaving scorch marks on the ceiling where they brushed the wood. It was then I witnessed the true face of the Duke of Dreams. A face half in darkness, eyes that glowed gold with magic and rage.

In a flash, Danrou was on her feet. She grabbed me, swung me in front of her like a shield. Her nails lengthened into claws—one set dug into my shoulder, the other set pressed against my neck.

"Step forward and I'll slice her throat open," she said coolly, her breath against my ear.

"Let her go." Jinglang stepped forward, hand outstretched. Lingwei had a dagger in hand, and looked as if she would love the opportunity to bury it somewhere in Danrou where it would hurt.

"So you already know what happened to Ruilan," Danrou said, amused. "It doesn't matter anyway. All of you will get what you deserve."

"If you harm her . . . ," Lingwei said slowly, her blade glinting.

"There are more plans for her yet." Danrou laughed, and she lifted her hand from my shoulder. With a flick of her wrist, her claws detached and shot in the direction of the door. They spun in the air and found their targets, striking the necks of Lingwei, Attendant Luo, and two of his companions.

The guards began to shake, unearthly gurgles emitting from their mouths. Attendant Luo clutched his throat. He made an awful, gasping noise as his eyes rolled into the back of his head. Lingwei too tried to fight it, but then dropped down to her knees. Darkness filled the whites of her eyes. Her features rippled and changed, her lips pulled back from her mouth and her teeth lengthened into sharp points.

Jinglang's sword was back in his hand, but it was Chenwen's terrified expression that I focused on.

"Jinglang . . . free me, now!" Chenwen cried. "They're Turning! Let me stop them!"

With another flick of her wrist, Danrou had something white in her hand. A feather. She tossed it into the air. There was a sudden flash, and I was blinded by the light.

"Stop her!" I heard Jinglang call, dimly, as if from a very great distance.

The air was filled with growls and the crunch of bones shifting out of place. Lingwei screamed, high and shrill. A battle cry. I was surrounded by the beating of many wings, and for a moment I felt like the poet in a vortex of butterflies—

Then I was high in the sky above the estate.

I tried to move, but white bonds held me fast, strapped me to the back of something moving. I looked to my left and right and saw an expanse of feathered wings. The estate grew smaller and smaller in the distance, until it was obscured by the clouds. We continued to rise and the air grew chillier. My breath misted in front of my face with every exhale. Tiny shards of ice pelted my face, beat against my body, and I shut my eyes to protect them. The air grew thinner, and it hurt to breathe. There was only gray mist and the steady beating of those great wings.

I must have lost consciousness sometime during that flight, for when I next opened my eyes again, rough hands tugged at me. The bonds were released. I was being lifted, then lowered. It was difficult to open my eyes, but I forced myself to.

Silver armor. Silver helmets, with decorations that lifted away from the ears like wings. Soldiers loyal to Lady Hè. She finally had me in her domain.

Beside me, a large eagle preened. This must be Danrou's Spirit form. She regarded me with a baleful glare, and I recognized that disdainful look. I didn't want to look at her or else I might do something unwise.

Under my feet were white paving stones. I was on a bridge with white stone banisters. The bridge led to the foot of a mountain, where a set of doors were carved into the stone.

"Will you walk, or must we carry you?" one of the soldiers asked me, the threat obvious.

"I can walk," I said. They placed no chains on me as I followed them down the path, other guards following me from behind. What did a Celestial have to fear from a Mortal girl?

Two fearsome stone dragon heads adorned the mountain doors, one on either side. Each held a single white orb in its mouth. The doors were so grand that it strained my neck to look up the entirety of their height. They opened before us, slowly, from within. I saw that it took three Celestials to push open each door.

From inside, a figure emerged, her silver robes trailing behind her.

The chamber within was a dome, a cave carved into the center of the mountain. I'd read about this place. One devoid of color and decoration, meant only for the pursuit of quiet meditation and reflection, to shed all Mortal desires and freedom from Corruption. To be pure of heart and mind. A True Celestial.

The Temple of Ordinance.

Lady Hè still wore her cloak of feathers, but upon her head was a jeweled headdress. When she turned her head, the light danced across the pale gems and the delicate silver chains that linked them together. A beauty that was glorious at first glance, but she could not hide the rot underneath. For some reason I thought of the birds in the garden who loved gathering their shiny baubles, and I tried my best to suppress the giggle that suddenly rose up in my chest.

She narrowed her eyes at me, her irritation obvious. "You seem to have a death wish, Mortal," she said coldly. "You forget your place."

A spear struck my back, and I coughed as the force of it dropped me to my knees. She wanted me humiliated. Again. But I no longer cared how I appeared in front of these Celestials. I didn't care for their tenets, their self-righteous misery.

"Did you complete your task at the estate?" Lady Hè asked. For a moment, I thought she was talking to me, but another voice sounded beside me. Soft and sweet, just like the first day we met in the courtyard.

"Yes, my lady," Danrou said reverently, having shed her eagle form.

"Four of the Meng Estate have been Turned. Soon, the Star of Protection will arrive with her acolytes, and whoever survives the slaughter will face the judgment of the tribunal."

It was true then. Chenwen wasn't the one behind the ravagers after all. It was Danrou, at the direction of the High Priestess. But why?

"They were people who you worked with, lived with, for years." I did not even bother to hide my disgust. "How could you be so heartless?"

"Back in the Spirit Realm I was a princess of the Bird Clan," Danrou sneered. "In the Celestial Realm I was nothing. A servant. And they made me bow to one of the Flower Clan. The Flower Clan! That girl wasn't fit to be anything, especially not beloved by those three."

"Ruilan didn't do anything to you," I whispered. "It was only ... jealousy."

Just a simple *Mortal* emotion. I started to laugh, and found I could not stop.

"Quiet!" Lady Hè struck me across the mouth.

Pain bloomed across my vision, sharp and red. The pain brought me back to myself, made everything else recede, and forced me to focus. They brought me here and I wasn't dead yet, so they must want something from me. If I could keep a cool head, I might be able to return to the Meng Estate in one piece.

I could have dignity even when brought down low—I'd learned that from my uncle. Now that I knew he could still be alive, I would keep on surviving, regardless of what they put me through.

"Bring her." Lady Hè turned away, and Danrou stepped forward to join her. The soldiers came up behind me, and because I did not want another spear in the back, I moved forward with them, through the great doors and then under the dome. Seven pillars rose around the room, upon which the characters for the emotions were carved.

喜怒哀懼愛惡欲

Joy, Anger, Sadness, Fear, Love, Hate, Desire

The Forbidden Seven. What they feared would engulf them, place them under threat of turning into monsters. But Chenwen somehow found a way to control them, and Ruilan found a way to survive as a ravager—though whether her life still remained in peril, I did not know.

In the center of the dome, there was a platform, around which the Ordinance soldiers stood like statues. Keeping watch. Something about that platform, that empty space that remained above it, chilled me, and I did not know why.

A chair was set up to the right, in front of the Pillar of Sadness. Lady Hè sat down with a sweep of her cloak. Danrou stood behind her, face expectant, as if she was looking forward to watching a great show.

Torture, then? Or something else?

I stopped before the platform and the guards behind me did not advance.

"I found your fortune in the Library of Souls," Lady Hè's voice trilled in the air, suddenly honeyed. "What a peculiar thread. A girl born to traitors, discarded to live upon the fringes of society, headed for a life of servitude and loneliness. How satisfying it would be to pluck it, to rid the Mortal Tapestry of such a blemish upon its radiant design."

I glanced at her. How she strummed her fingers along the curved arms of her chair, like she sat upon a throne, her delight at my upcoming punishment evident.

"The decision, sadly, is not one for me to make. But still, there must be a reason why a deviant thread would find their way to the Celestial Realm. It seems that you will fulfill a greater purpose after all." She smiled, but the amusement did not reach her eyes. "Do you have anything else to say before we send you to your wayward fate?"

"You set the ravagers upon the Meng Estate," I said. "Do you not worry what will happen to your children? To Jinglang and Lingwei?"

"When they professed to support their father and petitioned for justice for the Queen of Flowers, that was when I knew their minds have been twisted against me." Her face contorted, letting a glimpse of the rage that simmered underneath slip through. No matter how much she tried to preserve that perfect appearance, it always revealed itself. "If they survive the night, they will see for themselves the result of their despicable alliance."

Danrou still stood there, wearing the same grin that she wore the night of the party. Certain she had triumphed over me for the second time.

"And you . . ." Lady Hè's hand closed into a fist. "When the tower is done with you, you will be willing to say anything we wish for you to say. You will be our perfect puppet. That is . . . if you are able to walk out of there alive."

She nodded at the guard behind me. Hands shoved me forward. I fell toward the platform. I raised my arms to protect my head from cracking upon the stone, but instead I felt myself rising. I floated in the air, lifted upward by an unknown force. The top of the dome opened. I saw the shape of a golden flower. It bloomed, petals unfurling, pulling away until a portal was revealed.

I flew upward, into the light.

CHAPTER FORTY-TWO

IN ALL OF THE BOOKS, ALL OF THE SACRED TEXTS, they spoke of *the tower*.

The High Tower. The Tower of Suffering. Were they the same tower? Or different ones? Or did the tower change to suit whatever it was called to be?

I knew I was in the mountain, but when the portal closed beneath my feet, I was in a different space entirely—it was far more vast than even a mountain could contain. The night sky glittered above, but it seemed to be constantly moving. Stars arced overhead, rose and fell. They seemed to flare into something decipherable, but before I could read the words, they disappeared again. There was only one structure that stood lonely against that shifting sky.

A seven-sided tower. Each floor stacked upon one another, getting progressively smaller. There were windows, but there was no door. I turned to the right, and there the tower was again, before me. I turned to the left, and the tower was still there, at the center of my vision. It didn't matter where I turned, where I looked, the tower was there. It would be my only destination.

All the spinning around was making me feel sick, and I was only putting off the inevitable. I needed to get back and find out if Jinglang and the others were safe.

I walked forward. As I approached the tower, it seemed to grow larger and larger, until it loomed over me—

I blinked. The night sky was gone. The tower was gone. I was in a room with seven sides. No windows. No doors. I walked toward the wall, reached out to touch it—

I was a boy who grew up on the streets, who was kicked around like a dog. I ate whatever garbage I could find from the gutters and slept huddled under the eaves of businesses with owners who took pity on me. I had nothing of my own except the clothes I wore.

But one day I met my benefactor, who found me on the streets, cleaned me up and gave me a home. He trained me to fight and to climb and to steal. Until the day my training was done.

He brought me a boy who was once me. Scared and scrawny and eyes too large and squirming under his grasp. My benefactor gave me a knife and told me to kill him, to rid myself of my past life in order to be reborn.

I did not hesitate.

As the boy's lifeblood pooled under my feet, I felt the power of it. Power over another living being. One that I'd never had for myself.

This was Joy.

I was a woman who married a man out of duty. I endured the mistreatment from his mother, bore him two children. Had a house that we could be proud of, and when his mother was dead and buried, I thought I would finally be free.

Except then he brought his mistress home and said he intended to marry her, that it was his right as the man of the house. He said if only I'd kept him entertained, he would not need to take such drastic measures. That his mother was right—we should have never married.

I picked up the ax and sank the blade into his arm while he screamed. It took three good strikes to sever it from his body.

But only one to sever his head from his neck.

This was Anger.

I was a man who spent all of my meager earnings going to see the singer at the local teahouse. She met me at the back door and made me sweet promises about how someday, we would leave all of this behind us. She just needed to pay off her debt to the madam who owned her contract.

So I worked and worked to save up what I could for her freedom. But one day at the teahouse, I was warned by a man who said she had given him the same story. She was the darling of many more, all of the coin going into her own pocket, the madam taking her cut too.

She greeted me with a kiss that night and I put my hands around her neck and squeezed until the life fled from her eyes.

If I could not have her, then no one else could have her either.

This was Desire.

OVER AND OVER again, I lived these lives and these terrible fates. I crawled through the depths of despair. I endured pain and frustration and fury. I wept and screamed and ached for all of these lives. The decisions they made. To lie and kill and betray and hurt each other.

This was what they thought of us. The Celestials in their palaces in the sky, dictating how our lives would begin and end. Except this wasn't all there was to experience in the Mortal Realm. They'd taken all of the bitterness, the ugliness, and none of the beauty. I clung to the memories of the time I spent with my uncle and the House of Flowing Water, like a drowning person to a raft. I remembered laughter and camaraderie of the apprentices as we splashed one another in the main hall when we scrubbed the floors or paused in the midst of chores to listen to the wondrous sounds of opera echoing through the rafters. I recalled my uncle sharing with me his love of food, the burning delight of the first sip of peppery soup, crying as we took bite after bite . . .

Somewhere between Fear and Sadness, the span of forever or perhaps only two breaths, I heard a voice.

"Stand up."

I was on my hands and knees. My throat ached from screaming. My eyes struggled to adjust to the chamber, swollen as they were from all of the tears. Back to the room with the seven white walls and the white ceiling. The floor was cold beneath my hands. They should be stained with the blood of those I'd murdered. All of the horrible things I'd done.

"Did you hear me? Stand up!" The commanding voice was familiar. I looked up, stunned, to see Auntie Wu. I never thought I would see her again.

She extended her hand toward me and I took it. Her grip was ice cold, as chilled as the floor beneath my feet. She pulled me up to face her.

"Are you really here?" I managed to choke out through my shock.

She lifted her brow. "I'm only borrowing this face, child. I thought it would be better if I looked like someone you know, rather than take on an appearance that is incomprehensible to you."

"Who are you?"

"I'm the entity bound to this tower." A simple-enough explanation, though incomprehensible to me.

"You're a prisoner here?"

She shrugged. "One could say that." She gazed upon me with curiosity, as one might regard a lost, crying child who had stumbled into their path. "Out of all those they have sent my way, I've rarely encountered one such as yourself. A Mortal . . . 'in the flesh.'"

"Auntie Wu" grinned then, and that utterly predatory expression was so unlike my former mistress that I had to accept this was not the woman I knew.

"Not many of your kind would have survived my administrations, but you . . ." She ran her finger down the side of my cheek, the sharp edge of her nail threatening to slice open my skin. I flinched and pulled away, but she still regarded me with those wide, knowing eyes. "You are already halfway gone."

"Wh-what does that mean?" I sputtered.

"So many questions." She reached out again, and this time her touch lingered on my scar. I shivered at the intimate feel of it, but there was nowhere else in the room for me to go; my back was already against the wall. I watched her warily, this familiar unfamiliar woman. "Didn't he tell you? Every day you spend in the Celestial Realm, every time you enter the Dreaming, your Mortality leaks out of you in a steady stream. Drip, drip, drip . . ."

Time, I already understood, had its own meaning here. But I did not know what she was speaking of when it came to my Mortality. It reminded me again how little I knew, and that chafed still. *Foolish girl.*

"There's no need to be thinking that of yourself. Not when there are already many who would call you all of those things." She tsked, sounding very much like Matron, and a little like Uncle as well. I realized, a beat later, that she was able to read my mind. Read my every private thought.

"Oh, my dear." She waved a hand, dismissing my sudden panicked worry. "There is nothing I have not seen before. There's no need to be embarrassed. I've lived thousands of Mortals' lives. Thousands? Hundreds of thousands? They all taste the same, after a while.

"You've only had a brief glimpse of my repertoire," she said. "I carefully sift through those Mortal fates to cater to the specific tastes of the Celestials the priestess sends me. Torture is an *art* after all." She kept *smiling* at me, and I wished she wouldn't.

"What do you want from me?" I asked.

"As you tumbled through those many lives, I noticed you brought something into my tower." With the long fingers of her hand extended, the pouch containing all three memory jewels slipped out of my sash and floated toward her.

"Those are mine!" I protested as I lunged for them, but she snatched them out of the air and my hand came up empty. The jewels slid into her palm and she picked one up between her thumb and forefinger, held it up in front of her face.

"Memories, sealed and protected. Some, to pass on as a legacy. Others, eager to leave behind and forget," she said, slightly unfocused. "You should not have survived for so long, Guxue. You should have been executed next to your mother and father. A sorry reminder of what happens to loyal officials when emperors rise and fall."

The reflection of the executioner's face upon the polished blade. The rain that washed away our blood off the platform. I saw it happen before me, as it should have happened.

"You should have died under the claws of the ravager in the forest. You should have perished from a coughing sickness, the winter of your seventeenth year."

A winter that had the coldest temperatures on record for fifty years. A city frozen, with dwindling supplies. A house with many rooms, many young women, who slept next to one another at night, where it was easy for disease to spread. That was the fate that awaited me if I had refused the duke's offer.

"And yet . . . you continue to live. An unruly, stubborn thread." She tilted her head to one side. "Unnoticeable, utterly insignificant, and still, ever persistent in your survival."

With every word she spoke, I was certain she saw my existence as boundless suffering, and that I should be grateful for her assistance in ending my miserable life. Much like the High Priestess believed, but instead of the pale face of that haughty woman, it was the prince who I remembered. Chenwen and his usual look of handsome condescension, his flippant remarks on love and the Mortal weakness.

"Zhou Chenwen, yes!" Auntie Wu clapped, delighted. "How surprised I was to see him tangled in your fate, along with the other Celestials. How quickly it happened! Just one loose thread, and yet the effects upon the entirety of the realms! Staggering." She laughed, and I remained quiet. I didn't know how long she would keep me here, while the ravagers tore through Meng Manor. If there would be anyone left to save.

"Love. How it complicates things." She sighed, then her dark eyes regarded me once again, with that look of ancient knowing. "I'm here to make you an offer."

I suspected this was some sort of trick, a brief reprieve from the weight of those memories. To be given hope, only to have it snatched away. I suspected I had yet to see the true depths of their cruelty.

"Now, now." She placed her finger against my lips. "Listen before you refuse."

"Will you actually give me a choice?" I asked.

"There is always a choice," she said, suddenly serious. "I can promise you that."

The entity pressed her hands against the side of my face, like she was going to kiss me. I wanted to struggle, to resist, but I could not move. She leaned forward and touched her forehead to mine.

CHAPTER FORTY-THREE

"WHO ARE YOU?" I HEARD MY VOICE CALL OUT, echoing in that bright, empty room.

I was there at the making of the world.

I saw the scene before me. The girl I used to be, sitting in front of my uncle as he read from one of the classics, making me repeat the story of the origins of the universe.

"'Nüwa shaped the humans with her hands, and gave them breath from her lips,'" I recited. "'But the earth was unstable, and the elder gods determined a sacrifice must be made. One of them must give up their body so that the world could be given form.'"

I was selfish, for I carried a secret, and hid it from the other gods.

"'They drew lots, and it was the goddess Nüwa who was picked. The gods despaired, for she was one of the most beloved of them all. But she went willingly, knowing her sacrifice would ensure the survival of her beloved Mortals.'"

I wanted my child to be given a choice, just like the Mortals were given. Why were they given a choice, while the gods were burdened for eternity?

"'But the lots were rigged by the Deceiver, and when the ruse was discovered, Fuxi flew into a rage. The Deceiver cursed the Mortal Realm when she died, and they were riddled with disease, war, and famine.'"

I was cast out. They used the threat of my daughter's life for me to obey, and they broke me into pieces.

A scream shook the room. A great lotus spun above her, the rainbow petals burning with an orange glow. The unmaking of a god. She endured a pain that was just like the one Nüwa suffered. They took her daughter away.

"You are the Deceiver," I realized.

Parts of me were used to form the Barren Realm, a new plane to contain the imperfect first creations of the gods. Another part of me was kept in the High Tower, for the gods to utilize to maintain the realms. I was used to forge relics, to shape the Dreaming, and I slept . . . I slept for the longest time. Until he woke me.

I saw a man with twin flames of blue flickering in his eyes, levitating in the air. His power rippled around him, in flashes like lightning. There was something familiar about him, about the line of his jaw, the shape of his nose. Like someone I used to know. I watched him scream at the sky in rage and despair as he flew high above a tower. No, not a tower. *This* tower. Seven-sided rooms and seven floors high. A broken body at the foot of it.

The Flower Queen.

He pleaded for help from any who would listen. The other gods turned away, but I heard him.

"You have a choice," the Deceiver said to the Moon Sovereign, in that frozen moment in time. "I will reach through the Barrens to help you, but you will be despised forever, your memory tarnished."

He agreed without hesitation.

There was a rip in the borders between realms, and through that power, he was transformed. He became an unrecognizable beast that tore through the ranks of the Celestial army, and many bodies fell from the sky—

We returned to the white room, and she was Auntie Wu again. She was the one who helped him Turn, who brought ravagers back to the realms. I should hate her for it, and yet I knew the story was not so simple.

"We all have potential. Celestials, Spirits, Mortals, Demons, Ghosts . . . We all carry with us reminders of what we loved and lost. Do you know why the Moon Sovereign asked for my help? What he gave everything to save?" There was a trembling note of sadness in her voice.

"What?" I whispered.

"His son," she said. Just like how she ended up chained to this tower. Her daughter.

I saw it all for myself. In the skies above, they struggled to bring down the great ravager, but on the earth below, a small figure carried a baby away . . . Chenwen.

She nodded. "I watched over him, the best that I could, in the many years since the Moon Sovereign's passing," she said softly. "And I heard the rumors, the many things attributed to my name. I was not responsible. There are not many left who remember the part of me that remained here. I wondered about the strange things I witnessed, the peculiar stories I overheard, as the Celestials passed through my tower."

Did you hear? When they finally found the body of the Moon Beast, he had no heart. It had shriveled and died.

Did you hear? The pair of ravagers slaughtered a whole village in the Mortal Realm before the acolytes tracked it down.

Did you hear? The borders between the realms are weakening. It must be Demon influence.

"I realized the magic that held the Celestial Realm together is weakening, when it should have been stronger than ever. When the Jade Sovereign joined the Heavenly Mother in her crystal palace, another should have taken his place. The cycle should have started anew, the magic restored."

The room disappeared again. I stood on a stretch of pale sand, as far as the eye could see. Above my head, a white sun burned, but emitted no warmth. I waved my hand and the sand parted, revealing the body of a man with the shadow of a crescent moon upon his forehead. He appeared to be sleeping. I knelt down beside him and felt an immense sadness. With a hand upon his brow, I told him his son was safe, hidden in the Celestial Realm. From the corner of his eye, a single tear formed a luminescent pearl.

"You trust me?" I—no, the Deceiver—asked. The man had no response, and the sand closed over his body once again.

The Deceiver returned to the tower, her powers having grown in the years since the Flower Queen fell, and the borders more fragile now.

In that pearl, she was certain, would be the answer to the mysteries. She stepped into the memory.

The ravager that was the Moon Sovereign panted, tongue lolling out of his mouth. His chest heaved as he struggled to get to his feet. He tried, then fell, and tried again. His paws could find no purchase on the sandy floor. Above him, the Sky Sovereign wielded a sword, a fierce and terrible vision. Behind them hovered a rift in the sky, watching over them like the slit of a massive eye.

"I . . . I yield . . ." The body of the beast contorted and returned to the shape of a man. His clothing hung in tatters, his left arm limp at his side. He remained kneeling, legs folded underneath him. He no longer had the strength to stand.

The Sky Sovereign laughed. "Did you think it would be that simple?"

"I just . . . wanted her." The man strained to speak, every breath a struggle. "We asked for peace. Why did you refuse?"

"You have something else I want, something far more valuable to me than peace," the sovereign said. "I needed a reason to kill you."

The face of the Sky Sovereign peeled back and revealed the skull underneath. His skull was translucent, as if made from crystal. An orange light glowed within.

The Moon Sovereign recoiled in horror. "The Burning Lotus of the Heavenly Mother! You would defile the order of the realms . . ."

The face of the Sky Sovereign returned, impassive and cruel. "I found my power waning even though there was much left I wanted to accomplish. She called me to join her, but I was not ready. She forced my hand."

"You seek the impossible, and you will fail in this absurd quest," the Moon Sovereign scoffed, defiant.

"That is where you are wrong," the Sky Sovereign leered, and sank his sword into his opponent's chest.

The Moon Sovereign coughed, as his blood spilled upon the thirsty sands of the Barrens. "They will stop you."

"Let them try."

I KNEW SO little about the origins of the world, the conflicts between the gods, and yet I recognized the Sky Sovereign, who had welcomed the Celestials into the consort's palace. That laughing, jovial man who wanted me to play for him, who brushed aside Jinglang's request for punishment.

"But he's the Sky Sovereign," I whispered. "He is the ruler of the Six Realms."

We were back again in that small room. My head spun with all of the movement, all of the knowledge, and how insignificant I truly was in this war.

"He was the one known as the Jade Sovereign," the Deceiver said. "When his time came to retreat to the Palace in the West, he did not want to retire into obscurity. He pulled a hair from his head and formed it into the shape of a young man. From his throne, he guided his alternate self through the trials and through the court, gave him every advantage, until he was named a prince of the Celestial Realm."

How familiar this story. How those in power would always fight to stay in power. Lie, cheat, perform despicable acts, even as everyone below them suffered.

"He killed the Heavenly Mother and obtained her inner core, the only thing that can contain her magic—the Burning Lotus. He used it to form his new skull. It has given him access to immense power and held him together all this time, yet he's realized that so much power continually requires fuel. He must maintain it by ingesting Celestial magic."

Their inner core, the Celestial equivalent of their heart. He was *eating* them.

"And by helping the Moon Sovereign, I unwittingly aided him in this quest," the Deceiver sighed, regretful. "Where the Flower Queen died and where her son was born, red begonias bloomed, mingled with a tiny bit of Corruption that had found its way from the Barrens. It became a Celestial poison that causes them to transform into ravagers. More excuses for him to hunt down his own."

"Why tell me all of this?" I asked her, suspicious now. She was the Deceiver, the one destined to bring forth the Great Calamity. It was recorded in all of the history books, that one day she would return to seek her revenge.

"I've come to know many Mortal lives. I once despised your existence, believing you to be imperfect playthings of the gods. But now, I find your lives . . . interesting. How the decisions of Mortals, each one appearing to be insignificant, could yet yield astonishing effects. Your choices reverberate throughout the six realms, a chorus of life and death that causes ripples through time and space. So much potential for good, so much capacity for love, so much of myself . . . I see in you."

In her eyes, I saw clouds shift, the sun rise and fall, flowers bloom and wither—time's swift passing.

"If you want to help them, you have to make a choice," the Deceiver said, and in her expression, I caught a hint of pity.

She waved a hand and a portal appeared before us. We looked down upon the Meng Estate. I saw them cornered on the Platform of Forgetting, in the garden. The number of ravagers had grown from four to ten, all terrifying monsters of various shapes and sizes, baring teeth and claws. Chenwen with his flute, trying to control them with his magic. Jinglang with a sword in his hand, keeping them back. Which one of them was Lingwei?

"Soon the Sky Sovereign will descend upon the Meng Estate. He will reveal Chenwen's parentage and accuse him of Turning Celestials ravage, and he will tell them the Duke of Dreams assisted them. He will weave a tale of treachery and betrayal for the court to hear. These three are the only ones who still suspect there is something amiss in the court, the ones who still believe in the innocence of Meng Wujin."

Jinglang's father. The former Duke of Dreams.

The Deceiver nodded. "Yes. The one who carried the baby away from the battlefield, years ago. Who entered my tower, a few months prior, for asking too many questions. But now he's locked in a different space by the Sky Sovereign, somewhere even I cannot reach."

"What would you have me do?" I whispered, even though I already suspected the answer was one I would not want to hear.

"Set me free from this tower, and I will help you save them. I will teach you how to wield your own magic," she said. "It will be a return to the way things should be. Those in power must be torn down in order to achieve balance in the realms."

"Why me?" I asked, knowing there must be a trap in here, a ploy, and I just couldn't see it. "The Moon Sovereign still lives. You hold his memory jewel, so that must mean a part of him is still alive . . . somewhere.

Or why not another Celestial, one of the many who passed through the tower? They are more powerful than I could ever be."

"You viewed the memory within my own memory." The Deceiver smiled humorlessly. "The jewel faded after I viewed it, and he became a part of the Barrens. He was content, knowing his son yet lived, and that the knowledge he gleaned would be passed on. Just like the knowledge that was passed on by Meng Wujin, an understanding of the Jade Sovereign's treachery. To you, now, the next person who visited my tower."

But I was nothing. I was no one.

Her voice rang in the room, echoing all around me. "A girl who should have died many times in her short life, and yet still made it here. A Mortal who has traversed the barriers between realms. Who inspired a Celestial to love, despite him believing it contrary to his nature. How many stars had to align for you to stand here before me? And still, you doubt?"

CHAPTER FORTY-FOUR

BENEATH US, THE PORTAL CONTINUED TO SHOW ME
what was happening at the Meng Estate. The Sky Sovereign would hurt
those I cared for. The ones who had eventually welcomed me in, different as I was from them. How terrifying it was to trust in the unknown,
and yet I could not stand there and do nothing.

"Tell me what you want me to do," I said.

The being that wore Auntie Wu's face lifted her cupped hands and
offered me what was inside—a bloodred begonia, with a jewel in the
center, glowing softly. I knew what it was when it slipped into my hands,
for I had already felt the warmth and weight of it many times before.

I felt a trickle of fear at what was to come. Maybe I was dooming us
all. Maybe this was the unmaking of the world, a tragedy already foretold.

"Some of them . . . they still believe there is good in the world," I said.
"Those of the Transcendent Path. They may still be saved."

"If they do not stand in my way, then we can form a new balance."

I looked at the memory jewel in my hands. Such a small thing, I
had marveled once. The tear of a Celestial. "Who does it belong to?"
I asked.

"The Flower Queen. Shunying." She lifted my hands with her own,
bringing it closer to my mouth, and said, more urgently, "Make your
choice. Do you want the truth to be revealed?"

"Will it hurt?" I asked, childishly. *Physical, mental, and spiritual
agonies . . .*

"This will peel away your Mortality. You will be unraveled and then remade again." A pause, and then, "There is no going back. You will be Mortal no longer."

The weight of the jewel seemed to grow heavier, even though it was only my imagination. Everything it contained, the ability to save Jinglang, Chenwen, Lingwei. To become one of them. To have magic of my own. Was this what I wanted? To be able to protect my uncle, to meet his beloved, the Star of Fortune, to find out what happened to Ruilan and Zhuxi.

Those who fell because of a tyrant's desperate, pathetic attempt to hold on to his power.

I placed the flower upon my tongue.

"When the time comes, you'll know when to give it and who to give it to. Call my name when you are ready."

It tasted faintly of salt.

"Suirong." *A being of fire.*

Her face wavered, like ink dissolving into water.

"These, I return to you," she whispered, before she fully disappeared.

A necklace appeared around my neck, a thin chain upon which dangled three jewels that I had once pulled from my qín, the memories of a former Celestial.

I didn't know what sort of bargain I'd made, but I'd made my choice. Whatever happened, I had to live with it.

And there was always a price to pay.

I DREAMED WITH the certainty that I was dreaming. I was back at the Meng Estate, with all of its shadowy corridors and neglected beauty. But in this dream world, it appeared more derelict than I remembered. Cracks had formed in its walls; roots wormed their way through broken bricks. Branches and refuse littered the halls. I wandered through the manor, searching for the answer to the restless feeling inside of me.

Until, in the distance, I heard the strains of a song. A powerful strumming that emerged from what could only be the twenty-one-stringed zhēng. A fiery instrument that commanded even the loftiest performance halls. Where the qín was contemplative, the zhēng was an invocation. The qín looked inward, while the zhēng called out, demanded attention.

I stood at the entrance of Ruilan's garden and saw my qín up ahead, already set up under the eaves. Except waiting for me there in the garden was a sight that made me gasp in awe even as my knees quivered. She was a giant, taller than even the main building of the consort's glorious palace. Her enormous form filled the entirety of the space. She sat cross-legged, the great zhēng balanced on the walls of the manor.

Suirong.

Terrifying in appearance, her wine-dark hair was coiled, spilling over her shoulders like giant snakes. There was a large, vertical golden eye in the middle of her forehead, which peered down at me now, along with the pair that was where eyes would normally be. Her clothes were as red as her lips, rippling around her, blown by an unseen wind.

She had three gold bracelets on her arm, which clinked together as she cast her wrist across the strings of her zhēng. I was enveloped by a wave of sound, and I found myself lifted up, the magic depositing me before my own qín.

"Follow my lead," she commanded, her voice like the beating of many large drums.

The song that came from the zhēng sounded like war. Like the galloping hooves of a thousand horses. I listened for the underlying melody, a rushing current of a powerful stream that coursed alongside the stampede. I pulled it out and played in counterpoint to it, a bird that flew over the water. We played together and apart, wove in and out, two differing threads over the same cloth. She laughed then—I sensed her joy that I was able to keep up.

I knew then that something inside of me was changing, two dissonant sounds attempting to find a balance, moving together toward a final harmony.

Should I fear the loss of my Mortality? Or did my Mortal experience make me treasure it all the more?

After the call to war, the zhēng slowed, and from its strings came the sound of "Twilight's Begonia." As I played it, I experienced it for myself, the sorrow and regret of the Flower Queen's struggle. I saw her love for the man with the crescent mark upon his brow. Who taught her how to navigate the power of Corruption instead of fearing it. The forbidden magic that was a different form of power.

That great eye upon her brow stared at me, unblinking. *Do you understand now?*

The Celestials sought to rid the world of Corruption, and the Demons wanted to understand it. The Sky Sovereign feared what he could not understand, and when he learned of Chenwen's existence, he wanted to eliminate him.

Suirong taught me how to use the ebb and flow of the music to cast a net. How to use it to control and restrain, to lead and to push back. Through the music I understood how to heal, how to shift the clouds, how to travel through the realms.

The sound of the zhēng changed to a lullaby.

You have an affinity for the Dreaming. That was why you saw Ruilan, why you were able to find Zhuxi's memory. The Dreaming gives everyone a safe space to rest, to wonder, to heal, to recover.

She showed me how to traverse that other path, how the winding magic of the Dreaming was the backbone upon which the realms were formed. Another melody hidden in the song that echoed across the six realms. She showed me the memories Meng Wujin passed on to her before he was taken from the tower, in fear of what was to come. I caught glimpses of the boy Jinglang was then, darting in and out of the shadowy hallways of the Meng Estate.

"Can you save him? Can you free Jinglang's father?" I asked.

"I fear that he has become something else, warped by the influence of the Sky Sovereign's power . . . I don't know what has happened to him," Suirong told me. "This will be a test your Jinglang has to pass, eventually. He will have to face what his father has become and see who he will choose to be—his mother's son, or his father's."

She closed all three of her eyes and let out a soft sigh. Her zhēng remained quiet, her hands stilled in her lap.

"I've taught you all that I know. It's time for you to go into the Dreaming and seek him out. Show him what you have become. You will need him to free you from this tower."

TO BRING ME to the Dreaming, I needed a song that was able to soothe my nerves. I played one of the few memories of my mother, a song she hummed to me while I dozed, halfway between waking and slumber.

> *I've roamed for a long while*
> *Distant from the roads I used to run upon*
> *I've been searching for the flowers of my homeland*
> *It exists only in my dreams*

I opened my eyes and I was back in the streets of Wudan. Even as a yuè-hù, I was still free to roam through these roads if I was on House business. I ran through the twisted alleys and side streets, using them as shortcuts. My feet were dusty as they pounded the road, and when I flew out from the alley, I stumbled over a wheel that had protruded from a merchant's cart. The flower vendor smiled and called me a pretty lady, giving me a rose.

The stem of the flower felt so real under my fingers. I could feel the itch of the fur trim of my cloak against my neck. I passed through the gate of the House, flower still in hand. In the garden pavilion there were lanterns hung up on a stand, three by three. Each year we had our own festival in the courtyard of the House, and the other novices and apprentices would ponder the riddles drawn on the lanterns, hoping they could win the grand prize. I never had a hope of winning, but I liked to listen to how the others would cleverly deduce the solutions to the puzzles.

But within this dream, it wasn't the anticipation of the guessing that drew me in. He was the one who shone for me. The brightest star in my night sky.

Jinglang turned to me and smiled.

"I knew I'd find you here," he said.

When he held his arms open to embrace me, I hesitated, knowing this was only a distraction, a dream. But I leaned into him, and permitted myself this brief indulgence.

We clung to each other, knowing the dangers that waited us outside of this dream world, and yet we remained. After a moment, I tried to pull away, but he held me tighter.

"Even though I know we don't have much time, just allow me this," he whispered into my hair. "Just a bit longer."

Because I was weak, and because this was an irresistible lure, I kissed him, with all the longing that I'd held back these past few weeks.

He tasted so sweet, as we kissed each other, again and again. I wanted to stay forever, to wander these pretty streets, to lose ourselves in this city of pretend. I could see how easy it would be to fall into the promise of the Dreaming. I could see how someone could go to sleep and never wake up.

"We don't have much time," I murmured against his lips, even though I wanted to keep on kissing him.

"I know," he said reluctantly, his hands still in my hair. He looked at me with tenderness, with all of the things that he wanted to say. My hand found his, and I squeezed his fingers for strength. To convince him of what he needed to do next.

"Where did she take you?" he asked. "Are you safe?"

Reminded of the horrors that must have occurred while I was trapped in the tower, the garden of the House of Flowing Water melted away around us. We returned to the Meng Estate and stood on the Platform of Forgetting, surrounded by ravagers. Lingwei lay on the ground, her broken body feasted upon by giant crows. In the distance, Chenwen was being torn apart, limb by limb, by a pack of wolves that had tails like snakes and too many limbs. This was my dream turned into my worst nightmare.

After my time spent with Suirong, I could see him wield his magic. Saw how he used his power to reshape the nightmare, turn it into something else. The platform disappeared, the mist carrying away Lingwei and Chenwen. We were in his receiving room, where we had spent many hours, talking about poetry and sharing meals.

"Who are you?" he demanded then, his anguish clear. Like he didn't know whether to pull me close or push me away. "Are you actually her? Or something else deep in the Dreaming sent to torment me?"

"I am Guxue, once of the House of Flowing Water," I said. "I've come to collect on your promise." To return me to the Mortal Realm when all the memory jewels had been found. Except I can't go back. Not anymore.

I closed my eyes and drew upon my newly found magic then, conjured the necklace back to my neck and into this dreamscape. He lifted one of the jewels with his finger, and his touch made me shiver, made me feel slightly undone.

"Is it truly you?" he murmured.

"I am in the Temple of Ordinance," I told him. "Your mother sent me to the tower."

"The tower!" He drew in a sharp intake of breath. "They . . . they sent my father there. Have you met him?"

I shook my head. "I met someone else instead. The magic contained within the tower, it belonged to one of the elder gods, an ancient entity."

"No," Jinglang said, clasping my hand tight. "The High Tower changes your perception. Forces you to see things differently, to see it *their way*. It tries to mold you into what they want you to be. You cannot trust anything you see there."

I told him quickly of all that I had learned, of the true evil that lurked in the realm all of this time. Until his face grew pale with the reality that we faced. But I knew he believed me, believed that I was telling the truth, without hesitation. That trust made something inside of me sing, despite the immensity of the challenge before us.

"He is coming, with the Court of Stars," he whispered. "I sealed the estate, with Chenwen and Lingwei within. I remained outside and called for help through the Dreaming."

He turned his head, as if listening to voices I could not hear.

"They're here," he said.

The world rippled, the magic holding this space together weakening. "Wait," I gasped, but the table between us stretched, pushed me to one side and him to another. "The temple tower. That's where you'll find me. Please, Jinglang."

Then he was gone.

CHAPTER FORTY-FIVE

I WOKE UP COLLAPSED ON THE PLATFORM IN THE dome room, drenched in sweat and tears.

"She's awake, Priestess," the soldier above me said.

Lady Hè dug her nails into my arm and pulled me to standing, regarding me with the full force of her fury.

"Why is my son banging on the door of my temple?" she demanded. "How did you get a message out?" Her eyes narrowed as she took me in. I looked back at her, more awake than I had ever been, strangely calm. I felt her magic touch my mind, and I envisioned myself like a wall of stone. Cold, impenetrable.

"You're . . . you're . . ." Her chest heaved, the realization quickly flashing across her face.

"I've rid myself of the stench of Mortality," I said quietly. "Isn't that what you wanted?"

"You've been Corrupted," she gasped. "You're dangerous." With a flick of her wrist, chains wound around my neck, and she pulled my arms behind my back. I was still unused to my new body, and I did not know how to utilize the magic I'd been taught. I tried to see if I could remove my bonds, but they held fast.

Lady Hè let out a small sigh as she witnessed my attempt. "We'll return you to the tower. There must have been some mistake, some misunderstanding."

There was a boom from the entrance, and I turned to see pieces of those doors to the temple crumble. Jinglang strode in, soldiers behind him. These soldiers were dressed all in white, similar to what Lingwei had worn previously. Her fellow acolytes—part of the Celestial Army.

"I come here with a decree given by the Sky Sovereign and the Sky Consort," he said, scroll in hand.

The soldiers within the temple all dropped to their knees, and even Lady Hè had to bow her head in order to receive the decree.

"The Mortal Guxue, Winter's Wren, will be brought before the Court of Stars as witness to the trial against Zhou Chenwen. Such is the decree of the Sky Consort, Xuannu." He tossed the scroll at his mother's feet, and then bent over, gingerly picking me up in his arms.

"I'm sorry I arrived so late," he murmured, his eyes only for me.

"I'm glad you're here," I whispered back to him. I felt Lady Hè's cold gaze upon me as he walked out of the temple.

"You can close your eyes," Jinglang said, smiling a little, despite everything. "It might be your turn to feel a little motion sick."

We flew upon a conjured sword, what I previously thought was merely Chenwen's exaggeration. But as the stars and clouds flew past us, I did end up shutting my eyes so that I did not have to see that impossible movement and be sick. I felt him press his lips against my forehead. It was both too long and not long enough before Jinglang lightly landed upon the ground once again, and he carefully set me on my feet. He held my hand tightly in his.

The Celestial Court was gathered before the entrance to the estate. There was a seal upon the gate, one that glowed with Jinglang's magic, preventing us from looking within. The Sky Sovereign and Sky Consort were dressed in matching shades of regal white and gold. Their guards stood behind them, on alert. There were others there too, dressed in the colors that I recognized from the handbook. The blue of the Star of Governance. The black of the Star of Protection. I could only guess that these were the other members of the Court of Stars. In the distance, I could see more soldiers, dressed in white. One of the Celestial battalions, ready to be called forth to battle.

"Bring her here!" the sovereign called out. "I want to see her for myself."

A soldier took me away from Jinglang's side, and I could not help but look over my shoulder at him. My scholar. Who was not dressed for war. Whose exhaustion from these exertions of magic showed in the way he stood, in the lines at the corners of his eyes, in the way he clenched his jaw.

I was pushed forward, made to kneel before the sovereign and the consort, to look upon the evil that hid in plain sight.

"You who have brought so much trouble to the realm. Just a slip of a girl," he said.

Before, it had been difficult to gaze upon him, with his golden voice and his godly appearance. Now that I was remade into Celestial form, he looked like just another man. I lowered my gaze quickly, pretended to be subdued. I hoped he had not caught the hatred in my expression.

"The Mortal musician," the consort remarked. "Look upon me."

I raised my head at the command. Instead of shifting blue skies and moving clouds in her eyes, I saw the pale blue of a summer's day, but that was all there was. I wondered if she was aware of the sovereign's ambitions, if she had been part of his plans all along.

"You've changed!" she said, surprised. "What happened to you?"

"It is a sign of great blessings and fortune, Your Highnesses." It was Lady Hè again, who appeared beside me, all smiles and feathers. "I did as the sovereign instructed—I took her into the Temple of Ordinance. She went into the tower and came out changed. Someone who was lesser, transformed into a Celestial. The magic is returning to our realm. What was once lost can return again!"

"We will ascertain soon if this is a blessing . . ." The consort regarded me with caution. "Or a curse."

"The Temple of Ordinance!" the Sky Sovereign's voice thundered. "You are certain?" He slowly got to his feet, and I felt the overwhelming power of his magic. The burning fury of the sun. I saw him consider me, saw him weighing his options, and I felt the gathering of his magic, the build-up of smothering heat that would soon incinerate anyone who stood in his way.

I threw my hands up, and the blast struck me. A pure shock wave of magic that knocked me back. I landed on my side. I struggled to get up but could only get to my knees before his shadow fell over me. He trembled with rage, and underneath it all, I sensed his fear, could practically smell it.

The point of his spear was hot under my chin.

"Step back!" he commanded, one arm out. A ring of magic encircled us, a wall of flame that kept everyone else outside. "She is Corrupted."

"Your Highness!" I heard Jinglang call out. A plea.

"She is just a girl!" someone said. I could not tell who. But I knew the Sky Sovereign was willing to silence me before I had a chance to spill anything I'd learned within the tower. For he knew, just as I did, what was contained in there. And he could not risk it coming out.

Before anyone could stop him, he thrust the spear into my neck.

I felt the heat of it pierce my skin. I saw the madness in his eyes, the way he wished for me to die. I thought I heard Jinglang call my name, or perhaps I imagined it. What was the description I'd read? The Sky Sovereign wielded a spear that was said to be able to kill even the gods.

Soul Render.

Something inside of me fractured. The memory jewel.

The power hidden within it flowed into me. I could not contain it—
it was too immense. It spilled out of my body.

Vines and branches erupted from my skin, yet I felt no pain. I was
lifted from the ground as the branches grew into trunks and roots.
Flowers sprouted from my fingers, bloomed in my hair with a sweet
scent. I was there above all of the gathered Celestials, the magic writhing and growing around me. I looked down upon their faces: frightened,
curious, angry, confused. So many emotions. What they craved, what
they spurned.

I opened my mouth, but the voice that came out was not mine. I was
only the vessel, the speaker through which the memory was contained,
because I was now capable of wielding strands of the Dreaming.

"I am Shunying, once the Queen of Flowers, imprisoned by those
who I had considered my family and my friends. I forgive you for it, for
I know the truth still eluded you." Her voice quivered with emotion.
"This is the record of my final moments, for I know that the end is near.
I petitioned the Sky Sovereign for mercy. I knew I was with child. I told
him the baby that was coming could be a beacon for peace, a joining
of the two realms, Celestial and Demon. But he would not hear it. He
pushed me off the tower and left me there to die. Left me *and* my son to
die. Soon, that will be the end to this tragedy. My love and the life that
will never be . . ."

The branches and vines slowly lowered me to the ground, shrink-
ing away to nothing. The flowers wilted and fell around me, the petals
disappearing when they touched the earth. The magic faded from my
throat, leaving behind a feeling of emptiness and regret.

The consort turned to her husband, confusion upon her face. "Is this
true?"

"She spews only lies," the sovereign raged. "Everything out of her mouth is a falsehood. Look at her! She has been overcome by the Corruption!"

"She carries with her the evidence of her lies!" Lady Hè ripped the necklace off my neck and held it high for all to see. "The truth of it, as revealed by my loyal servant."

Danrou was there, standing with the Ordinance soldiers. She stepped forward and bowed before the court. "One of the jewels will show the truth. Zhou Chenwen is the result of a tryst between a Demon and a Celestial. He controls the ravagers that have so plagued the realms. He controls them with a flute made of bone."

"Your Highness!" I cried. "I beg of you—"

"Silence!" Lady Hè interrupted me. "You stand accused. How dare you speak!"

"But I do not." Jinglang strode forward and bowed before the consort. His mother sputtered, but the consort silenced her with a raised hand. "Your Highness. The truth is sealed within the manor. It will be revealed when you see who still survives within."

The Sky Consort regarded him with a thoughtful look.

"Who has the most to gain? And the most to lose?" he asked.

They stared at one another for a moment as she pondered these questions. Finally, the consort gave a nod, and then turned to the court to address them. "When Jinglang breaks the seal, we will see what emerges. If Chenwen has survived, we will hear him speak. There must be an explanation for all of this."

The Sky Sovereign, seeing the nods of the members of his court, frowned. "We will see then," he said, even though his frustration was still evident. "We will see what's contained within."

Jinglang bowed, and then he gestured toward the gate. The seal on it cracked. Bright light shot through the seal, until the magic that contained it slowly dissipated. The gate opened slowly. The courtyard, or what we could see from this perspective, was empty. Jinglang returned to my side. I could sense the tension under his arm when I took it, and we followed the court.

The first wave of soldiers entered the courtyard, spears raised, advancing slowly. The sovereign and his consort behind them, then the rest of the court.

We were past the second gate when something shrieked overhead, and there was the sound of the beating wings.

Chenwen walked over the bridge that connected the garden to the manor. Something eased inside of my chest when I saw him, and beside me I knew that Jinglang felt similar. Chenwen remained whole. Unharmed.

"Ah, Grandfather," he said, greeting the sovereign with that signature mocking bow. "Disappointed to see me?"

CHAPTER FORTY-SIX

THE HATE ON THE SKY SOVEREIGN'S FACE WAS clear. "I should have drowned you when I had the chance," he snarled.

"How did you hide who you were?" the consort asked, realization dawning upon her. "You've never shown anything but an affinity for the magic of the Flower Clan."

"It was sealed away, hidden," Chenwen said. "Until it was time for me to know." He held up both hands—in his right, a flower bloomed, and in his left, a blue-green flame burned. Some of the members of the court gasped. What little knowledge of Demons that I gleaned from the history books, I knew that one of their rumored powers was described as an "unearthly flame, a perversion of the natural order that corrodes everything it touches."

"There was so much that had been kept from me," he said, closing his fist, and the flame disappeared.

"The comingling of Demon and Celestial blood is forbidden!" the Sky Sovereign roared, the spear now aimed at its new target. "You will bring forth the Great Calamity!"

"That was what was foretold, wasn't it?" Chenwen laughed, as if delighted by the prospect of a fight. *The very air will tremble with the beating of wings, and ravagers will fill the skies.*

Behind him, three ravagers lifted into the air, rising from the depths of the manor. A leopard with an eagle's head tipped its head back and let out a scream. The beast next to it had similar wings, but the face and body of a monkey, its arms so long they extended almost to its feet. The final beast was a bull, but it had two heads that split from the thick stalk of its neck, and four wickedly sharp points at the end of its curved horns. Its wings were attached to the back of its stout legs instead of its back.

With a shout, the soldiers all readied themselves for battle. The battalion that had remained at distance descended upon the grounds of the estate from the sky, called forth by a single gesture from the Star of Protection.

"You're not hurt?" Jinglang regarded me with wonder. I shook my head, still amazed I had faced Soul Render and lived. His hand in mine, we moved to join Chenwen before the manor entrance.

"Brother!" Chenwen said with a grin, then greeted me as well with a bob of his head. "Lady Xue." He did not seem bothered by the force that was soon to be descending upon him. Beneath the shadow of those great wings, the ravagers were indeed a ferocious sight. But still, it seemed so few against so many.

We turned to face the Celestial Court, the Sky Sovereign's face contorted in fury at being opposed, his handsome features twisted and warped by hatred. The consort stood off to the side, with a furrow in her brow, expression still pensive.

"I hold no loyalty to this court any longer," Jinglang said, voice quiet but firm. "I've seen how it treats those we are supposed to protect."

The Sky Sovereign scowled. "Then you will be punished, just like your father, just like your misguided mentor!" He turned with a sweep of his arm and addressed the court, every bit the commander. "This is the example of the plight of the Demon Realm. They continue to send ravagers to plague our borders. This is why Spirit children no longer feel safe. They are the reasons why the Mortals cower and speak of monsters from the mountains."

"Lingwei!" Chenwen called out.

The eagle-form ravager spread its wings and landed on the other side of him, joining our line. She bowed her head before Chenwen, and he offered the flame to her. It bounced from him to her wing, enveloping her in a sheath of blue. Then black holes began to appear, as if the fire ate away at her, consumed her until there would be nothing left by ashes.

The Celestials that witnessed this were horror-stricken, and my stomach turned a little, knowing the deadly power of the Corrupting Flame. But then the flames faded away into nothing, revealing at their center the figure of a woman. Lingwei emerged, serene and unscathed. Not even a smudge upon her face or a singed strand of hair to indicate that she had been burned at all.

"But how is that possible?" the Star of Balance asked, his curiosity finally piqued. He seemed willing to listen to his acolyte, unlike the others who still regarded her with suspicion.

"Commander." Lingwei bowed first, then addressed him with grave seriousness. "I am here to tell you that all we know about ravagers is a lie. It is not a path of no return like we had initially believed. It is . . ." She frowned, searching for the words to describe it. "It is a *Transformation*," she finally said. "A raw instillation of magic, permitting the body to shapeshift, but the mental strain is immense. It was difficult to keep hold of who I was, and I could see how, without assistance, one could easily succumb to the influence of others."

"You mean . . ." The Star of Balance recoiled at this revelation. "All those that we have put down . . . Those ravagers we have slain without this knowledge, believing them to be lost entirely . . ."

Jinglang's hand tightened on mine, and I knew he was remembering the ravager he had slain and mourned back in Wudan.

"The blood of so many," Chenwen said, as the gathering looked upon one another in discomfort. "We were all ignorant to this, save one."

He pointed at the Sky Sovereign, who looked back at him impassively.

"You have no proof." The Sky Sovereign pursed his lips, regarding him with derision. "This has no basis in reality. It is the sort of illusion created by Demons to stir up dissent in the realm, to ensure we are weakened and ripe for invasion!"

"You speak of the influence of Demons, and have made every attempt to prevent us from making contact," Chenwen said. "Why don't we allow them to speak for themselves?"

"I'm sorry, Commander, for what I am about to do," Lingwei said, and then before he could stop her, she raised her arm and sent a bolt of power toward the sky.

"What are you—"

A rift appeared above the manor. Small at first, only the size of a single person, but then it grew larger, expanded, and became a portal before us.

A woman came through first, astride a black winged horse with claws for hooves. She was striking in appearance, with high cheekbones and thin lips. She wore a headdress of silver that gleamed with jewels. She was clad in armor, with a resplendent violet cloak that rippled behind her in the wind. Though she did not have the mark of the crescent moon on her forehead that marked the reigning Moon Sovereign, I recognized the etchings on her armor. Mó Jūn. *The Demon Lord.*

On another monstrous steed beside her was a second woman, whose beauty was of a softer sort. She wore a gown of pale lavender, with silver embroidery down the sleeves and skirt. Upon her head was a crown of flowers, woven into her hair. A ruler and her consort.

I recognized the young woman in lavender immediately. Older now, yes, her features stronger, more defined. Her hair not wild and tousled, but loose and flowing over her shoulders. The one whose presence lurked among these halls, who I'd thought of as my rival once, whose shadow I had befriended. Jinglang also straightened, and I knew he recognized her too, for he whispered her name beside me.

"*Ruilan.*"

The Star of Protection's eyes flashed as magic crackled between her hands and she rose to meet this rift in the realm. "Meng Lingwei! Your titles will be stricken from your name from this point forth. You have betrayed the oath you swore to protect the Celestial Realm. How dare you open the borders and disrupt the balance? Acolytes, to me!"

She advanced upon the Demons emerging from the portal, but Lingwei did not falter. Her sword raised, she stood there, battle ready, prepared to defend the visitors who slowly descended from the rift to land upon the earth with their own sort of grace. But I could not reconcile that group of warriors with what I had imagined Demons to look like, for they were all impossibly beautiful in my eyes. It was only the pattern of their armor, the designs upon their robes, the rich hue of the fabric, that separated them from the Celestials. In the folktales they were hideous, deformed by the Corruption, but that was obviously a lie.

"Protect them!" Chenwen called out. The two-headed bull snorted, and landed heavily on the ground before Lingwei and the group of Demons. It pawed the earth and lowered its head, pointing its sharp horns as a threat to anyone who approached.

"You see?!" the Sky Sovereign shouted for all to hear. "He commands them. He is the one who directs the ravagers to do his bidding. He has bent the knee to the Demon Lord, his true lineage!"

The one he called the Demon Lord came forward, a smirk on her lips. "It is you who cannot control the ravagers you create. Your power is weakening, and you can only hold on to your throne through lies and manipulation to hide your waning power."

The eyes of the Sky Consort flashed, and she was the one who walked forward to face the opposition. "It is well known that the ravagers came from the fall of the last Moon Sovereign. It was his blood that contained the Corruption, that resulted in the ravagers returning."

And it was the consort of the Demon Lord that dismounted and walked forward to face her, head held high.

"You saw me Turned," Ruilan said, her voice ringing and clear. Not with the authority of the woman at her side, but with a conviction that made everyone listen. "I will tell you now. It was a Celestial's hand that forced me to ingest the begonia flower. It was a Celestial who poisoned me and forced me to Turn."

The Sky Consort blinked, confused. "Ruilan? No, we saw you fall off the Platform of Forgetting . . ."

"I fell into a place between realms," Ruilan said softly, "and it was the Demons who found me, healed me and returned me to myself." She gazed upon the Demon Lord beside her with love, and the Demon monarch regarded her with returned affection.

"That is impossible!" Danrou shrieked. "You died! *You died!*"

"It was her hand that fed me the flower," Ruilan said coldly. "She was the one who Turned me."

Jinglang spoke next. "You were a servant of my house. You betrayed the one you professed your loyalty to and fed her poison. You watched as she suffered and said nothing. Who directed your hand? Who is it you work for?"

Danrou's mouth twisted into a sneer. "How much I had to endure while working on this pitiful estate. The foolish pursuit of the former duke. Ruilan's fate was a warning, that even those who lived within the protected sanctuaries of the Celestial estates could fall." She shook her head. "Still, you continued on and brought this Mortal creature to foul the air with her presence."

"She conducts herself with honor and dignity," Jinglang said. "Two words that could never be attributed to your character."

Danrou laughed. "She may have turned herself into a Celestial, but no one will forget her wretched origins, I promise you that. Just look at what happened to Zhuxi." From her satisfied expression, I knew then that she'd had a hand in his demise as well. I wanted to reach over and wring her neck.

"Look at her," she mocked me. "So wounded, so helpless." Then her eyes hardened as she looked at the two of us, standing together. "If I must serve, I will serve someone worthy of the power."

"We know whose orders you follow," Chenwen said, then looked upon Lady Hè, challenging her to dispute his claim. "Your Eminence, you provided the poison. You tried to recruit me into your cursed plot."

So that was why Danrou was elusive in the reason as to why she had to communicate with Chenwen in private. Not a desire for a tryst after all—something far more sinister.

"Well?" the Sky Consort demanded. "Do you deny it, Lady Hè?"

"All I have done, I have done for the sanctity of the realms," she sniffed, head held high, still unwilling to admit fault.

Guxue, I heard a voice call at the back of my mind, a reminder of what I had left behind in the Temple Tower. *It is time.*

I was a voice for the Flower Queen, but that was not enough. The Celestials continued to squabble, to point fingers at one another, while nothing was ever resolved. The origin of the lies had to be exposed.

I let go of Jinglang's hand, and used my magic like a whip. I called for my qín, and it spun through the air to me like a falling star. It was time for me to stand on my own. To show them what I'd learned, what I had become.

"Stop her!" I heard the sovereign roar. I could hear the cry of the battalion leader as they called for archers to prepare, to draw their bows and ready their arrows, to rain them down upon my head.

"Help her!" It was Ruilan who called out for me, and the Demon Lord moved from her side, launching herself to meet the attack. The arrows flew toward us, but the ruler of the Demons cut them down with a conjured blade, showering the earth with sparks.

The qín settled against me. The stand and the bench rose to meet me, conjured easily by a thought. With a shout, Lingwei also rose up to meet the wave of Celestial soldiers that advanced.

This was where I had to decide: Did I trust Suirong? All the legends, the scrolls, the stories passed down to us warned of her capacity for deception. Here was the point of no return.

But I would have to risk it all.

I balanced the qín against my arm, and I cast my magic across the strings, strumming the full chord, just like Suirong had taught me. The magic exploded outward, me at the center. It went in a rippling wave through the crowd, knocking some of them over. Celestials fell, into one another or upon the ground. The note went on and on, and I heard it for what it was. Another sort of beacon.

Before the note faded, in the distance came the strumming of a zhēng.

A call, and a response.

The ground began to shake beneath our feet.

"The Temple of Ordinance is no more," Lady Hè declared with horror. She looked at me as if she saw me for the first time, truly saw me for what I was. "What did you do?"

CHAPTER FORTY-SEVEN

SUIRONG APPEARED THROUGH THE CLOUDS. IN front of one of the elder gods, even Celestials had to tremble. Her true form was still awe-inspiring, terrifying, just like I had witnessed even after my Mortal eyes were replaced. She made the manor before her appear like a toy house, and all of us like dolls for her amusement.

"The Deceiver!" the Sky Sovereign challenged. "We must rally against her, or else she would destroy us all!"

The Celestial soldiers regarded one another, uncertain, afraid.

"All I seek is balance." Suirong leaned over, casting a dark shadow across the entirety of the courtyard. Her true voice was like the sound of a thunderstorm, like waves crashing against the cliffs, all fury and destruction. "Relinquish your hold upon the realms. It is enough."

But the sovereign barked orders at the archers to ready their arrows and, with a wave of his hand, unleashed the first round of them. Suirong did not even flinch as the arrows simply passed through her. She was there, but not entirely.

"Will you lend me your Cleansing Flame?" Suirong addressed the Lord of Demons, extending her hand. With a nod, the Demon conjured the blue-green fire and it leapt from her hand to the palm of the god.

Suirong brought her wrist up to her chin and extended her hand toward the Sky Sovereign. Pursing her lips, she blew, and the fire flared around the Sky Sovereign. He clutched his face, mouth open in a silent scream, as the fire burned around him, and he aged before our eyes. His beard turned gray, and lines rapidly appeared on his face. White streaks went through his hair and turned his brows white. His cheeks became sunken, gaunt, until he appeared as skin stretched too tight over the crystal skull, with cavernous deep eyes that emanated fury. The orange fire burned within.

"The Jade Sovereign," the Star of Balance recognized and named him, stunned by this revelation.

"He holds the Burning Lotus." The consort trembled then, seeing the true depth of the horror before her. She sank to her knees. "Goddess, forgive me."

The Burning Lotus was the relic of the Heavenly Mother. With it, she was originally able to shape the realms. She was the one who took Nüwa and used her to build the Mortal Realm. She was one of the first gods, who remained to provide guidance to those who came after. I remembered when I witnessed its fearsome power in Suirong's memory. The terrifying magic that unraveled her body, pulled her apart.

That he wielded it now meant she was no longer. Now they all bore witness to the truth that I had learned back in the tower.

Instead of being cowed, the skeletal figure threw his head back and laughed.

"You wish to reveal a secret of mine?" he said, addressing the god. "Then I will reveal a secret of yours."

With his spear he shot a bolt of power to the heavens and opened up another rift above the rooftops of the Manor of Tranquil Dreams. This time, instead of an assembly of Demons, a large vessel of translucent crystal came out, similar in hue to the crystal skull, glittering with rainbow light. It circled above him, spinning. There was darkness inside of it, something hidden inside of the murk, but I could not see what it was. Only that it emanated a dark power.

The Sky Sovereign rose above the heads of the other Celestials, moving forward to meet the vessel.

"All of the heartblood of the Celestials I've gathered, waiting until it was the right time," he said.

Ravagers emerged through the rift from which the vessel originated. A one-eyed dragon with talons like an eagle. A fanged deer with two pairs of large golden eyes on its chest. A peacock who fanned out its tail feathers, and below each of the many blinking eyes was a mouth, from which protruded the forked tongue of a snake. These were larger— much larger than the ravagers that were beside Chenwen. They howled together, a hungry, desolate sound.

"No . . . ," Suirong whispered. She raked her hands across the entirety of the zhēng, casting a wide net of magic. Most of the Demon forces and the Celestial Army were knocked back and away. They were flung over the courtyard of the birds, pushed out to fall into the forest beyond. "Seal the estate, Duke of Dreams! Fulfill your calling as the Keeper of the Dreaming! Seal the estate, or all will be lost!"

Jinglang heard the call. He sat down upon the earth, took a deep breath, and pressed his palms together. He sent his magic to join hers, until the dome descended upon us, but this time it locked us in with these new ravagers. His lips continued to move, mumbling the chants that would hold the protections in place.

The vessel tipped, and a torrent of red poured from within, drenching the body of the Sovereign. The scent of blood and magic filled the air. His body contorted, bones cracking, new limbs emerging from him, until he too was an amalgamation of parts. A head perched upon a gray, skeletal body that sat cross-legged, levitating in the air. More arms than I could count bursting from his chest and back, and at the center of each palm, there was a spinning, moving eye. When he turned, I saw he had two faces. The Jade Sovereign and the Sky Sovereign. The old and the young.

"I spent the entirety of my long life attempting to ward off the inevitable." He laughed. "But now I see this is what I was intended to be. My final form. I *am* the Great Calamity. Bow down to me or be destroyed!"

Various forms continued to slither out of the rift. Too many tails, fangs, wings. Creatures slithered, crawled, and scurried down the underside of the dome, but the magic prevented them from escaping. What Celestials and Demons that were trapped inside drew their weapons and attempted to fight them off. The air was filled with the screams of battle.

"That is a portal to the Barren Realm," Suirong warned. "The monsters that reside there will be drawn to the living energy of the other realms. More of them will come soon. We must protect the duke at all costs. He is the only one that can contain them."

Hearing her speak, the Dual Sovereign gave a grin, and said with both of his voices joined, "Were you not looking for balance, Deceiver? Our ravagers will consume everything in their path. They will not discriminate between Mortal or Celestial. The world will begin again, and we will become the Supreme Ruler."

"Protect Jinglang!" Chenwen gave a battle cry as he directed the ravagers that were loyal to him to circle the still form of the duke.

Lingwei whistled and Bailu's large form swept down overhead, snatching one of those smaller ravagers from the sky and crushing it in his sharp beak. With a leap, she jumped on top of Bailu's back and her blade was a gold arc across the sky as she cut down the ravagers. The two other ravagers loyal to Chenwen followed.

"Do you not recognize your father, Jinglang?" the Dual Sovereign gloated. "The former Duke of Dreams in all of his glory!" The one-eyed dragon roared and picked up two soldiers, who screamed in his grasp before being crushed between his jaws.

Between his protectors, Jinglang grimaced. He'd tried so long to save his father, only to see that he had already been Turned.

The hunger of the swarm was the gnashing of teeth, the skittering of claws on stone, the rapid beating of wings.

"We will not let them through!" The Demon Lord clashed with the ravagers as they flew toward the portal to the Demon Realm, looking to escape. Ruilan, with a gesture, began to slowly seal the opening with her magic.

"How do we know if they are a monster from the Barrens or if they are a Celestial who could be saved?" Lingwei cried despairingly as she fought them in the air.

"We may have to choose." The Demon Lord swung and chopped off the wing of a passing ravager. It howled as it fell to the ground. "Sacrifice them or be overwhelmed as well. There are too many of them."

There is a way, Suirong's voice resounded in my head, and I looked up to see her meet my gaze. *I will break the vessel from which he draws power. It is now the only shard of me that still exists in all the realms after the tower was fractured. You will send the ravagers back to the Barrens, for they will listen to the power of your qín.*

It was a wild plan, but it was time for wild plans. The rift must be sealed. A large claw emerged, straining the sides of the portal to the Barrens, ripping it farther open. What other horrors would fly out from those depths?

You must call for them to attack him. Both Celestials and Demons. Only when they join their forces can they succeed.

Convince two realms who had been at war to cooperate, while using my newfound magic to direct monsters back to the realm where they came from. Simple.

I sat down beside Jinglang in the circle that was protected by Chenwen's prowling ravagers. I placed the qín upon my lap, readied myself to play the most important song I had ever played in my brief existence.

Suirong reached across the entirety of the sky and caught the vessel in her hand.

The Dual Sovereign turned, fear flashed across both of their faces, old and young, as their body ascended toward the god.

"You cannot do this," the Sky Sovereign said.

"To break the vessel would be to rid yourself of any chance of returning," the Jade Sovereign said.

"It is the only thing that tethers you to this plane of existence!" they screamed, joining their voices.

"All of you, Children of Nüwa, hear me!" Suirong called out, her voice ringing through the din of battle. "You have known me as the Deceiver and have had to bear my curse. This, I cannot undo, but I will make amends."

With an expression of peace on her face, she crushed the vessel. It broke into pieces and scattered into the crowd below. The sovereign howled, falling toward the earth. The ravagers fluttered about, disoriented and confused.

"You must attack him with all of your combined magic." Suirong's great face twisted with agony as she pointed at the form of the Dual Sovereign, falling like a star. "Only then could he possibly be weakened."

The Demon Lord did not hesitate. She raised her hands and sent her magic coursing toward the sovereign. It was tinged violet, a dark stream of power. The remaining Demons rallied around their ruler and added their magic to that stream as well.

"Your Highness?" I called out. The consort stood there, frozen, looking upon the battle before her. She blinked, once, twice, then she gained a look of grim determination.

"Celestials, we will not fail the realms again! We are all Nüwa's children. Join me!"

The scattering of Celestials also focused their magic and sent it arcing in a white beam toward the Dual Sovereign, until he was caught, suspended in an orb of light and shadow.

Chenwen and Lingwei dropped down beside me. They sensed I needed them, even though I had not called for their help.

"What do you need us to do?" Lingwei asked.

"I have to send the ravagers back to the Barrens," I said. "They will try to stop me."

They exchanged glances, and then nodded grimly.

"We will help you," Chenwen said.

I looked over at Jinglang, who still had his eyes closed. Protecting the other realms.

The song I chose was "Light's Eminent Arrival," a spirited tune that was like sunlight streaming through clouds, dancing off the sparkling surface of the water. I imagined the light spinning through the ravagers, directing them to the portal. Not one of control, but one of gentle persuasion.

Follow me, the song beckoned.

And the ravagers listened.

"Stop her!" The Dual Sovereign screamed from within his orb, but he could not move from where he was trapped.

The largest, most fearsome ravagers turned away from the call of the song to follow the bidding of their master. But Lingwei was there, with Bailu beside her, warding off their attacks. Chenwen brought his flute to his lips and joined his melody to mine, made it stronger, more irresistible.

The strum of another instrument entered our song—another Demon who left their ranks to assist us instead. I saw in her features echoes of the Demon Lord. The lift of her brows, the shape of her face, the waves of her dark hair. This must be someone in her family, and it lifted my heart to know that not all Demons were as consumed with hatred for the Celestials as the Celestials appeared to be for them. She inclined her head and acknowledged me as she joined me with nimble fingers upon a kōnghóu—a kind of harp that I had only ever read about, never seen played. Its lovely sound sparkled in contrast, as if light had broken through the surface of the water, illuminating the ocean. Air and water, a scattering of light above and below.

A nagging thought prickled at the back of my mind.

Suirong said this would be the way to weaken the Sky Sovereign.

But how could we *defeat* him?

CHAPTER FORTY-EIGHT

I FELT THE FLOW OF TIME SLOW TO A TRICKLE. TIME could not be stopped altogether; I had learned from Suirong when she taught me how to use magic. It was a balancing force for everyone, even the gods.

Suirong leaned over me, but she was fading. She had destroyed her remaining tie to the realms with her own hand. *You will have to make a choice.* She hung her head, as if she regretted what she was asking of me.

How difficult of a choice would this be, if it would protect the other realms, save those I cared about?

Slowly, I watched Lingwei bury her sword in the side of a ravager. Blood arced in the air as the beast thrashed in pain.

Ah. Everyone dreams. Celestials and Mortals and Demons and Spirits. Did you already forget? The Dreaming is a part of the realms and yet apart from it. The Jade Sovereign's survival is intricately tied to the Burning Lotus. When the skull is shattered, the Lotus will emerge. It is also known as Realm Shaper. It can create realms or destroy them. That is his final gambit.

The lone Keeper walked the Dreaming, kept us safe on the other side of the tapestry. The loss of a single life, versus so many others.

The duke.

My duke.

Suirong's gaze pierced mine. *You see?*

Oh.

I recognized what she meant, and despaired. There had to be another solution.

Soon they will not be able to hold him.

Celestials and Demons alike strained, joining forces to keep him contained. The Sky Sovereign howled within the orb, sending his own magic outward, trying to break free.

Why was I the one to choose?

Your friends can send the ravagers through the portal, lead the others to safety. But you are the only one remaining who has the affinity for the Dreaming and can repair it. You will be the one to walk the path as the Keeper, because there will be no one else strong enough to bear it. Also, it is not solely your choice . . . He has already given an answer.

I gazed up at her, the god who was said to be the source of Mortal suffering. The one who cursed us and wished us ill. Who had wandered through our dreams and our memories, our highest highs and our lowest lows. Who found us worthy. She had almost disappeared.

I pushed my qín off my lap and went to sit in front of him. His lips still moved, holding the ward that sealed us in, protecting the realms.

I can give you a moment. Just a breath.

I cupped his face in my hands, leaned in, and touched my forehead to his.

IN HIS DREAM, we were beneath a tree. The summer breeze made the leaves above our heads dance. I sat cross-legged, leaning against the trunk, while he sprawled on the ground in front of me, head in my lap. His eyes were closed, the picture of contentment. A rare moment of peace that we never enjoyed together.

"I should have told you about every dream," I whispered to him. "Every wild and impossible dream I wanted to share with you." The question he asked me once.

If I were only a Mortal girl, and he my Mortal lover, where would we go?

I would walk with him on the glowing streets of Wudan during the lantern festival.

I would drink tea with him in a mountain teahouse.

I would play a duet with him on the shores of the Yinyang Sea. Me on the qín, him on the xiao.

I BLINKED AND the moment was gone. I dreamed of a thousand lifetimes, and it would not be enough.

My hands held his and I could not bring myself to let go. But I knew what awaited me. I would have to put all of the magic that Suirong taught me about the Dreaming to use. Jinglang would have to destroy the Dreaming, himself within it, to contain the Sky Sovereign and the remaining ravagers, and from the ashes, I would have to restore the paths connecting the realms, to prevent them from falling into one another.

One last time, I brushed my lips against his. When I leaned back, I noticed something gleaming in the corner of his eye.

It fell into my hand. A memory jewel.

Lingwei pulled me away. We rose high into the air, toward the glittering portal to the Demon Realm, where Ruilan and the Demon Lord still stood guard. In the distance, the orb shattered. The Dual Sovereign emerged, his many hands clawed as he hurtled toward us with murderous intent.

Chenwen rose to meet him, Soul Render in hand. With one clean swipe of that blade, his head severed from his body. He flew up to join us as the skull shattered behind him, and the body of the one he used to call *Grandfather* fell from the sky. He did not look back.

The Burning Lotus spun in the air, glowing gently, its rainbow petals tinged with an orange hue. Jinglang rose to join it in the air. He reached up and caught it in his raised hands, expression reverent, eyes still closed, and head lowered. It looked as if he was accepting it as an offering or about to place it upon his head like a crown.

A brilliant light emerged from the lotus. The last thing I saw before the portal closed was Jinglang's face, still and serene, at peace with the choice he made. To destroy the Dreaming with the power of the Burning Lotus. To prevent the Jade Sovereign from ever returning to threaten the realms once more.

Someone I loved, taken away from me *again*.

I flew for a time upon Lingwei's back, the world racing past us in a blur. Her swan shape had changed, merged with her ravager form. The webbed feet had been changed to an eagle's talons, and leopard spots bloomed across her wings. I was lowered gently to the ground after Lingwei landed. I looked around and found myself in a garden. Above us was a peculiar violet sky. The blue-green grass was cold under my hands. I couldn't resist dropping to my knees and running my fingers through it, to ensure that it was real. The bushes beside us drooped with large, heavy white blooms. The air was thick with their floral scent.

"We'll help you." Lingwei knelt before me. Half of her cloak hung in tatters, and her arm appeared to be at an odd angle. Her face blurred as I struggled to hold my tears back at the sight of her injuries. She placed a hand on my shoulder, ever so gentle. Like she was afraid I would shatter into pieces just like the crystal skull.

"It will take time," Chenwen told me, collapsing to the ground beside me as well. His hair mussed, face smudged, legs sprawled out before him without a care. There was a scorch mark on his chest plate. Still the image of the defiant prince.

Time for what? To rebuild? Or to recover from what we'd just lost? Lingwei gathered me into her, and Chenwen leaned closer to rest his head on both of our shoulders, putting an arm around us as well.

I allowed myself to relax into their embrace, to know that even though I lost Jinglang, I wouldn't be alone. Not anymore.

THE DEMON REALM offered us refuge. To recover and recuperate from the resultant shock wave of magic that had rocked the entirety of all the realms when the power of the Burning Lotus was unleashed.

Ruilan pulled me in and hugged me like a sister after I explained to her that I had already met a fragment of her memory she'd left behind at Meng Manor. The striking and intimidating Demon Lord was introduced to me as Ziyan. I also met Ziyan's younger sister, Yueting, the one who had played the kōnghóu with me on the battlefield. Her demeanor was significantly less icy than her older sister, and she played the eager hostess, wanting to show me everything in the palace. She spoke often of their younger sister, who had gone traveling for a time, and who I would meet when she came back from her journey.

Chenwen and Lingwei, after giving me a few days to rest, found me in my rooms at the palace and promised me a "surprise." Knowing Chenwen's tendency for mischief, I was immediately wary, but Lingwei promised me it would be worth the effort.

I followed them on a conjured sword of my own, even if I was a bit unsteady in my flight path, now that I could wield Celestial magic. We hovered over a clearing in a secluded forest. There was a small vegetable garden, a plain bamboo cabin beside it. Two people sat in front of it, bent over a game of Go.

When one of them looked up, shielding his eyes from the sun with a fan, I almost fell off my sword in astonishment. They were both standing when we landed, and one of them opened his arms in greeting for me to rush into them.

"Xue'er!" He murmured above me as I squeezed him tight. The scent of camphor tingled my nose. As familiar as the rest of him.

"Uncle," I choked out.

"Let me look at you!" he said, pulling back but still holding me by the elbows, examining me from head to toe. Over his shoulder, I saw the face of the former Star of Fortune. He gave me a nod. I felt like I already knew him, from the memory jewels and from Jinglang's stories, even though this was the first time we'd met. Then his face stretched into a smile, and he embraced us together, his happiness evident.

Two of those who I thought were lost had been returned to me. United under a strange violet sky, the hope a tentative peace across the Six Realms could be brokered to create a new world. A world where a Demon could fall in love with a Celestial, and a Celestial could love someone Mortal-born.

"Well, come! Tell me everything!" Uncle demanded, tucking his arm into my elbow and pulling me along. "We've been waiting a while. The food is getting cold!"

Later that night I sat there in their cabin, my stomach full after the feast. I was content, looking at the faces of my friends and family around the table as Uncle told us the story of how they were spirited away to the Demon Realm in his usual exaggerated manner. He had us all howling as he described them kicking and screaming all the way, Elder Gao next to him providing comedic demonstrations of the events. Chenwen shook his head in mocking protest, while Lingwei chortled in delight.

As they chattered and bickered next to me, I reached for the most precious jewel, hidden in my sleeve. I clutched it tightly in my hand, to remind myself that it was still there. It pulsed in my palm, to the beat of my own heart.

As long as this remained, I dared to hope.

CHAPTER FORTY-NINE

IN THE ENTIRETY OF THE SIX REALMS, NO ONE
dreamed for one hundred and eighty days.

FINALE

WHILE THE DREAMING WAS BEING REMADE, THE Sky Consort granted me a temporary residence in the Crystal Palace. No sign of the Heavenly Mother was found there in those gleaming, silent halls.

Every so often, when I wanted a break from my duties, I would return to the site where the Meng Estate was formerly located. Here, I found no trace of the Burning Lotus. That magic must have been consumed when the Sky Sovereign, the Meng Manor, and its duke were devoured.

Where the manor and its gardens once stood, there remained only a brilliant green meadow, a great tree with red blooms and leafy branches standing at its center. It reminded me of the meadow where the Spirit Tree was located, though I've still yet to visit. Once I had made an off-handed remark in one of my letters that I wished to look upon it, and he remembered in that final moment. This dream he left behind for me.

I sat there at the foot of the tree and conjured up my qín. I ran my hands over its smooth surface, its warm, comforting familiarity. Even though I could have requested one of the relics of the Celestial vaults, in which there was a multitude of magical qín for me to choose from, I preferred my own. I had tried to return it to Uncle Gao once, and he laughed.

"That qín has been transformed just as you have been," he told me. "It chose to remain at your side. I could not keep it, even if I tried."

Upon the back, where the carving had once read: *Mountains High, Swift Streams*, it now had four different characters:

長夜孤雪

A Long Night, Solitary Snow.

Since our first meeting, we have played duets together many times, with my uncle as our happy audience. But this song, I played alone, for no one else to listen.

From my hands came a gentle melody. The boat upon the lake. The girl waiting for her lover to come. The memory jewel began to glow where it rested in the hollow at the base of my throat, dangling from the thin chain around my neck. The rest of the world faded away as I entered the memory.

Jinglang was in the study of his residence, brush in hand. He lifted his head when he heard the sounds of the qín, somewhere in the distance. He laid down his brush and stood up, drawn by the call of the music.

Through the trees he saw her, in the Pavilion of Expectant Frost. Her hair tied back simply, trailing down the graceful curve of her back. Each note lingered upon the strings, a mournful call, just like his gaze lingered upon her every time she appeared.

He should walk away. He turned, and yet, he glanced back. She looked luminous and lovely in the moonlight.

Someone he could possibly love.

The song drifted away, like the small boat carried away by the current. My heart ached as I touched the pearl, a reminder of all that had passed. I never wondered how he appeared so quickly to save me when the ravager came down from the mountain, not long after I arrived at the estate. When I was angry at him for lying to me about the Celestial Realm. He expressed his admiration for my music, and I thought that was all it was.

With a wave of my hand, I put away the qín, and conjured up a small table. Brush and ink. Paper.

My beloved Jinglang,

Soon it will be spring again in the Mortal Realm, and I will travel to visit my uncle and Uncle Gao at their new estate in Fengshan. Chenwen will meet us there, and you know that he will be as annoying as ever. He still constantly reminds me of the debt I owe him for hiding them in the Demon Realm when they were under threat from the Jade Sovereign, who was certain they knew about his devious plans.

It will be a nice reprieve from the ongoing reconstruction of the manor. I believe you will be pleased with the progress we've made so far. I think you will especially like the archive wing. I've split it into several rooms, one for music, the other for poetry. I am eager to fill the shelves to replace your father's lost collection. I'm still searching for Zhuxi, but a part of me wonders if he does not want to be found. For out of everyone in the entirety of the Six Realms, he would be the one who has the ability to hide from the reach of the Dreaming.

Relations between the Celestial and Demon Realms remain strained, but there's been some progress made between the courts. The Celestials are considering adapting some of the features of the Demon court, such as appointing a Council of Advisers. Change is difficult, as you once told me. I witnessed it for myself.

There is still no sign of the former sovereign, or a trace of Suirong. We will wait and see though, and keep vigilant.

Like each and every letter before this, I still have hope a part of you is out there. If you can hear my song, it will bring you home.

Yours,
Xue'er

After ensuring the ink had dried, I folded the letter upon itself. Just like the many letters I'd sent out before, I hummed the song, gave it a small tendril of my magic. It changed in form, growing wings, until it became a butterfly. Its wings flapped, then it lifted into the sky and headed for the horizon. It would carry my message to a distant corner of the realms.

Where someday he would wake from his long slumber, dreaming of butterflies.

AUTHOR'S NOTE

The gǔqín (古琴, "ancient qín") is a Chinese musical instrument with a three-thousand-year history. It is also known as the "seven-stringed Chinese zither." It was the favored instrument of scholars, and playing it was seen as a refined practice, associated with poetry and philosophy. I have chosen in my story to refer to the instrument as "qín," as that would be its common name.

Several poems featured in the story were written by Tang Dynasty poets, or I had written with inspiration from the Tang poetry tradition.

The poems that were translated are listed below and accompanied by their translations:

霜月 - 李商隱

初聞徵雁已無蟬，百尺樓南水接天。

青女素娥俱耐冷，月中霜裏鬥嬋娟。

Frost Moon—Li Shangyin

When the cicadas have quieted, the migrating geese begin their call

From my view upon the high tower, the land meets the sky upon the horizon

Both the Goddesses of the Frost and the Moon endure the chill

Hard to say who is the victor, the beauty of the moon or the frost?

古朗月行 - 李白

小時不識月，呼作白玉盤。

又疑瑤台鏡，飛在青雲端。

仙人垂兩足，桂樹何團團。

白兔搗藥成，問言與誰餐？
蟾蜍蝕圓影，大明夜已殘。
羿昔落九烏，天人清且安。
陰精此淪惑，去去不足觀。
憂來其如何？悽愴摧心肝。

On Observing the Moon—Li Bai

As a child I had no name for the moon, called it a plate of white jade

Suspected it may be a Celestial mirror, flying amidst the faraway
   clouds

The Celestials dangled their feet from the sky, as the osmanthus tree
   grew round

The white rabbit ground the immortal pill in the mortar, who was it
   intended for?

The giant toad took a bite, the moon is no longer whole

Houyi had already shot down nine suns, created peace for those on
   earth

As the light of the moon fades, reminds us we should soon depart

But worry still descends, how can I bear to leave? This sorrow sinks
   deeper into my heart.

水仙謠 - 溫庭筠
水客夜騎紅鯉魚，赤鸞雙鶴蓬瀛書。
輕塵不起雨新霽，萬里孤光含碧虛。
露魄冠輕見雲發，寒絲七柱香泉咽。
夜深天碧亂山姿，光碎平波滿船月。

Melody of the Water Immortals—Wen Tingyun

A late-night guest approaches on the water, riding a red carp

A mythical bird and twin cranes announce his arrival from a faraway
   land

The air stills, the freshness of the rain clears the sky
The solitary radiance of the moonlight can be seen over a great
distance
Fog skims over the mountain tops like strands of fine hair
From the cold strings of the qín, the sound of a fragrant spring
emerges
Darkness of the evening obscures the beauty of the mountains
Moonlight fills the boat like scattered pieces of jade

The song "The Tragedy of Consort Xiang" was an old gǔqín piece from a song collection of the Ming Dynasty with no attributed author as it draws from a legend that originated from the Han Dynasty (湘妃怨). The text of the first verse, as recalled by Xue, is as follows:

落花落葉亂紛紛，終日思君不見君。

腸欲斷兮腸欲斷，淚珠痕上更添痕。

Swirling flowers, falling leaves, mark the days I've dreamed of my
king but have not seen him
The pain inside like my organs severing, my tears leave ever-
deepening scars

Any references to Chinese mythology, folk religion, astrology, and numerology were adapted for the purposes of the story and have no connection with real-world practices or beliefs today.

ACKNOWLEDGMENTS

The writing and publishing process for *Song of the Six Realms* was just as terrifying and wonderful to embark upon as I remember when I first wrote *A Magic Steeped in Poison*. Thank you, dear reader, for picking up this book and taking a chance on this story! And thank you to the booksellers, librarians, and influencers who have helped it along on its journey.

I still remain in awe of the many steps that it takes for a manuscript to turn from a dream to the book in your hands today.

Thank you to my editor, Emily Settle, for your care and insight into Xue's story and your assistance in helping me polish it. I'm extremely lucky to have you as my editor!

Thank you to my agent, Rachel Brooks, who continues to champion my books and remains my fierce advocate. I'm so grateful that you're in my corner!

So much appreciation to the Feiwel & Friends team. Thank you especially to: Jean Feiwel, the amazing publisher of a diverse imprint with many authors I admire, as well as Avia Perez, Senior Production Editor, and Jackie Dever, my copyeditor, for helping me deal with the challenges of formatting Chinese characters, poems, and my often-nonsensical choices re: capitalization.

Thank you to the dream team in marketing and publicity at Macmillan and Fierce Reads: Morgan Rath, Sara Elroubi, Gaby Salpeter, Leigh Ann Higgins, and Nicole Schaefer, for your tireless efforts in getting my books out to the world. I'm in awe of your boundless enthusiasm for the books under your wing. Also many thanks to Raincoast and my publicist Erika Medina for all your help with my Canadian events!

Thank you to Rich Deas and Maria W. Jenson for the art design and to Sija Hong for illustrating another glorious cover. I'm so proud to have this beautiful art as the first impression for *Song*!

Thank you to my UK editor, Michael Beale, for your notes that made me tear up and feel like you truly understood what I was trying to achieve with this story. And to the Titan Books team for your support!

Deep thanks and appreciation to authors who I admire tremendously: Axie Oh and Sue Lynn Tan, for taking the time out of your busy schedules to blurb my book. I'm excited to continue to fangirl over your current and future stories.

Much love for The Jianghu Discord. I so appreciate the safe space where we can chat about C-dramas, poetry and translations, and the diaspora experience.

Many thanks to Yilin Wang for sharing your knowledge and for your assistance in my poetry translations. Here's to more hot pot and debates on obscure philosophical references! I can't wait to support your books.

Thank you to Nafiza Azad and Roselle Lim for being there still after all these years. One day we will have our eating retreat reunion! I look forward to celebrating many more of our books together.

Thank you to Maya Prasad for all of our sprints that encouraged me to keep writing even when the words were difficult to find.

Many, many thanks to Justin Ho for your detailed and insightful notes, and for sharing wonderful folktales for me to explore further.

To my daughters: Lyra, for your boundless creativity. I love how you have embraced your writing as your own; Lydia, for your brilliant smile. I'll never be tired of reading stories to you.

And finally, so much love to my husband. My #1 supporter as we continue upon this wild ride. Can't imagine doing all of this without you.

GLOSSARY

Term	Chinese	Pronunciation	Meaning
jī lǐ	笄禮	jī lǐ	A Coming of Age ceremony for young women.
jiaoliao	鷦鷯	jiao liáo	A small bird known as the Eurasian or Northern wren.
kōnghóu	箜篌	kōng hóu	A vertical stringed harp.
liánwù	蓮霧	lián wù	A fruit shaped like a bell, commonly called a "wax apple."
qílín	麒麟	qí lín	A golden hooved creature with the head and antlers of a dragon.
qín	琴	qín	A seven-stringed instrument played by plucking, known as gǔqín (ancient qín) in modern times.
shīfù	師傅	shī fù	A mentor who has accepted a student and is oath-sworn to the responsibility of their instruction.

sìhéyuàn	四合院	sì hé yuàn	A family style of manor, with four wings surrounding a large interior courtyard. Each wing could also have its own private courtyard or garden hidden within.
xiao	簫	xiāo	A vertical flute, usually made of bamboo.
yuè-hù	樂戶	yuè hù	One of the lowest ranks in society, many restrictions were placed upon their freedoms. Often the wives or children of disgraced court officials, and they often became entertainers or prostitutes.
zhēng	箏	zhēng	A plucked, stringed instrument played with finger picks. Also known as the Chinese zither.
Ziwei Guard	紫微軍	zǐ wēi jūn	A battalion within the Celestial Army
zhīyīn	知音	zhī yīn	A term for a person of intimate understanding. "The one for whom my soul resonates."

CHARACTER NAME PRONUNCIATION GUIDE

Name	Chinese Name	Pronunciation
Anjing	安菁	Ān Jīng
Bailu	絎鷺	Bǎi Lù
Boya	伯牙	Bó Yá
Chidi	赤締	Chì Dí
Danrou	單柔	Dān Róu
Datou	大頭	Dà Tóu
Dee (Matron)	狄(大姊)	Dí (Dà Jiě)
Feiyun	飛雲	Fēi Yún
Fuxi	伏羲	Fú Xī
Gao Qiqi (Mentor)	高啟期(師傅)	Gāo Qǐ Qī (Shī Fù)
Guxue	孤雪	Gū Xuě
Kong Yang	孔陽	Kǒng Yáng
Meng Jinglang	孟景朗	Mèng Jǐng Lǎng
Meng Lingwei	孟凌薇	Mèng Líng Wēi
Mili	米莉	Mǐ Lì
Nüwa	女媧	Nǚ Wā
Ruilan	芮蘭	Ruì Lán
Shunying	舜英	Shùn Yīng
Su Wei	蘇微	Sū Wēi
Suirong	燧融	Suì Róng
Tang Guanyue (Uncle)	唐關月(舅舅)	Táng Guān Yuè (Jiù Jiù)
Xidié	喜蝶	Xǐ Dié
Xuannu	玄女	Xuán Nǚ
Wu (Auntie)	吳(大娘)	Wú (Dà Niáng)

Yingzi	影子	Yǐng Zi
Zhou Chenwen	周晨文	Zhōu Chén Wén
Zhuxi	竹溪	Zhú Xī
Ziqi	子期	Zǐ Qī

PLACE NAMES OF NOTE

Place Name	Chinese Name	Pronunciation	Location
Archive of Dreams	尋夢館	*xún mèng guǎn*	*Library where dreams are catalogued*
Fengshan Teahouse	鳳山(茶樓)	fèng shān (chá lóu)	A traveling teahouse named after the mystical "Phoenix Mountain"
Hall of Heartfelt Dreams	夢心樓	*mèng xīn lóu*	*Main hall of the Manor of Tranquil Dreams*
Manor of Tranquil Dreams	夢幽府	*mèng yōu fǔ*	*Also known as the Meng Estate*
Pavilion of Expectant Frost	待霜亭	*dài shuāng tíng*	*Along the back wall of the manor, at the foot of the mountain*
The Kingdom of Qi	齊(國)	qí (guó)	Mortal Realm
Residence of Fateful Dreams	夢緣堂	*mèng yuan táng*	*North wing of Meng Manor*

*Italics are locations within the Meng Estate

Place Name	Chinese Name	Pronunciation	Location
Residence of Hopeful Dreaming	夢盼閣	*mèng pang é*	*East wing of Meng Manor*
Shandong School	杉東(琴院)	shān dōng (qín yuan)	A school for students of the qín, located in Wudan
Shanyang Academy	山陽(學院)	shān yáng (xué yuàn)	A once-renowned academy of the arts that is now closed
Wind-Swept Pavilion	風吹亭	*fēng chuī tíng*	*Across the bridge at the far side of the garden*
Wudan	霧丹(市)	wù dān (shì)	An eastern city in the Kingdom of Qi
Xingfu Forest	杏福(樹林)	xìng fú (shù lín)	The royal forest in the Kingdom of Qi

Thank you for reading this Feiwel & Friends book.
The friends who made

SONG
OF THE
SIX REALMS

possible are:

Jean Feiwel, Publisher

Liz Szabla, VP, Associate Publisher

Rich Deas, Senior Creative Director

Anna Roberto, Executive Editor

Holly West, Senior Editor

Kat Brzozowski, Senior Editor

Dawn Ryan, Executive Managing Editor

Kim Waymer, Senior Production Manager

Emily Settle, Editor

Rachel Diebel, Editor

Foyinsi Adegbonmire, Editor

Brittany Groves, Assistant Editor

Avia Perez, Senior Production Editor

Follow us on Facebook or visit us online at mackids.com.
Our books are friends for life.